THE GATHERING FLAME

"You've made a name for yourself, Captain Metadi," the Domina Perada said. "They say you are something more than a successful pirate—"

"Privateer," he corrected. "I bear letters of marque and reprisal."

"My apologies, Captain," Perada said, her expression unruffled. "Privateer. If the newsreaders don't lie, you have proven yourself able to meld independent raiders into a fleet and carry the war to the enemy."

"Enemy?" Jos Metadi shook his head. "No. Enemies are personal. None of this is personal with me. I take prizes—rich ones—and I take them for the goods and merchandise they carry. If your sources are any good, they should have mentioned that I don't fight warships when I can help it."

"You fight when you must, and you win when you fight." Her voice remained composed. "I have decided. You are the man who will return with me to Entibor and, once there, make a warfleet for me."

"You've decided, have you?"

**Also by Debra Doyle and James D. Macdonald,
from Tor Books**

*The Price of the Stars
Starpilot's Grave
By Honor Betray'd*

THE
GATHERING FLAME

Book Four of
Mageworlds

Debra Doyle and
James D. Macdonald

A TOM DOHERTY ASSOCIATES BOOK
NEW YORK

This is a work of fiction. All the characters and events portrayed in this book are fictional, and any resemblance to real people or incidents is purely coincidental.

THE GATHERING FLAME

Copyright © 1995 by Debra Doyle and James D. Macdonald

All rights reserved, including the right to reproduce this book, or portions thereof, in any form.

Cover art by Romas

A Tor book
Published by Tom Doherty Associates, Inc.
175 Fifth Avenue
New York, NY 10010

Tor® is a registered trademark of Tom Doherty Associates, Inc.

ISBN: 0-812-53495-6

First edition: July 1995

Printed in the United States of America

0 9 8 7 6 5 4 3 2 1

CAUTIONARY PROLOGUE

"What you have to realize, son, is that almost all of the people who were there at the time are dead. And everybody who's still alive is lying to you about something."

—General Jos Metadi to an unknown interviewer, some time after the end of the First Magewar.

I. Galcenian Dating 974 a.f.
Entiboran Regnal Year 38 Veratina

Errec Ransome—late of Ilarna, now copilot and navigator of Jos Metadi's *Warhammer*—ran up the broad staircase of the Double Moon two steps at a time. In the public rooms behind him, the sounds and smells of raucous celebration filled the air like thick smoke. Metadi's privateers had come back again to Waycross, and the party had just begun.

They'd had a good run this time. Nobody had gotten blown up—except for Celeyn, and that was his own damned fault—and the Mageships had dropped out of hyperspace right where Errec had told Jos that they would: cargo ships, big and arrogant, full of the treasures of half a hundred worlds. The Mages hadn't expected serious trouble at a neutral planet so close to their home territory, and they'd counted on the warships escorting them to take care of any trouble that did occur.

They'd been wrong. The Ophelan system was a long way from the main privateering lanes. That was why the cargo ships had chosen it for their fuel and repair stop before heading back across the gap between the Mageworlds and the civilized galaxy. But Ophel wasn't so far away from civilization that Jos Metadi couldn't persuade other privateer captains to follow him there. When the cargo ships and their escorts made the translation from hyperspace, it wasn't just *Warhammer* that waited at the drop points for them: it was a whole fleet.

Now that the voyage was over and the share-out done, most of the privateers seemed intent on spending their cut of the proceedings as fast as possible, with the eager help of every bartender and brothel keeper in Waycross.

Jos Metadi had already banked most of his portion—he hadn't made it out of the Gyfferan slums, and into command of his own ship, by being careless about finances— but even he hadn't banked it all. The captain liked money, and with good reason, but he also liked the undoubted pleasures that money could buy.

The Double Moon sold most of them. Ransome was aware, as he hurried up the carpeted staircase, of the seething, sweating presence of the establishment's other patrons. He ignored the pressure of their unspoken desires, and made his way down the narrow, red-carpeted upstairs hall.

Translucent glowcubes in filigree holders marked each door, but Errec didn't have to read the brass plate outside number seven to know that he'd found the right room. He pounded on the polished wood with his fist—pounded hard, because the Double Moon had extensive soundproofing underneath its old-style façade—and shouted, "Jos! Are you in there?"

The answer came back, muffled by a treble thickness of wood and insulation: "Go away, Errec. I'm busy."

"Jos, there's a girl downstairs!"

"There's a girl right here. Go away."

Errec tried again. "The one downstairs wants to talk to you!"

"One minute!"

Errec laughed under his breath and started back down the hall to the stairs. Jos was likely to take more than a minute to disentangle himself, and somebody ought to keep the lady amused while she was waiting.

The private room downstairs was furnished with carved wooden furniture upholstered in crimson velvet. The lady herself—fair and petite in a full-skirted gown of frosty blue—sat bolt upright in one of the high-backed chairs, knees together and hands on knees. A formal mask of black velvet covered her face from well above the eyebrows to halfway down her cheeks. Her mouth looked young, though; surprisingly young, for the aura that surrounded her.

Iron, thought Errec. *This one is iron.*

He wondered if the two gentlemen standing with her realized it. They were both older than she was, but seemed to have little else in common beyond a firm conviction that being here at all was a very bad mistake. One of them—a large man, dark and heavily muscled, with strength and training apparent even beneath his fashionable clothing—stood on the far side of the room, his back against the wall, in a position that afforded a clear view of both doors. Whatever this one's title might be, Errec decided, his work was the selective application of violence in the lady's interest.

The other man was slight and grey-haired, dressed in plain dark clothing cut out of good cloth. He stood at the lady's left shoulder and gazed about with a quizzical air, as if he'd never been in a place like the Double Moon until this evening. An old family retainer, was Errec's conjecture, keeper of the young noblewoman's reputation . . . or at least, considering where they all currently were, of her virtue.

In spite of Waycross's bad name for violence, the three carried no obvious weapons. That meant they assumed power—and people with so much unconscious surety of their own power, often had it.

Errec stepped across the threshold. The heavy door swung shut behind him. "Captain Metadi will be with you soon."

The woman nodded. Ice-blond hair in an elaborate set of curled braids swayed with the motion. Her eyes behind the mask were a bright, startling blue. She said nothing.

Errec was aware of the younger man's assessing gaze: was this one potential trouble, the bodyguard was wondering, or was he a person of neither threat nor consequence? A spacehand's coverall didn't argue for much by way of wealth or position, and—like the woman and her escorts—Errec Ransome didn't carry any obvious weapons.

He ignored the two men and spoke to the woman directly. "What is the nature of your request for Captain Metadi?"

The bodyguard's dark face grew even darker. "That is a matter for Her Dignity to discuss with the captain himself."

"I'm Metadi's copilot," Errec said. "I'll learn about the whole business soon enough."

The bodyguard folded his arms across his chest and set his jaw. "Her Dignity wishes it this way."

The door to the private room opened again as they spoke.

"You can tell Errec anything you can tell me," said a familiar voice. As always, Jos Metadi's words had a strong down-home Gyfferan twang, even when he was speaking careful Galcenian. "He'll need to know anyway, if the 'Hammer's going to be part of it."

The lady spoke for the first time.

"Leave us," she said. Her voice was clear and well bred, with an accent that Errec didn't recognize. Her blue eyes swept from the bodyguard to Errec and back. "What I have to discuss with Captain Metadi, I will discuss with him alone."

Her other escort, the older man who stood at her shoulder, looked distressed. "My lady—"

"You too, Ser Hafrey," she said, over his protest. Then, turning again to Metadi, she went on. "I have hired a room, Captain, for three hours' time. I'm told that's the usual span you linger with a woman here."

Metadi shrugged. If he was surprised—and to Errec, who was as familiar with his moods and expressions as anybody living, he didn't seem to be—it didn't show on his face. "Sometimes more, sometimes less," he said. "It depends. Lead the way."

The woman stood, her long skirt rustling with the movement, and crossed the room to the inner door. With her hand on the lockplate, she paused.

"Wait for me outside," she told her escorts. "I'll join you afterward. Now, Captain—"

Jos moved to follow her, catching Errec's eye as he did so. "Same thing," he said; and added, in the thick portside Gyfferan that served as the 'Hammer's business language, "See if anybody on the street knows what's going on here, would you?"

Errec nodded. "There's a café," he replied in the same tongue. "The Blue Sun. I'll start there and meet you afterward."

The Blue Sun wasn't far—a short walk along the noisy, garish Strip. When he got there, the main dining room was crowded with newly paid free-spacers. Some of them had come to get a cheap meal and a stiff drink before embarking on their evening's carousal. Others—the ones that Errec was interested in—were there to buy or sell things of value, information included.

He slid into the first open booth he came to, inspected the menu pad, and signaled for plain bread and cheese and a mug of the local beer. He was in the mood for something quite a bit stronger, but it looked like he'd be holding down this booth for quite a while.

Three hours, he thought, and laughed again, softly, to himself. If the lady was pretty and skillful, Jos sometimes took all night.

Jos Metadi, more amused than not by developments so far, nodded at Ser Hafrey and the bodyguard and followed the young woman into the private room. The door—an automatic one this time, unlike the old-style wooden panels that adorned the more public areas of the Double Moon—slid closed behind him.

The room contained a small table and two chairs, in the same curved and ornamented style as the furniture of the outer chamber. Heavy brocade curtains obscured the dim alcove in one corner. His interest, already piqued by the lady's mask and her brace of escorts, quickened even further.

Whatever she's got in mind, he thought, *it's not the usual.*

The lady sat down in one of the chairs, and waved a hand at the other. "Captain Metadi," she said. "Pray be seated, and let us talk."

For a fraction of a second, Jos thought about accepting her invitation at face value. Then he decided to push things a little instead. The lady wanted something from him; he might as well let her know that the price wouldn't be low. He moved over to the table and stood behind the empty chair, resting his hands on the carved arch of its high wooden back.

"First things first. The mask has to come off. I don't make deals with anyone I can't see."

Her mouth curved in a faint smile under the black velvet. "Fair enough, I suppose."

She reached up and undid the tabs holding the mask in place. The black velvet slid away; she caught the mask as it fell, and placed it on the table in front of her.

"There," she said. "Shall we proceed?"

Jos looked at her. She was younger than he'd expected, considering the weight of authority in her voice, with fair, unblemished skin. The contours of her face were clean and pure, saved from arrogance only by the warmth of her mouth and the vivid blue of her eyes. Her brows and lashes were darker than her hair, ash blond rather than ice. His glance continued appraisingly downward. She was pleasingly buxom, and he found himself imagining—he wrenched himself back to the present, hoping that the track of his eyes had gone unremarked.

"I'm afraid that you have the advantage of me," he said, pulling out the chair and seating himself as he spoke. "You know me—by name and reputation, at least. But I don't know you."

The lady regarded him for a moment before seeming to come to a decision. "Very well. I am Perada Rosselin, Domina of Entibor, of the Far Colonies, and of the Space Between."

Entibor? thought Jos, keeping his expression unchanged by an effort of will. Since becoming a privateer, he had needed to learn who ruled which planets, and something of their alliances. The whole tangled nest of them made his head ache sometimes. *Who's ... yes, Veratina. Whoever this is, though, she sure as hell isn't Veratina. But if the old woman's dead ... I thought that Veratina's heir was a schoolgirl on Galcen.*

He looked again at the lady across from him, and revised his estimate of her age downward by several years. At her majority, clearly, or she wouldn't be claiming the title ... but closer to girl than woman. Not yet twenty, Galcenian, that much was sure.

Don't let her age fool you, hotshot. This girl's been training to sign death warrants since the first day her pudgy little fist could hold a stylus.

He leaned back in his chair. "Well, then, Domina," he said. "What is it that you need me to do?"

"They told me you were quite the direct man," said Perada. She sounded amused. "I see that they were right."

"Deal with me honestly, and I deal honestly in return. But until I know what you want from me, there's nothing else I can say."

"What I want," she said, and for the first time hesitated, as if marshaling her arguments. "You've made a name for yourself, Captain Metadi, and not merely on Gyffer and Innish-Kyl—the newsreaders on Galcen talk about you as well. They say you are something more than a successful pirate—"

"Privateer," he corrected. "I bear letters of marque and reprisal."

A whole sheaf of them, in fact, from the Citizen-Assembly on Gyffer and a host of other sources, including the Galcenian Council and the Highest of Khesat—and Veratina Rosselin herself, by way of House Rosselin's ambassador on Perpayne. But if the young woman across from him didn't know that, Jos Metadi wasn't going to tell her. Knowledge was power, and it was never a good idea to give away power to somebody with whom you were trying to strike a deal.

"My apologies, Captain," Perada said, her expression unruffled. "Privateer. And something more. If the newsreaders don't lie—and I have excellent sources who say that they do not—you have proven yourself able to meld independent raiders into a fleet and carry the war to the enemy."

"Enemy?" Jos shook his head. "No. Enemies are personal. None of this is personal with me. I take prizes—rich ones—and I take them for the goods and merchandise they carry. If your sources are any good, they should have mentioned that I don't fight warships if I can help it."

"You fight when you must, and you win when you fight." Her voice remained composed. "I have decided. You are the man who will return with me to Entibor and, once there, make a warfleet for me."

The certainty of it nettled him. "You've decided, have you?"

"You will be amply rewarded."

"I have enough money," he said. "And if I want more, I know how to get it. I don't need to cramp my style by putting myself under anybody else's command." He stood up. "I'm sorry, but there's no advantage for me in taking your offer. Now, if you'll excuse me—"

"No," said the Domina. "I have not given you leave."

"I didn't ask," he said. "I'm a free citizen of Gyffer, and nobody's subject. Which means I come and go as I please, and right now it pleases me to go."

"Wait!"

He paused, one hand on the door. "I told you, I don't want money."

"Money isn't the only reward." Her blue eyes were very bright. She reminded him of a gambler just before the last card went down. "Name your price, Captain. I can meet it."

"Sorry," he said. "But I don't play cards with somebody else's deck."

He pressed the lockplate to open the door. Nothing happened. He turned back to the Domina.

"I hope you're the one who set the door to lock behind

us," he said. "Because otherwise, I think we've got a problem."

Ser Hafrey gave the Domina and the merchant-captain plenty of time to begin their discussion before he made any move to leave. He checked the lockplate on the private room first, to make certain that all was in order, then moved toward the outer door.

As he did so, he ignored the other man in the room. As Minister of Internal Security for Entibor, Nivome do'Evaan of Rolny shouldn't have come on this journey in the first place. He should have stayed behind on Entibor to make ready for the Domina's accession. But the Rolnian had insisted; had, in fact, exerted the considerable political power of his office to force himself onto the mission.

Perhaps it was better to keep Nivome busy close at hand, where his schemes for advancement could be watched and countered, rather than leaving him to work his machinations in the palace undisturbed. Nevertheless, Hafrey found the minister's self-interest distasteful—and felt, therefore, no obligation to tender his associate any more than the minimum of deference.

Stepping past Nivome, the armsmaster opened the door and glanced out into the hall. As he had expected, *Warhammer*'s second-in-command was nowhere in sight. Hafrey stepped back into the room and closed the door before addressing the Minister of Internal Security directly for the first time.

"The copilot's away. We should be going as well."

The minister's expression of disapproval didn't change. "You, maybe. I'm staying right here."

"The word Her Dignity used was 'leave.' "

Nivome didn't move from his position against the wall. "The Domina of Entibor should not be wandering the streets of Waycross unprotected."

Ser Hafrey allowed himself a faint smile. "I doubt that she will be."

He bowed—the slight inclination of formal politeness, nothing more—and added, "Nevertheless, we must all comport ourselves according to our inclinations. I'll wait for you at the ship."

The armsmaster departed from the Double Moon without looking back, and made a slow and introspective passage through Waycross to the docks. All along the dockside thoroughfares, the ranks of grounded starships waited in their bays, each enclosure separated from the next by privacy walls looming even taller than the ships themselves.

The gates of *Warhammer*'s bay stood open. From the look of things, the Innish-Kyllan dockworkers had begun to off-load cargo while the captain and his copilot worked off their nerves and excess energy along the Strip.

Ser Hafrey lingered in the shadows for a while, watching as the skipsleds ran in empty and departed stacked high with shrouded loads—the pick of the loot from Metadi's Ophelan run. The worklights mounted on top of the privacy walls were harsh and blue–white, mimicking in their spectra the suns of another world.

Warhammer was an ugly vessel, at least to the armsmaster's exacting eye—a huge, flattened disk that stood on heavy metal landing legs. Its cargo doors gaped open, with ramps leading down to the floor of the bay. A shower of blue–white sparks rained from the underside of the freighter, where somebody was making repairs to the skin of the ship.

After a few minutes Hafrey moved away again, continuing toward his own ship: an Entiboran Crown courier, small and fast and discreetly armed against the day when speed alone would not answer. He showed his identification to the scanner at the entry force field and walked through the main passageway to the bridge. Once there, he settled back in the command chair, laced his fingers in his lap, and closed his eyes, calming himself and bringing his thoughts into a better order.

If all went well, he told himself, matters would proceed as he intended. If not, then he would deal with reality as it developed. Ser Hafrey was old—far older than he gave others to understand, or than he ever admitted even in his most private thoughts—and he had schooled himself long ago to accommodate the universe when it decided to change itself around him.

"Whoever locked the door," Perada said, "it wasn't me."

She regarded the captain uncertainly as she spoke. She'd been expecting an older man; not as old as Ser Hafrey, perhaps, but at least someone well into the middle of life. Jos Metadi, however, looked barely a decade older than she was herself.

Tall and tawny-haired, he wore dark trousers and a spidersilk shirt underneath a crimson velvet coat fastened with massive gold buttons. An odd combination, she would have thought—but thanks to Ser Hafrey's preliminary report, she knew that rich, almost gaudy, clothing was the traditional mark of a prominent captain, an advertisement of his success in the same way that the heavy blaster, its holster tied down to his thigh, was a mark of his violent profession.

Metadi had come a long way in a short time, then, and he wanted to go even farther. A good sign, she hoped. Just the same, he was an untried quality. Veratina's court on Entibor hadn't contained anyone like him; neither had the finishing school on Galcen. She drew a breath and tried for a note of careful detachment.

"You say we might have a problem?"

He glanced at her again and nodded. "I'm not sure if you're the target, or if I am, or if it's the two of us together—but I'm feeling more like someone has me locked and tracking with fire control than makes me comfy."

"Oh." At least, she reflected, Captain Metadi had spoken of "we" and "us." Maybe there was a chance she could bring him around after all.

Great-Aunt 'Tina would be furious—the Head of House Rosselin taking a Gyfferan nobody for Consort!

She was willing to go that far if she had to. Ser Hafrey hadn't approved of the idea when she'd broached it to him on the hyperspace run to Innish-Kyl, but he knew better than to gainsay the Domina on a dynastic matter.

Captain Jos Metadi was not, after all, simply a Gyfferan nobody. His family and his early history might be untraceable—if Ser Hafrey said that a man's lineage was obscure, no conventional records check was going to provide the information—but his current fame and his known accomplishments were matters of established fact. Jos Metadi was, by anybody's reckoning, the foremost captain among the privateers of Innish-Kyl, and the only one who had proved consistently able to bring other ships under his command.

If he can do it for a rabble of pirates, she told herself, *he can do it for me.*

Meanwhile, the captain was rummaging under the tapestries that covered the walls of the private room.

"Damned thing's back here somewhere," she heard him mutter under his breath. He let the tapestry drop back against the wall. "I wasn't counting on a room with only one way out."

"My fault, I'm afraid. Ser Hafrey insisted—the better to control the circumstances of our discussion, he said."

"I hope he hasn't controlled us right into a bloody ambush," Metadi commented. His Gyfferan accent was stronger than it had been, and there was an edge to his voice that hadn't been there when he came in. "I suppose he insisted on scanning the room for spy-eyes and snoop-buttons?"

"Of course," she said. "But there weren't any."

"No electronics." Metadi was prowling about the perimeter of the room, looking for she didn't know what. "Then how would they . . . hah!"

He'd come to the alcove with the bed, where heavy curtains swagged across the entrance partly hid and partly revealed the cushioned interior. He seized the fabric of the curtains with one hand and jerked it aside. Light came into the alcove from the glowcubes that illuminated the room itself, and Perada saw with a faint sense of shock that the entire back wall of the alcove was a single large mirror.

She blinked, and swallowed. "What? Surely you don't—not now?"

Metadi wasn't listening. He picked up one of the high-backed wooden chairs, lifted it over his head, and threw it full-force into the alcove. The chair hit the mirror with a tremendous splintering crash. Shards of silver-backed glass fell down like spangles onto the bed below. Where the mirror had been, Perada saw an empty hole—and beyond that, a small room with walls of dead black, and a pale, clerkish-looking man with an expression of intense surprise on his otherwise unremarkable face.

"One-way glass," said Metadi. He'd drawn that heavy blaster she'd noticed earlier, and was pointing it at the clerk—which explained, Perada thought, why the man hadn't made any attempt to run away. "I expect that news of our chat is all over Innish-Kyl by now. In a week most of the civilized galaxy will know about it. In two, even the Magelords will know."

"You expected something like this, didn't you?"

"Let's say it doesn't surprise me very much."

By now, Metadi was inside the black-walled cubicle, presenting the frightened clerk with a close-range view of his blaster. "Maybe our friend here is nothing but a random pervert who bought himself an evening at the peep show—but it's a lot more likely that he's a paid spy."

The clerk turned even paler than before. "No, no . . ."

"A pervert, then," said Metadi. "In that case, gentlesir, it will only increase your enjoyment if I tie you securely before we go."

He glanced about the little room, frowning slightly. Perada thought that he seemed to be looking for something.

"The curtain ropes," she said. "Will those do?"

"Good thinking. Pull 'em down."

The ropes were thick and sturdy underneath their velvet casings. Perada worked quickly, and soon had an armful of them ready to pass across the glass-strewn bed to Captain Metadi, who holstered his blaster and set about binding the unfortunate clerk.

"There," he said when he was done. He looked down at the clerk, now trussed and tied like a fowl for the roasting.

"I wouldn't struggle, by the way, if I were you. You'll only strangle yourself."

"He isn't struggling," Perada felt obliged to point out. "He's too scared."

"Smart man," Metadi said. He extended a hand to help her scramble over the couch. "There you are, Domina. Let's go."

PERADA ROSSELIN—five years old, her pale yellow hair barely long enough to make into braids—shivered as she made her way carefully along the second-floor ledge of her mother's manor house. She wished she'd remembered to wear a jacket. The late-spring sun of Felshang Province looked bright and warm, but outside, and this high above the ground, the wind was cold.

She'd reached the ledge quite easily, by climbing over the sill of the casement window in the upstairs guest bedroom next to the nursery. Because it was the smallest and most inconvenient of the empty rooms, nobody had ever noticed that the force field over the window opening didn't work anymore. The ledge itself was over a foot wide, and the big bluestone statues that stood along it at intervals were tall enough to hide a small person from anyone looking up from below.

Just the same, she'd taken care not to be seen. *She* knew that she wasn't going to fall off the ledge, but she also knew that none of the adults in the house would ever agree. If anybody suspected that the ledge, with its high, windy solitude and its view of the fields and vineyards of Felshang, was her secret haven, then the window in the empty room would be locked and the force field repaired—and Perada would be taking all her meals in the nursery until Mamma decided she'd grown up enough to know better.

So Perada was always very quiet, and very cautious, when she went out onto the ledge. Especially today. She made her way on hands and knees past the nursery windows, and eased herself an inch at a time across the carved stone lap of the statue on the southwest corner. At last she came to a spot outside the open windows of her mother's study.

She squeezed herself into place beyond the outflung pane of the open casement, in a nook sheltered from the wind by the hunched shoulder of a bluestone gargoyle. She didn't normally risk coming so far, but today she had a special reason. She wanted to listen to what Mamma and Dadda were talking about when she wasn't there.

Dadda had come down from the capital by aircar that morning—in the middle of the week during school season, which wasn't usual for him—and all through lunch he and Mamma had spoken to each other in worried-sounding half-sentences. Perada had understood without asking that they didn't want to talk about it in front of her—whatever "it" was that could make Mamma look frightened and solemn and excited all at once—but they were talking about it now, in Mamma's study.

"She won't do it," Mamma was saying, and Perada knew that they were talking about Great-Aunt Veratina. Not just at the Felshang manor house, but everywhere, "*she*" in that tone of voice always meant the Domina of Entibor: a tall, hatchet-faced woman with iron–grey hair and pale, cold eyes, loved and feared and hated and worshiped in almost equal proportions by everyone in Perada's life.

"It's not a matter of 'won't,' " Dadda said. Dadda was Owen Lokkelar, a professor of galactic history at Felshang University and Mamma's husband by ·commoners'-rite. "She *can't* do it."

"Can't do what?" Mamma sounded angry—and afraid,

too, which made Perada, crouched out of sight on the ledge, hug her knees and shiver. "Can't come out and say what everybody from here to the Far Colonies knows perfectly well already—that she's as barren as a parched field and has been for the last thirty-seven years?"

Barren ... Perada had heard that word before, when the nursery maid and the majordomo were talking in the hallway while they thought she was napping. "A bad thing," the majordomo had said; "no vigor left in *that* line, anyone can see it. Not like our own lady."

"She can't afford to make it official," Dadda said. "As soon as she does, the factions will start pressing on her twice as hard."

"I don't blame them," said Mamma. "You know how people are about things like that, even in this day and age. If she doesn't either step down or name somebody capable, they'll start blaming the House for every disaster that comes along."

"After word of this gets out, she won't dare name anyone," Dadda said. He'd started using what Perada thought of as his teacher–voice, the one that her mother always listened to. "She's broken tradition—which most people could forgive her for; this isn't five hundred years ago—and she's failed at it, which nobody is ever going to forgive."

Nobody said anything for a while. Perada wished she dared look in through the open window and see their faces—she could almost always tell from the faces what people were thinking. At last her mother said, "If she doesn't name anyone, it all comes down to the closest heir left. Now that the Chereeves are out of the picture, with that oldest girl of theirs cutting her braids so disgracefully, exactly who might be closest is a matter for discussion."

"It won't be for long." Dadda sounded worried, which wasn't like him. "It's going to be the Blood Tontine all over again."

"Not for me," Mamma said. "I'm out of all that."

There was another long pause, and then Dadda said, very quietly, "But should you be?"

Mamma sighed. "Damn you, Owen. I was afraid you

were going to come around to that. You know what it'll mean, though."

"I know," Dadda said. "One of the Urnvards would be a good choice, I think; or Gersten Kiel, if you prefer. He's produced nothing but girls so far, and he did well enough for 'Rada."

"Mmm. I'd hoped that maybe you—"

"Not when the stakes are so high. If you want to play at all, you can't make any sentimental choices."

"No." Mamma's voice sounded tight and brittle, like sugar candy drawn out fine and ready to break. "The question is, do I want to play?"

There was another long pause. "For the sake of your House, Shaja . . . I think you have to."

II. Galcenian Dating 974 A.F.
Entiboran Regnal Year 38 Veratina

THE SECRET room had a hinged door with an old-style mechanical latch, leading into a narrow service hallway dimly lit by a flickering low-power light panel. Metadi latched the door behind them from the outside.

"That should buy us a minute or two," he said. "Now, let's see . . . if I'm not lost, the rear exit to this dump should be down that way."

"I don't believe it," Perada said, after an unsuccessful struggle against her baser impulses. "You really do know the back door of every bordello in Waycross."

The captain threw a quick glance in her direction. "People say that about me, do they?"

She didn't know what to say in reply—most of Nivome and Ser Hafrey's comments on the subject of Jos Metadi had been even more uncomplimentary than that. But the captain had already found what she supposed was the way out, another hinged door set flush with the grimy plast-block wall of the service corridor. He set his hand against it, pushed, and the door swung open.

"This way, Domina."

She followed him out into what looked—and smelled—like a back alley, full of slimy puddles and malodorous garbage bins, illuminated only by the occasional blue safety glow. She wrinkled her nose.

"It's not as clean as the front lobby," Metadi said, as if he'd seen her change of expression. "But it's probably safer at the moment."

Something hot and bright red zinged past them before he finished speaking, and the plast-block next to Perada's head bubbled up and blistered from the sudden intense heat. She drew breath to exclaim something—she wasn't sure what—only to have most of the wind knocked out of her when the captain pushed her full-length onto the reeking pavement of the alley.

Another instant, and he was on top of her, a warm and solid weight, with the gold buttons of his fine velvet coat digging into the flesh along her spine. Any urge she might have felt to protest died as soon as she realized that his entire body was between her and the source of the unexpected attack. For attack it was; Metadi had his blaster out and in hand, and she heard footsteps approaching, sounding rapid but at the same time cautious. She felt the captain's free hand on her shoulder, pressing her down . . . *Stay quiet.* She had no trouble in interpreting the wordless command. *Don't move.*

Perada endeavored not to breathe.

The footsteps drew closer—coming to check on the kill, she supposed. Then the weight on her back lifted as Metadi rolled away. A loud, high-pitched buzz sounded from close overhead, followed by the pop-and-flash of an exploding glow. She turned her head sideways as much as she could without raising it above the pavement, and saw Metadi, now in deep shadow, fire the heavy blaster twice more down the alley.

The whole exchange, from the first shot to Metadi's last, had taken only a few seconds. The owner of the footsteps was nowhere in evidence. Metadi rose out of the half-crouch from which he had fired, and held out a hand—presumably, Perada thought, it was safe for her to get up. She took the offered hand, and stood.

Her mask was gone, forgotten and left back in the Double Moon. The blue dress—carefully chosen for the interview just past—had lost several of the tiny, hand-sewn buttons that gave the bodice its exquisite fit, and she didn't want to think about what nameless substances might have been ground into the delicate fabric. On the other hand, she was alive, when she might well have been otherwise; and the understanding of it filled her with a peculiar sense of exhilaration.

"Time to leave this place behind," the captain said. "Even in Waycross, if you fire a blaster somebody eventually shows up to investigate."

"How soon is 'eventually'?" Perada inquired. Getting arrested was something that Nivome and Ser Hafrey could extricate her from, but they'd exact a high price for their complicity in such an escapade. Legal entanglements, then, were best avoided.

"Soon enough that camping out at this address isn't a good idea," said Metadi. "Where were you supposed to be meeting your two buddies after our chat was over?"

She gestured at the building behind them. "In there—the front lobby."

"No good, I'm afraid. You came here from off-planet; is your ship waiting for you dirtside, or up in orbit?"

" 'Dirtside'? Oh. Down here, yes." She paused. "I'm sorry I can't give you any better directions—I never expected the need."

She heard him laugh quietly in the dark.

"Domina, if I can't find a ship when it's in port, I'll eat my pilot's license. I'll get you home safe—it's the least I can do." Blaster in hand, he started down the alley in the direction from which the shots and footsteps had come.

"That way?" she asked, hesitating. "I thought . . ."

"So did they, probably." He paused, then reached into his coat pocket and pulled out a second, smaller blaster. "But in case they didn't—did that finishing school you were at teach you how to work one of these things?"

She shook her head. "I'm afraid the curriculum didn't include a course in heavy artillery. Sorry."

Metadi pressed the weapon into her hand anyway. "It's easy," he said. His hand was warm over hers. "You hold it here, and when you want to shoot it, you press on this stud here with your thumb. Whatever's standing in front of the bell goes away."

"How about aiming it?"

"No time to practice that—just don't point it at me."

She hefted the blaster. It had an oddly heavy feel to it for its small size, and she felt inclined to treat it with considerable respect. "Is there a—what do you call it? A safety mechanism?"

"I've already armed it."

"You seem to have thought of everything," she said—and at that moment the back entrance to the Double Moon flew open and a voice shouted, "It's them! Stop them!"

"Come on," Metadi said, and sprinted for the mouth of the alley. Perada gathered up her skirts with her free hand and followed after him. Somewhat to her surprise, nobody shot at them from either direction.

When they reached the juncture of the alley and the street beyond, she understood why. The man who'd carried her message upstairs to Captain Metadi was standing there waiting for them, leaning on what she thought at first was an Adept's staff.

Surely not, she thought, and then saw that the staff was a bar of plain metal, such as anybody might pick up and wield. Three men lay motionless on the pavement nearby, their weapons fallen from their hands.

"I thought you'd given up that sort of thing," Metadi said. There was a note in the captain's voice that Perada couldn't quite identify, as if he'd touched on something that was an old issue between him and his copilot.

The other man—Errec Ransome, that was his name— glanced sideways at the bar of metal, and shrugged. "One uses the tools that come to hand. I'll deep-space it once we leave orbit, if it makes you happier."

"Up to you," Metadi said. "But we'd better go."

He started down the street at a brisk pace, threading his way through the press of vehicles and pedestrians. Nobody seemed to notice his blaster, still at the ready in his hand, or perhaps nobody cared. Nor, to Perada's relief, did anybody seem to notice her: the blue spidersilk gown was a good deal more formal than what passed for the usual female garb in this part of Waycross, but the mud-stained fabric and ripped bodice—and the blaster Metadi had given her—apparently sufficed to camouflage the fact.

"So what happened?" Ransome said to Metadi. "Get into trouble again?"

Again? wondered Perada, but Metadi didn't break stride.

"Some kind of misunderstanding," he said, hurrying through the noisy crowd. Ransome matched his pace easily, but Perada—shorter than both of them and hampered by the long skirt of her gown—had to half-run to keep up. "What about you? Find out anything?"

"Quite a bit," Ransome said, followed by something in the unfamiliar language he and the captain had spoken together earlier. Perada wondered if it was the copilot's birth-tongue that he and Metadi used for privacy's sake, or the captain's.

Another cry of "There they are! Over that way!" made itself heard above the noise of the crowd. Metadi looked in the direction of the shout.

"Uh-oh," he said, picking up his pace. "Security goons. Time to get scarce."

"But you said—" Perada began, at the same time as Ransome said, "What about her?"

"She comes with us," said Metadi. "We had an interesting conversation after you left."

"And that made people madder at you than wrecking fifty Mage warships did?"

Fifty? Perada wondered breathlessly—she was running in earnest now, gripping the blaster in one hand and her skirt in the other. Her soft blue slippers would never recover from this expedition through the trash and slime of Waycross's port quarter.

Boots, she thought. *I'm going to need boots.*

She heard the whining, zinging sound of blaster-fire again a second later; the bolts of ugly red light came near to hitting more than one of the people thronging the busy street. The crowd thinned out almost instantly, in what she supposed must be a local survival skill, and Metadi paused long enough to turn and fire back.

"Teach 'em to keep their damned heads down, anyway," he observed; and then, in response to Errec Ransome's question: "Looks like it did. All I know is that somebody sure as hell didn't like what the lady had to say."

Amid the welter of broken glass on the floor of the Double Moon, Festen Aringher rolled onto his back. The curtain cords that bound him were tight, but the privateer captain, while thorough and efficient, had not been as ruthless as his words had implied—so long as Aringher didn't mind cramped muscles, he wouldn't choke himself by moving.

He inched back with his shoulders, trying for purchase against a wall. Bits of glass crunched underneath the heavy broadcloth of his coat and scraped against the bare skin of his wrists and hands. He winced as his movements ground the splinters even deeper, but he didn't stop.

He needed to find a shard of glass long enough to cut through the cords around him; with luck, he wouldn't slash any important blood vessels at the same time. Once he'd done the first loop, the rest of the escape would be tedious, but not difficult. Some minutes later he had moved all the way against the wall, and had gotten several small and annoying cuts on his hands and arms in the process of attempting to sever the cord. Otherwise, he was no closer to freedom than he had been when he started. He stopped working, intending to catch his breath for a few seconds before starting over.

Only then did Aringher notice that he was being watched.

A slender woman wearing a coronet of dark braids stood with crossed arms in the broken frame of the mirror.

"Mistress Vasari," Aringher said. "I should have known you'd take an interest in tonight's proceedings eventually. You didn't consider untying me, did you?"

"Briefly. But you looked like you were having so much fun I decided to let you go on." She looked around the tiny, black-walled room. "I didn't think that you were interested in this kind of thing."

"I'm not," he said. "Come on, untie me."

"If you insist." She knelt behind him, and he felt her fingers tugging at the knots. A little longer, and he was free.

She helped him to his feet. He stood massaging his wrists and shrugging his shoulders, trying to get back the circulation.

"If you don't get off on this," she said finally, "then what's the point?"

"All in good time," he said, flexing his stiffened fingers. Most of the cuts had stopped bleeding, and the blood had started to dry. He took a few seconds to glance around the inner room where the Domina and Captain Metadi had held their conference. Except for the torn bed curtains and the broken glass—and a black velvet mask lying forgotten on the table—no evidence remained of that earlier encounter. Aringher contemplated the mask for a moment, then almost absentmindedly picked it up and stowed it in his jacket pocket. One never knew when such things might come in useful.

"I learned something tonight," he said, "that may be to our advantage."

"Right. How do you feel about getting out of here, now that you've learned it?"

"Highly positive," Aringher said. "I believe I've exhausted all the possibilities of the current situation."

The two walked together into the outer room. Vasari pursed her lips thoughtfully. "What are the odds that the first person out in the hall gets picked up by Security?"

"About fifty-fifty," Aringher said. "Did you bring a blaster?"

"Better yet. I brought two."

"You know me too well, I'm afraid. Well, nothing for it."

He took the weapon from her outstretched hand, and pressed the lockplate enough to disengage the bolt. Then he kicked the door, making it fly open, and in the same movement threw himself out into the hall in a low, flat dive. The action brought him up against the far wall, lying prone with his blaster leveled toward the farther reaches of the Double Moon.

Nothing else happened. The hall was deserted.

"Do you know how silly I feel lying here?" he asked, after a little while.

"I have my suspicions," she said. "Shall we away?"

Aringher pushed himself back up onto his feet. "Your place or mine?"

"Yours is closer."

"Then let's go."

A short walk later, the two of them were safely ensconced in Festen Aringher's apartment overlooking the Strip. Monitors and projectors flashed against three of the four walls in the main room, filling the place with a babble of images and sounds. Aringher had stripped off his jacket and shirt and was busy applying antiseptic to his cuts. Mistress Vasari sat curled up on the divan watching him.

"Time for a talk," she said. "What brought you to the Double Moon, and how did you end up in such an undignified position?"

"You see before you," Aringher said, "a martyr to the cause of a more equitable galactic polity. I came to the Double Moon because I had heard that Captain Metadi made Waycross his usual port of call, and the Double Moon his usual site of recreation, after a successful voyage. As it happens, I desired speech with the good captain on a certain subject."

"Dare I ask?"

"My unending search for truth, beauty, peace, wisdom—"

"Money."

"There is that," he admitted. "But we never spoke, Captain Metadi and I, except informally in passing. Before I could arrange a meeting, I heard that someone of considerable importance was already in the building in search of the good captain, and an interview between them was to commence in mere minutes. As I soon discovered, that someone was the Domina of Entibor herself."

"Veratina?" Vasari looked surprised. "I know the old lady has an eye for well-set-up young men, but—"

"Your gossip is sadly out of date, my dear. Veratina's dead, and the new Domina is a schoolgirl fresh out of the Delaven Academy on Galcen."

"She's not wasting any time, then, is she?"

"Indeed not," said Aringher. "Which stirred my curiosity a great deal, let me tell you. 'Why,' I asked myself, 'should this person be seeking that person?' Motives interest me, so I decided to find out—and what I learned is that an innocent, beautiful . . ."

"Rich."

". . . rich young woman desired to contract an alliance with an old, deceitful—"

"Spare me. Jos Metadi is younger than you are."

"Details, details. What counts is that the new Domina appeared to have reached the same conclusion I had, of the need for this particular man in that particular job at this very time. Not only that, she had learned, as had I, the best place to find him—and while I had determined to wait until he was finished with other business before pressing my case, she was bolder. In short, the sly minx outmaneuvered me."

Vasari smothered a laugh. "That has to be a first."

"Regrettably, it isn't." Aringher sighed theatrically. "Yet while I couldn't be the earliest person to open negotiations with Captain Metadi, I was admirably positioned to become the best-informed. And what I learned is that neither Metadi nor the young woman really wanted to make the bargain. I was mentally rehearsing my own presentation to the captain, setting forth our cause in terms based on my new knowledge, when . . . well, I've seen people be manipulated before . . ."

"You've done your own share of manipulating."

"True, I confess," said Aringher. He shrugged, grimacing a little as the motion tugged at the cuts along his shoulder blades. "At any rate, just as it appeared that no agreement could be reached between the two of them, another party decided to take a hand in the proceedings. Subsequently I was discovered. The rest you know."

" 'Another party'?" Mistress Vasari's eyes gleamed with a businesslike curiosity. "Mages, do you think?"

"I doubt it, my dear. The captain and the young lady are still alive, and the Double Moon is still standing. Considering the magnitude of the grudge the Mages must hold against Jos Metadi, any attempt at revenge would involve considerably more than a locked door and, from the sound of it, a few poorly aimed blaster bolts in a dark alley."

"Well, it wasn't me, I assure you."

"I never thought for a minute that it might be."

"Go on."

Aringher put away the bottle of antiseptic and pulled on a fresh shirt. "Anyway, somebody else wanted the deal to go through—so they arranged an attack, in order to make the Domina and Captain Metadi allies by sharing a common danger. But not, mind you, too *much* danger. In fact, the more I think about it, the more I believe that the whole purpose of the exercise was to separate the Domina from her escort, and to throw her into the company of Jos Metadi."

"Tricky, tricky," Vasari said, in approving tones. "Who was it?"

"My question precisely." He slipped on his jacket and began doing up the buttons. "And I believe that the answer can be found on Entibor."

The Armsmaster of House Rosselin was still sitting in the courier ship's command chair when Nivome returned.

"So there you are," the Rolnian said. "Asleep."

Hafrey opened his eyes and turned them toward the Minister of Internal Security. "Not sleeping," he said. "Thinking. A practice I would recommend to you."

"This isn't the time for sarcasm," said Nivome. "There

was violence at the Double Moon—the Domina is missing, perhaps even dead."

Hafrey regarded the dark, heavyset Rolnian dispassionately. "I think I can ease your mind somewhat concerning Her Dignity's whereabouts. If you would accompany me?"

"Of course," Nivome said. "Lead the way."

The two men left the ship, retracing Ser Hafrey's course to the shadows outside the docking bay where *Warhammer* had rested not long before. The worklights along the top of the privacy walls were dark, and the blast doors were shut. The dockworkers and their skipsleds had gone on to another ship and another cargo, leaving silence behind.

"It's empty," said Nivome. "They've already lifted and gone to orbit."

"True enough." Hafrey let the implied complaint go unanswered. "If you would be patient a while longer—"

He busied himself at the juncture of the wall and the blast door. After a few minutes he gave a brief nod of satisfaction, and stepped back. In one hand he held a small black cube, scarcely a thumbnail's length on a side. He offered the cube to Nivome.

"You may examine the record, if you like."

Nivome picked up the spy-eye, but didn't bother to look at it. "You're too sure of yourself. What have you arranged for me to see?"

"I? Nothing. But if you watch, you will see Her Dignity enter the ship in company with Captain Metadi."

The Rolnian clenched his fist around the black cube. "You're her guardian, and you approve of this?"

"She is the Domina," Hafrey pointed out. "And Entibor is most decidedly not Rolny. It is not for us to approve or disapprove."

The armsmaster paused to allow the reproof time to sink in. Nivome do'Evaan had a good deal of native shrewdness and physical courage, along with vaulting ambition and a high opinion of his own worth—a mixture of qualities that had made him useful to Veratina in her later years. Domina Perada, Hafrey was relieved to note, was proving herself less easily impressed by his talents—physical and otherwise—than her predecessor had been.

"In any case," Ser Hafrey added, "so long as the Domina reaches Entibor in good time, no one will care what happened on Innish-Kyl."

"Metadi's copilot knows about it. If *he* knows, so will the whole ship's crew, and half the port."

"Ah, yes; the Ilarnan. An interesting fellow, that one. But I don't think he'll talk." Hafrey stepped away from the sealed blast doors and the empty bay. "Enough chatter. Are you satisfied?"

Nivome remained unmollified. "I still want to check out the Double Moon."

"If you like," replied Hafrey, unperturbed.

They turned to go. But in that moment three men emerged from the shadows before them—portside bullyboys, from their clothing. All three of them had blasters ready.

"Ah," Ser Hafrey said. "Good evening, gentles all."

"Hands up," said the biggest and tallest member of the trio. He lifted his blaster by way of emphasis. "You're coming with us."

Nivome made a grab for his jacket pocket and one of the gunmen shot him down. He collapsed, holding his belly and gasping in pain. Hafrey glanced in his direction and raised his hands.

"Search them," ordered the man who had spoken before.

Hafrey submitted to the search calmly. Nivome, however, came close to choking as the other two thugs hauled him upright and went through his clothing piece by piece. They removed both the spy-eye and the needler he'd kept hidden inside his jacket, then dropped him onto the pavement.

The leader glanced over at Ser Hafrey. "Come on, you."

"Of course," said Hafrey mildly. "Those of us who are professionals understand such things."

He took a step forward. At a nod from their leader, the two gunmen who had been searching Nivome fell in like guards, one to either side of the armsmaster. A heartbeat later, the one to Hafrey's right dropped his blaster.

The heavy-duty Gyfferan Special fell to the concrete with a metallic clatter, loud in the silence of late-night portside. The man looked startled and opened his mouth as if to speak, but nothing came out except a gush of foamy, bright-red blood. He collapsed to his knees, then toppled forward onto his face, blood pooling under his head.

Ser Hafrey reached out and tapped the number-one thug on the shoulder. The man sat down heavily, his arms and legs splayed out like the limbs of a rag doll. Now only the gunman to Hafrey's left remained standing. He held a blaster in one hand, but he wasn't moving, and his eyes were large and dark with fear. Hafrey's left hand rested against the man's neck.

"Did you know," the armsmaster said conversationally to the man sitting helpless on the pavement, "that there are over two hundred pressure points on the human body—points which, properly manipulated, can cause anything from paralysis of half-a-minute's duration to symptomless death eight hours later? In your case, your arms and legs will remain useless to you for a bit, although your eyes and ears will serve you well enough. In the case of your comrade—" Ser Hafrey nodded at the man who stood sweating beside him. "—I am not going to use pressure points at all. Rather, this is a mechanical."

This was something metallic and glittering, barely visible for an instant between Hafrey's fingers.

"Now," said the armsmaster to the man beside him, "I want you to place your blaster underneath your chin, pointing up toward the top of your head."

The man was pale and shivering, but his arm responded, lifting the weapon and pushing the muzzle into the soft skin under his jaw.

"I don't approve of people who attempt violence toward me or my associates," Hafrey said. His tone was, if possible, even milder than before. "I want you to press the firing stud."

There was a wash of crimson light—the close-range aura of a blaster firing on full power—and the man's head exploded outward and back, leaving a gory crater where the dome of the skull had been. A shiny metal wire protruded from the top of the curdled, blackened mass inside.

Incredibly, the man still stood, his blaster pressed up against his chin and a thin curl of smoke drifting away from the entry burn.

"Steam explosion," Ser Hafrey explained. "Very messy."

He withdrew his hand from the neck of the standing man, taking with it a long metal object that had been buried point upward in the man's neck. As he did so, the bit of wire disappeared from above the dead man's ruined skull, and the lifeless body crumpled to the pavement.

Hafrey made the metal spike disappear. "You'll notice that you are beginning to regain feeling in your hands," he said to the third man, who remained sprawling half-paralyzed on the ground. "Please signal this by releasing your weapon."

The man's right hand twitched, and the blaster hit the ground.

"Excellent. Now I want you to stand up."

The man stood, not looking at either of his former companions. Hafrey nodded approvingly.

"Very good. Now go home. Don't come back, and don't signal or talk to anyone along the way. If you do, I'll see that you regret it. I assume I have made myself clear?"

The man nodded.

"Then go," Hafrey said.

The man left. Hafrey waited until he was out of sight, then turned his attention to Nivome. The Rolnian was still curled around himself on the pavement, his eyes tight shut and his breath coming in shallow gasps. Hafrey regarded him without emotion.

"Get up," the armsmaster said.

Nivome shook his head without rising. "I need a medic."

"I don't think so," Hafrey said. "Professionals don't bother with using low power unless they want the target to stay healthy. You've only been stung, not hurt."

"I might have known," grumbled Nivome, as he rolled up

onto his knees—and stared, wide-eyed, at the carnage around him. "Lords of Life! What happened?"

"I am the Armsmaster to House Rosselin," Hafrey said. His voice was cold. "Did you think it was merely a customary title? I tell you now, do not play tricks like this with me again. Try it on Entibor, and it won't be your hirelings that suffer."

Jos Metadi: Gyffer
(Galcenian dating 959 A.F.; Entiboran Regnal Year 23 Veratina)

SUNSETS OVER Telabryk Spaceport were always a dirty red from the smoke and debris that the belching jets threw high in the atmosphere, and the twilights sparkled with more than stars as the orbiting dockyards and constructories caught the last of the falling sun. Josteddr Metadi, age twelve and newly enrolled in local politics as a ward heeler's apprentice, didn't have the time or the inclination to appreciate the harsh beauty of the Gyfferan skyscape. Jos had responsibilities to consider: passing out flyers in the neighborhood elections; putting up stickers and posters on walls, utility posts, and recycling bins; tearing down or covering up similar posters for the political opponents of Rorin Gatt.

Jos considered himself lucky to be employed, not caring that his job existed only because under Gyfferan law a minor couldn't be forced to give testimony in court. He didn't need the work—the Citizen-Assembly wouldn't allow a legal resident of Gyffer to starve or freeze or go homeless—but the Citizen-Assembly made no effort to keep anyone from getting bored, either. And even at the age of twelve, Jos Metadi found boredom intolerable.

Running errands for Gatt provided more than enough novelty to keep anyone happy and occupied. Today Jos's route took him to the shuttle platforms of Cronin Ogilvid, where he would scout out locations for one of Gatt's cronies to give a speech and organize the shuttleboppers.

Jos stood outside the automatic gate of the shuttle platform and wondered how to get inside without an authorization. He looked up at the gate—no, that wasn't any good. Too many ID scanners and spy-eyes for Jos's comfort. He circled the platform, checking the perimeter fence line in hopes that the barrier might turn out to be more symbolic than real.

This fence, though, looked tight all the way around, probably to keep Ogilvid Enterprises from being sued right down to its socks if an unauthorized visitor happened to get fried in the exhaust from a shuttle's engines.

Jos went back to the front entrance and took a second look at the autogate. Maybe he didn't have the right ID-scan to get through, but that didn't matter. He knew lots of ways to beat an ID lock. Which trick he used would depend on what sort of traffic went through the gate.

He could watch for someone to show up with a day pass, then steal the pass—but that risked detection and capture and a prolonged social-development session in the hands of Telabryk's Underage Client Services Department. Or he could wait until the gate opened for somebody legit, then duck through before it closed; that way was safer, but likely to require more than one try before he achieved success. Safest and easiest was to make friends with someone who would let him in. . . .

"Here now, lad," came a voice. "What are you doing here?"

The accent wasn't local—not Telabryk dockside, or Telabryk District, or even the smoothed-out speech of the politicians and holovid news announcers.

Off-worlder, Jos thought, and smiled up at his ticket through the gate. "Please, my daddy works in there, and I have to take him a message. Will you help me look for him?"

The worst the man could do was say no. But if he said yes, Jos was in, and free to fade from sight a moment later, then scout the place out and slip away.

"Yes," the man said. He had to be a spacer, Jos thought—the local dockhands and mechanics wore the same kind of loose, drab-colored coverall, but all of them talked straight Gyfferan. "I think you should look for your daddy. Come with me."

The man palmed the lockplate and the gate swung open. Jos stuck close as they walked through. *Give it a twenty-count,* he decided; *then run.* He'd reached "eighteen" when the man's hand came down on his shoulder and caught him in a tight grip.

"Come with me," the man said. "If you don't yell you won't get hurt."

Jos tried to pull away, but the man's grip was too tight. Another fractional amount of pressure, and the bony fingers would meet under his collarbone.

He's got to let go soon, Jos thought. But he didn't. The cruel pressure never let up, forcing Jos into a half-run to match the man's longer stride.

They were heading for a shuttle, an ugly, battered craft. Jos made one last effort to twist away before he was forced inside, but it didn't do any good. The grip on Jos's shoulder tightened so fiercely that tears of pain started in his eyes; then the man half-marched, half-pulled him up the shuttle ramp into the craft's dark, evil-smelling interior.

Jos had seen enough and read enough, in his sporadic and eccentric self-education, to know that the padded bedlike thing the spacer strapped him onto was an acceleration couch. He heard the man speaking over a comm link to somebody called Gyfferan Inspace Control. Then an enormous roaring sound filled the shuttle, and a vast weight pushed him down onto the couch.

After a long time the weight lifted, and he felt another, different kind of sensation, as though he were infinitely light and not connected to anything. If this was what spacers meant when they talked about breaking loose from dirtside gravity, he wasn't surprised that they seemed to like it so much. He'd have enjoyed the feeling himself, if he hadn't been so worried about what was going to happen next.

He heard the man speaking over the comm link to a merchant ship called the *Quorum*. They were talking in spacertalk—whatever the language was that gave the man his distinctive accent—but it sounded enough like dockside Gyfferan that Jos could pick out some of the words. Or maybe dockside lingo was half spacer-talk already, since everybody else on Gyffer made a big deal out of not being able to understand it.

The shuttle docked with *Quorum*, and the man unstrapped Jos and took him aboard the merchant ship. The ship had gravity, but not much. Jos kept taking steps that were too big or too forceful, so that only the man's pincer grip kept him from floating up and colliding with the ceiling. The grip hurt more than it helped, and it made him angry as much as it hurt: what was the point of it, now that he had nowhere to run?

Another man was waiting for them on board the ship. This man looked Jos over, then spoke rapidly to his captor in spacer-talk—too rapidly for Jos to follow, this time. Then he turned back to Jos.

"You listen, boy," he said in badly accented Gyfferan. "You do what we say, you get along. I'm selling you to a good master somewhere else and you're doing fine. You don't, you remember: food on my ship belongs to me, water on my ship belongs to me, air on my ship belongs to me. You want me to take 'em away, you piss me off. Once is all it takes."

III. Galcenian Dating 974 A.F.
Entiboran Regnal Year 38 Veratina

THE HEAVY push of acceleration eased off at last. Perada felt a momentary sense of dislocation, a kind of sliding sideways without any physical motion, and recognized it as the privateer ship's translation into hyperspace. The pilot had gone straight from boost to orbit to a jump without pausing. She drew a deep breath, unstrapped her safety webbing, and sat up on the acceleration couch.

Hafrey, she thought, would be pleased. The side journey to Innish-Kyl hadn't gone entirely according to the plan she had worked out soon after leaving Galcen—she was forming the distinct impression that other people's plans didn't work too well once Captain Metadi became involved—but her situation was already better in several respects than it had been a few weeks before.

"Matters are approaching a crisis," she remembered Hafrey saying after he told her that Great-Aunt Veratina had died. *"You may find that presenting yourself as the late Domina's acknowledged heir is not enough. The people of Entibor must be convinced that you are capable of taking active measures."*

"Well," she muttered as she swung her legs down to the metal deckplates, "I've certainly made a decent beginning."

She stood for a moment with her feet apart, getting her bearings in the 'Hammer's common room. The air in the ship smelled recycled—the same faint, persistent odor of sweat and grime that she'd noticed aboard Ser Hafrey's courier, but stronger here. Scratches and dings marred what she could see of the dull-grey bulkheads. The glow of the overhead light panels failed to penetrate into all the corners—or where the corners would have been, if the room hadn't been circular.

Perada was, for the moment, alone: Captain Metadi and his second had left the compartment as soon as she'd strapped herself in, heading through the forward passageway to what she supposed must be the bridge. Similar exits led away to aft, port, and starboard along the starship's horizontal plane, and an opening in the bulkhead near the acceleration couches gave access to a fifth, vertical passage. Two more openings—one with a door, one without—pierced the bulkhead between the forward and the starboard exits. Ladderlike handholds for zero-g work ran along the tops and sides of the passageways.

In addition to the acceleration seating, the common room held a circular table with chairs bolted to the deck around it. From the table, she could see that the nook beside the forward exit held a cramped galley. Somebody aboard Warhammer took an interest in cooking, she decided; the light panels were brighter inside the galley, and all the surfaces were clean.

The smell of cha'a reminded Perada that she hadn't had anything to eat or drink since Hafrey's courier had touched down on Innish-Kyl. In the excitement of the past few hours she'd forgotten about such mundane matters, but now that she had the leisure to notice them, she became aware that she was both hungry and thirsty. Thanks to the mysterious assailants at the Double Moon, she was also grimy, ragged, and slightly bruised. Not at all the picture of a proper Domina after Great-Aunt Veratina's manner—but that was all right. She wasn't planning to be another Veratina anyway.

In the meantime . . . cha'a.

She went into the galley. The cha'a pot was easy enough to locate—its red On light was glowing. That left finding a cup or a mug of some kind. She tried one of the cabinet doors. It was unlocked, but instead of cups the shelves inside held square flat boxes of commercial space rations and smaller, oddly shaped jars and bottles of condiments, some of them labeled in Standard Galcenian, others in languages she didn't recognize. She knelt down to open one of the lower cabinets.

Maybe in here—

A deep, wordless roaring interrupted her search. She tried to stand up and back away at the same time—a pointless exercise, given the dimensions of the galley, but considering the huge, scaly creature that stood blocking the entrance, she felt compelled to try. The creature advanced a step toward her and she took another step away, hoping without much optimism that she didn't look as scared as she felt.

Then a pleasant soprano voice spoke up from farther back in the common room. "Oh, for heaven's sake, Ferrda, let her find her own cup."

The scaly one rumbled something in reply and backed out into the shadowy common room. He—or she; Perada couldn't tell—was replaced by a thin, birdlike woman wearing a black velvet vest over a loose white shirt, and dark trousers tucked into high leather boots. The woman also wore a matched pair of medium-weight blasters, rigged with the butts turned forward.

Perada reminded herself forcibly that these people were, after all, privateers. *What was it Ser Hafrey said? "Only one step up from pirates, and that a short one."*

She inclined her head politely. "Well met, gentlelady."

"I suppose you're the passenger the captain mentioned," the woman said. There was a faint accent to her Galcenian, as though she'd been speaking the common language of the spaceways long enough to lose all the identifying marks of her native tongue, but not the last lingering traces of it. "I'm Tillijen, number-two gunner. That was Ferrdacorr, ship's engineer. Come on out, and I'll introduce you."

"I'd be honored," Perada said—this was no time, she suspected, to stand on precedence and insist that any honor from the encounter was likely to flow the other way. She made a vague gesture at the cha'a pot. "But—"

Understanding lit up the woman's features. "That's right—you were looking for cha'a. Cups are in that cabinet over there. Take one of the ones with blue rims. They don't belong to anyone."

"Thank you."

The woman faded out of the compartment as silently as Ferrdacorr had done. Perada found a cup and poured some cha'a. She didn't want to bumble around hunting for fixings—she looked undignified enough already—so she took it brown. With the mug in her right hand, she headed back into the main compartment, trailing her left hand against the bulkhead as she went. Ferrdacorr and the woman were sitting at the mess table, watching her.

"I see you've been under way before," Tillijen said.

"I've been in space, yes," Perada said. She took one of the empty seats at the mess table. "To and from school on Galcen, mostly."

"Well then. Welcome to our merry crew. Like I said, this is Ferrdacorr, son of Rillikkikk. Ferrda, for short."

The green scaly one made a rumbling bass noise.

"He says he's pleased to meet you," Tillijen said.

Ferrda said something else, this time directed to the gunner.

"It was a loose translation," she replied. "She's new here."

Again a deep noise.

"Oh, all right." Tillijen turned back to Perada. "He says, 'Another damned thin-skin. I hope she doesn't get in the way.' "

Perada gave the scaly crew member a polite smile and pretended she hadn't heard the translation. "Well met, Gentlesir Ferrdacorr."

"Just a hint," Tillijen said under her breath. "If you're going to smile at him, for heaven's sake don't let him see your teeth. Ferrda's used to us, but some of his people are a bit touchy about things like that."

Ferrdacorr leaned back, smiled, and showed his teeth.

Perada sipped her cha'a and said nothing. School life on Galcen had taught her a number of lessons—among them, that deliberate provocations were best ignored. Maybe *Warhammer*'s engineer had a real problem dealing with anyone who wasn't big and green, or maybe he had a warped sense of humor. Either way, she didn't gain anything by rising to the bait.

Moments later, the sound of boots on the ladder rungs in the vertical passageway heralded a new arrival, a slender woman with ivory skin and a great deal of curly dark hair. She swung out of the passage and leaned up against the bulkhead beside it, hands thrust in trouser pockets, and sang in a clear alto voice:

> *"Come all ye remittance men, listen to me*
> *I'll give you advice of such use as I may,*
> *That you will be guided and not go astray*
> *When you enter the life of a spacer."*

The singer's accent was different from Tillijen's, as well as being a good deal broader. Like the number-two gunner, though, the dark woman had on what Perada guessed were port-liberty clothes—emerald spidersilk and black moiré satin, this time—and another matched pair of blasters. She nodded to the three sitting at the mess table, and kept on singing.

> *"First mind you don't stay down in Waycross too long;*
> *The water is bad and the liquor is strong;*
> *As you have to drink something, you're sure to go*
> * wrong,*
> *And ruin your life as a spacer."*

She pushed herself off of the wall with her shoulders and walked over to the table. "I'm Nannla," she said, putting out her hand. "You?"

Bemused, Perada took it. "Perada Rosselin," she said; and added, prompted by what impulse she wasn't sure, "My friends call me 'Rada."

Tillijen gave the other woman a curious look. "So what was the concert in honor of?"

"Our sudden departure," Nannla said. "And our new guest."

"I didn't have time to ask, before," Perada said. "Where are we supposed to be going?"

I hope I haven't miscalculated everything, she thought. *If it turns out I'm being kidnapped instead of rescued, Ser Hafrey is* never *going to let me forget about it.*

Ferrda rumbled something short. Tillijen shrugged.

"We'll find out soon enough," Nannla said. "When the captain tells us."

The door leading from the common room to the forward areas opened with a snick and a thud. Perada turned toward the sound, and saw the door sliding closed again behind Jos Metadi and Errec Ransome. Errec headed into the galley and emerged with two cups of cha'a. Metadi took one of them and slid into a seat at the mess table. Ransome remained standing, cup in hand—nobody at the table looked surprised or offended, so Perada guessed that the practice was customary with him.

"So, Captain," said Nannla, after the two men had settled themselves. "What's the good word?"

Jos took a long swallow of his cha'a. "The good word is, we're on our way to Ophel."

She stared at him. "Ophel? Are you crazy? We were just *at* Ophel. We stole a bunch of stuff from there, and we blew up everything that we couldn't steal—do you think we're going to be welcome?"

"I thought you and Tilly might be wanting to go back," Jos said. "Because we'll be going to Entibor soon, and, you know . . ."

He made a vague gesture with one hand that Perada didn't have any trouble interpreting: *Let's not talk about it in front of the passenger.*

Nannla shrugged, and the discussion might have ended on that ambiguous note—if Tillijen hadn't half-risen in her seat, her pale eyes bright with indignation.

"Is that how it is, Captain?" she demanded. "When things get interesting, you want to jettison us?"

Metadi shook his head. "That's not it," he said. "I didn't want to make the two of you uncomfortable, is all, or get you in some kind of trouble."

"Who's going to notice me in this rig, after all these years?" Tillijen asked.

The woman's faint accent had gotten stronger and more familiar as she spoke—in response to stress, maybe, or to the subject matter. Strong enough to recognize, in fact. With an effort, Perada kept her reaction from showing on her face; privateers came from everywhere, after all, and what did it matter that the *'Hammer's* number-two gunner was Entiboran?

"Depends on what you mean by 'notice,' " Metadi said. "You may not be able to get out of . . . social obligations."

Tillijen laughed. "You know me, Captain. I can get out of anything."

"It's your call," said Metadi. "But if you honestly don't have a problem, I'd rather keep you and Nannla both. I've never seen a better pair of gunners, and that's a fact."

Nannla gave the captain a half-bow; hard to do from a seated position, with one hand wrapped around a cup of cha'a, but she managed. "And we've never seen a better captain."

"That's right," said Tillijen. "So what's the new plan—straight on to Entibor?"

"We might as well. I'm sure the Domina wants to get there as soon as possible."

Perada looked down for a moment at her cup of cha'a. *This is it,* she thought. *Now's when I find out whether I'm a passenger, a prisoner, or a—a business partner.* She looked up again, and took a deep breath.

"I'm not certain that I do want to go to Entibor," she said. "There's another place I need to stop at first."

The glance Metadi gave her was sharp and alert. "Where?"

"Have you heard of a world called Pleyver?"

"Yes. Tricky place to get in and out of. There's a field around it that blocks hyperspace engines, and realspace navigation through the local system is obscured by gases and such. I don't go there unless it's absolutely necessary."

"Ah," she said. "Does knowing that there's money involved have anything to do with making it absolutely necessary?"

He gave a short laugh. "Almost everything."

"Good. Because there's money on Pleyver."

"Yours or somebody else's?"

"Somebody else's," she said. "An old school friend of mine lives on Pleyver. The money belongs to him—or at least, to his family."

Ferrda hooted softly and growled something under his breath. Jos glared at the big saurian. Tillijen and Nannla both laughed, though, and even Ransome smiled. Perada raised her eyebrows at Tillijen.

"He wants to know if you're planning to borrow the money or steal it," the gunner explained.

"Well . . . what I really need to get on Pleyver is advice."

"Don't sit with your back to the door," Nannla said promptly. "Never volunteer. When in doubt, wear your good clothes."

Perada stifled a giggle. Ser Hafrey had warned her that showing amusement at the wrong moment could be dangerous—and Great-Aunt Veratina had never smiled once in all the times Perada had seen her.

Or maybe Aunt 'Tina never thought anything was funny. I hope I don't get like that.

"Political advice," she said. "The situation with the Mageworlds isn't getting any better, you know."

"We'd noticed," Metadi said.

"You already know what I want to do about it," she said. "The offer stands."

Ferrda made a rumbling noise that Perada didn't have any

trouble interpreting as one of curiosity. The captain reddened.

"I'll explain later," he said hastily. "Meanwhile—anybody have an objection to Pleyver?"

Nannla and Tillijen shook their heads, and Ferrda gave an almost human shrug. Metadi looked at his copilot.

"Errec?"

"Will it help us kill Mages?"

"I was hoping you could tell me about that."

The copilot shook his head. "It's up to you this time—I can't see anything one way or the other."

"Fine." Metadi set down his empty mug and stood up. "Then we're going to Pleyver. All of you get to your places and strap in. I'm going to drop out and change course."

Perada glanced over at the acceleration couch she'd left only a short while before, and started to rise. Metadi put out a hand to stop her.

"I thought I'd let you use my cabin," he said. "The transit to Pleyver's long enough that you'll need someplace better to sleep than in here."

"What about you?"

He shrugged. "There's a spare bunk in number-two crew berthing. Errec snores, but I can live with it."

"If you're sure—"

"I'm sure." He strode over to the door beside the galley nook and hit the control button on the lockplate. "I'm clearing the lock for you—as soon as the door gets your palm-scan you'll be the only one who can open it. My cabin, and everything in it, is at your disposal. Places, everyone!"

With that he turned on his heel—rather too quickly, Perada thought—and strode off toward the bridge.

"You heard the captain," said Errec. Ferrdacorr headed aft, and the two gunners looked at each other, stood, and made for the vertical passageway. Nannla began climbing the ladder upward, and Tillijen swung into the shaft leading down.

So Captain Metadi makes all his jumps and dropouts fully armed, Perada thought. She understood a little bit about the way such things worked—enough to know that the extra power drain would call for expert shiphandling on the captain's part, and to appreciate what the choice said about Metadi himself. *He trusts a lot in his own skill ... and he counts on the universe to give him nothing but unpleasant surprises.*

Of the 'Hammer's crew, now only Errec Ransome remained in the common room. "Will you require help getting strapped in, my lady?" he asked. Like everyone else in the privateer's crew, he spoke Standard Galcenian with a strong planetary accent.

And all of them different, thought Perada. *I have to get Jos Metadi—anyone who can make a crew out of four foreigners and a scaly green whatever-he-calls-himself can make a unified fleet for the civilized galaxy.*

"I think I can get myself ready this time," Perada said. She paused. "If it isn't too personal a question—may I ask where you come from?"

"Ilarna, my lady."

Ilarna, Perada thought. *The Mages captured Ilarna four years back. The rumors were very bad.*

She looked over at the copilot. Errec had gathered up the empty cups from the mess table and carried them to the galley. His expression told her nothing.

"Can I help you with those?" she said.

"No, thank you."

He began stowing the cups in the washer. A moment later, Jos Metadi's voice came over the common-room audio link: "Everyone strap in and strap down. Errec, get on up here."

"I have to go," Errec said, coming out of the galley. "And you'd better do what Jos says. Transitions can be rough."

Perada palmed the lockplate of the captain's cabin. The black plastic pad clicked and flashed, and the door slid open briefly before sighing closed again behind her. She didn't put a lot of faith in Metadi's assurance that from now on it would only open for her. The captain could probably get in with an emergency override any time he wanted to. But the gesture had been a kind one all the same.

The cabin held an acceleration couch—the fastenings were simple, almost rudimentary, and she strapped in quickly. She doubted that Captain Metadi had ever used it; she couldn't imagine him staying locked up in his cabin while the ship was maneuvering. Once she was strapped down, she glanced about the cabin, looking for more indications of Metadi's character.

There wasn't much. The forward bulkhead of the compartment was lined with locking drawers from deck to overhead. To the right, the outer bulkhead held closet doors. And that was it. Other than a holocube and a reading light in a niche by the bed, the cabin was a simple, unadorned bit of cubic.

The only extravagance, if you could call it that, was the bed itself—neatly made, and wide enough for two. The wall nearest the bed held a set of monitor screens. As far as Perada could tell from the numbers and letters scrolling up them, they echoed the bridge and engineering readouts.

So Jos Metadi doesn't like to do without information, Perada thought, *even when he isn't on watch. Ser Hafrey says that the captain has a reputation for being lucky; if he does, it's because he makes his own luck.*

As she watched, the lines of type on the monitors slowed down, and one of the screens began to blink. A wave of nausea swept over her. The whole ship vibrated, and somewhere outside in the common room something fell over with a *whump*. Another line of monitors lit up with what looked like status lights. Most of the lights glowed a reassuring green, but one red light kept blinking on and off and sounding a persistent bell-tone with each blink.

She didn't know what that meant—other than nothing good—but she did know all the standard starship general-alarm signals, and this one wasn't any of those, which meant it was probably safe to get out of the webbing. She unstrapped and stood up—in time for a sudden thrust to knock her staggering. She grabbed the back of the couch for support, biting back a less-than-ladylike remark as she did so. The red light changed to green and the bell-note stopped.

Perada got her balance again—keeping a hand near the bulkhead to catch herself if she needed to—and moved over to the closet doors in the outer bulkhead. The captain had put the whole cabin at her disposal, and she couldn't wear her current garments all the way to Pleyver; with any luck, there'd be something in the captain's locker that she could wear instead. She pulled open one of the closets, and discovered that it wasn't a closet at all, but a refresher cubicle.

Even better, she thought, and began unbuttoning the bodice of her torn and mud-stained gown. *First a bath, and then something clean to wear.*

The 'fresher turned out to hold the only other touches of luxury in the cabin, a freshwater shower hookup and a bulkhead dispenser for what looked like real soap. Perada looked at them both wistfully, but opted for the sonics instead; she wasn't sure if her free hand in the captain's cabin extended to wasting the ship's water. Sonics were good enough, anyway—she'd known a few people at school who actually preferred them—and they had the added virtue of speed.

She hit the On switch and stepped into the shower compartment, feeling the dirt and grime of her excursion into the back alleys of Waycross fall away from her as the vibrations excited the grease and soil molecules. She unbraided her hair and fanned it out with her fingers to release any dirt that might linger there as well. One of the sonic projectors was slightly out of balance; it made her teeth on the left side hurt a little.

Once she was clean and her hair was back up in braids again—simple plaits this time, no point in formality here— she checked the other closets. Most of the clothes hanging in them were plain and dark, like the wardrobe of a sober Gyfferan man of business rather than an Innish-Kyl privateer, and all of them were far too large. She eventually settled for a bathrobe of nubbly brown cloth over a loose white shirt that came down to her knees. The combination wasn't especially becoming, but it would do until she could get some clothes of her own.

She opened the cabin door and padded barefoot into the common room. The deckplates felt cold underfoot, but that couldn't be helped; her slippers had mud inside them as well as out, and she didn't want to put them back on. The common room turned out to be empty except for Tillijen, who took one look at Perada and shook her head.

"Oh, dear," said the number-two gunner. "Jos didn't tell us you came aboard without any luggage. You come with me. We'll go through the slop chest and see about getting you outfitted like a real spacer."

"Where is everyone else?" Perada asked. "Still at their stations?"

"That's right," said Tillijen approvingly. "I'm off right now—we dropped out of hyper in a quiet sector, so the captain's only keeping one gunner on duty, and Nannla's got it. As for Jos and Errec, they're hard at work plotting the course to Pleyver, and Ferrda hardly ever leaves engineering."

"Really?"

Tillijen nodded. "Really. I was amazed when I saw him a bit ago. He couldn't wait to see you, I expect."

"I'm that odd?" Perada frowned. "Or is he one of those people who have a fetish about gawking at anybody who comes from a ruling House?"

"A Selvaur care about thin-skin royalty? Not likely. No, it's ... oh, never mind. Come along. I believe we have some clothes that might fit you." Tillijen paused. "If you're going to dress like a member of this ship's crew, you'll want guns. I think I have something that I can lend you until we get to Pleyver, but you'll probably want to buy your own once we're there."

"My own what?"

"Your own blaster. You can't be a free-spacer without one." The 'Hammer's number-two gunner chuckled. "Nannla has a song about it, of course. In the meantime, come along."

Perada shook her head uncertainly. "I'm the Domina of Entibor. I don't need guns."

"Everyone is someone," Tillijen said. "And at the moment you're a spacer. Come along."

They went.

Errec Ransome: Ilarna
(Galcenian Dating 970 A.F.; Entiboran Regnal Year 34 Veratina)

IT WAS good to be home.

A year at the Retreat on Galcen was supposed to be an honor and a privilege, but Errec Ransome hadn't enjoyed the time he'd spent away. Like any true Ilarnan, he preferred his own world and his own place, and he'd never grown accustomed to the stony bleakness of the Guild's main citadel, hidden away in the northern mountains of Galcen's emptiest continent. Even in midsummer the stone walls of the Retreat—ten yards thick at the base, and not much thinner above—drained the heat out of anything living; and in winter, when the north wind shrieked around the ancient fortress like a lost soul, nothing in the galaxy could make it warm.

The never-ending chill had seeped into his bones, settling there so deeply that he thought at the time the cold had gone away. *I was wrong,* he thought sleepily. *I grew accustomed, that's all. It took coming home to feel the difference.*

Amalind Grange had never been a fortress like the Retreat. Ilarna had always treated its Adepts kindly, and the Grange had been a manor house and farm before a local squire had given it to the Guild as thanks for aid in some long-forgotten difficulty. The outbuildings had been converted into dormitories and guesthouses, and the manor house itself was given over to Guild business from root cellar to attic, but the Grange remained as it had been built, a place of comfort and solid prosperity. Even in the darkest part of winter, with snow lying thick on the rolling countryside all around, and a cold wind as biting as any on Galcen whistling outside the leaded glass of the windows, Amalind made a cozy shelter for those within.

Snow was falling, a steady quiet hiss against the curtained windowpanes. The bedchamber—one of many such little rooms in the uppermost story of the Guildhouse—had a small fireplace against one wall. A ceramic heat-bar glowed a dull red against the stone. Errec could see it from the bed. The room wasn't as large as the guest chamber he'd lived in for a year on Galcen, but the size of the room didn't matter. He would have traded the Retreat's massive austerity for this snug corner of Amalind Grange on any one of the days he'd spent away.

For home, he thought, stretching out luxuriously under the rough wool blankets. *And a chance to sleep without having bad dreams.*

The Guildhouse had sent him to Galcen to study. The senior Masters said that he had a talent for advising rulers, and that it should be trained. He'd found out for himself that Power and the government on Galcen were not always in harmonious accord. The help that Galcenian Adepts stood ready to provide to the civil authority often served a double purpose.

"Thus," he remembered one of Galcen's Adepts saying, in the course of a long discussion, *"favors are owed, and respect is maintained."*

"It's not respect," he'd said. *"It's fear."*

The other had made a dismissive gesture. *"They come to the same thing."*

He'd let the subject drop, though not without wondering what use the senior Masters on Ilarna intended to make of his hard-learned skills. He wondered even more, now that he was home. In the refectory at dinner, the long tables where the apprentices and junior Masters sat had buzzed with rumor. Some said that the Master of the Ilarnan House was even now working out an arrangement with the government ... there was a threat of raiders from the outplanets, people said, and the Adepts were needed to help counter it.

I'll find out what's going on tomorrow, he thought, and turned over onto his left side, away from the glow of the heat-bar. He slept deeply and without dreams.

IV. Galcenian Dating 974 A.F.
Entiboran Regnal Year 38 Veratina

I N COMPANY with Tillijen the gunner, Perada went through the used clothing in *Warhammer*'s slop chest. The collection appeared to go back several decades at least. The overalls and work clothes hadn't changed style much, but some of the port-liberty clothes reminded Perada of galactic fashions from her grandmother's day. She tried on several of those, as much for the amusement of dressing up as for any other reason, but none of them fit—the original owners had all been either taller or heavier than she was, and some of them had possessed what she could only regard as eccentric taste.

Finally Tillijen pulled out a set of newer garments from the back of the locker. "It'll have to be these," she said. "Put them on, and let's see how they do."

Perada took the lacy white blouse and the ankle-length skirt of supple black leather and regarded them uneasily. This outfit was no leftover product of a bygone era. Whoever had left the garments behind had done so in the recent past—almost certainly since Jos Metadi had become the

'*Hammer*'s captain. But they were, as Tillijen had said, the only clothes that fit.

"I'm afraid we don't have a proper pair of boots for you," the gunner said. "You'll have to make do with sandals until we get to Pleyver. Now, about the blaster—"

Perada regarded the gunner dubiously. "Are you sure I need one?"

"Flatlands is a rough town," said Tillijen. "And the '*Hammer*'s got a reputation to maintain."

"What is it—'armed and dangerous'?"

"Well-armed," said the gunner. "And *exceedingly* dangerous."

Perada thought about the combination. "I can live with that," she said finally. "You said you had something I could borrow—?"

"It's in my locker," Tillijen said. "Come along."

Number-one crew berthing had bunks and acceleration couches for two occupants. Perada noted with interest, however, that only one of the bunks appeared to be in use. The other held an eclectic assortment of hats, holocubes, musical instruments, and stuffed plush animals, all held in place behind a net of zero-g webbing. Tillijen went to one of the bulkhead lockers and took out a small blaster.

"You'll want a shoulder holster for this," she said. "Nannla used to have . . . ah, here we go. What the well-dressed young lady wears to a gunfight."

There was a full-length mirror bolted onto the inside of the locker door. Perada looked at herself and smiled. In the long skirt, with her hair in two plain braids hanging down past her belt, she looked both several inches taller and quite a bit older.

The hooting sound of a klaxon came over the cabin's audio link, and a red light started flashing above the door.

"Ah," said Tillijen. "Looks like Jos and Errec have found us a course. Time to strap in for the run-to-jump."

The transition this time was smoother. Once the hazard light over the door had quit flashing, Tillijen said, "Well, let's give the others a look at you," and led the way back out into the common room.

Two of the *'Hammer'*s crew members were there already. Errec Ransome sat at the mess table, and Nannla lounged on one of the acceleration couches. The gunner regarded Perada's costume with approval.

"Not bad," she said. "Needs a hat, though."

"I don't like hats," said Perada. "I keep taking them off and losing them."

"Hatpins," Nannla advised; and Tillijen said, "Practice. You don't want to leave the Iron Crown behind you someplace and lose it, too."

"No chance of *that*," Perada said. She eyed Tillijen curiously. "You're Entiboran, aren't you?"

The gunner didn't answer.

"Time for another of Auntie Nannla's Etiquette Lectures," Tillijen's partner said after several seconds had gone past. "Never ask a spacer where she's from. She'll tell you if she wants, but you mustn't ask."

Perada felt herself blushing. "Sorry."

"It's all right," Errec Ransome said. "Everybody's new once."

She glanced over at the *'Hammer'*s copilot, who had answered without hesitation when she'd asked him about his own origins a short time before. *Is the difference because Tillijen and Nannla think they have something to hide,* she wondered, *or because Errec doesn't think of himself as a spacer? And if he isn't a spacer, then what is he?*

She remembered how she had thought, for a few seconds in the alley back on Innish-Kyl, that the metal bar he'd used as a weapon was an Adept's staff. And the way Captain Metadi had spoken to him about the diversion to Pleyver, as if expecting that Ransome might have knowledge that others didn't . . . but why would an Adept give up the staff and the name and the respect of the galaxy, to sign on as a privateer?

To kill Mages, she realized at once. *I don't know about Tillijen or Nannla or Ferrdacorr, but Errec is one member of the* 'Hammer'*s crew who came to Captain Metadi for the same reason that I did—because nobody else is fighting the enemy the way the enemy needs to be fought.*

* * *

At the Entiboran Fleet Base on Parezul, true dawn was almost an hour off, but the working day had already started. Base Commander Frigate-Captain Galaret Lachiel was not a young woman—her short black hair was liberally streaked with grey—but she was still a handsome one, and she wore her dark red uniform with undeniable panache. She also prided herself on working harder, and keeping longer hours, than any of the junior officers under her command.

Gala had almost finished her usual early-morning scan of the sensors in the OutPlanet Review Sector when she heard the swish-snick of the door behind her. Turning, she nodded at the stocky, brown-skinned man who had entered. "Morning, Tres. You're up early."

A quick grin flashed underneath the newcomer's dark mustache. "No earlier than you are."

As commander of the Parezulan Sector Squadron, Captain-of-Corvettes Trestig Brehant had authorization for the sensor area on the base. Out of courtesy, though, the squadron commander usually waited for Gala to pass along the reports. The fact that he'd come dirtside in person piqued her interest.

"*I'm* not bunking up in high orbit," she pointed out. "Unlike some people I could name. If something's got you worried . . ."

"Rumors," he said. "Speculation that the Mages are gathering in force out by Monserath. Nothing definite, but persistent enough to make me want to take a look at the raw sensor data."

Gala regarded him thoughtfully. Tres had never been stupid; if he thought there was a reason for checking this morning's reports, he was probably right. She turned to the nearest comp station and began punching up the intelligence reviews. Even the most recent one was already out of date, but it was better than guesswork.

"Let's see," she said, running a finger down the screen. Her fingernails were blunt and neatly trimmed. In her youth she had bitten them, but she hadn't given in to the impulse for almost twenty years. "This sector has been quiet. Unusual activities anywhere we have to worry about—none."

Brehant didn't look satisfied. "Anything from Home Fleet?"

"Nothing."

"I haven't heard anything either. And frankly, I don't know whether to feel worried or relieved." The Captain-of-Corvettes glanced about uneasily, as if concerned that a spy had appeared by magic to listen over his shoulder. "Central is a snake pit all the time anyway, and right now it's even worse."

"I know," said Gala. Her agreement was more heartfelt than possibly Brehant realized—House Lachiel's political standing was sufficiently high that one of her cousins had been a minor political casualty in the succession struggle a few years back. She'd cut her own braids when she joined the Fleet, and never regretted the choice. "But so far they've—"

A beeping noises cut her off in midsentence, and the comm panel began to spit out a sheet of flimsy. Gala looked over at the message header—FROM: ENTIBOR CENTRAL; TO: COMMANDER FLEET UNITS PAREZUL; INFO: COMMANDER, OUT-PLANETS COMMAND; REFERENCE: GENERAL ORDER 672; HANDLING—and grimaced.

"They must have heard us talking," she said. "Priority transmission. Eyes only."

"Do you want me to leave?" Brehant asked.

"Don't bother. Just let me have a look at it first." She pulled the flimsy out of the printer and read it, frowning. "I wonder . . . this isn't more than a couple of days old. Central must really be concerned."

"What is it?"

Gala passed over the slip of flimsy. "Nothing that you'd think was worth a max-pri override—it's a standard request-for-information on privateer activity."

"Privateers?" He shook his head. "Haven't dealt with any. Central doesn't trust them."

"Central doesn't trust anybody. The Crown backs a few

of them, though, or used to. Mostly to spite Central, I think."

"They're a bunch of damned irregulars," said Brehant, frowning. "Out for the money and unreliable as hell."

"Good fighters, all the same," she said. "From the reports, it sounds like one or two of them have managed to run fleet actions against the raiders."

"Well, I'm glad somebody is." Brehant handed back the slip of flimsy. "But it should be us, not them."

"You won't get any argument from me on that," Gala said. She took the flimsy and stowed it in her tunic pocket. "But those aren't our orders, and these are. Can you put a lock-and-trace on ships operating out of Innish-Kyl?"

"The ones who come into our patrol area, yes," he said. "Which they generally don't, thank fortune. Now, if they wanted reports of Mage activity . . . anything from the probes?"

Gala laughed. "Back to that, are we?" She waved a hand at the row of monitor screens. "What you see. All quiet in Parezulan space."

"Which is why you're up every morning before daybreak checking the sensors?" Brehant shook his head. "You don't believe that, Gala, any more than I do. You're tracking something. Give."

No, Gala reflected, Tres Brehant had never been stupid. She smiled in spite of herself, but only for a few seconds. She had other things on her mind.

"All right," she said. "I don't know if this is significant, but it worries me: when I chart where things are moving, and where the last raids were, all the lines of transit go right through this sector."

"Parezul's on the arc to a lot of places. It's why we're sitting here." Brehant moved over to the comp station and called up more of the intelligence reports. "Let's see what else we've got in the civilized galaxy this week."

Brehant scanned the material for several minutes in silence. Then his eyebrows—dark and bushy, and always mobile—went up toward his hairline. "Here's an odd one—from Innish-Kyl, no less. A movement report from a Crown courier. In port for under twelve hours, heading to Entibor, in passage from Galcen with a stopover. Do you know how far Innish-Kyl is from being the most efficient course from Galcen to Entibor?"

"Of course I do. But when I run across items like that, I try not to speculate. The Crown doesn't like snooping."

Brehant cast a sharp glance in her direction. "So you saw it, then."

"Of course."

"Anything else in the traffic?"

She shook her head. "Nothing."

"Then let's go have a cup of cha'a. Your galley ought to have the morning supply ready by now."

"The truth comes out," said Gala. "You only love us because the cha'a brews up better with natural groundwater."

Brehant laughed. Over on the communications panel, a message light blinked on and started beeping.

"Courier coming in," Gala said. "With news."

A few minutes later, the comm panel beeped and chittered and extruded another curling slip of printout. This time Gala beckoned for Tres to come up and look at it along with her. They read it together in silence. Finally the squadron commander sighed and stepped back.

"That's it, then," he said. "What we were both watching for. Mage raid on Tanpaleyn."

Gala crumpled up the scrap of flimsy, then reflexively smoothed it out again. "Damned poor report. Nothing on strength or type of units. With no more information than that, all we can do is detach a scouting and security force."

"I can handle that," Brehant offered. "The squadron hasn't had enough work lately anyhow. We could use the exercise."

"Thanks, Tres." Gala punched the comm button for the duty officer. "Get Lieutenant Verris out of bed and tell him to come in here. I want nearspace monitoring stations up and active."

"So we watch and wait. Do you think that's enough?"

"It'll have to be," she said. "The Mages'll be gone from

Tanpaleyn by the time anyone gets there anyway. They know what our reaction time is better than we do."

"Don't they though." Brehant straightened his shoulders. "I'd better get back to orbit and start my run out toward the drop points. Later, Gala."

"Later."

Gala turned back to the sensor screens. The door snicked open and shut and open again as Brehant hurried out and the newly awakened Lieutenant Verris hurried in, hastily sealing up the front of his uniform tunic.

"Good," she said to the lieutenant. "You're here. Get on the boards—I want the monitors set to extreme range and top sensitivity, and I want somebody watching them every minute."

"Extreme range and top sensitivity, aye." Verris began entering the changes as he spoke. Without glancing up from his work, he asked, "What am I supposed to be scanning for, anyway?"

"Anything that looks suspicious. The raiders have hit Tanpaleyn."

There was a sound as if Verris had bitten off a startled oath. Gala tried to remember if the lieutenant had friends or family on the colony world, but she couldn't recall. The sensor room fell silent except for the click-clack of Verris's fingers on the comp-station keyboard.

She watched the lieutenant at work for a little while, then turned away and brought up the massive holochart that filled most of one wall with a schematic representation of Entibor's colonial space. In silence, the base commander put in the contact report from Tanpaleyn, so that the colony system showed up in the chart as a point of bright red light. Trestig Brehant and his squadron, presumably in hyperspace transit, she marked with a thin line of pale blue dots. Then she waited.

Twenty minutes later, another courier showed up. This one reported a Mage raid at Ghan Jobai. By now the sensor room was full of men and women in uniform, watching the monitors and keeping the communication links open. Gala entered the contact from Ghan Jobai on the chart; behind her, as she punched in the data, she could hear the comm panel spitting out yet another incoming message.

She never did have time to go for a cup of cha'a. Eventually a runner from the galley brought in a carafe of fresh-brewed. She poured some into one of the unwashed mugs left in the sensor room from the night before, and drank it down without tasting it while she stood with Lieutenant Verris and contemplated the holochart.

The lieutenant said, "I don't like the looks of this, Captain. They're attacking in too many places all at once. Raiders don't—"

"If these were raiders, we'd have a report of at least one of them breaking off. No—" Gala pointed at the spangle of systems in Entibor's colonial protectorate. More than half of them were flashing red. "This time they're moving in to stay. It's the big push."

The lieutenant nodded. Whatever the news of the first attack had meant to him, by now he had himself well under control. "That's what I thought. What do we do now?"

"They want us to split up," Gala said. "Which means it's the single worst thing we can do. We're going to take the entire fleet and hit one of their groups, then do it again for the next one. And the next."

A siren began hooting in the hall outside the sensor room, and a voice came over the audio link.

"Mage raid," it said. "Mage raid."

"Where?" she demanded—though she knew, already, what the answer was going to be.

"Right here!"

An exclamation from one of the technicians at the sensor screens drew Gala's attention, and she strode over to see what had caused the reaction. It was as bad as she'd imagined. The entirety of nearspace was full of Magebuilt warships, and more of them were dropping out of hyper every minute.

Gala grabbed up the link handset for the base comms and flipped the setting to All.

"Launch, launch, launch," she said. "Duty courier, make for Entibor. Inform Central of our situation and status. All hands report to your vessels. All ships on the ground, make orbit as soon as your crews are aboard."

She turned to Lieutenant Verris. "You have control on the ground. Keep comms up; coordinate task elements and evaluate data as available. I'm taking command on-scene."

That taken care of, Gala left the sensor room at a dead run, heading for the launching field and a shuttle to take her up to her flagship, the Entiboran Fleet Cruiser *Opal Wind*. She had reached the main doors of the headquarters building when a series of powerful blasts from the field outside jammed the doors open and filled the passageway with curling dust. Where the nearest shuttle had stood on landing legs a minute before, only a crater remained.

"Bastards!" she yelled at the unseen raiders, somewhere up above the stratosphere of Parezul. The energy strike had taken out not just that one shuttle but every vessel remaining on the surface at Parezul command.

Gala turned back toward the inner recesses of the building, hoping that communications were up. Because whether they were up or not, it looked like she was going to have to fight her fleet from right here.

"The problem is," Tillijen said, after the silence in *Warhammer*'s common room had drawn out long enough to become awkward, "we all got shorted on our portside liberty."

"Damn straight," said Nannla. "I don't know about you, Errec, but Tilly and I had a room booked downtown for two nights—at a good hotel, too, none of your sleazy shankhalters—and *somebody* owes us a party."

Tillijen nodded. "It'll be a while before we hit Pleyver . . . plenty of time to relax and make ourselves some of the fun we didn't get a chance to have back in Waycross."

Errec smiled slightly. "If the captain agrees, why not?"

"Agrees to what?" The door leading to the cockpit slid shut behind Captain Metadi. "If it's a party you're talking about, I say we haven't had a good one in a long time. Somebody go tell Ferrda, and I'll break open the grog locker."

It might have been a drill, Perada reflected. The *'Ham-

mer's crew responded with practiced ease: Errec headed off toward the engineering section; Nannla and Tillijen disappeared into number-one crew berthing and emerged burdened with what looked like half their collection of musical instruments. Captain Metadi, meanwhile, opened a cabinet in the galley and brought out the first of a whole series of bottles. By the time he was finished, there was a small thicket of them in the center of the mess table—Felshang claret from Entibor and straw-colored spring wine from Low Khesat; amber-tinted brandy from the Galcenian uplands; a square unlabeled bottle of something purple, stoppered with an ugly spongewood plug.

"Quite a collection," she said, after he had gone into the galley again, this time for a half-dozen glass tumblers. "You didn't buy them all in Waycross, surely."

"Only a fool buys any more liquor in Waycross than it takes to get drunk there," the captain said. "Most of these are souvenirs."

Errec Ransome came back into the common room, followed by Ferrda. The ship's engineer carried what looked like a bundle of sticks under one arm; on closer inspection, the bundle turned out to be a kind of bellows-pipe. Perada had heard similar instruments before, at traditional-music festivals on Galcen, and schooled herself to smile—without showing her teeth—no matter how badly the Selvaur played.

She needn't have worried. Ferrda handled the instrument like a master. The first tune he played was one that she recognized. Nannla had been singing it earlier. Now the dark-haired woman used a small hand drum of animal hide stretched over a pottery base—Perada had seen it, tied up behind zero-g webbing in the unused bunk, and had wondered what it might be—to beat out a rhythm behind the Selvaur's melody while the others sang.

> "After moving your cargo with infinite pains,
> You find that your debts are the whole of your gains—
> Just buy yourself guns with the cash that remains
> And finish your life as a pirate."

"I'll drink to that," said Tillijen, when the song was finished. "What do you say, Captain—full glasses all round?"

"Sounds good to me," Metadi said. He lined up the six tumblers in a row on the mess table. "Let's see ... the Entiboran first, I think, in honor of our passenger."

He poured out a half dozen equal portions of the claret and handed one to Perada. "You'll have to tell me if it's any good or not," he told her. "I've never had enough of it to judge."

She inhaled the scent of the claret. "It's certainly not rotgut," she said. She took a sip and let the taste warm her before going on. "I'm not that knowledgeable myself— enology wasn't a formal part of the school curriculum any more than sharpshooting was—but I'd say you made a good investment. Where did you pick it up?"

Jos and Errec glanced at each other. "Off a Mage cargo carrier," the captain said finally. "Somewhere beyond Ninglin. I don't know where they got it—none of us could read their manifests."

"Oh," Perada said. She gazed at the claret a while longer, then tilted back her glass and drank it all. She set the tumbler down on the mess table with a thud. "Better us than them."

Ferrda rumbled something approving, and the others laughed. Tillijen refilled the empty tumblers, then tilted her chair back and started singing a rousing ballad in a language that Perada didn't recognize, though Metadi apparently knew it well enough to join in with Nannla on the chorus. Errec Ransome didn't sing this time, only smiled and poured Khesatan spring wine into the empty tumblers.

The spring wine had bubbles in it, and a taste like an explosion of flowers. At formal receptions on Galcen, during her last year at school, Perada had sipped it out of thimble-sized crystal glasses after the Khesatan fashion. The experience hadn't prepared her for dealing with *Warhammer*'s more generous portions. She decided that she didn't care.

She drained her glass and let the bubbles float upward and go off in her head like fireworks, while the music went on and on. Errec Ransome was singing now, and the drink in the tumblers was Galcenian Uplands brandy, harsh and powerful like the northern hills it came from. Errec's song was one that Perada recognized from her schooldays; it came from those same hills, and she wondered where and when he had learned it.

> "Oh three they drew and two he slew
> And one he wounded deep.
> The youngest one threw down his blade
> And bitterly did weep.
>
> "He's taken out his little knife,
> He's gripped it fast and high.
> 'And though you were my own blood kin
> This night you'd surely die.' "

It was an old song, one of the dark and bloody ones, and he sang it alone, with no accompaniment except for a wandering countermelody on Ferrda's pipes. He finished, and drank off the tumbler of brandy that had waited on the mess table in front of him while he sang.

The glasses were empty again. Nannla unstoppered the square bottle of purple liquor and poured out six equal portions. Perada noticed the others looking at her expectantly.

My turn, she realized. *They want to see if I can fit in, or if I'm nothing but a passenger who happens to own a couple of star systems.*

She picked up the tumbler and sipped at the purple liquid—it had a strong, almost medicinal flavor, and it stung going down—while she tried to think of some tune that wouldn't be more suited to a garden party than to a shipboard singalong. In the end she gave up trying—*Can I help it if everybody I used to know was respectable?*—and sang "Bindweed and Blossom" as she'd learned it from Gentlelady Wherret in music class at school. Nobody laughed, and she wasn't surprised to hear Tillijen singing the chorus along with her.

Most of the purple liquor had vanished from her tumbler

while she did her thinking earlier. She swallowed the drop or two remaining, and looked over at Jos Metadi.

"It's your turn," she said.

He shook his head. "Not me. I'm the only one on board with no voice."

"You can't get away without doing something." She turned to Nannla and Tillijen. "Isn't that right?"

Tillijen nodded solemnly. "That's right."

The number-two gunner was definitely tipsy, Perada decided—well, so were they all by now, even the captain.

Even me.

She looked at Metadi. "You said that everything in your cabin was at my disposal."

"That's right."

"Then come and prove it to me," she said. "Now."

For a long moment he said nothing, and she feared that she'd lost her gamble at the very beginning—*He's an off-worlder, remember; you can't expect him to understand*—but then he rose and held out his hand.

"Whatever you say, Domina." His Gyfferan accent made the word into two syllables—"Dom'na"—but she found that she didn't mind. "And whatever you want. Now."

Perada Rosselin: Galcen
(Galcenian Dating 963 a.f.; Entiboran Regnal Year 27 Veratina)

PERADA HAD never seen any place like the spaceport at Galcen Prime. Nothing on Entibor came close. The immense dome of the Grand Concourse covered an area so big that she could scarcely see the edges of it. Everywhere she looked, she saw signs—flat ones displayed on the walls and the floor and the kiosks that rose up from the concourse like a field of mushrooms; brightly colored half-rounds in shop windows; and free-floating holos filling up the air beneath the dome like pictures painted with light. A lot of the signs had writing on them that she couldn't read, which frustrated her; she'd known how to read signs back home on Entibor for over a year, and it looked like she was going to have to start all over again.

She tugged on Dadda's coat sleeve and pointed at the nearest sign. "What does that say in real writing?"

"It *is* real, babba—it's in Galcenian, that's all."

"But what does it say?"

Dadda said something that sounded like *"frunds kovitten atteki,"* and Perada shook her head. Her two braids—down to her shoulders now—swung back and forth with the motion.

"No. I want to hear what is *says*."

Dadda sighed. "It says 'ground transportation this way.' "

"Then why don't they write that?"

"Because we're on Galcen, babba, and they write the signs in Galcenian."

"Am I going to have to learn that, too?"

"You'll have to, I'm afraid. The school you'll be going to takes its students from all over the galaxy, so they all have to speak Galcenian in classes and with each other."

"Why?"

"Because otherwise nobody would be able to talk at all."

"No," she said. "I mean, why don't they talk *real* talk, like at home?"

"Everybody talks real talk," Dadda said. "But the talk is different in different places. So they use Galcenian when they're not at home."

Perada thought about this for a while. She was about to resume the argument—why should all these people she'd never met talk to each other in Galcenian, which sounded funny, instead of learning how real people talked?—when the glidewalk came to an end. The archway ahead of them had a greyish shimmer across the opening and a scanner set into the wall beside it; Dadda showed a wafer of white plastic to the scanner and the force field came down.

The hairs on her arms rose up and her skin tingled a little when she passed through the opening. On the other side of the archway was a room with a couple of chairs, a low table, and a green plant in a pottery tub. A thin, white-haired woman in a black dress rose from the nearest chair as they entered.

"Gentlesir Lokkelar," she said. "I am Zeri Delaven."

Zeri Delaven's words had a strange rhythm to them, but nothing stranger than the way people from some parts of Entibor talked when they came to Felshang Province. Perada felt vindicated—people on Galcen didn't have to speak the funny-sounding language of the signs if they didn't want to. She opened her mouth to say so, then thought better of it. The white-haired woman had a look about her that made Perada think silence might be a wiser idea.

"Mistress Delaven," Dadda replied. "This is the student Lady Shaja wrote to you about: the Damozel Perada. We ... Shaja and I ... hope that she'll be happy here."

Zeri Delaven fixed Perada with a penetrating glance. "We can't guarantee happiness, I'm afraid. But that she will learn, and that she will be safe—those things, Gentlesir Lokkelar, we *can* promise."

V. Galcenian Dating 974 A.F. Entiboran Regnal Year 38 Veratina

T HE *'HAMMER* dropped out of hyperspace after a journey of some two weeks. Perada was in the cockpit for the dropout, on the foldaway acceleration couch behind the two main positions. The navigator's seat, Jos Metadi had called it; unused these days, since Errec Ransome was both copilot and navigator. Not even an Adept—and Perada felt increasingly sure that the Ilarnan was, or had been, a member of the Guild—could sit in two chairs at once.

She had traveled through hyperspace before, but only on commercial spaceliners and, rarely, on Entiboran Crown couriers like *Crystal World*. Neither the spaceliners nor the courier vessels allowed passengers onto the bridge, although she supposed that as the Domina she could insist on the privilege. It pleased her that Jos Metadi had granted the favor without having been asked. She was careful to stay quiet and out of the way, like an honored guest at an unfamiliar ritual.

"Dropout . . . now," said Metadi.

The opaline pseudosubstance outside the viewscreens

went away, replaced by starry blackness. In the distance—
near? far? Perada couldn't guess; she didn't know how the
terms worked, out here in deep space—she glimpsed something that looked like a tangle of colored light.

"All right, Errec," Metadi said. "How close did we get?"

"Optimum range for the Farpoint beacon."

"Good. Let's talk to the nice people."

Perada watched the captain's hands playing over the *Ham-*
mer's comm panel. She'd heard of Farpoint, the manned
beacon at the outside edge of Pleyver's Web. The three-
dimensional maze of fluctuating magnetic fields that encircled
the system blocked all hyperspace transit. Farpoint marked
the earliest possible hyperspace translation for outbound craft,
and the nearest point of dropout for new arrivals.

"Farpoint, Farpoint," Metadi said over the comm link.
"This is Freetrader *Warhammer*. Request permission to
make transit to Pleyver."

"*Warhammer*, this is Farpoint," came the reply, made
faint and scratchy by the shifting electromagnetic discharges
of the Web. "Interrogative do you require a pilot, over."

Metadi and Ransome looked at each other. The captain
raised an eyebrow. Ransome shook his head. Metadi turned
back to the link.

"Farpoint, negative, over."

"A pilot is recommended. Entering without a pilot requires you to make formal statement holding harmless
Pleyver Inspace, over."

"Statement made. I hold Pleyver Inspace harmless."

"Roger, copy all. Interrogative how many individuals in
your crew, so we know what priority to put on rescuing
you?"

Metadi and Ransome looked at each other again. "Total
of six aboard," the captain said.

"Roger, copy six. Permission granted to enter the Web.
Good luck, Captain, over."

"Roger, out." Metadi switched off the link. "Now comes
the tricky part."

"What's that?" Perada asked.

"Getting through the Web without having an accident on the way in," he said. "Those fields are hell on electronics, and they change all the time. We've got a fairly recent update—I bought a copy off of Sverje Thulmotten back during the payout for the Ophelan run—but that doesn't mean something hasn't changed in the last couple of months. We'll have to keep our eyes and ears open the whole time."

"Wouldn't it be easier to hire a pilot?"

"Pilots cost money," Errec Ransome said.

"If that's the problem, I can—"

"So could I, if I wanted to," Metadi cut in. "For what it cost me to get that coursebook from Sverje, we could have hired us a couple of pilots. But you hire someone, and the first thing they want to do is plug their book into main ship's memory and record the run. And *nobody* does that on a privateer ship who isn't a member of the crew."

"I see," Perada said. Security in all its forms was no stranger to her. The school on Galcen had gained its reputation as much for the safety it provided for its students as for its unquestioned academic rigor. The students, in their turn, had honed their skills against that same unrelenting watchfulness—she'd seen what could happen when a curious mind came too near something that was locked against intrusion.

So Jos Metadi was a cautious man, and not an overly trusting one. She'd guessed that much already, but the confirmation pleased her. If he intended to survive at court—and if he fell in with her plans, he would have to survive there in order to accomplish anything—he would need that caution.

"Shutting down vulnerable systems," the captain said. "Now."

He flipped a switch, and the *'Hammer'*'s comp screens went dark. Nothing reminded alive on the main console except a few red and green lights and a scattering of readouts from what Perada hoped were navigational sensors.

Errec Ransome slid open the drawer underneath his side of the console and took out a flat tablet not unlike a newsreader. A length of thin cable dangled from one side; on the other a stylus hung from a coiled-wire leash. He plugged the cable into one of the receptors on the bulkhead next to the copilot's position, then swept the stylus across the face of the tablet. The surface lit up, as a reader would; but Perada, craning her neck for a look, saw that instead of the familiar news-service logo the tablet's opening screen displayed a crudely drawn hand transfixed by a bloody dagger.

She must have made a noise without intending to, because Metadi chuckled. "I guess Sverje doesn't like snoops."

"Wouldn't a simple 'keep out' have sufficed?"

Errec Ransome glanced back at her over his shoulder. She saw that he, too, looked faintly amused. "I've met Thulmotten's crew," he said. "For that lot, this *is* a simple 'keep out.'"

"I see," Perada said again. "You certainly have a . . . colorful . . . group of friends and acquaintances."

"Shutting down nonessentials, now." The captain flipped another switch on the main console. About half the telltales flashed from green to red. "Errec—how's the coursebook?"

"Interfaced and running. So far, it looks like Thulmotten didn't cheat us."

"He knows what I'd do to him if he tried. Recording?"

"As full a transcript as we can get with most of our sensors off-line."

"Good. We can sell the update later if we need the cash." Metadi glanced over at Perada. "It'll be pure old-style piloting from here on in: running through realspace with half-witted comps and half-blind sensors and a coursebook that was outdated as soon as it was made. So I'd advise you to stand by and be ready for anything."

"I understand, Captain," she said. "Pray carry on—I have every confidence in your abilities."

And so does he, she realized as he went back to his work. *He's looking forward to making this run—it's difficult, and he's good at it, and there's nothing in the galaxy that's quite as much fun as a combination like that.*

"Shields full," said Metadi. He flipped another switch. "Now. Gunners on station?"

"Present," came the voices over the audio link. Perada recognized Nannla's warm alto and Tillijen's lighter, higher tones, the feed from the two separate gun bubbles combining in harmony. Then Nannla added, in solo voice, "Orders, Captain?"

"You know the drill. Sensors are down, except for the basics. Keep your eyes open and let me know if you spot anything, especially aids to navigation."

"Rules of engagement?"

"Anybody can shoot at us once. Make sure they don't get a second shot." Metadi paused and added—mostly for her benefit, Perada suspected—"Not that anyone's likely to try. Fighting in the Web would be more of a mess than anything I'd like to think about."

"Understood, Captain," Nannla said, and Tillijen echoed her, "Understood."

The cockpit was silent. The swirling colors of the Web grew nearer as the hours and minutes passed. And then, before Perada expected it, they were in.

In the Palace Major of Entibor, on its hill overlooking the streets of the greater An-Jemayne metropolis, the ceremonial torches of scented heartwood smoked in their wall sconces in the public corridors. Discreetly, behind embroidered cutwork wall hangings and pierced metal screens, the palace's environmental systems labored to keep the air clean enough for the household electronics to do their work undisturbed. Farther back in the palace, among the family rooms, glowcubes and light panels shed a dim and respectful light. The old Domina, Veratina, lay in the bed in which she had died, waiting beneath a stasis field until the new Domina should come home.

In another room nearby, Ser Hafrey sat among his racks of antique weapons, looking out over the spires and rooftops of central An-Jemayne. He fingered a plutonian equalizer—a beautiful thing, handmade out of ebony and adamant—and spoke to the man who had come to visit.

"I am uneasy with the reports of Galcenians here in the capital," Hafrey said. "Can't we gain access to them somehow? Are they all incorruptible? Surely one of them has, if not a secret vice, at least a tragic flaw?"

"No," said Meinuxet. The armsmaster's chief agent was a small man with a thick crop of burnished red hair. "Or if anybody has one, we haven't discovered it."

Hafrey regarded his visitor with an expression of grave concern. "Reports of failures among my own people distress me."

Meinuxet shrugged. "What can I say? The Galcenians on-planet don't talk much about their business. But they never try to hide anything, either. They're open, they're hospitable, they're friendly—they do everything but invite our people to move in with them and read their mail."

"It could be," said Hafrey, "that the Galcenians are nothing more than what they seem to be—businesspeople, scholars, travelers, diplomats."

The agent shook his head. "I'll believe that story when you do. Not before."

"Then discover their purposes," Hafrey told him. "If they won't lay plans in private where we can dig them out, learn how they manage to lay their plans in public."

"Armsmaster," Meinuxet said, "let me travel to Galcen. Maybe I can pick up their trail at that end, if I can't unravel it here."

"No," said Hafrey. "I can't spare—"

A knock sounded on the door.

"Enter!" Hafrey called.

The door opened and another messenger stepped into the room—a woman in Fleet uniform this time, with short dark hair.

"Armsmaster," she said, "I have word from Central Command."

Hafrey looked at her with mild curiosity. "And it is—?"

"That a special watch has been placed on the privateers of Innish-Kyl."

The armsmaster frowned slightly. "I gave no such orders."

"No. The order came from Fleet Admiral Pallit."

"*I* am responsible for the safety of the Domina," Hafrey said. "Not Pallit."

"The fleet admiral claimed that his order was given for purposes of general security," said the woman. "And he would not let himself be dissuaded."

"Pallit . . . Pallit," said Meinuxet, after the other agent had finished speaking. "Whose creature is he?"

"The fleet admiral has strong ties to the bankers' guild," Hafrey said. "And the bankers are entirely too friendly with our friend from Rolny." The armsmaster paused, and smiled faintly. "I think I know who set the fleet admiral hunting down this particular trail. There's no harm done, though, if Pallit is allowed to proceed—but with caution. He doesn't need to catch any privateers, only to watch them. For they do, in fact, bear watching."

Both agents nodded, and Meinuxet said, "What about my request?"

"To go to Galcen?" Hafrey shook his head. "The Galcenians would eat you alive and pick their teeth with your bones. The Adepts there are strong, and ambitious, and unscrupulous. Any two of those qualities would be troublesome. Taken together, they are deadly."

"I'll ask again some other time, then," said Meinuxet, unperturbed.

"Feel free to do so." Again Hafrey smiled faintly. "In the meanwhile, practice your skill in drawing secrets out of slabs of granite, so that someday you may work on those Galcenians who happen to be available here on Entibor."

Meinuxet bowed and left.

"And now you," Hafrey said to the woman, after Meinuxet had gone. "Aside from Pallit's rather ill-advised set of orders, how are things at Central?"

"No different than while Veratina was alive."

Hafrey's lips tightened slightly. "A sinkhole of bubbling rivalries, then. Well, use what influence you have to build loyalties to the young Domina. She will arrive soon, and bring with her what I hope is good news."

"Do I dare to speculate?"

"If you think it's necessary," said Hafrey. "It should be enough to say that she is not Veratina."

"Ah," said the woman. She looked pleased. "I take your meaning. In *that* case, there'll be no problem raising support. Do you know if she plans to take an official consort? That would guarantee at least one faction on our side."

"I have hopes," the armsmaster said. "But Her Dignity is young and headstrong—"

"*And* the Domina."

"Yes, and the Domina. Which means that almost anything is possible, and it will be our duty to see that her person remains safe throughout. For now—return to Central, and carry on with your mission."

After the woman had left, Ser Hafrey turned back to contemplating the racks of weapons before him. He selected one at last—an energy lance, of Gyfferan mass-manufacture but an excellent weapon nonetheless—and settled it on his shoulder. Then he too left the room, and made his way to the Royal Firing Range, where one of the late Veratina's nonsuccessive relatives was awaiting his daily lesson in marksmanship.

In the Web, the space outside *Warhammer*'s viewscreens was full of swirling, glowing clouds of dust—or at least something that looked like dust to Perada's untrained eyes. She knew that in deep space any estimation of distance and proportion was unreliable at best; the clouds, vague and insubstantial though they appeared, could be in reality the size of continents, or of entire worlds.

Some of them, it seemed, even had names: Farren's Lurk, Longstrands, the Gulper. That last one, she suspected, had a ruder name when well-born passengers weren't around. She kept her amused speculations to herself, though, because the Gulper was apparently also a serious hazard, and one which—if Sverje Thulmotten's coursebook held good—had shifted its position since the last time Jos Metadi took the 'Hammer through.

The captain sat leaning forward, one hand on the power controls and the other hovering above the steering panel.

"Come on, baby," he muttered. "Where's the damned beacon?"

"Should bear one-five-two, plus two," Errec said, not looking up from the coursebook. "That's off by five point eight from last time."

"I'm not picking up anything. Think it's moved again?"

Errec closed his eyes and his face went blank. To Perada he looked for an instant like a painted ivory carving of himself—warm and lifelike, but empty. She glanced over at Metadi, and caught the captain watching his second-in-command with something that looked very much like concern.

Then Errec came back into himself from wherever he had gone, opened his eyes, and said, "No."

"Damn," said Metadi. "If Sverje rigged that coursebook, I'll—"

"Beacon in sight," Tillijen called over the internal link. "Bearing one-five-two, plus two."

Some of the tension went out of Metadi's posture. "Good eyes, Tilly. I have it on the board now. The signal's weak, though—remind me to put in a report to Inspace when we hit Flatlands. They need to send out a repair crew."

It was some minutes before Perada herself saw the beacon: a patch of pulsing color against the greater display of the Gulper itself. The only way she could be sure which spot of light was the beacon—and she *wasn't* sure, not really—was that it throbbed to a regular beat, rather than drifting apart and solidifying again like the cloudy mass behind it.

"Leave the beacon to port ventral," Errec said. "Change course to six-eight-six."

Metadi touched the steering controls briefly. "Speed?"

"Speed's fine. I see us on track, on time."

"Very well."

Perada leaned back and watched the swirls of red and blue mist outside the cockpit windows. The masses of light took on fantastic forms, like the pictures she had found in the clouds over Felshang when she was little, but at the same time they looked like rocks, hard and broken and nowhere near as pretty as clouds. And all the while the colors shifted and changed.

Once another ship passed by—a big spaceliner, seeming almost close enough to touch, although Perada knew it must be some miles distant. The vessel appeared without warning, looming up out of the ever-shifting layers of cloud, pushing its way through, long tendrils of mist flowing back along its body as it headed outward past them. And all the while Ransome kept scanning the coursebook to follow their transit, while Metadi watched the way and the two gunners called contacts.

The morning in Wippeldon was bright and clear, rain-washed and sun-dried. Gentlesir Festen Aringher and his friend Mistress Vasari stood at the rail of the portsled carrying them away from the spaceliner's grounded shuttle and looked about.

"Entibor at last," Aringher said. "Entibor after a full night's sleep, which is even better."

"Do you suppose that *The Milliner's Daughter* is any good?" Mistress Vasari asked, with a nod toward the row of advertising flats that ran down the center of the portsled. "I could use some entertainment."

"Something advertised to new arrivals? I have my doubts. But I'm sure a bit of searching will reveal rare delights of entertainment."

"Something advertised to off-worlders would suit me fine."

"Where is your sense of adventure?"

"Packed in the bottom of my suitcase."

"The younger generation. I despair."

" 'Younger generation,' hah. You're the same age as I am."

"I," he informed her, "am wise beyond my years. But now, I fear, it's time for us to depart."

They descended from the portsled and made their way through the open doors of the main concourse toward the luggage recovery point. Aringher took Mistress Vasari's hand as they walked, and squeezed it gently.

"I hope that Customs isn't too punctilious," he said, as his fingers moved in the rhythmic patterns of the pressure-code.

Trouble here. Look how many slots there are on the logboard, how few in and out ships posted.

Vasari laughed at him. "What have you got to worry about? This isn't some dreary outplanet where everything's illegal."

Maybe it's a slow day, her hand replied against his.

I don't think so. "I don't know how you feel about some total stranger pawing through your good socks, but I don't like it." *I think there's a problem.*

"Poor dear." *What kind?*

"You mock me. But see how you feel when it's *your* frilly underthings spread out across the table." *Too early to tell. But keep close and keep your eyes open.*

"Always such concern," Vasari said aloud. "Let's go straight to the hotel as soon as we're checked through. I want to freshen up before I look around Wippeldon."

Customs proved strict but courteous. When the inspection was over, Vasari and Aringher collected their baggage, summoned a hovercab, and entered the bustle of spaceport traffic. They were bound for lodgings on the slopes of Mount Kelpen, a little to the local south of the spaceport—a remote spot, yet one from which they could watch the activity at the port.

"Might as well hang 'we're spying' signs around our necks," Vasari had complained to Aringher when she first learned where they would be staying.

"No," he'd replied, "the thing is, we *aren't* spying. So anyone who thinks that we are is plainly mistaken. But from little mistakes—well, I grieve to see my fellow-creatures make mistakes, but they're all instructive, don't you agree?"

"Instructive," Vasari had muttered at the time.

And "Instructive" she muttered again now that they were here, threading through the outskirts of Wippeldon and onto a narrow road leading up into the foothills. They went straight to the lodge on Mount Kelpen, in case someone was following or taking interest in a pair of well-to-do visitors from Galcen. When they arrived, their accommodations proved luxurious enough to raise Vasari's eyebrows.

"Who's paying for this?" she asked, once they were ensconced in a double suite on the most exclusive floor of the best wing.

"I am, my dear. Don't you recall my granduncle's legacy?"

"I didn't even know that you had a granduncle."

"I was devastated, I assure you, to learn of his untimely death. But enough about such sorrowful matters—we have work to do."

Vasari shook her head and wandered off to unpack. In the meantime, Aringher opened the doors onto the balcony. He sat there sipping a room-service mixed drink and looking out over the valley with a pair of binoculars set to Record All. When Vasari emerged from her rooms, Aringher rose, and offered her a clone of his own drink.

"Thank you," she said, and downed it at a gulp.

"You never were such a hard-drinking woman before," Aringher said. "What happened?"

"I never traveled with you for this long before," Vasari replied. "Shall we go?"

"Certainly." He held out his arm, she took it, and together they ambled from the suite and down to the lobby below.

"It occurs to me," Vasari said a while later, as they walked through the streets of Wippeldon, "that if we linger on Entibor for very long, at some point the Domina may see us."

"Quite likely," Aringher said. He fed a coin into a news kiosk and waited for the printout, then flipped through the pages of flimsy as they walked. "Why should I be concerned if the Domina sees us?"

"Because she might recognize you."

"I doubt it. I'm not wearing the same clothes. But even if she does—what could she possibly say?"

"Nothing," Vasari admitted. "If you're not worried, we might as well move on to the capital."

"Whatever for?"

Vasari raised her eyebrows. "Why *did* you decide to come to this planet?"

"To attend the annual chamber-music festival," said Aringher with a straight face. "And you?"

"As it happens," she said, "I have letters of introduction to some of the very best people. My relatives back on Galcen are most anxious that I should pay the proper courtesy calls."

"The rooms at the lodge are booked for a week. No refunds."

"Let your great-uncle's legacy worry about the bill," Vasari said. "We don't want to miss the accession ceremonies. You can stare at the scenery later, if that's what amuses you."

"Since you put it that way—"

"I do. And I must admit, a chance to go shopping in the capital would be nice."

Aringher nodded. "I wouldn't mind that myself. To AnJemayne, then; and we'll see what happens once we're there."

After several hours of watching the shifting colors of the Pleyveran Web through the *'Hammer'*s viewscreens, Perada grew restless and went back into the body of the ship. The lights were out in the common room, and the gravity was off. Part of saving power, she supposed. She made her way to the galley, pulling herself along with the ladder rails set in the overhead. Then she made cha'a, transferred it to a zero-g flask according to the helpful instructions on the side of the pot, and took the flask back with her to the *'Hammer'*s cockpit along with a handful of drinking bulbs.

She arrived in time to hear a perturbed rumble coming up on the comm link from the engineering spaces.

"I know, Ferrda," the captain replied. "Just hold them together for two more hours. That's all I need." He glanced over his shoulder at Perada. "Thanks ... I could use a mug of cha'a."

Perada filled two of the drinking bulbs and passed them

to the captain and Errec Ransome. "Should I take some to the others, too?"

He nodded. "Tilly and Nannla, anyhow. Ferrda's not going to want anything until we get through."

Perada went back through the common room to the access tubes for the gun bubbles. She went down first—or the direction that would have been down, had there been gravity. Tillijen was there, looking out through the curved armor-glass walls of her bubble, spinning in the gimbal-mounted seat.

As Perada came through the hatch, the number-two gunner keyed on her headset.

"Beacon coming up—one-two-one occulting, green. Bearing zero-niner-zero."

She clicked off and spun around so that she looked upward into the tube. "Cha'a," she said, extending an arm for a drinking bulb. "Your Dignity, you're a lifesaver."

Perada blinked. *She must be tired. That's the first time she's slipped and used proper form.* Aloud, she said only, "My dignity isn't quite up to managing zero-g in skirts, but it'll survive."

The gunner leaned back in her seat and took a long pull of the bulb of cha'a. "How's everyone else holding up?"

Perada looked down at the gunner. *Of course, from her point of view it probably feels like I'm looking up. Unless she's worked in zero-g so often that she doesn't think about "up" and "down" any more.* "All right, I suppose. Gentlesir Ferrdacorr seems worried about the engines."

"Ferrda always worries about the engines. He's got a point, though."

"Are the engines likely to present a serious problem?"

"Not unless we get unlucky," Tillijen said. "But this junk out here—" She waved her free hand at the glowing masses of light outside the bubble. "—it's hard on everything. And the engines can't be shielded, so they take more damage than anything else."

"If getting through the Web is so difficult," Perada said, "I'm surprised that anyone bothers to visit here at all."

"That's because you haven't seen Pleyver." Tillijen

sighed. "It's a lovely world, almost as pretty as—well, never mind. And rich, too; lots of natural resources, and right on the route from anywhere to anywhere else. Whoever was the first one to find it, though, coming through this soup—"

The clouds of light parted, and there was the system spread out below them—the central sun and the planets, with Pleyver close at hand.

"It's beautiful," Perada said.

"It surely is," Tillijen said. She keyed on the headset again. "Pleyver in sight. Numerous ships in orbit. I make two lifting."

She turned back to Perada. "No offense, but I think you ought to take Nannla her share of the cha'a and then go strap down. Pleyver was all right the last time I was here, but things can change fast these days. If any old friends or casual acquaintances are waiting for us, things might get rough."

ERREC RANSOME: ILARNA
(GALCENIAN DATING 970 A.F.; ENTIBORAN REGNAL
YEAR 34 VERATINA)

ERREC WOKE abruptly, as if from a sudden
noise—heart racing, breath suspended. For a
minute or two he lay quiet and listened, but his ears caught
nothing beyond the usual sounds of the Amalind Grange
Guildhouse late on a snowy winter's night.

His mind catalogued them all, and found them harmless.
A faint rattle as the wind first gusted, then died, then gusted
again: lozenges of window glass stirring in their leaded
frames. Distant, muffled creaks and snaps: house timbers
flexing and shifting as the building settled into the cold of
the night. And underlying everything, a steady, peaceful
rhythm—the breath and heartbeat of every living thing sheltered within the Grange's wooden walls.

Why, then, had he awakened?

Not from a nightmare ... he knew the feel of that too
well, after his time on Galcen. Such awakenings always
held as much relief as they did leftover apprehension, and
there was no relief for him here. Whatever had brought him
to full consciousness out of an untroubled sleep, he felt sure
that it had come from a source outside his own mind.

And it was continuing. He sensed it—a thrumming in the air, a vibration along his nerve ends like the note of the lowest string on a megaviole. He sat up and looked around the bedchamber. Nothing had changed since he'd composed himself earlier and dropped off to sleep. The heat-bar, its ceramic element a dull red against the shadows, glowered at him from the hearth like a slitted, malevolent eye.

There was no point in trying to go back to sleep. He'd experienced fits of wakefulness before, and knew that there was no help for the affliction except to rise and walk it off. He pushed aside the blankets and began getting dressed: the trousers and shirt from his formal blacks, that he'd hung over the back of the bedside chair a few hours ago; a pair of warm socks; the leather boots he'd bought off-planet.

Then he reached out for his staff, and drew a sharp breath. The six-foot length of Ilarnan whitebole wood was vibrating under his touch.

He jerked his hand away. When he touched the staff again, he felt only the cool smoothness of the wood beneath his fingers. He told himself that he had imagined the brief sensation; that the illusion, and the sudden waking that had preceded it, were the products of unresolved tension—the legacy of a stay on Galcen that had not brought him the knowledge he had expected to gain.

I didn't imagine it, he protested to himself. *Whatever I felt, was real.*

But if it had been real, why wasn't every Master and apprentice in the Amalind Guildhouse as tense and wakeful as he was? The situation bore investigating. He picked up the staff—with some trepidation, but it continued to behave like ordinary inert wood—and stepped out of his bedchamber.

The air in the hall was chilly and unmoving, unstirred by drafts. The only light came from a blue low-power glowcube set above the stairwell. Errec considered for a moment, then ducked back into his room and took down his dark woolen night-robe from the hook on the back of the door. He belted on the robe over his shirt and trousers and, feeling somewhat warmer, continued his explorations.

All the doors up and down the central top-floor hall were

shut. He eased the nearest one open. A gentle snoring met his ears. He took a step forward, calling a faint light into his staff. The sleeper turned over restlessly—even that much change in the flow of Power was enough to disrupt the slumber of a sensitive Adept. Errec recognized Allorie Sandevan, the youngest daughter of a banking family from the southern continent. She'd been a senior apprentice when he left for Galcen, and living in the long dormitory instead of the main house. He remembered Allorie as being one of the best students in her year; it was inconceivable that the menace he had felt—if it had been real—would leave her asleep.

For a moment he debated waking her, but in the end he stepped back into the hall and closed the door, leaving her undisturbed. There was no point in forcing anyone else to share his midnight prowling. He moved off quietly down the hall.

Thick black velvet curtains hung across the end of the hallway opposite the stairwell. Errec knew that they masked a small, windowed alcove—in warmer weather, a good place for solitary meditation, or for looking out over the fields and outbuildings. He let the faint glow from his staff die away, and slipped in between the velvet folds.

Outside the windows, heavy, silent flakes of snow fell onto the rolling hills of the Amalind district. And as quietly as the snow, but vastly more ponderous, the wing-shaped black raiding ships were lowering themselves to the ground on glowing nullgravs.

VI. Galcenian Dating 974 A.F.
Entiboran Regnal Year 38 Veratina

J os Metadi brought *Warhammer* down into the
secured landing area near Flatlands Portcity.
The final approach to Pleyver-had gone without a hitch. Nobody had jumped him on the way out of the Web, or demanded that he submit to boarding and inspection, or any of
the other bad things that could happen to a more or less
law-abiding privateer outside his normal range of operations. Flatlands looked like a safe port, at least for now;
Errec and the others could finish up their interrupted dirtside
liberty while he kept an eye on the Domina.

"She'll need help," he said to Errec. They were in the
'Hammer's cockpit, shutting down the systems after an un-
eventful touchdown. "Flatlands may be safe, but that
doesn't mean it's the sort of town she ought to be running
around in all by herself."

"You think so?"

Jos didn't know whether to call Errec's expression
amused or not. A lot of Errec's reactions were like that—
off-center, somehow—and it didn't do any good to try and
figure them out, because you couldn't.

"Yeah," he said. "I think so. She hasn't been out of school long enough to dry off behind the ears."

Errec shrugged. "Don't underestimate her, is all."

"You sound like you don't trust the lady very much."

"It's not a matter of trust. She'll keep her bargains. But—"

"But what?"

"She wants something from you. She came to Waycross on purpose, trying to get it, and she won't have forgotten about it just because the two of you have been sharing a bed ever since we lifted from Innish-Kyl."

Jos looked at his copilot thoughtfully. Such blunt speaking wasn't like Errec. Most of the time the Ilarnan was reserved about such matters, especially compared to Ferrda and the two gunners. "You think I'm making a mistake, going along with her like this?"

"I can't tell." Errec sounded doubtful, not evasive. "All I know is that there's pain and trouble in it for somebody, somewhere along the line."

"I suppose you think I ought to drop her as soon as we get to Entibor."

Jos wasn't surprised to find himself disliking the idea. Perada Rosselin was a warm armful, and good company no matter how many star systems she happened to own.

Errec shook his head. "Nothing so easy. There's pain and trouble that way, too."

"Fine," said Jos. "Then I'll do what I please and to hell with the omens."

"Not omens," Errec said. "Patterns. Currents. The universe moves, and sometimes the path is visible."

"Whatever," said Jos. He'd given up trying to follow Errec's explanations a long time ago. "Come on, let's go tell the others they can get ready for a good time portside."

Perada was already waiting in the common room. It looked like she was planning to go incognito again: she didn't have the velvet mask anymore, but she'd improvised something almost as effective with a sheer black scarf and one of Nannla's hats. She wasn't wearing braids, not even the two long schoolgirl plaits; instead her unbound hair flowed down past her belt in a long, pale waterfall.

His breath caught at the shimmering beauty of it, and at the memory of what it felt like, falling down around his face in a silken curtain. He forced his mind back to practical matters with some difficulty.

It's part of the incognito, he reminded himself. *She's taking it a lot more seriously this time.*

He found his voice. "You're going to make contact in Flatlands with your old school chum?"

"That's right," she said. "All I need to do is find a public comm-link kiosk. Garen can arrange everything once I get in touch."

"Garen?"

"Garen Tarveet. He left school a half-year before I did."

"Tarveet . . . if the newsreaders don't lie, your pal's family owns half of Pleyver. Maybe more than half, by now."

"I suppose so," she said. "That's not what I need to talk to him about, though."

Jos hazarded a guess. "Politics?"

"And long-range plans. He used to have some good ideas; now it's time to see if he believes in them."

Plans, Jos told himself. *Remember what Errec said, hotshot—this one has plans.*

Maybe so. That doesn't mean she ought to be out on her own in Flatlands without somebody to look out for her.

"If you're going to wait around the transport hub for a pickup," he said, "you'll need to have somebody with you."

He half expected her to protest. She didn't, though; just looked at him through the concealing swathe of gauzy scarf. "Do you really think so?"

"Yes."

"Very well. You may come with me."

" 'May'?" He felt his skin redden. "What do you mean, *'may'*?"

"If you like." Her smile under the veil had a mischievous quality. "Wear plain clothing and don't talk to anyone. They'll think you're my bodyguard."

Jos considered several different replies and gave up on all

of them. "Right," he said finally, and ducked into his cabin to change into one of his talking-to-bankers outfits. He'd had the jackets on those cut to hide a small blaster up the sleeve or in a shoulder holster—tailors in Waycross were used to requests like that—but this time he decided to be obviously armed instead, going with his familiar Mark VI heavy, belted low and tied to his thigh.

"Excellent," was all the Domina said when he returned. "Shall we go now, or wait for the others?"

"No point in hanging around," he said. "Let's go."

There was a comm-link kiosk at the edge of the landing zone. The slot called for three Galcenian decimal-credits, or two Pleyveran tiles, or one Mandeynan tenthmark. Jos wasn't surprised to find out that the Domina didn't have any one of those. A quick search through his own pockets produced a handful of Innish-Kyllan cash-tacs and a crumpled Galcenian twenty-credit chit.

"We need to find a money changer," Jos said. "Usually I keep enough local currency on hand to get off-port wherever the 'Hammer's docked, but Pleyver's not one of my normal stops."

The exchange booth turned out to be some distance away. Perada didn't complain, in spite of the hot sun. What Jos could see of her face behind the concealing veil looked thoughtful. She didn't comment on anything until the Pleyveran Guaranty Trust logo on top of the currency-exchange booth came into view.

Then she said, "People shouldn't have to go through this every time they come into port."

"Changing money isn't that big a problem," he said. "You learn to deal with it."

"Maybe," she said. "But everything's like that. All the worlds have their own coins and their own languages and their own fleets. Any time two systems want to work together on something—like fighting off the raiders, for example—the project dies because they can't agree on whose things to use."

"Lords of Life," he said, half amused and half disbelieving. "The Domina of Entibor is a Centrist."

"I am *not!*" she said. "But something needs to be done before the civilized galaxy gets carried off to the Mageworlds piece by piece."

Jos couldn't deny the truth of her last statement, especially since he'd caught himself thinking the same thing more than once over the past few years. His home world of Gyffer had a strong fleet, built up and kept ready to protect the planet's orbiting shipyards and the factories below; but was that fleet strong enough to hold off the raiders if they attacked full-force?

Once he'd changed the twenty-chit, things got easier. The Guaranty Trust booth had a public comm-link, so they didn't have to hike back before Perada could make her call. She had the call-code memorized, too, which made him wonder exactly how well she'd known this Garen Tarveet before he left school.

She kept the hush screen turned on, so he couldn't hear what she said over the link, but when the screen went off she came out smiling. "It's all arranged," she said. "A driver from the estate will meet us here in half an hour."

"Local or Standard?"

She frowned slightly. "He didn't say . . . I suppose we'll find out when the driver gets here."

"Unless your friend's a spacer," Jos said, "I'll bet he meant local."

Free-spacers all over the civilized galaxy used Galcenian time for the same reason they used the language of the Mother of Worlds: there'd be no doing business otherwise. He was no Centrist himself—not many Gyfferans were—but he could see why some people found the concept attractive.

The hovercar showed up in a little under half an hour by the local-time clock on the wall of the currency exchange. A liveried driver got out and gave the Domina a respectful bow.

"Gentlelady Wherret?" he said.

"Yes," said Perada.

"The young gentlesir regrets that he could not meet you himself. He awaits you at the estate."

"Very well."

The driver opened the door of the hovercar and looked at Jos expectantly. So, after a moment, did Perada.

Right. You're the bodyguard; you're supposed to check things out for her first.

Feeling a trifle absurd, he stepped up to the open door and peered inside. As far as he could tell, he was looking at an ordinary unthreatening hovercar—except for the luxury, which was enough to make a poor boy from the Gyfferan dockyards nervous all by itself. He stepped back and nodded to Perada. She gave him a polite but distant smile in return and got into the plushly upholstered passenger compartment. He decided that bodyguards were supposed to stick close to the body they were guarding, and followed.

That was apparently the right move; the driver swung the door shut without comment, and Perada was smiling. There was armor-glass an inch thick between the passenger compartment and the driver's seat, but Jos didn't trust it for an instant.

"Gentlelady Wherret," he said. He let a faint hint of disbelief tinge his voice, but nothing more.

Her blue eyes danced with mischief behind the veil. "Yes."

He wanted to say *How did you come up with* that *for an incognito?,* but he didn't dare.

"Be careful," he said instead.

They both fell silent. The ride from the aptly named Flatlands Portcity to the Tarveet estate took over an hour, leaving the open plain and following a broad river westward into rolling hill country. Jos decided that the driver must have been ordered to take the scenic route. Either that, or they were in trouble—*I'll give him another fifteen minutes to get us anyplace, and then we're getting out of here if I have to shoot the door open.*

Such drastic measures turned out to be unnecessary. Five minutes later, local time, the hovercar passed through a pair of elaborate wrought-metal gates and started down a long driveway lined with tall, fan-shaped flowering trees. A large manor house of pale grey stone stood at the end of the drive.

The hovercar settled onto the combed sand with the faintest of crunching noises—the sound of fine particles compacting under the car's weight—and the driver got out and swung open the passenger door. Cool air scented with flowers rolled in from outside. Night had fallen while they were making their way from the port, and the sky burned with the colored streamers of an auroral display.

Perada looked at Jos. He took the hint—*Time for the bodyguard to go first and draw enemy fire if there is any*—and got out of the hovercar. Perada followed, emerging onto the driveway in time for a lanky youth in dark blue velvet to come running down the broad steps of the manor house and throw his arms around her.

" 'Rada!" he exclaimed. "I never expected—how *wonderful* to see you again!"

The Domina had pulled off her veil and was hugging him back. "You haven't changed a bit, Garen. I'm glad to see you, too. I need your help."

The young man let her go and stepped away—not very far away, though, and he was looking only at her. Jos and the driver might as well have been part of the landscape.

Skinny twerp, Jos thought. *Whatever she wants him for, it can't be his looks.*

Garen Tarveet was only about a year older than Perada, if that; his thin frame had some of the lingering gawkiness of late-adolescence. His limp brown hair fell down across his brow and got in the way of his eyes—which were themselves a watery and unattractive grey. He wet his lips in a nervous gesture.

"I'll help you however I can, 'Rada—you know that—but I have to know what's going on first."

"Veratina's dead."

Tarveet made a startled noise. "But she wasn't even eighty yet—what happened?"

"I don't know," Perada said. " 'Natural causes,' according to the armsmaster, but that could mean almost anything. I'll find out more when I get to Entibor." She fixed Tarveet with a challenging glance—the same all-or-nothing look she'd worn back at the Double Moon—and said, "What's important now is that I'm the Domina. And everything we used to talk about on Galcen is possible."

Thinking about it afterward, Jos decided that he had to give Garen Tarveet points for guts. It was one thing to have big ideas and spread them out on the table to impress a pretty girl, but something else altogether when the pretty girl showed up later and expected you to follow through.

Tarveet blinked and swallowed hard. "There's a lot of people we'll have to talk to first. But I think we can do it."

Perada smiled. The effect was dazzling. "I knew I could depend on you, Garen. But it was a long drive from the spaceport; is there some place I can go to freshen up before we start working?"

"Of course," Tarveet said. The two of them headed up the steps of the manor house, arm in arm.

Feeling out of place, Jos followed.

In the far western highlands of Galcen's northern continent, a winter storm howled across the black walls and looming towers of the Adepts' Retreat. Snow and ice covered the narrow road that led up from the village of Treslin in the valley below; snow and ice blanketed the pocket-sized landing field that linked the Retreat to the outer world by air. Nobody was going to enter the Retreat, or leave it, until the weather broke.

Within the stone walls of the fortress, however, Galcen's Adepts contrived to keep themselves warm. Force fields shimmered across windows that had once been nothing but open slits hewn through massive blocks of stone; heat-bars glowed on every hearth. In the windowless inner rooms that housed the record-keepers for the Guild, where the winter cold should have penetrated to the bone, heavy-duty climate-control systems kept the area warm—not for the comfort of the Adepts who worked there, but for the sake of the equipment that they tended.

Two of the Retreat's senior Adepts stood by the main comp console, leaning on their staffs and watching the apprentice who had drawn today's round of data work. The apprentice was accustomed to working unsupervised—she was qualified to handle the comps, and the task at hand was not an urgent one—and the set of her shoulders as she went from comp screen to keyboard and back again betrayed both annoyance and unease.

A name came up on the main screen. RANSOME, E.; ILARNA.

Another dead one, she thought. Most of the Ilarnans were, or as close to it as made no difference. But she was too conscientious to mark the owner of any name as dead without a proper check, especially with Master Otenu and Master Faen breathing down the back of her neck. She touched the key to begin the search.

Behind her, she heard Otenu murmur, "Ransome. He studied here for a while, did you know?"

"Yes," said Faen. A pause. "But he was on Ilarna."

"Are you sure? I always wondered—the dates were so close—"

Too close, thought the apprentice. The first information had already come up on the secondary screen: records of the Red Shift Line, showing that the spaceliner *Fleeting Fancy,* on a regular run from Galcen to Ilarna, had carried one Errec Ransome as a passenger—putting him on-planet a full day and half a night before the attack.

She felt Master Faen leaning to peer at the screen over her shoulder.

"You see," Faen said to Otenu. "He was there."

"At the spaceport," Otenu said. "The Ilarnan Guildhouse was in broad countryside—farming country. I remember him saying so once. He missed it, I think, while he was away."

The apprentice felt sorry for Master Otenu; it sounded like Ransome had been a friend of his. But another scrap of data was scrolling up onto the secondary screen: the deposition of an Ilarnan refugee and former spaceport worker, who remembered renting a long-range aircar to an Adept fresh home from Galcen, said aircar to be returned at the rental franchise in the town of Amalind Under.

"That's it," said Faen. "Unless something happened to that aircar between the spaceport and Amalind Under, he was at the Guildhouse when it fell. And there were no survivors."

"His body was never found."

"Neither were half a hundred others," Faen said. "Remember—everything that the raiders couldn't take away, they burned."

Master Otenu moved restlessly. His shifting about made the apprentice nervous, and she wished that he would stop. She had the feeling that the senior Master was the reason both Adepts were here and bothering her at her work—Otenu was looking for something, and she didn't know what.

Maybe Otenu doesn't either.

"Ransome makes me too uncomfortable for someone who's supposed to be dead," Otenu said finally. "I dreamed about him last night."

She heard Master Faen draw a sharp breath. "I see."

"He came to me in my dream and tried to warn me of something," Otenu said, "but the thing itself I couldn't hear."

"How do you know it was a warning, then?"

"It felt like one." Otenu paused. "And you will admit, I think, that if anyone had the strength and the talents to escape the killing on Ilarna, it was Ransome."

"I defer to your judgment on that," Faen said. "You worked with him and I didn't." Another pause. "What was he like?"

"Very strong," said Otenu. "And not always subtle—he came to his talent late, after working for several years as a common merchant-spacer out of his home world. As for his particular gifts—you know as well as I do what Ilarna sent him here to learn."

No, thought the apprentice. *What?* But neither Adept seemed willing to pursue that part of the discussion further, and her curiosity had to remain unsatisfied.

"If Ransome *is* alive," Faen was saying, "then where is he? None of the Guildhouses have reported seeing him, and no Guildmembers. If he were alive and free, he would have contacted the nearest Guildhouse. He has not done so—therefore, either he is not alive, or he is not free. And in either case," Faen concluded, "he is lost to us."

"You forget one other possibility," said Otenu. "It could be that Ransome is alive, and does not want to be found. And in that case—"

"I agree," said Faen. "In that case—unlikely as it may be—in *that* case, it is imperative that we bring him back."

The apprentice stifled a sigh. The name RANSOME, E., still glowed on the console's main screen. She hesitated a little longer, then keyed in the necessary commands.

RANSOME, E; ILARNA.
STATUS: MISSING.
SEARCH: ACTIVE.

The interior of the Tarveets' manor house was as luxurious as the hovercar had been, and even more elaborate. Jos decided after a few minutes' reflection that the Double Moon back in Waycross wanted to be someplace like this when it grew up. Garen Tarveet, in his dark blue velvet, looked right at home. Perada, however, looked somewhat out of place. Jos couldn't tell if it was her clothes—she was wearing the pick of the *'Hammer*'s slop chest, along with Nannla's hat and Tillijen's spare blaster—or that he'd gotten used to seeing her in plainer settings than this.

The second possibility made him uneasy. In the privateering life you took the good times as they came, and you certainly didn't turn down a sporting invitation from a girl whose personal wealth was enough to buy an entire planet on the open market. But you didn't dare let yourself get used to having someone around—do that, and when they were gone you didn't just miss them, you hurt all over.

Garen Tarveet and Perada went into a long, open room full of cushioned furniture made of some kind of knotty, light-brown wood. Jos followed—since nobody stopped him, he supposed that as a bodyguard he wasn't officially there—and took up a position near the entrance, where he could watch the doors and windows while he kept an eye on the Domina and her friend.

The two former classmates had settled down on a couch at the other end of the room, screened from direct view by a small thicket of potted plants and hanging ferns. Jos wondered, briefly, what the room was used for when the family's son and heir wasn't occupied in making conspiracies in it. A game room, maybe; he spotted what looked like a four-high pushball cube down at the far end, behind another obscuring mass of greenery, and not far from where he stood was a low table about the right size to display a draughts board and opposing control pads.

Jos was tempted to try out the table himself, but refrained. Bodyguards didn't do that sort of thing—and besides, he was too busy trying to overhear what Perada and Tarveet were saying to each other with their heads so close together. The young man's dull brown hair was all but touching Perada's lighter tresses, and she was whispering something in his ear.

The few scraps of conversation that carried as far as the entrance, however, didn't sound particularly loverlike:

". . . can you get access . . . ?"

". . . nominal control of the off-world properties . . ."

". . . Galcen?"

"No choice. But . . ."

The talk went on like that for some time. Then, abruptly, both Perada and Tarveet stood and left the room by the inner door. Since he hadn't been told to do otherwise, Jos followed.

They were going deeper into the manor house, through hallways and corridors that grew more elaborate as they went along. Plain flagstone flooring gave way to polished wood, and then to rugs—if such a homely term could be applied to the precious fabrics that covered the Tarveet family floors. Jos recognized the carpet underfoot as Ilarnan mille-fleur knotwork, exquisite and damn-near priceless—the *'Hammer* had taken a couple of bales of the stuff off a Magebuilt cargo hauler a while back, and the sum Errec

Ransome had named as its fair value had staggered everyone on board.

I've seen old spacehands retire rich on money like that. And Errec never would take his share of it.

The corridor ended in a set of heavy double doors, done in dark wood with enameled trim. The doors swung open, and Perada turned to Jos.

"Wait here," she said, and turned away without pausing for a reply.

The doors closed again behind the Domina and Garen Tarveet, leaving Jos alone. As instructed, like a proper bodyguard, he waited. And waited, staring at the swirls of blue and cream and gold on the door panels, while the evening wore on. He would have checked his chronometer, or started pacing, or gone ahead and pushed open the doors in spite of his instructions, but all of those things were off limits in his current role.

Not that he wasn't tempted.

You don't know what's going on in there. She could be in all sorts of trouble.

Right. Or maybe she and her pal are having dinner with his family, and the last thing she needs is for you to come charging in waving a blaster right in the middle of the salad course.

He'd about decided to open the doors anyway, and to hell with it, when a maidservant in livery approached and said, "Come with me."

Jos shook his head. "My, uh . . ."—what *was* the right word?—"my employer told me to wait right here."

The maidservant looked amused. Jos found out why a moment later, when she handed him a folded slip of cream-colored notepaper. He unfolded it and saw three sentences, written in a firm, round hand: *You're as suspicious as your friend Thulmotten. It's all right. I'll be with you later. —P.*

He refolded the slip of paper and tucked it into his inside jacket pocket. "Lead on," he said.

The maidservant started off down a service passage, narrower and darker than the elegant public rooms that it connected. Jos followed, feeling lighter of heart than he had for some time. The reference to the front page of Sverje's coursebook had eased a worry that he hadn't been aware of until it was gone: that the Tarveets or somebody in their employ had seized Perada and tried to fob off her bodyguard with a forged note.

The maidservant led him to a room containing a bed, a chair, and a dressing table—all good quality, but plain.

"You'll be spending the night here," she said, and closed the outer door behind her as she left.

Jos looked about the room. It was about the same size as his cabin aboard *Warhammer*, but not as well designed: all the furniture sat in the middle of the floor instead of tucking itself out of the way in nooks and alcoves, and wall space that could have housed useful built-ins was wasted on a window and two inner doors. One door, upon inspection, led to the refresher cubicle; the other proved to be locked from the other side. All in all, the setup was less than what he could have bought for himself in downtown Flatlands after a halfway decent run.

So this is what personal bodyguards rate by way of quarters, he thought. *I believe I'll stick to privateering.*

He sat down in the chair and waited. According to his chronometer, an hour, Standard, passed by without incident. Then two hours. At last, when it became obvious that he wasn't going to be called for or even fed, he turned off the lights and stretched out fully clothed on the bed.

Some time later, he woke to the sound of the inner door swinging open in the darkened room. He didn't make any sudden moves, but had his blaster aimed before the door was all the way open. Then a familiar presence settled down on the mattress next to him. He slid the blaster back into its holster.

"Thank goodness *that's* over," Perada Rosselin said. "I thought I'd never get away."

He put an arm around her and leaned his cheek against her hair. She smelled nice—no flowers or perfume or anything, just girl. "I was afraid you'd decided to spend the night with your friend instead."

She gave a sleepy giggle. "Garen? He has clammy hands. And his mother's a horror."

With Perada curled up beside him, Jos could afford to feel magnanimous. "Don't be too hard on the poor kid. He can't help his mother—or his hands, either. When I was his age, I was even worse."

"I don't believe that for a minute."

"Truth," he said. "But I learned better."

"You'll have to show me what you've learned some time." She yawned. "But not tonight, I think. I'm so tired I'm falling over when I try to stand up. If you don't mind just keeping me company—?"

"We'll keep each other company," said Jos. And wondered, as he drifted off to sleep a few minutes later with her head pillowed on his shoulder, if he hadn't already grown too used to Perada Rosselin for his own good.

Perada Rosselin: Galcen
(Galcenian Dating 963 a.f.; Entiboran Regnal Year 27 Veratina)

MAIL DELIVERY at school came once a day, in late afternoon after all the classwork was done. It didn't matter whether the news from home came as voice chip or compressed-text, as printout flimsy or calligraphed parchment; everything came first to Mistress Delaven's office and passed under Mistress Delaven's eye. What Zeri Delaven judged safe and fitting, she distributed. The rest—or so dormitory rumor had it—she kept, and presented years later to the departing student in one fat, long-outdated bundle.

Perada Rosselin didn't know if she believed the story or not. After almost six months of schooling, she could speak and understand enough Galcenian to follow the classroom lessons—the teachers always talked slowly and explained everything at least twice—but the conversation of her fellow-students still at times confused her.

And you can't ask anyone for help, she thought. That lesson, at least, she'd guessed at without having to be told. *Or they'll know for sure that you don't know.*

But today it didn't matter. She had a letter from Dadda:

real ink on real paper, in a stiff white envelope sealed with his university ring. The letter had come from Entibor on the diplomatic courier—Mistress Delaven had said so—and the Entiboran ambassador had put it into the Galcenian Planetary Post, and the GPP had carried it by aircar, hovertruck, and speederbike to the mailbox in Mistress Delaven's office, and Mistress Delaven had given it to her.

Perada clipped the envelope onto the back of her text reader and hurried for the big dormitory room she shared with three other primary-class girls. She didn't like any of them—they were all Galcenian, and the way they spoke to each other, a quick slide and patter of words with all the important syllables missing, wasn't anything like the way her teachers said that the language was supposed to go.

She didn't think the other girls liked her, either.

As soon as she reached her desk, she tore open the envelope. When she saw the writing inside, she felt a sharp sting of anger: more Galcenian! But the seal and the writing were Dadda's, so—slowly and clumsily—she began to read:

My dearest babba:

Mistress Delaven said that I should write to you in Galcenian to help you learn faster, and I think that she is right. Besides, I need the practice myself. If I make any mistakes, I know that you will tell me, since you speak the language every day with your friends.

But that is not what I am writing to tell you. The real news is that when spring comes in Felshang this year, you will have a new baby sister. Gersten Kiel is her gene-sire, as he was yours, so she will probably look a lot like you once she is grown. We are all very happy, and your mother is well. I hope that you—

She never got to read the rest of the letter. The door slid open and two of her roommates came in—the worst two, as bad luck would have it. Elli Oldigaard was the oldest of the four girls who shared the room, a second-year student whose father did something important with other people's money in Galcen Prime, and Gryl was Elli's most dedicated follower.

Perada tried to tuck the sheet of notepaper out of sight underneath her text reader, but it was too late. Elli had spotted it.

"Oooh, look who's got mail!"

Elli's long fingers darted out and snatched up the letter. Her dark eyes flicked over the lines of writing.

"Oooh!" she said again. Perada wanted to hit her. "Somebody's mamma is going to have a baby!"

"You give that back!"

Perada grabbed for the note. Elli danced back out of reach, laughing.

"You didn't share, so it's mine."

"It's *mine*! My dadda sent it to me!"

"He's not your father," Elli said—the older girl was speaking clearly, so Perada knew she was meant to understand. "The letter says he isn't."

"He is so!"

Elli shook her head. "Is not. It said right there in the letter: your father is somebody called Gersten Kiel."

Perada felt tears of frustration coming to her eyes. Galcenians were *stupid*. "It did not say that. Gersten Kiel isn't my dadda, he's my gene-sire, my—"

She was speaking Entiboran now, because Galcenian didn't have the right words to say it—if the words had been the right ones, Elli would have understood when Dadda used them. She gave up trying to explain and made another grab for the note. Elli tossed the sheet of paper to Gryl, saying something as she did so in that too-fast, too-mixed-up kind of Galcenian that the other girls spoke with each other, and Gryl threw the letter down the waste-recycling chute.

Perada slapped Elli across the face.

Elli screamed.

Gryl shouted, "I'm going to tell! I'm going to tell!"

"I don't care!" Perada shouted back at her, and ran out of the room.

She was all the way down the hall and halfway down the main stairs—not knowing where she was heading or what

she was going to do when she got there—when she ran
headfirst into Mistress Delaven coming up.

"Now," said Zeri Delaven in a dreadful voice. "What has
disturbed the tranquillity upstairs?"

It was no use keeping secrets from Mistress Delaven. The
students said she read minds, and Perada believed them.
She told the whole story—letter, waste chute, slap, and all.

"I see," said Zeri Delaven. Perada couldn't tell what she
was thinking. "Come with me."

Perada followed Mistress Delaven to the small room near
the school office where students waited for interviews, and
sometimes for discipline. The door slid open when Mistress
Delaven touched the lockplate.

"Stay here for now," Zeri Delaven said. "I need to have
a word with Gryl and Elli."

Perada went into the room and the door slid shut behind
her. The soundproofing was thick; she couldn't hear if Mistress Delaven, on the other side of the door, went away or
not.

The waiting room held only a couple of desks and, today
at least, one boy. He was about Perada's age, or a few
months older, and he looked as if he'd been crying. He was
new, Perada thought; at least, she'd never seen him before—
and it was usually the new students who cried.

For a long time she didn't say anything. But Zeri Delaven
didn't come back, and the quiet room was lonely even if it
did have somebody else sitting in it.

"Did you just come here?" she asked finally—in Galcenian.

The boy looked at her and swallowed hard. His face was
blotchy and his eyes looked puffed—yes, Perada decided,
he had definitely been crying.

"Today," he said. The words came out slowly, with long
spaces of thought between them. "From Pleyver. And I
can't. Understand. *Anyone!*"

His accent, Perada thought happily, was even worse than
hers. *But there's two of us. And if we stick together, Elli will
have to leave us alone.*

"Don't worry," she said. "I'll help you."

VII. Galcenian Dating 974 A.F.
Entiboran Regnal Year 38 Veratina

Jos Metadi opened his eyes. The ceiling seemed too far away, and it took him a few seconds to orient himself. He wasn't on his ship or in some portside flophouse—the high overhead that had at first startled him told him as much.

That's right. Perada's buddy Tarveet and his family's little place in the country.

He rolled onto his side. From the new position, he could see that the morning had dawned a wet and sullen gray. He felt like he'd slept in his clothes—which turned out to have been the case—and his face felt scratchy.

Wonderful. Wrinkled clothes and a face full of stubble. And I'm supposed to convince the locals that I'm the Domina's professional bodyguard.

Thinking of the Domina caused Jos to look for the first time at the place beside him on the bed. Perada was gone. He felt a wrench of dislocation that was almost physical.

You knew it would be like this, he told himself. The reminder didn't help. He grunted and rolled out of bed. *No point in lying here.*

He stretched and ran his fingers through his tangled hair. A quick look around the room showed him that nothing obvious had changed since the previous night. The inner door was locked again on the far side. The refresher cubicle, fortunately, was not; he had a long, luxury-loving shower underneath what seemed like an unlimited supply of hot water, and felt somewhat less out-of-focus as a result.

He put his old clothes back on for lack of anything better. Then—seeing no point in another several hours of idle waiting—he slid open the room's outer door.

A stack of trunks and boxes filled most of the service hallway. Shipping labels on the boxes declared them to be the property of The Royal Party of Entibor, and enjoined the recipient to Hold For Arrival. A quick look at the routing codes told Jos that the boxes had been sent from Innish-Kyl on the same day that *Warhammer* had left.

Whoever posted these, he thought, *knew that we'd be coming next to Pleyver.*

Years of working the dubious side of the spacelanes had given Jos a deep-rooted mistrust of mysterious packages that appeared at convenient times. He pulled the top sheet off the bed, twisted it, and tied it to the handle of the uppermost case. Then, standing around the corner of the open door, he gave a quick jerk to the improvised rope. The case fell from the stack onto the floor.

As far as he could tell, nothing else happened. No explosion, no noxious fumes. *So far, so good.*

Feeling a bit foolish, he dragged the case over to the window where the light was better. If his hosts had wanted to kill him—or Perada—they'd had a dozen chances already. And they weren't likely to pick a method that would require them to replace all the wall hangings afterward. But feeling foolish didn't stop him from rigging a remote-release on the box's catch, or from taking shelter behind the far side of the bed while he used it.

The top of the case cracked open—nothing more. Nevertheless, he waited for several minutes before walking over and lifting the lid. Inside the box he found a layer of women's clothing, with a card and a sealed envelope lying on the top.

He picked up the card. It was small and rectangular, cut from thick, heavy stock, with an elaborate crest in raised gold. Underneath the crest was a handwritten note, in Galcenian:

> *You are wise, Captain, to take precautions. Few things are what they seem. The young Domina's continued safety is of the utmost importance. I congratulate you on the care you have taken thus far, and wish you every success in the future. Awaiting your arrival at Entibor,*
>   *I remain, your servant, &c.—*

Beneath the note, by way of signature, was an elaborate swirl of Entiboran script—initials, it looked like, worked into some kind of design. Jos frowned. As a privateer and sometime trader, he had first-glance recognition of any number of seals, sigils, chops, and trademarks, and casual knowledge of a great many others. None of them matched the one he was looking at.

He laid the note aside with a sense of unease. Whoever had sent the Domina's belongings to Pleyver must have known in advance that she would come here, and that he would be coming with her. Jos didn't like the idea of somebody being able to predict his movements with that much accuracy. He made his own living by knowing where the Mageworlds ships would be, and when, and had no desire to play the victim in someone else's ambush.

I'll have to talk to Errec about this, he thought. *See if he's noticed anything funny going on.*

He picked up the envelope. It was thick, as if it contained many sheets, and the same hand that had written the note had inscribed on the front: "To: Perada Rosselin, Dom. Ent., F.C., S.B." A line of Entiboran script, written with the same firm elegance, ran beneath the address, and the unfamiliar sigil-signature was sketched across the seal on the other side.

He heard the faint creak of the inner door swinging open,

and looked up. Perada had come back from wherever she had vanished to while he was asleep. She wore a wide-sleeved white bathrobe, and she looked like she'd washed her hair and put it into braids while it was wet.

"Good morning, Captain," she said. She craned her neck a little to get a better view of the letter in his hand. "What do we have there?"

Jos nodded toward the partially open box. "Looks like you don't have to go shopping in Flatlands," he said. "Somebody knew that you were coming."

"Oh, dear. That could be awkward. Unless—"

She held out a hand and waited, eyebrows lifted in polite inquiry. Jos took the hint and passed over the envelope.

"Want me to open that for you?" he asked, as she turned it over for a closer look. "It could be rigged."

Perada smiled. "Spoken like a true bodyguard. But it isn't necessary. I recognize the mark." One neatly trimmed fingernail tapped the unfamiliar sigil. "It belongs to Ser Hafrey, armsmaster to my House."

The name sounded familiar to Jos. A moment's thought, and he remembered: she'd used it once in Waycross, talking to her brace of escorts, the thick-necked bruiser and the one who looked like a retired schoolteacher.

"Which one was Hafrey?" he asked. "The young guy?"

Perada's lips twitched in amusement. "No."

That'll teach me not to trust in appearances, Jos thought. Aloud, he said, "You told the armsmaster you were coming here?"

"No—I didn't decide until after we were away. Until you mentioned Ophel, in fact. Up until then, I'd thought that you would be making course for Entibor."

Once again Jos felt the stirring of unease. The armsmaster, it seemed, was an unknown quantity, and one who didn't match his outward seeming. *I definitely have to talk with Errec about all this.*

"Then how did he—?"

"Hafrey is like that," she said. "He makes it his business to know things that other people don't."

"For your benefit?"

Perada shrugged. Jos couldn't be certain, but he thought that he sensed in her manner an uneasiness similar to his own. "He's always been loyal to the House. Veratina trusted him."

"Do you?"

"I don't know," she said. "I suppose I do."

She opened the envelope and drew out several sheets of paper covered with Entiboran script. Jos left her reading it, and went back out into the service hallway. He'd thought earlier that he'd recognized one of the pieces of stacked luggage, and he wanted to see if he'd been right.

He had been. Sitting on the carpet next to the Domina's pile of trunks and footlockers was a duffel from *Warhammer*, with an address tag dated from the day before. There was a note on the back of the tag, written in Tillijen's firm hand: *"If you're planning to spend the night, boss, I thought you might like your tooth cleaner and a change of clothes."*

Jos shook his head and picked up the bag. There was no mystery about this one, other than how Tilly had found out where he was going. He supposed that Errec had been involved somehow—this Hafrey wasn't the only one good at that sort of thing.

First the armsmaster, now my own crew members, he thought. *If it's so damned easy to figure out what I'm going to do next, I sure wish that somebody would let me in on the secret.*

Because I haven't got the foggiest idea.

In her office at the Entiboran Fleet Base on Parezul, Captain-of-Frigates Galaret Lachiel swallowed the dregs of her latest mug of cha'a. She was starting to feel worried. Parezul had beaten off the first wave of raiders—and the second wave, which had hit a few days later—but Gala wasn't inclined to call the accomplishment a victory. She'd lost too many ships and seen too many others crippled, and not even knowing that she'd swapped the Mages one-for-one in losses could make her feel good about the overall situation.

Parezul lay near the end of a long supply line; only Tres Brehant and his squadron patrolled farther out. Without more ships and fresh crews, Gala knew that neither she nor Brehant could bear up for long under repeated attacks from the Mageworlds. She'd tried her best to get the supplies and reinforcements that Parezul needed, but her best, it seemed, had not sufficed. The requests she'd sent to Central had been acknowledged, and nothing more.

Veratina Rosselin—damn her barren bones—couldn't have picked a worse time to die. Central wasn't going to bother itself with thinking about Mages when there was a new Domina to worry about instead. Gala knew what that meant, too.

They'll leave us hanging out here. And when the Mages push in past the outplanets and start raiding An-Jemayne, they'll blame us for not keeping them away.

Unless somebody did something, the situation could only get worse. Already the even flow of trade and communications—the constant back-and-forth of raw materials and finished goods, of news and entertainment and simple gossip—had been disrupted by the repeated attacks. The next stage wouldn't be long in coming: unable to rely on the Fleet for protection, the colonies would begin to slip away from the influence of their mother world.

Gala wondered if Entibor's outplanets were the only target in the current raiding campaign, and decided that she wasn't going to find out while it still mattered. If raiders had struck the Khesatan colonies, the Highest of Khesat wasn't likely to pass along the news.

And Central, damn them, wouldn't bother to tell me even if they did happen to know. Just like they sure as hell haven't mentioned the situation to any of our so-called allies.

Base Commander Galaret Lachiel thought about the future she saw coming, and decided she didn't like it.

I can't fight this war single-handed with my head stuffed in a sack. Something has to change.

She left her office and went down the hall to the base comms center.

"Captain Brehant's squadron should be coming into orbit shortly," she told the crew member on duty. "Send word to his flagship that I will be coming aboard for a private conference."

Most of Entibor's western hemisphere lay in darkness. In a fashionable block of houses in central An-Jemayne, a shuffling noise disturbed the predawn quiet. An instant later there came a flash of light and a rolling boom, and a section of wall collapsed inward in a cloud of dust from broken stonework.

Dark-clad figures carrying blasters and energy lances slid into the building through the smoke of the explosion. As soon as most of the haze had dissipated, Ser Hafrey left his position on the far side of the street and entered the ruins as well.

"You shouldn't have come," Meinuxet said, coming out of the wreckage to join him. Shadows obscured the features of the armsmaster's chief agent, but his voice sounded concerned. "There could be traps or snipers—and we haven't evaluated the structural damage yet, either."

"Let me judge how much peril to place myself under," Hafrey said. He gestured Meinuxet aside and moved farther into the broken room.

The whole chamber had been painted and hung in black, except for a white-painted circle on the floor in the center of the room. The circle was surrounded by candles, now extinguished. The heavy smell of wax hung in the air, masked by the acrid, throat-catching smell of the explosion and its attendant dust and smoke.

Hafrey reached out with thumb and forefinger and pinched the candle near its wick. The wax deformed easily.

"They were here," he said. "Not more than five minutes before the raid began. They were here."

"All the exits were watched, and the street has been cordoned off," Meinuxet said. "They won't get far."

"You can believe so, if you will," Hafrey said. "But I suspect that the truth will be far otherwise."

He turned to go. As he stepped out through the shattered

wall and into the street, a hovercar pulled up in a hiss of nullgravs. The door of the vehicle bore the crest of the Minister of Internal Security. Hafrey watched, unsurprised, as a familiar heavyset figure unfolded from the hovercar's passenger compartment and strode forward to meet him.

"Nivome," he said, and made a half-bow.

The younger man didn't bother to return the armsmaster's greeting. "What is the meaning of conducting violent operations in my area of control?"

"You were informed prior to the raid."

Nivome glowered, unmollified. "You made sure that the message reached my desk so late that I couldn't countermand it."

Hafrey shrugged. "I did all that I was required to do."

"Your damned high-handedness is going to get you in trouble someday, old man." Nivome's glance slid sideways toward the rubble. "What did you find?"

"What I expected. That there are Mages conducting their rituals on our planet."

"You arrested them?"

"No. They escaped."

The Rolnian's lip curled. "Did they get away by accident," he wondered aloud, "or was it another one of your everlasting plans? If state security wasn't at issue, I'd have you put on public trial."

"As you will," Hafrey said. "When the Domina arrives, you are invited to lay all of your grievances before her."

Nivome gave the armsmaster a look of disgust. "And while she's missing—thanks to you!—you seek to wear the tyrant's robes in An-Jemayne, is that it?"

"It is whatever you wish it to be. Good day, sir."

Ser Hafrey bowed again and walked off, pulling the hood of his cloak up and over his head to guard against the chill of dawn. Behind him, pale smoke drifted away in curls from the empty building.

"I've already located and disabled Central's snoop in this compartment," Captain-of-Corvettes Trestig Brehant said, as soon as he and Gala were together in his private cabin. "I have a feeling that you're about to suggest something dangerous."

"I am," Gala said. She'd perched herself on the edge of Brehant's bunk. The cabin only had room for one chair, and Tres was sitting in it. She was aware in the back of her mind that most of the ship's crew were going to suspect that she and the squadron commander were lovers—*Better that,* she thought, *than the truth.*

She pushed the thought away and grinned at Brehant. "Tell me, Tres—how do you feel about rank insubordination?"

His eyebrows rose in surprise. "Depends on who's being rank about it."

"Me, probably."

Brehant laughed aloud. "You'd have to go pretty far— you've got a fair amount of credit to drew on around here. With me, anyhow."

"I wasn't thinking about you."

"Oh, damn. And here I thought something interesting might come out of this mess after all."

She laughed in spite of herself. "Tres, you're incorrigible. If things weren't so serious, I might even take you up on that offer . . . but right now the raiders are bleeding us like sucker-flies, one bite at a time."

"No argument there from me." His mobile features changed, becoming sober again. "What's the odds they're planning to drain us dry and knock down the empty shell?"

"I don't take bets like that," Gala said. "I'll tell you something else, though: if we don't take out their staging bases, there's no way that we can stop them. And nobody has the foggiest idea where the raiders are coming from, unless you count 'from the Mageworlds' as a workable set of navigation coordinates, which I don't."

Brehant's dark brows drew together in thought. "You say *we* don't know where the Mageworlds are—but I'll bet my paycheck against yours that the privateers have a pretty good idea. Maybe we should go find ourselves some privateers and ask."

"I have a better idea," said Gala. "It's what I came here to talk with you about, in fact—"

"Took you long enough to get around to it."

"I had to work up my nerve first."

He made a face of astonishment. "Nerve? You?"

"Wait until I'm finished, Tres." She drew a deep breath. "I'm thinking that I ought to go to Central and ask *them* where the Mageworlds are. And ask them a few more things while we're at it—like why they haven't sent us the reinforcements we've asked for, or the intelligence we've asked for, or anything else we've asked for, ever since the raids began."

Brehant gave a long, admiring whistle. "That's nervy, all right. It won't work, though. Central doesn't listen to lowly line captains from the outplanets."

"Maybe not. But somebody has to make the attempt."

"Two somebodies," he said. "If you're hell-bent on throwing your career down the waste chute, then I might as well throw mine in after it."

On the seventeenth floor of the Markey's Prime Hotel, not far from the Art Institute of Flatlands, morning sunlight slid in through the drawn curtains and touched the pillows of the large double bed. Tillijen sat up and stretched.

Warhammer's number-two gunner felt well rested and satisfied with herself and the universe. She had spent a marvelous first night of liberty, not at all unhappy with her impulsive decision to send the captain a change of clothes. Errec had helped a lot there—the *'Hammer*'s copilot was good at locating people, an odd gift to encounter in such a reserved and solitary man.

Ransome was like that, though, she reflected; quiet, and talented in strange ways. Even the thick bulkheads in *Warhammer*'s berthing spaces couldn't hide the fact that sometimes he screamed in his sleep. Tillijen had never asked him why. The spacelanes had their own etiquette, as rigid as any court's—and as Nannla had said, such things weren't done.

At least he was unbending a bit as time went on. He was

a lot more relaxed now than he had been when Jos first brought him aboard. And he'd proved his worth. He found Mages.

She swung her legs over the side of the bed and stood up. Pulling on a light robe, she went over to the window and drew the curtain a little aside. Flatlands Portcity spread out beyond the glass. The metropolis lived up to its name, being flat and uninteresting with an uninspired style of local architecture. She let the curtain fall back into place. Time to get dressed for the day.

This morning, she and Nannla planned to go to the Art Institute. Pleyverans didn't have much of a name for producing great art, but they did have a considerable name for making money, and the collection of off-world objects at the Flatlands Institute was well spoken of in the better guidebooks. After that, well . . . other things of interest would surely present themselves. A restaurant, perhaps. Tillijen had never been to Artha and had never found an Arthan restaurant on any of the worlds she'd visited. The Flatlands Directory in the hotel room listed no fewer than three.

An evening began to take form in her mind as she headed over to the closet where she'd stowed her portside clothing. A call to the ship after breakfast, to let Ferrda know where they'd be, then off into Flatlands . . . there was something lying on the carpet inside the door.

Tillijen changed her path from a direct course toward the closet to approach the vestibule. The object on the carpet was an oblong of cream-colored paper—an envelope. Tillijen frowned. She didn't recall an envelope being there the night before.

She reached out one toe and pushed the corner of the envelope. It slid a bit. She pushed again, this time getting her toe under one corner, and flipped the envelope over. The other side had lettering on it—*Warhammer*, in square Galcenian capitals.

Tillijen left the envelope lying on the carpet. Instead of going to the closet, she made her way back to the bed, where Nannla lay with a pillow pulled across her face. Tillijen pushed her friend on the shoulder.

"Time to wake up, Nannla," she said, in the Ophelan patois they spoke when they were alone. "I believe that the morning has become interesting."

The bedclothes twitched, and Nannla's voice came muzzily from underneath the pillow. "What could possibly be interesting about mornings?"

"I have a mystery for you. Someone's sending us letters."

"What's so mysterious about that?"

"Get up and find out."

Nannla pulled the pillow aside. "All right. Half a moment while I put some clothes on."

A few minutes later, both women were dressed and standing together in the vestibule. The envelope lay where it had landed when Tillijen flipped it over. Nannla regarded it with a speculative expression.

"Sure isn't from anyone *I* know," she said after a while. "How about one of your friends?"

"Both of them know how to find me if they want to. They don't need to sneak around Flatlands being mysterious."

"You've got a point." Nannla looked at the envelope a while longer. "Maybe we should leave it right there and go on about our business."

Tillijen raised an eyebrow. "And let the hotel servants pick it up instead?"

"I suppose not," said Nannla, with a regretful sigh. "You will be careful opening it, won't you?"

"Of course. You know me."

Tillijen pulled a pair of thin leather gloves out of her jacket pocket and slipped them on. Then she drew a small knife from her boot top and, stooping further, picked up the envelope by one corner. She slit the envelope and shook out the card it contained, a sheet of stiff paper covered with flowing script.

"Well, what is it?" Nannla demanded. "A ransom demand, a death threat, or an invitation to the ball?"

"None of those," Tillijen said. She put the card back into the envelope and crumpled both together. "It's a—" she dropped out of Ophelan for a few syllables, then stopped and started over again, stumbling a little as she translated the awkward bits. "It's a—you might call it an Announcement of Expectancy—in the name of the Domina of Entibor."

"Does that mean what I think it does?" Nannla looked shocked. "Our little Perada?"

" 'Our little Perada,' indeed," Tillijen said. "Her family are cousins to mine—and she's not that little, either. Do you know who these things usually go to?"

Nannla shook her head. "Enlighten me."

"The Announcement of Expectancy," said Tillijen grimly, "goes to the closest female relative—or, absent a relative, the closest female associate—of the lady's consort."

"Oh, my," said Nannla. "Jos."

Tillijen nodded. "Jos."

By the time morning came to the Strip in Flatlands Portcity, most of the bars and lounges had closed until the next night. Those places that remained open, like the Meridian Grill, tended to do as much trade in cha'a and breakfast as they did in stronger stuff. Breakfast, however, wasn't what Errec Ransome had come for.

Left on *Warhammer* with only Ferrda for company, he'd awakened early and found himself unable to get back to sleep. Fearing to sleep, if truth be told; the nightmare had been a bad one this time, and he could feel it waiting to snatch at him again if he gave it the chance. Something about the Web passage had triggered a memory, and Errec didn't want to go looking for what the memory might have been. He'd made that mistake before, and he hadn't liked the places the search had taken him.

But now the memories were coming back unasked, peeking and grinning at him from the shadows like gargoyles. A shift of light as he crossed the threshold of the Meridian Grill made the pushball cube in one corner transmute for an instant into a monstrous, looming threat before resuming its proper shape. He shuddered reflexively, then made his way to the counter and put down a five-tile note.

Errec took the glass of blue sparkly stuff he got in return—overpriced, he was certain, but after *Warhammer*'s last run he didn't lack the money—carried it to the end of the bar, and began to sip.

The drink was powerful and the taste was smooth. He sat back, trying to relax. This early in the day the Grill wasn't crowded, but enough people came and went that he didn't need to fear being alone. He sipped his drink and let the potent liquid push his memories down to where they wouldn't bubble up to disturb his waking thoughts.

A while later—how much later he couldn't be sure, but he had a vague recollection of a second drink, and perhaps a third, being placed before him—two men walked into the bar and took seats at the other end. They called for hot food, eggs and fried bread and thin slices of cured meat, and for mugs of stimulants. These two weren't here to forget, but to stay close and stay sharp.

Errec saw the two men, and he saw as well the changeable patterns of not-color overlying their presence in the universe. The shift in his vision didn't surprise him very much. Whenever he let himself go like this the auras came back, the first of the symptoms that had driven him—a merchant-spacer, a qualified navigator—to seek out the Adepts of Ilarna for training. His curiosity stirred a little: these men had the auras of those who are to die soon, and who suspect that they are fated.

Errec didn't do anything as obvious as turn his attention to the two men, but he listened to what they said. They spoke in the harsh, unmelodious local tongue. Despite his best intentions—maybe because he was so relaxed by the drinks, maybe because he was unable to ignore the source of his pain like another man would be unable to avoid the temptation to press on a rotten tooth—he let the thoughts behind the others' words take image in his own mind, as he had been trained to do, another life ago, on Galcen.

The images now were unimportant. Women, money, work—the corruption of officials and the recalcitrance of space engines—nothing surprising. Errec stretched out a tendril of awareness and entered the mind of the nearer of the two.

The man he violated never noticed. Errec looked on as if from a distance at what he himself was doing, feeling a mild surprise that he should be doing it again. He wouldn't have done it, not for cash nor friendship nor for any vows, except that he was too tired and a little too drunk, and something about the men belied the ordinary nature of their conversation. He could handle both of them at once, if need be, but one should be enough. . . .

He added a bit of compulsion to his invasion of the other's mind. *Talk about what you're doing here,* he pressed the man. *Talk about the schedule for today and the next day.*

It was easier now than it had ever been. Errec sat back and sipped his drink. The conversation at the far end of the bar went on at his direction while he listened to the images behind the words: ships lying in ambush, guns, secret orders, an armed freighter named *Warhammer* now standing on its landing legs at Flatlands Field, and the ambush—capture—killing of the Domina of Entibor.

Jos Metadi: Freetrader *Quorum*
(Galcenian Dating 959 A.F.; Entiboran Regnal
Year 23 Veratina)

SOMEWHAT TO his own surprise, Jos found that he liked being in space. During the brief time he'd worked for Rorin Gatt in the port quarter, he'd seen shuttles and stargoing craft lift off from Telabryk Field every day, and had sometimes wondered what it would be like to make such a journey himself. He'd never expected to find out—he didn't have the family connections to get himself into a work-and-learn berth, or the money for regular schooling, and he for-sure didn't want to join the Gyfferan Local Defense Force and pick up his qualifications that way. Thanks to the greed of the *Quorum*'s master and crew, he'd gotten off-planet anyhow.

Jos didn't waste energy on gratitude. He'd seen and heard enough in the dockside quarter to know what sort of "good master" the captain intended to find for him. Most free-spacers liked their hookers and joyboys fully-grown and Gyfferan-legal, but some didn't—and anything that enough people wanted, somebody in port would set up a pleasure-house to provide. Underage Client Services broke up such establishments as fast as the UCS inspectors could find

them, but not all the civilized worlds were as fastidious as
Gyffer.

If the captain of the *Quorum* sold him into a house like
that, he wouldn't last long. The boys in such places never
did. So he concentrated on getting as much entertainment as
he could out of his time in space, and didn't think about the
future at all if he could help it.

With the exception of the officers' quarters and the bridge
itself, Jos had the run of the ship—not because the captain
and the crew felt any kindness toward him, he knew that,
but because they found it easier to let him fend for himself
in crew berthing and the ship's mess than to take care of a
prisoner. He wasn't old enough to be dangerous; and as for
trying to escape, it wasn't like he had anywhere to run.

He spent most of this time down in the engineering control room. The *Quorum*'s chief engineer and his assistant
were, if not friendly toward their unwilling passenger, at
least tolerant as long as Jos didn't get underfoot. Mostly
they ignored him, and he soon found that he could sit in a
corner and read tech manuals by the hour without being noticed. The manuals were homemade hardcopies, thick bun-
dles of printout flimsy clamped together in grubby plastic
binders. Jos listened to the interchanges between chief and
assistant, and learned that main ship's memory hadn't func-
tioned reliably for some time; the hardcopy manuals served
as a backup in case of failure.

The manuals were written in Galcenian, the spacer-talk
he already knew in bits and pieces from working around the
docks. The alphabet turned out to be almost the same as the
Gyfferan one, and when the spacers' language was written
down a lot of the words looked almost the same as Gyfferan, even though they sounded different.

Most of the diagrams didn't even need words at all. With
enough study and the right tools, Jos decided, a smart
dirtsider would be able to reset *Quorum*'s hyperspatial reference block himself, or mend a leaky tube lining, or adjust
a safety override. And getting the tools would be easy. The
tool cabinet on *Quorum* didn't lock properly—it had been

jammed in the open position years ago, and had never been fixed.

Sloppy, he thought. *When I have a ship of my own . . .*

It was the first time he'd given a name to what he'd been wanting ever since the moment when he felt gravity let go: not home or safety, but freedom.

The realization almost came too late. From the crude jokes and half-understood comments made in his presence, Jos knew that the captain and his second played this game whenever a likely prospect fell into their hands, and they had regular buyers in almost every port. *Quorum* would be dropping out of hyperspace over Cashel in eight days—and once the ship made orbit, his relative liberty would come to a sudden end.

Eight days, he thought, and turned back with renewed concentration to the diagrams in the manual on tube-lining inspection and repair. *I only have eight days.*

VIII. Galcenian Dating 974 A.F.
Entiboran Regnal Year 38 Veratina

JOS PUT on fresh clothes out of the bag that Tilly
had sent: another of his respectable dirtsider
suits, made out of plain dark cloth in the conservative
Galcenian style. He was glad she hadn't taken the notion to
send along his usual portside liberty togs—he was moving
among merchants now.

He kept the blaster, though. As the Domina's bodyguard,
he might need to use it.

When he left the refresher cubicle, he saw that Perada
had finished dressing as well. She wore a loose gown of
filmy blue cloth, and had redone her hair into a half-dozen
narrow braids. She wasn't wearing Tilly's extra blaster any
longer, though, and Jos decided that he missed the effect.

"Time for breakfast," she said. "Nothing formal—we're
joining Garen in the sunroom."

Jos nodded and followed her out. He wasn't surprised
when the Tarveet family's notion of informal dining turned
out to involve a room the size of *Warhammer*'s number-one
hold, with three of the four walls and part of the roof made
out of glass. A sunken pool occupied half the floor space;

a table and chairs stood nearby, along with a serving cart loaded with plates and urns and covered dishes.

Garen Tarveet sat waiting for them at the table. *Waiting for the Domina,* Jos corrected himself. *The bodyguard isn't really here, remember?*

In more ways than one, it looked like: whoever had set up the breakfast had put down place settings for two, not three. Perada looked in that direction and raised an eyebrow. Then she turned back to Tarveet, who came hurrying forward to meet her with both hands extended.

" 'Rada!" he exclaimed. "You're looking well this morning."

She took his hands and smiled. "Oh, I *am* well, Garen. And your hospitality is a delight to experience ... but I thought I said that Captain Metadi would be joining us."

Tarveet glanced over at Jos. His eyes widened and his cheeks flushed bright red. " 'Captain'? But I thought—"

You thought I wasn't important enough to count, Jos finished for him, but didn't say it aloud. The young man's obvious embarrassment in front of the Domina looked too painful for him to make it any worse.

"He probably thought you meant after breakfast," Jos said to Perada. "Mixed signals, that's all."

"Yes," said Tarveet. His gratitude for the escape hatch Jos had provided was as transparent and almost as painful as his embarrassment had been. "I'd misunderstood ... I'll get someone in here right away...."

Tarveet hurried over to a comm plate set into the far well and began speaking sharply and earnestly into the audio pickup. While he was occupied, Perada moved a step closer to Jos.

"That was kind of you," she said under her breath.

"He's a good kid. There's no point in making him feel bad."

They didn't have time to say anything more. Tarveet had left the comm plate and was coming back to join them.

"The table will be ready in a minute," he said. "I'm truly sorry, Gentlesir Metadi."

" 'Captain,' " Jos said. "Owner and commander of the armed merchantman *Warhammer*, Suivan registry." ·

"*Warhammer.*" Tarveet's expression changed abruptly, from embarrassed to excited. "*Warhammer*—you're the privateer captain who raids the Mageworlds convoys! 'Rada, you should have told me sooner. We could have planned something—"

"Not while your mother sat there watching us like a State Security agent," Perada said. "That's why I wanted to wait until this morning. I hope she's back in Flatlands by now?"

"She went back after dinner last night," Tarveet said. He grimaced. "But she left me a long list of instructions on how I'm supposed to treat our honored guest."

"I hope food was on the list," Perada said. "Because right now I'm starved."

"Feeding you was definitely one of the things I was supposed to do," Tarveet said. While they were speaking, a small parade of kitchen servants had come and gone. The breakfast table now had chairs and settings for three. "Oh, good—it's fixed. 'Rada, Captain Metadi—if you'd care to join me?"

They sat on folding wooden chairs for their poolside breakfast. The food was good: grilled meats and fresh-baked pastries, both plain and sweet. Perada hadn't lied about her appetite. Jos made a hearty meal himself, relishing a change from the *'Hammer*'s space rations, but the Domina outdid him.

Tarveet sat and watched them, without doing much more than pick at the food on his own plate. At length he said, "I've done everything I could manage from here. About the war, I mean."

Perada swallowed a last bite of pastry. "Already?"

"It wasn't hard," he said. "I've had it planned out for a long time, remember? The accounts on Suivi were already there, so I didn't need to waste time opening them."

"Ah—*those* accounts." Perada turned to Jos. "They were part of a galactic economics project, back at school. We were supposed to close them all out after we got our grades, but some people didn't."

Jos wasn't surprised. Numbered accounts on Suivi Point had made it easy for money to change hands—and forms, from one planetary currency to another—ever since the former asteroid mining settlement had opened up its first banking house. He had a couple of those accounts himself, for that matter, one for his personal funds and another for *Warhammer*.

"Dahl&Dahl?" he said, naming the most freewheeling of the Suivan mercantile houses. Tarveet and Perada looked startled, and he knew he'd guessed right.

"They handle some of House Rosselin's private finances," Perada said. "Offworld investments, mostly."

"They handle a lot of other stuff too. Some of the people who deal with them are a bit rough around the edges."

Perada seemed amused. "Are they your bankers, too, then?"

"No," he said. "I like my bankers dull and respectable, thank you."

"Dull and respectable won't work for what we're doing."

Jos looked from the Domina to Garen Tarveet. *If I didn't know better,* he thought, *I'd say the pair of them were planning to steal a whole lot of money from someone.* He wondered how much that course in galactic economics had taught them—and why the ruler of an entire planet would need any more money than she already had.

He didn't have a chance to ask. Tarveet put aside the pastry he'd been crumbling onto his plate and said, "What I was going to say was, I don't think you'd better stay here much longer. Mother wasn't pleased—she believes that as long as Pleyver stays out of galactic politics, the Web is enough to keep us safe—"

"And I'm too political for her?" Perada's expression of injured innocence was a work of art.

"Well . . . yes. And if you stay, she'll think you're trying to—to corrupt me into an off-world alliance."

"Marriage, you mean?" Perada asked.

Tarveet blushed furiously. "Yes. And she's dead set against anything like that. If she ever finds out how much I've done already, she'll probably disown me."

"Ah," said Perada. "You're right, then; I should leave here as quickly as possible." She turned to Jos. "Captain—how soon can *Warhammer* lift from Flatlands?"

"Right after I buzz the ship and tell Ferrda to start calling the crew in from liberty," he said.

"Good," she said. "We'll do it. And this time we go straight to Entibor."

It was one thing to determine upon rank insubordination and near mutiny, Galaret Lachiel discovered, and quite another to hammer out the fine details of the enterprise. Several hours after resolving to take on the higher powers at Central Command, she and Captain-of-Corvettes Trestig Brehant were still hard at work in Brehant's quarters.

The task that she and Tres had set for themselves was complex. A planetary base, its associated fleet, and an entire roving squadron could not be abandoned to fend for themselves. The two captains had to name acting commanders; had to issue standing orders with instructions on what to do if the raiders came back, and on what else to do if they didn't; and had to come up with a plausible excuse for leaving Parezul in the first place.

"Not that having an excuse is likely to do us any good if the Mages hit while we're gone," Gala said. Her initial surge of energy had faded long ago, leaving only a fatalistic resolve. "They'll court-martial us for sure."

"Don't worry about it," Tres advised. "If Central feels like court-martialing us, they'll do it whether the Mages hit Parezul while we're gone or not."

"You're probably right." She uncurled from her cross-legged position on the foot of the bunk and stretched, feeling the crunch of knotted muscles in her back and shoulders. "All the same, if I'm going to get killed, I'd sooner have it done to me by the folks on the other side."

"So would I, but we may not be able to afford the luxury." Brehant set aside the data tablet he'd been working on. "I think we've taken care of everything we can here; time to figure out what we're going to tell Central after we show up on their doorstep all unwelcome and uninvited. Whatever we do, it'll need to look believable from this end, for morale's sake."

"Good point. And if we can make it something that'll get us past the first five or six layers of security, so much the better." She began pacing back and forth across the tiny rectangle of deck space that Brehant's cabin afforded. "How about letting the word get around that we're carrying sensitive intelligence for personal contact transmission?"

Tres nodded. "That'll even justify taking one of the fast couriers and piloting the ship to Entibor ourselves—no point in pulling some poor kid down the waste chute along with us—and if we talk fast and look arrogant it might even get us all the way in to the fleet admiral."

"You do the fast talking," Gala said. "I'll handle the arrogance." She smiled, letting her teeth show like a Selvaur from Maraghai. "I can play 'my relatives outrank your relatives' all the way *up* to the fleet admiral if I have to."

Brehant shook his head in mock disapproval. "That's not going to make you any friends in the High Command."

"So nobody comes to the bye-bye party before they shoot me for treason. It doesn't matter, as long as somebody at Central listens to us first."

The ride back to the airport from the Tarveet estate was a short one—Jos supposed that the driver had instructions not to take the scenic route this time. Young Tarveet had made his good-byes to Perada after breakfast, back in the sunroom. If the Domina felt disappointed that her old school friend wasn't going to stand on the front steps and wave farewell as the hovercar pulled away, she didn't show it. She looked cheerful and pleased with herself, in fact; whatever she'd come to Pleyver for, she'd obviously found all of it she needed.

Politics, Jos told himself. *Remember that, hotshot. Where she comes from, they play politics like Tilly and Nannla play two-handed kingnote. And that happy little smile means she's getting ready to reach out and scoop up the pot.*

Be glad you're leaving her behind on Entibor; these people gamble for higher stakes than you can afford.

The hovercar passed through the gates of the spaceport without stopping for an ID or customs check. Jos wondered if Tarveet had arranged everything with an advance comm call, or if the hovercar's relay transponder had some kind of "don't even think about stopping this one" code embedded in it.

Before long the hovercar reached the quarter of Flatlands Field given over to independent merchant craft, and pulled up at the safety line. The 'Hammer stood on her landing legs in the middle distance—far enough away to make for a longish hike, especially with the Domina's newly acquired luggage. Jos noted with gratitude that Nannla had thought to bring out one of the nullgrav skipsleds and wait with it.

The 'Hammer's number-one gunner looked worried about something, though. *I'll have a talk with her as soon as we've got the luggage stowed,* he thought. *It's no good jumping into hyper with an unhappy crew.*

The hovercar stopped and the door swung open. Jos got out first—as long as he was on Pleyver, he might as well keep on playing the bodyguard—and stared at the by-now-familiar figure standing on the pavement. Garen Tarveet.

"What are *you* doing here?" Jos demanded.

"I'm coming with you to Entibor."

"Like hell you are. I didn't sell you passage."

"I have the money—" Tarveet began.

"You don't even have a carrybag."

Tarveet looked scared but stubborn. "I didn't dare pack anything. Somebody would have tried to stop me."

Perada took a step forward. "Captain—"

Jos cut her off with a sharp gesture. "Let me guess," he said to Tarveet. "Your family doesn't want you off-planet."

The young man nodded. "There's a lot of stuff I can't access from here—it's blocked, and Mother likes it that way. Once I'm away from Pleyver, though, I can get at everything."

You have to give him credit, Jos thought reluctantly. *It takes nerve to make a decision like that on a moment's notice.*

"You're throwing in with the Domina, then?" he asked.

"That's right."

" 'That's right, *Captain*.' " Jos folded his arms across his chest. "Let me explain a few things. First off, I own my ship free and clear. There's nobody anywhere I have to answer to. And second, there's no law past high orbit. What I say, goes." He paused and fixed Tarveet with a penetrating glare. "Think fast—can you live with that, or not?"

Tarveet blinked a couple of times but didn't hesitate. "If it gets me off Pleyver, I can live with it."

"Good. Hop on the skipsled and let's get going."

It didn't take long to pile the Domina's luggage onto the sled. Nannla raised an eyebrow at the amount of it, but said nothing to Jos until the sled had lifted off the pavement. Then, under the hum of the nullgravs, she murmured, "Good thing you called us in when you did. There's trouble."

Jos closed his eyes briefly. *Dirtside liberty—I swear hunting Mages is safer.* "Didn't everybody make it aboard in one piece?"

"As much in one piece as we ever are," Nannla said. "The problem's Errec. He says he heard something on the Strip."

" 'Says'?" Jos frowned. "Come on—you know Errec doesn't lie about stuff like that."

"Right. But catching a line or two of portside gossip shouldn't have brought him back to the ship looking like death on a holiday, either."

"Damn. Where is he now?"

"In the common room. Tilly's pouring cha'a and soberups down him, and he says he'll be all right in time for lift-off."

"I'll be the judge of that." Jos waited impatiently for the skipsled to reach *Warhammer*'s loading ramp. He jumped off the sled before it stopped moving, speaking over his shoulder to Nannla as he did so. "Get the passengers and their gear strapped and stowed. I'll handle Errec myself."

He took the ramp and the inner passageway at a run, slowing down as he slapped the lockplate to open the common-room door. Inside, Tilly and Errec sat on opposite sides of the mess table. Jos caught Tilly's eye and jerked his head back at the door.

"Go help Nannla with the passengers," he said. "Get everything ready for lift-off."

Tilly nodded and hurried out. Jos went into the galley nook, poured himself a mug of cha'a, and slid into the chair the number-two gunner had vacated. Then he braced himself and took a good look at his copilot.

Nannla hadn't exaggerated. Errec was always pale—he came by it naturally, like a lot of Ilarnans—but right now he looked downright bloodless. He sat gazing into the middle distance, barely seeming to notice when the captain sat down across from him.

Jos spoke quietly. "Nannla tells me you've got some news."

Errec gave a brief nod. "I was at the Meridian Grill. Two pilots . . . there's going to be an ambush . . . somebody paid them to kill us all."

"You don't think it was just portside bragging?"

"No."

"Hard to see why they'd be talking, if it was real."

Errec shuddered convulsively. "They weren't talking."

Jos thought about that idea for a minute, and decided to leave it lying right where it was. *Some things aren't healthy to know too much about.*

"Right," he said. "Any word on who's behind it, or when it's supposed to happen?"

"The Web. As for who—" Errec shrugged. He'd gotten some of his color back, and his voice wasn't as tight. "We're dealing with paid help. They didn't know who was behind the offer, and they didn't care."

"Mages?"

"I don't think so. It didn't smell that way." Errec looked down at his mug of cha'a as if noticing it for the first time, then swallowed the contents at a gulp. "Whoever it is, they want to kill Perada—but they don't want it to look like Pleyver's to blame."

* * *

Perada had expected to ride out lift-off on the acceleration couch in the captain's cabin—or, possibly, on one of the couches in the common room, along with Garen Tarveet—but that didn't happen. She'd known for a while that something was wrong, ever since Nannla and Captain Metadi had started their low-voiced conversation on the sled ride out to the ship. She hadn't been surprised when Metadi dashed off as soon as they reached the 'Hammer's ramp, leaving the trunks and boxes to get put away by Nannla and their owners. Garen had opened his mouth to protest—as if he hadn't carried his own day pack on field trips back at school!—but she'd stepped on his foot before any sound could come out.

They'd almost finished stowing the luggage, under Nannla's direction, when an alarm sounded over the ship's audio system, followed by Jos Metadi's voice saying, "Places for lift-off, everyone. Passengers to the bridge."

" 'Passengers to the'—what's going on?" Garen asked. "Is something wrong?"

"I expect you'll find out when Jos is ready to tell you," said Nannla, dogging shut the airtight door of the cargo space as she spoke. "But I wouldn't waste time on questions."

Perada grabbed Garen by the sleeve and pulled him along with her toward the 'Hammer's cockpit. "Come on."

The air on the bridge was thick with tension. Metadi and Errec Ransome were running down a checklist of some kind and frowning as they worked; Metadi waved a hand at Perada and Garen without turning around.

"Both of you strap in on the navigator's couch. It'll be snug, but nothing you can't manage." He flicked on the switch to what Perada guessed was the ship's internal comm system. "Nannla, Tilly—ready on station?"

Perada heard the gunners replying "Ready" over the link as she and Garen strapped themselves into the empty couch. As Metadi had predicted, it was a close fit.

"Get your elbow out of my ribs," she muttered in Garen's ear. "If you don't, it's going to poke clear through to my spine when we lift off, and I'll have bruises for a week."

He squirmed into a new position under the safety webbing, and Perada breathed more easily. Garen Tarveet had been her good friend and fellow-conspirator ever since she'd found him crying in Zeri Delaven's office all those years ago, but he had sharp elbows.

"What are we doing crowded in here anyway?" he complained under his breath. "They've got more couches—I saw them."

This time the captain did look up from his work. "There's a chance we might have some trouble out in the Web. I want to be able to close down the nonessential life-support systems if I have to. Now shut up."

Garen didn't say anything for a while after that. Perada wondered if he'd been frightened by the prospect of trouble, or frightened by Jos Metadi.

Metadi, she decided. *Garen hasn't been on the 'Hammer long enough to understand what's normal and what isn't. But people were shooting blasters at us in the streets when we left Waycross, and Jos didn't talk about shutting down systems then.*

If knowledge is such a great thing, then why doesn't having it make me feel better?

"What's wrong?" Garen whispered.

She shook her head. "Nothing."

Jos Metadi and Errec Ransome kept on working their way through the lift-off checklist. "Engines?" Metadi said.

A growl of Selvauran came over the internal comms.

"Good. Shields?"

"Repaired and ready," Errec said.

"Good," said Metadi again. He reached out and flipped more switches on the control panel. "Combat overrides, off."

Perada felt Garen stiffen with surprise. He drew a sharp breath. She shook her head furiously—*No! Be quiet!*—before he could speak, and Metadi and Ransome kept on running down their checklist.

"Coursebook?" the captain asked.

"On-line. Linked and logged."

"Roger. Let's talk to Port Control."

Perada lay back on the acceleration couch, gazing at the access panels and instrumentation that filled all the overhead space, and listening to the talk back and forth between Captain Metadi and Flatlands Port Control. Finally the colloquy ended, and Metadi did something to the controls that caused the freighter to shift position, tilting its leading edge upward.

Forward nullgravs, she thought. The change in position was a lot more apparent here in the cockpit that it would have been to someone back in the main part of the ship. *We're getting ready to lift.*

"All right, people," she heard Metadi saying into the audio link. "Stand by for lift-off—we'll take it nice and easy this time, no reason to let anyone know we're nervous. Ten ... nine ..."

On "one," the deep full-throated roaring of the *'Hammer*'s realspace engines filled the cockpit. Perada felt the acceleration couch begin to vibrate in sympathy, and the pressure of the lift-off pushed her down and down and down—

The sky went black, laced with colored fire outside the viewscreens. Then, suddenly, the acceleration ceased, and she could breathe again.

"Heading for orbital approach to the Web," Metadi said. "Calm and normal, but everybody keep your eyes open."

"Captain," Errec Ransome cut in. "Someone's broadcasting on fire-control frequencies."

"Got a position on 'em?"

"No, they aren't pointing our way."

Nannla's voice came over the internal link. "Captain— I've got four single-seat fighters rising from orbit."

"Stand by," Metadi said. "If they get too close, you can shoot, but make sure your first shot misses. Errec—can you get an ID on them?"

"No match in ship's memory."

Next to Perada, Garen made a convulsive effort to sit up, thwarted by the safety webbing. She turned her head around to stare at him. He was pale and sweating—tension had al-

ways done that to him, even back at school—but the look
on his face was something that went beyond fear.

"Captain Metadi," he said. It came out as a faint croak.
Perada shook her head at him, but he swallowed audibly
and spoke again, louder. *"Captain Metadi."*

"Later," Metadi said without turning around. "Errec—"

Garen drew a deep breath and said in a rush, "Captain
Metadi, I think I know who sent those fighters."

As soon as he'd spoken, Perada knew it, too. *His mother
never did like me. Now that I'm the Domina, she thinks I'm
dangerous enough to kill. Flattering, I suppose, considering
I haven't even been crowned yet. . . .*

Metadi, from the sound of it, hadn't taken long to reach
the same conclusion. "Your family's taking the direct approach to getting rid of your off-world connections?"

"I think so."

"Think they'll call off their hellhounds if we let them
know the family son-and-heir is on board?"

Perada felt the webbing shift and stretch around her as
Garen shrugged. "I don't know."

"It's worth a try. I'm setting the audio pickup on High—
talk loud, and let them know you're here."

She heard Garen swallow again. Then he started speaking
in a high, strained voice: "This is Garen Tarveet of Tarveet
Holdings. I am a passenger on this vessel. Go back to the
surface. I say again, *go back to the surface.*"

"No reply," said Errec, after several minutes had passed.
"And they aren't changing course, either."

"That's it, then," said Metadi. He glanced back over his
shoulder at Garen. "Looks like you've been disinherited,
Gentlesir Tarveet—and I think the party's about to get
rough. Gunners, stand by."

"Captain," Errec broke in, "I've worked out the intercept
point on those fighters. It's inside Web space."

"I wonder if they've got a few more friends waiting
around for us inside?" Metadi said. "I'll bet you a round of
drinks that they do."

"You know I don't bet when I'm sure to lose. . . . Contacts astern show up Doppler."

"We'll get to the Web before they do," Metadi replied. "Shields full. Taking down sensors and external comms, now." The cockpit dimmed as screens and readouts went dark all over the control panel. "Give me a DR track."

"Bearing niner-six-one to first aid to navigation," Errec said.

"Good. Beacon in sight—Damn!"

The dimly lit cockpit filled for an instant with lurid purplish light.

They're shooting at us, Perada thought. *We could get killed up here.*

For some reason, the prospect was worse than the idea of getting killed by blaster-fire had been. At least in Waycross she'd been able to do something about the threat; here, she could only lie in her cocoon of safety webbing and watch.

Another flash of light washed over the viewscreens, and she felt the *'Hammer* shudder as the shot connected.

"The shields are taking it and holding," Metadi said. "Errec, where's that beacon?"

"Coming up on it bearing one-one-niner range twelve. Mark in five seconds . . . four . . . three . . . two . . . now—"

—and the glowing obscurity of the Web was all around them.

Jos Metadi: Freetrader *Quorum* (Galcenian Dating 959 A.F.; Entiboran Regnal Year 23 Veratina)

FREETRADER *Quorum* dropped out of hyperspace over the Casheline system and began her approach to planetfall. Observers at Cashel Inspace Control, monitoring the readouts from a mixed array of orbital and groundside platforms, followed the subsequent events in almost-realtime.

The starship held a course that would bring it to Cashel's primary spaceport of Venfy Kai. At the outermost edge of planetary atmosphere, a streamer of gas burst out of *Quorum*'s ventral side, sending the vessel tumbling. As the ship grew more and more unstable, a single lifepod blasted free of the main hull. Moments later, *Quorum* disintegrated into a spray of hot metal fragments that lit up the night sky over thirty degrees of arc.

The pod used its jets to push away from the path of the burning wreckage. After the pod had fallen some distance into Cashel's atmosphere, it fired jets again to retard descent, then deployed its chutes. Slowed and supported by a billowing spidersilk canopy, the tiny craft came down to

within a few hundred feet of the surface, where it fired its
jets again to achieve a braked landing.

When the team from Fire and Rescue reached the grounded
pod, they found it intact and already open. A very young man
with tawny hair and changeable hazel eyes sat on the ground
nearby. Nobody else from *Quorum* appeared to have survived.

"Your name?" the leader of the Fire and Rescue team
asked.

"Pel Cendart," the survivor said. "Engineer's apprentice.
From Wrysten."

Fire and Rescue entered the survivor into their records
under the name he had given. They had little choice, since
a search of the area revealed no other members of the vessel's crew, and all of *Quorum*'s records had perished in the
upper atmosphere. If Cendart looked a bit young for his
post—well, it wouldn't be the first time a space-happy kid
adjusted his personal file in order to qualify for working papers. Nobody could prove anything, and Wrysteners tended
to be on the small side anyway.

The Casheline branch of the Spacers' Aid Society took
the survivor in, providing him with fresh clothes to replace
the torn and grease-stained garments he'd been wearing
at the time of the fatal accident. They also supplied him
with a dummied-up ID and a temporary apprentice's card, to
tide him over while Fire and Rescue awaited confirmation
of his name and status from Central Records on Wrysten.

Interstellar mail was slow, and the Spacers' Aid Society
lacked the resources for faster linkups. Several weeks after
the query went out, a return message arrived from Wrysten:
no person using the name Pel Cendart and having the survivor's physical characteristics had ever passed through Central Records there, much less put in for an engineering
apprenticeship.

The Society notified Fire and Rescue, who notified Security. But by the time the team from Security arrived at the
Spacers' Hostel, Jos Metadi was long gone—his share of
the insurance money from the wreck of *Quorum* in his
pocket—and was working in the engineering boards of a
free-spacer bound for Innish-Kyl.

IX. Galcenian Dating 974 A.F. Entiboran Regnal Year 38 Veratina

THE *'HAMMER'*'s viewscreens filled in an instant with the glowing colors of the Web. Perada thought that she could hear each individual breath and heartbeat in the crowded cockpit. Garen Tarveet, strapped in beside her on the acceleration couch, was shivering and sweating at the same time. His flesh felt cold and clammy wherever her skin touched his. She didn't think the reaction came from fear, though, or at least not from fear alone; he must not have believed that his family would disown him.

Captain Metadi monitored the few readouts that still glowed on the command console. If Perada hadn't seen him watching the same board on the way to the Flatlands, she might have been fooled. He reached out with one hand—tension evident in the line of neck and shoulder—and keyed on the intraship comms.

"Engineering, bridge. Take all safety circuits off-line. Give me maximum power."

A rumble of Selvauran came back over the link.

"Not rated maximum," Metadi said, his voice preternaturally steady. "If what you give me is even a hair less than the absolute most you can squeeze out, then it wasn't the maximum. We're in trouble."

More rumbling in Selvauran.

"Trust me, Ferrda. They can handle it. Give me the power." He clicked off the link and spoke to Ransome without turning his head. "Errec, I need another beacon and I need it fast—this is no place to be flying blind. There's too much hard stuff out there to hit."

"It's even worse than that." Garen's whisper was a thread of sound in Perada's ear, but she felt sure that both the captain and the copilot could hear it. "The way the Web warps things, you'll keep going in circles forever if you don't find a beacon. Not even inertial navigation works."

"Don't worry," she murmured back. "I'm sure Captain Metadi can get us through."

She hoped that he could, anyway. In the next instant, a crashing shudder ran through the ship, rattling the 'Hammer's strength members and making the metal deckplates flex and vibrate.

Metadi picked up the intraship comm. "What was that? Anybody get a visual?"

"Something hard nailed us on the ventral side," came back Nannla's voice over the link. "Doesn't look like any real damage—shields took it. How are those fighters coming along?"

"They're still with us," Metadi said. "Errec, I need that beacon *now*."

Perada glanced over at the copilot. Errec Ransome's face was pale and intent. One hand kept Sverje Thulmotten's coursebook balanced on his lap, and the other hovered over the controls on his side of the command console, without quite touching anything. His eyes were closed.

"Fighters gaining," said Metadi. "Errec . . ."

"Give me the helm," Ransome said.

"You got it," Metadi said. The captain let go the controls on his side and leaned back. "Navigator has the helm."

Perada heard Garen draw a sharp breath. " 'Rada—his eyes are shut!"

"I know. Don't distract him," she whispered back.

Ransome's free hand remained poised over the control panel for a second, then came down. The glowing mists outside the viewscreens blurred and slipped away upward as *Warhammer* swooped in response. He touched the controls twice more, bringing the ship first left and then right, twisting the *'Hammer* like a corkscrew through the dust clouds of the Web.

Tillijen's voice came over the intraship link. "Beacon in sight. Occulting one-four-three, bearing six two seven plus five, range unknown."

"Mornim's Range Beacon," Ransome said, opening his eyes. "Jos, you have it."

"Got it," Metadi said, as the copilot turned his attention again to the coursebook. "Gunners, look sharp—I'm starting to get a signal off of something that isn't Mornim's Range."

"I have them," said Tillijen over the link. "Unknowns coming up fast behind. No ID signatures, but they sure look like they're—"

A purplish-pink light washed over the viewscreens, and the deckplates vibrated. A row of lights on the control panel bobbled as *Warhammer*'s guns fired in response.

"—hostile," Nannla's alto voice finished her partner's sentence. "If you call shooting at us 'hostile.' "

"Counts in my book," Metadi said, not taking his eyes from the control panel. "Keep 'em off us, and stand by for a ride. Errec—where does Thulmotten say we go next?"

"Three five seven," Errec said. "But it's calculated for a lot lower speed."

"Figure me something better, then. I'm not slowing down."

The steady growl of *Warhammer*'s engines increased to a roar. Perada felt herself pressed first sideways against Garen, then down into the padding of the acceleration couch as Metadi worked at the controls. Tillijen's voice came over the intraship link.

"If you're trying to outfly them, boss, forget it. Those guys are lots more maneuverable than us."

"Have they fired on us again?" the captain asked.

"Negative, but they're hanging out there in visual range. I think they're trying to see what we're up to."

"Good luck to 'em on that," Metadi said. "Right now I don't know myself. Errec, where's the next beacon?"

"We should have picked it up already."

"Negative on beacons," Metadi said. His voice had an edge to it that hadn't been there before. "Give me a recco, Errec. Do it now."

"We're overshooting Thulmotten's coursemarks. I recommend we reduce speed."

"Noted," Metadi said. "Now, what's your real recco?"

"Maintaining current speed ... Try coming to—let's see—six-eight-zero in thirty seconds. On my mark. Stand by. Mark."

Metadi's shoulders flexed as he hit the controls, pushing *Warhammer*'s nose down. A fantastic structure of glowing greens and threads of swirling gold passed over their heads in the viewscreen as they ran down into a clearer portion of the Web.

Seconds passed. Perada listened to her heart beating, dividing up the time into even intervals like the strokes of a clock. At last Ransome said, "No beacon. We should have had it by now."

"We're lost," said Garen. He didn't make any effort to keep his voice low this time.

"At least we're taking the Happiness Boys down with us," Metadi said, gesturing with his thumb over his shoulder, back in the general direction of the fighters. "I always wanted to go to Hell with an escort."

"Beacon in sight," Nannla called over the intraship link. "Bearing niner-six-niner."

Metadi straightened. "Where away?"

"Dead astern. Looks like we overshot again."

"Coming around, then," Metadi said. "Here we go."

Again he touched the controls. The streamers of glowing dust outside the viewscreens swirled into a vertiginous blur as *Warhammer* spun on its vertical axis. The freighter slowed, moving stern-first, then started back along its original track.

"Beacon on the scope," Tillijen said over the link. "You make the characteristics?"

"I have them," said Ransome. "We're a long way off track."

"Put me back on, then," Metadi told him. "And get it right this time."

"Working," said Ransome, at the same time as Nannla said, "Here come the hostiles," and the 'Hammer's viewscreens lit up with the flash and dazzle of energy gunfire.

Perada's acquaintance with deep-space gunnery was limited to holovid dramatizations. Even that scant knowledge, however, was enough to tell her that the 'Hammer's guns weren't working as they should have in normal space. Beams that should have been straight became bent and twisted, sometimes moving in corkscrew patterns, sometimes appearing as sine waves, sometimes vanishing altogether at one place and reappearing somewhere else.

The guns of the pursuing craft weren't working any better, but their pilots seemed to have at least some idea of how and where to shoot to get hits. Warhammer's metal structures rang with the vibration as the freighter's shields took the energy bolts and held up against them.

Garen was right, Perada thought. The Web changes everything. No wonder so many Pleyverans are isolationists, if they've got all this between them and the rest of the galaxy.

The intraship link clicked on, and the cockpit filled with an agitated roaring from the engineering compartment. Metadi broke into Ferrda's rumble of complaint in midstream.

"I don't like this either. But we have to live with it. Keep up the power!"

Tillijen's voice cut in—"What's that coming at us from the starboard?"—followed by Nannla's—"I don't know, it looks solid"—and a heartbeat later the viewscreens filled with something that looked like, but probably wasn't, a sheet of green marble shot through with polished copper strands. It was enormous, threatening, and eerily beautiful, all at the same time. Perada held her breath as Metadi hit the controls and the 'Hammer veered left and downward while the looming wall of color kept on coming at them like the face of a cliff—and then they struck.

There was no impact, nothing but a dazzling cloud of tiny points of light, green and orange and white like a many-colored blizzard. They passed through into an area of clear space with the fighter craft barely out of range behind them.

"Vela's Curtain," said Ransome. His voice sounded relieved but a bit shaky. "Not the usual angle to take for passage, but it worked this time."

"You did good," Metadi said. "We even pulled a bit ahead of the opposition. All we have to do now is stay ahead of them for the rest of the run."

How long the Web-run out of Pleyver lasted, Jos was never quite sure. Sverje Thulmotten's coursebook gave a time of fourteen Standard hours for the jumpbound leg, but Sverje hadn't had Errec Ransome to find the beacons for him. When *Warhammer* emerged from the Web near the Farpoint beacon, the console chronometer gave their time-in-transit as eight hours, Standard, and the beacon's time-tick put them at six point five.

Split the difference and call it seven, he decided uneasily. The Web did things like that to chronometers sometimes; nobody knew why. The coursebooks and navigation manuals talked about "unstable space-time anomalies," which as far as Jos could tell meant that the supposed experts didn't know why either.

One of the fighters had stuck with them all the way. Jos spared a moment for admiration of the pilot's skill and persistence. Then he put the *'Hammer* onto a straight-line run for the nearest possible jump point into hyper. The Pleyveran didn't try to follow; like most craft of its kind, it had no hyperspace capability. *Warhammer* made the jump, and the stars outside the viewscreens blurred to opaline nothingness.

Only then did Jos relax enough to start putting the non-essential systems back on line. He turned around to address Perada and her friend Garen Tarveet, crowded together under their safety webbing on the navigator's couch. The

Domina appeared pale but cheerful; young Tarveet, on the other hand, looked wretched—not surprising, considering he'd just been emphatically disinherited.

"Life support's back on for the common room and the berthing spaces," Jos said. "You two might as well go aft and make yourselves a bit more comfortable. I'm going to drop out, set course for Entibor, and make another jump."

They both started hastily unstrapping. Jos thought he heard Perada murmuring something about getting to the 'fresher cubicle, but he couldn't be certain. He'd already turned his attention back to the command console—the board was lit up from top to bottom with damage-control reports from the reactivated sensor system.

We got off easy, he conceded to himself. *A hell-run like that one could have shaken loose a lot more than it did.*

He glanced over at his copilot. Now that the white-knuckle work was over with, Errec looked sick and exhausted.

"You, too," Jos said. "Go sack out before you fall asleep at the console and I have to get Ferrda to carry you out of here. I can handle the drop-and-jump and get us on autopilot by myself if I have to."

Errec hesitated for a second, as though he might protest. But he lacked the energy even for that, apparently; he gave a weary shrug, unbuckled his safety webbing, and left the cockpit.

Working alone, it took Jos some time to bring the starship out of hyperspace, get a good jump point for Entibor, and make the run. Finally, though, he was able to engage the autopilot and unstrap his safety webbing.

He stretched and sighed. All the others were probably sacked out by now, and he was almost as tired as Errec himself. After the adrenaline charge of the Web-run, though, he'd need a mug of cha'a in order to wake up enough to get to sleep. He headed for the *'Hammer*'s galley, where the cha'a pot should have a few drops left in the bottom.

Nannla and Tilly were waiting for him in the common room. "Boss," Nannla said, "we've got to talk."

"Now?"

The two gunners looked at each other. He thought he saw Tilly nod slightly at her partner.

Then Nannla nodded at him. "That's right, boss."

"It's important," Tilly added.

"Let me get some cha'a first, then."

He moved past them to the galley nook and poured the last of the cold cha'a into his favorite mug, a rough piece of blue-glazed pottery from a Mageworlds tradeship. He'd taken the ship years ago, on *Warhammer*'s first privateering foray, and had sold all the loot but that. He carried the cha'a back to the mess table and sat in his usual chair.

"All right," he said. "Tell me what's up."

This time Nannla nodded at Tilly, and Tilly spoke. "It's about the Domina."

"What about her?" Jos asked. "Is it bothering you that she's from Entibor?"

"It's not that. It's—Captain, she's pregnant."

Jos took a careful sip from the blue-glazed mug. He'd hate to drop it and break it, after all this time . . . it was a lucky souvenir, almost . . . "What do you mean, 'pregnant'?"

"The usual, I suppose," said Nannla. "You know, going to have a baby. Roughly nine standard months after we left Waycross."

"Nine," said Jos.

"Give or take a week or two."

He put the mug down on the table, and his hands down flat to either side of it. He didn't need to ask why the gunners thought he might be interested in the news. But there were still questions.

"How did you find out?" he asked. "If it's true."

Tilly produced an envelope from her jacket pocket and dropped it onto the table. "She sent us a formal announcement, that's how. And before you ask me why—it's because that's the way things are done on Entibor."

"We're standing in for the female relatives you haven't got," Nannla explained. "That's what Tilly says, anyhow, and she ought to know."

"Right." Jos shook his head slowly. "Would you believe

me if I said I asked . . . and she said I didn't have to worry about it? Otherwise, I would have—"

"We believe you," Nannla said.

"She was telling the truth," Tilly added. "You *don't* have to worry about it. She's the Domina of Entibor."

Jos gave up and put his head in his hands. "I'm missing something," he muttered. "Tilly, you're going to have to tell me what it is that I don't get, because I can't figure it out for myself. I think the Web must have scrambled my brains."

Tillijen sighed. "I'll do my best, Captain, but it's complicated. The first thing you have to know is that the old Domina—Veratina—didn't leave a direct heir. Not for lack of trying, either. But she couldn't. Nothing ever lasted more than a couple of months, if it got that far."

"Barren as a brick, in other words," said Nannla. "Which Tilly claims is seriously bad luck for Entibor in general."

Jos looked at Tilly. "I didn't know you believed in luck."

"I don't. But a lot of people on Entibor do believe in it. And if people *think* that a thing is so, they're going to *act* like it's so. Public morale on Entibor's been twitchy as hell for, oh, the last twenty-five or thirty years, maybe more— and now here comes a brand new Domina, right when the Mageworlds raiders are starting to show up in force. If this new Domina turns out to be barren, too . . ."

"Riots in the streets," said Nannla. "Sabotage in the factories. Dry rot in the roofbeams—sorry, I got carried away there."

"What's important is that people are worried," Tilly said. "And the best way for the new Domina to reassure them is to come up with an heir . . . or at least a—the closest word for it in Galcenian would be 'placeholder,' I suppose—a firstborn who doesn't inherit for some reason . . . as soon as possible. But she needs to prove that she can reproduce."

As soon as Metadi came into the captain's cabin, Perada knew that the gunners had told him everything. She felt a certain amount of relief and satisfaction—she'd thought that Tillijen could be relied upon, and was glad to see herself proved right—but more than that, she felt worried. Metadi was a Gyfferan, after all; even if he understood what had happened, that didn't mean he understood why it had to happen according to the proper form.

She'd been lying on the bed, letting her stomach settle after the long, tense run through the Web. When the door snicked open, she sat up, curling her legs under her. Metadi let the door close behind him and stood with his back to the metal panel.

"Well," he said finally. "What is it I need to do?"

She swallowed. This was going to be harder than she'd thought. Jos Metadi wasn't Nivome, whose ambition kept his mind focused on his own advantage to the exclusion of everything else, and he wasn't Garen, who had been her friend for so long now that some things didn't need explanation at all. She would have to proceed very carefully.

"Nothing. I said that you didn't have to worry."

"That doesn't matter. I can't just leave you to it."

"Didn't Tilly explain? Entibor and House Rosselin take care of their own; there's no obligation on you."

She watched his face intently as she spoke. The relief that she half-expected to see never came; instead, Metadi's eyes darkened.

"No obligation. And no claim, I suppose."

"No," she said, watching him. Now his face showed no expression at all, not even the watchful but slightly amused detachment he'd presented to the world while he masqueraded as her silent bodyguard. "Nothing. Except what you choose."

"Oh. I have a choice, then."

"Yes."

"Tell me about it."

Perada was reminded, suddenly, of their first conversation in the private room at the Double Moon. Jos Metadi had been wary and unrevealing then, too, though not as rigidly self-controlled. And she had been more sure of herself then. She wished she had the black velvet mask back again; the effort of keeping her face from betraying anything made her whole body ache from the tension.

"I am the Domina of Entibor," she said. "No child of mine will ever need anything that Entibor can't provide. But what Entibor needs ..." She let the sentence hang unfinished.

He picked it up almost at once. "What *does* Entibor need?"

"A strong hand in the Fleet," she said. "And more ships than the raiders—many more." He hadn't expected that, she could tell; the glint of curiosity came back into his eyes. She went on. "We worked it out, Garen and I, while we were at school: what the raiders would have to do in order to win effective control over the civilized galaxy. And then we looked closer, and saw that they were doing it already."

"Strike and then retreat," he said. He was looking interested in spite of himself. "Never attempt open battle against a larger force than your own. Break apart the galaxy a planet at a time."

"You've seen it, then. You understand."

"Dom'na, I've been fighting them ever since I got my own ship. If I didn't see it, I'd be dead by now."

"That's *exactly* what I mean!"

In her excitement, she forgot herself enough to bounce on the mattress of the bunk for emphasis. She caught herself at it, and felt her face redden. The corners of Metadi's mouth curved upward for a moment.

She took the slight change of expression for a good sign and continued hastily, "Nobody at Central Command thinks that way. I've heard the reports, and I know. Even if I could find them more ships somehow, they wouldn't understand the right way to use them."

"And you think I might."

"I know that you would.

He chose to ignore her last statement. "Where do you count on getting more ships from? You can't build a fleet from scratch in less than a couple of years, even if you fill every construction dock from here to Gyffer."

"I know," she said. She hesitated, then decided to tell him something more of the truth. "That's why I had to talk with Garen. With his share of the money from Tarveet Holdings,

and the money belonging to House Rosselin, I think I can
hire the privateers out of Innish-Kyl. Regular pay plus whatever prizes they can take. What do you say, Captain?"

Again he almost smiled and then seemed to think better
of it. "I say that we've come back around to our talk in the
Double Moon. Why should the privateers give up making
their own decisions and put themselves under some
chairbound fossil?"

"They shouldn't. That's why we need you. The privateers
will come and fight for you when they won't come for anyone else. And whether they fight for you or not, they *all* believe in taking the war to the enemy."

"That's a lot of faith to put in someone you don't even
know."

"I told you before, I've seen the reports. You may not
own more than one ship yourself, but you've been leading
fleets against the raiders for two or three years now."

He made a sharp, dismissive gesture with one hand. She
would have felt discouraged, except that it was the first time
he'd moved since taking up his position inside the closed
door. "Believe me, Dom'na, it's not my pretty face that
brings them along. When they go with me, they come back
rich if they come back at all."

"And what if you could offer them a guaranteed profit—
plus a chance of coming back rich? Would they go with you
then?"

Metadi laughed. "For a bargain like that, most of them
would probably sign on with the Lords of Death."

"You understand me, then."

"I understand why you want me to do it. But I don't
know why I should bother." He paused and looked at her
narrowly. "Unless it has to do with those choices you mentioned."

She drew a long breath. "If you like—if you agree—I can
name you Consort, and General of the Armies of Entibor."

"You put a high price on me, don't you?" There was an
edge to his voice that she couldn't identify. "What does all
that involve, besides the obvious stuff?"

" 'General of the Armies' is a courtesy title," she said. "But it would give you rank, if you needed it. 'Consort'—"

"That's the one I want to know about."

"I thought it might be." She wet her lips. This was even more difficult than she had expected. Galcenian was a stupid language; it was hard to translate the formal words. "As Consort, you would be father to any children I might have, and would give me your aid and support in whatever should be necessary, until I should say otherwise."

" 'Aid and support,' eh?" The edge had left his voice, replaced by a note of grim amusement. "That's a phrase for it I haven't heard before."

Again she felt herself blushing. "Captain, you are incorrigible."

"Everybody needs a hobby." He pushed away from the door, and half-turned to set his hand on the lockplate. Over his shoulder, as the panel slid open, he said, "You drive a hard bargain, Dom'na. But this time I'm going to take your deal."

The Armsmaster to House Rosselin sat in his chambers overlooking greater An-Jemayne. So far, the city outside his workroom window had stayed calm and free of civic unrest—though the longer the interregnum stretched on, the shakier that calm became. Fortunately, he reflected, the Palace had not fixed a date on the public calendar for the new Domina's arrival from Galcen; the populace in general remained unaware that her prolonged absence was something that nobody—except, perhaps, for the Domina herself—had intended.

Hafrey frowned slightly. It should have occurred to him that Perada Rosselin might have ideas and plans of her own. The time she had spent on Galcen had made her half an outworlder in her thinking, and less predictable on that account than Veratina had been. He himself was a flexible man, capable of changing when the situation demanded change; but not all the members of the palace staff or Central Command could say as much.

The door to his private workroom chimed in a familiar pattern, and Ser Hafrey abandoned his meditations.

"Come," he called.

The door opened to admit the dark-haired young woman in Fleet uniform who had visited his workroom before.

"I have news," she said. "Interesting developments at Central Command—two of the commanders from the Parezulan sector have shown up at Central uninvited. They insist on speaking with Admiral Pallit."

"Ah." Hafrey allowed himself a bit of private amusement. He had dealt with Pallit before. "And how is the fleet admiral reacting to this ... irregular procedure?"

"So far, he has put off meeting with them."

"Typical," observed Hafrey. "And the commanders—who are they?"

"The Parezulan base commander and the CO of the sector squadron: Captain-of-Frigates Galaret Lachiel and Captain-of-Corvettes Trestig Brehant."

"Unknown quantities," Hafrey mused aloud. "How are they taking their reception?"

"Badly," the woman said. "Their comments verge on insubordination; they say outright that Pallit is mishandling the conflict with the Mageworlds raiders. And Captain Lachiel, at least, is a woman of good family, with palace connections."

Hafrey shook his head. "If Pallit doesn't meet with them soon, then, a confrontation is bound to occur—and the fleet admiral's reaction to unexpected developments is regrettably conservative. If he feels threatened by our Parezulan friends, he is quite likely to order their arrest for mutiny under the military code—their arrest and, since we are in fact if not by declaration in a state of war, their summary execution."

"I hope not," said the woman. "That would be a shame." When Ser Hafrey looked at her curiously, she said further, "Some of us at Central feel that the captains have a point. About the war with the raiders, that is."

"You count yourself in that party?"

The woman flushed slightly. "I hold by my oaths, Armsmaster. But philosophically—yes."

From his expression, Ser Hafrey might have been amused.
"I don't require my agents to be mindless blocks. So long as
you are loyal, your philosophy is your own concern."

"Thank you, my lord."

"I am not anyone's lord," Hafrey said, perhaps more
quickly than he should have. Then, more slowly, "I serve."

"As do we all," said the messenger in soft agreement.

"Go, then," Hafrey said, "and find a way for me to speak
in private with these insubordinate captains. But hurry; the
fleet admiral's patience is even more limited than his understanding."

Perada Rosselin: Galcen
(Galcenian Dating 964 a.f.; Entiboran Regnal Year 28 Veratina)

PERADA GLANCED from the packing list in her hand to the open carrybag on her bed. She had trouble believing that everything on the list would fit into the carrybag, but Zeri Delaven—who had made the list—said that it would. Mistress Delaven also said that anyone old enough to be a student at the academy was old enough to start learning how to pack a carrybag.

The "do-your-own-packing" rule wasn't an unbendable one, at least for the younger students; Perada knew that if she messed up badly enough, one of the teachers would help her finish the work. But Elli Oldigaard had given up with *her* bag not even halfway full—and Perada was determined to succeed where Elli had failed.

Mamma and Dadda will be proud of me, she thought. *Packing all my own clothes—and even a present for the baby.*

Perada had made the mobile in art class out of cut paper and black string, after Gentlelady Otalh, the art teacher, had said that babies liked to watch bright moving objects. She slid the pieces of the mobile into a stiffened envelope and tucked it into the side pocket of the carrybag.

She hoped that little Beka would like the present. This between-terms vacation—the first time she'd been home to Entibor since coming to Mistress Delaven's—would also be the first time she met her new baby sister. She hadn't seen Mamma and Dadda since coming to Galcen, either, except for the picture postcubes that sometimes came in the mail.

I wonder if everybody at the house will think I talk funny, after speaking nothing but Galcenian all year long?

The door to the room slid open. She turned, expecting to see Elli or Gryl. The newcomer wasn't one of the girls, though, or even Garen Tarveet on a surreptitious visit from the boys' wing—it was Zeri Delaven herself. Perada felt a twinge of uneasiness. Mistress Delaven never came into the students' rooms except, on rare occasions, to enforce discipline.

But Perada's conscience was reasonably clear. She hadn't fought with Elli for months, and hadn't broken any other rules lately that she knew of. So she smiled politely at the head of the academy and said, "Good morning, Mistress Delaven. Don't worry—I'll be packed soon. I don't want to miss the shuttlebus to the spaceport."

Zeri Delaven sighed, and Perada noticed for the first time that she was frowning. "I'm afraid I have some very bad news for you, my dear."

Perada's faint sense of uneasiness congealed into a gelid lump somewhere under her breastbone. The sort of bad news that Mistress Delaven had to bring in person usually meant that people left the school suddenly and didn't return—and that wasn't fair, not when she'd finally started understanding real Galcenian and Elli wasn't winning all the fights anymore.

"Mamma doesn't want me to come back after the vacation is over?" she asked.

Mistress Delaven looked right at her, not away like most grownups did when they were about to say something they knew you weren't going to like. "No, dear," she said—and that was another thing; Zeri Delaven never called *anyone* "dear"—"you'll be in school here after vacation. But I'm afraid you won't be going home to Entibor this year."

Perada sat down on the edge of the bed. Her knees felt wobbly. "But I have to go . . . I have to take my baby sister her present, the one that I made . . . Mamma *said.* . . ."

Her voice trailed off. Mistress Delaven was shaking her head.

"No," said Zeri Delaven.

And in careful, painful words, she explained to Perada that Mamma and Dadda and the new baby sister—whom Perada would not ever see—were all dead. And Great-Aunt Veratina, who was Perada's official guardian, thought that her youngest great-niece should stay at school on Galcen.

After a while Mistress Delaven stopped talking and went away. When she was gone, Perada took the bright paper mobile out of her carrybag and tore it apart, one piece at a time, snapping the thin black string so hard that it cut her fingers and made them bleed. But she didn't cry.

X. Galcenian Dating 974 a.f.
Entiboran Regnal Year 38 Veratina

CENTRAL COMMAND Headquarters for the Entiboran Fleet was a sprawling complex, almost
a city in itself, that lay beyond the outskirts of An-Jemayne.
Visiting officers' quarters occupied an older building, dating
from the early Redactionist period, full of high ceilings and
tall narrow windows, with not a sliding door in the place.
Galaret Lachiel had never cared for the style—she had no
use for nostalgia, and little patience with those who did—
but after more than a week spent waiting in those taste fully
appointed rooms, she was beginning to actively loathe it.

Today, as they had every day for the past ten days, she
and Trestig Brehant prepared to spend their waking hours in
the long drawing room on the building's first floor. A
holovid viewer set against one wall provided entertainment
of a sort; so did a draughts table and several decks of cards.
Other officers came and went, but Gala and Tres held themselves apart—it wouldn't be fair to implicate the others in
what might be treason just for a few minutes of idle talk.

Gala fetched a deck of cards from the games cabinet by
the western windows, shuffled, and began to deal. "Double

tammani this morning, I think. An octime a point for stakes?"

"Dangerous high living," said Brehant. "You're going to clean me out entirely if we keep this up much longer."

"Don't worry." Gala picked up her cards and studied them. "We aren't going to be here long enough for you to go under."

"You've gotten word from Pallit?"

"No. But if we don't hear something today, I'm going to make a few comm calls." She smiled briefly. "My family owes me a thing or two, and it's time to start calling the favors in."

Brehant's eyebrows twitched downward in concern. "That could get sticky. Politics and all."

"I know. But we can't wait here forever." She started to pull the first of her discards from her hand, then stopped and laid the cards facedown on the table. At the far end of the room, the main door had swung open. A junior officer with staff insignia on his collar came up to the card table.

"Captain Lachiel, Captain Brehant," he said. "If you would come with me—"

Finally, Gala thought. Tres had laid down his cards as well; she put them all back into the box without looking at the hands she had dealt. As she worked, she said to the junior officer, "Are you taking us to talk with Admiral Pallit?"

The young man shook his head in what looked like genuine ignorance. "Captain-of-Frigates, I don't know."

Gala looked at Tres. The junior captain gave an almost imperceptible shrug. She turned back to the messenger.

"Let me put these cards back in the cabinet and we'll be right with you."

A hovercar waited at the edge of the lawn outside the visiting officers' quarters. Gala recognized the Palace arms on the passenger door. A quick glance over at Tres showed that he'd seen the blue-and-silver blazoning as well.

Whoever wants to see us, it isn't the fleet admiral. She slid into the rear seat of the hovercar. Tres followed. The messenger got into the driver's seat, and the vehicle slid into motion. Gala leaned back against the seat cushions and tried to relax. *I knew I was going to wind up playing politics. But I hadn't expected the politicians to find me first.*

The hovercar sped through the Headquarters complex and out past the guards at the main gate. Some time later, after a silent and uneasy ride first through the countryside and then through the crowded thoroughfares of An-Jemayne, they emerged from a tangle of narrow streets into a vast open area paved in white stone and set about with marble statuary. On the far side of the plaza rose a massive structure, also of marble, with many glittering windows: the Palace Major of the Ruling House of Entibor. Gala had been inside the palace walls once in her life, at the obligatory court presentation after her commissioning, and recalled almost nothing of the experience, except that her brand-new uniform had scratched the back of her neck all during the ceremony.

On that occasion, the new-minted officers had entered the palace by the state entrance, passing through massive bronze doors ornamented with bas-relief panels depicting the unification of Entibor. This time, however, the hovercar glided to a stop underneath a minor portico at the end of the palace's eastern wing. The door through which the messenger escorted Gala and Tres proved to be of plain wood bound with iron—old enough to be preserved and restored, but not a work of art.

The two captains wound up in a small chamber deep inside the palace. There were straight-backed chairs of carved whitebole wood lining the walls, and a low table with nothing on it in the middle of the carpeted floor. Their guide showed them into the room without explanation, and left them there.

Gala looked at Tres, not daring to say anything in case of snoop-buttons, then folded her hands on her lap and waited. That was obviously what the room was for, and if service in the Fleet had ever taught anyone anything, it was how to wait.

Eventually the room's inner door opened to admit a slight, grey-haired gentleman. Gala didn't know him, which meant he wasn't Fleet and wasn't connected by blood to any of the noble houses. He bowed; she and Tres rose and bowed also.

"Captain Lachiel," he said. "Captain Brehant. I am Ser Hafrey, Armsmaster to House Rosselin; I serve the Domina."

"We all do," Gala replied, still standing. "What is it that you need from Captain Brehant and me?"

The older man made a gesture toward the chairs. "Please—seat yourselves, and tell me what's brought you so far from Parezul without orders."

Tres Brehant spoke up then, for the first time since the messenger had come for them at the visiting officers' quarters. "What we've got to say is meant for Admiral Pallit. He's our senior officer, and he has the right to hear us before anyone else does."

"I understand," said the armsmaster. "But I may perhaps be of some assistance, if you allow it."

Gala lifted both hands briefly, palms-up like a petitioner. "Then will you help us speak with the admiral? We have so little time—"

"My influence with the Fleet is limited," Hafrey said. "But here at court I can expedite measures, or bring them to the attention of the Domina."

"Is the new Domina on-planet?" Tres cut in. "The last I heard, she'd been sent for, but that was all."

"He's right," said Gala. "We got the word on Veratina as soon as it happened, more or less, but we never heard anything about a coronation."

Before Ser Hafrey could answer, the outer door of the room flew open with a bang of wood against wall. A dark, heavily muscled man strode in, followed by a pair of palace guards carrying energy lances.

Nivome, thought Gala unhappily. *If he's mixed up in this, we might as well say good-bye to the idea of talking to Pallit.*

The Rolnian-born Minister of Internal Security had been the old Domina's last lover—strong rumor said that he'd wanted the name of Consort, but that Veratina had been too canny to give it to him—and he was no friend to the Fleet.

Gala wasn't surprised when Nivome pointed a forefinger at Ser Hafrey and said, "You're exceeding your authority again, Armsmaster—and this time I've caught you."

Hafrey inclined his head, like someone receiving an awkward compliment. Nivome's forefinger slewed around to point at Gala and Tres.

"And you two have been aiding and abetting him." Nivome looked over at the guards, then jerked his head toward the two captains. "Take them away."

Ser Hafrey watched without comment as Nivome's guards took Lachiel and Brehant out of the room. The pair of officers were in no immediate danger. Entibor's Fleet cherished zealously the right to discipline its own, and Captain-of-Frigates Lachiel, at least, was well connected enough that the Interior Ministry wouldn't dare risk her convenient disappearance. Achieving the duo's ultimate disgrace and execution would take time and effort—resources that Nivome shortly might find himself unable to spare.

After the door had closed behind the two captains and their escort, Hafrey turned back to Nivome.

"You mistake yourself," he said quietly.

"I don't think so," Nivome said. "Not this time."

"I plead ignorance. Enlighten me."

"Don't make a joke of it, old man. There's nothing funny about treason."

"True enough," said Hafrey. "Am I a traitor, then?"

Nivome glowered. "You're conspiring with mutineers who've deserted their stations during a time of peril. When the Domina returns, she'll have your head displayed in a stasis box right next to theirs."

"That will be as the Domina wishes," Hafrey said. "In the meantime, gentlesir, pause and reflect a while on past experience. Do you truly intend to make me your enemy?"

Nivome said nothing for several seconds, and his face darkened. But whatever his faults, the Rolnian had never lacked for nerve. He gave a harsh laugh, and said, "I can't make what already exists. Enjoy your power while you have it. Once the Domina returns, your time is done."

"You're ambitious," Hafrey observed mildly. "But your intelligence gathering is not what is should be. Perhaps you haven't heard—a free-spacer named Metadi entered Entiboran space this morning. Even now he and his crew are landing at the royal port."

Nivome's features grew even darker with anger. "Metadi," he said. He spat the word out, like a curse. "The gall of that man passes all belief . . . the royal port!"

"And why not?" Hafrey said. "He has the right; he is carrying the Domina on her ascent to the Iron Crown. And more: the Domina asserts that she is, at this moment, gravid."

There was a long silence—an instant, Hafrey knew, in which anything could happen. He readied himself for action, if action should be needed.

Then Nivome seemed to relax, and his high color faded somewhat toward normal. "Good . . . good. This should at least convince the populace that the Domina Perada is no Veratina as far as *that* problem goes."

"True enough," Hafrey said. He regarded Nivome with an unsympathetic eye. "But if you see yourself as the next Consort, your sources have failed you and you need to develop new ones."

"What do you mean?"

Hafrey shrugged. "Only that Captain Jos Metadi requested official transport to the capital for the Domina and her Consort—and you are already here. Moreover, when Captain Metadi spoke with Inspace Control, he styled himself General of the Armies of Entibor."

Nivome made a choking sound, and his right hand clenched into a massive fist. "Metadi . . . !"

"Don't do anything hasty," Hafrey said. "Shall we go out and greet the Domina on her arrival? For myself, I'd prefer to have you alive and active about your duties for the next part of the history of Entibor, but be assured that if you are otherwise my plans will not be seriously discommoded."

He bowed and walked past Nivome as if the larger man weren't there. Two more palace guards waited outside the door. The armsmaster walked past them as well. They fell into step a pace behind Hafrey as he walked down the passageway, seeming unsure whether they were supposed to arrest him or provide him with a guard of honor. All of them, including the now-silent Nivome, proceeded through the palace's inner corridors to the entrance by the former stables, where ground transport from the ship would soon be arriving.

Moments later the side door of the old stables slid open and admitted a hovercar in the blue and silver of House Rosselin. The car grounded there, and out of the passenger compartment stepped Perada Rosselin, with Captain Jos Metadi and another, much younger man behind her, one at each shoulder.

Hafrey recognized the second man as the heir to Pleyveran-based Tarveet Holdings. Garen Tarveet had been at school with Perada on Galcen; perhaps, Hafrey reflected, they had become closer friends than he had thought. Or perhaps not. Young Tarveet looked as if he'd worn the same suit of clothing all the way from Pleyver, and his face was not that of a happy man.

The armsmaster bowed—the full bow of profound respect. "Welcome to your world, Domina."

Perada's face revealed nothing, though she smiled at Nivome with the same bright goodwill as she had shown to the Rolnian on Galcen, before she had decided on the diversion to Innish-Kyl. She inclined her head in a well-schooled response to the armsmaster's greeting.

"Ser Hafrey," she said. "Gentlesir Nivome. I apologize for making such an informal arrival—but there's a great deal of work to be done, and much less time than I'd expected to do it in. I want to get the ceremonial part over with as soon as possible."

This time it was Nivome's turn to bow. "Everything is arranged, Your Dignity. Veratina's funeral rites need only your presence in order to begin."

"Take me to her, then," Perada said. "We'll have the public burning tonight, in the Grand Plaza. Meanwhile—" She glanced at Ser Hafrey, and the armsmaster saw that while she was smiling, her gaze was sharp and intent. "—General

Metadi has business of his own to take care of. See to it that he gets whatever help he needs."

She left on Nivome's arm, and Hafrey watched her go. The Ministry of Internal Security reckoned among its visible duties the supervision of those Palace departments which worked with ceremony and protocol, and if the minister himself—now that his ambitions had come to naught—resented the effort he'd expended in making everything ready, he didn't show it.

When the palace doors had closed behind Nivome and the Domina, Hafrey turned back to Jos Metadi. The privateer captain was dressed in all the customary finery of his trade—crimson velvet and gold buttons and high, polished boots, with a heavy blaster in a leather holster tied down to one thigh. Hafrey, who had long since investigated Metadi's habits, knew that the gaudy display was not put on by chance. Away from the privateer ports, the captain dressed as soberly as any man of business from the Gyfferan merchant class.

This man denies nothing, the armsmaster thought. *He changes nothing. He believes that etiquette and protocol will change themselves instead to suit him.*

And his belief in his own luck is strong enough that he may indeed be right.

Hafrey kept his thoughts to himself, as he had always done. "Welcome to Entibor, General. I am at your service."

"The first thing I need is a translator," Metadi said, in passable Galcenian—grammar and syntax were clear enough, but overlaid with a strong home-world accent. Some people at the Domina's court would find it amusing; but Hafrey doubted that Metadi would care. "For Galcenian and Gyfferan both. If the translator knows something about life along the spacelanes, that's even better."

Hafrey nodded. He'd heard more outrageous requests in his time, from men and women far more nobly born than Captain—now General—Jos Metadi. "When will you require the translator?"

"Right now," Metadi said. "If I'm General of the Armies of Entibor, then I'm going to inspect my command."

* * *

Fleet Admiral Efrayn Pallit frowned at the sheets of flimsy scattered across his desk. Ever since word of the young Domina's arrival in-system had reached Central, he'd been working on the Fleet's official message of greeting. First impressions were vital, and Her Dignity was something of an unknown quality—*All those years on Galcen,* Pallit thought uneasily; *as if Entibor didn't have enough good schools of its own*—the combination made him bite the end of his stylus and strike out line after line.

And there was his own court presentation speech to polish after this message was done, not to mention some appropriate remarks of condolence for the old Domina's public burning. *So much work; so little time.* He had waited too long to begin. He had, perhaps, not believed that she was going to come? He wished that he could assign writing the messages to a subordinate—but that would reveal his lack of preparation. That would give someone power over him. He turned back to the message blank.

The sound of voices outside the closed door of his office broke into his concentration. Someone was talking very loudly. He couldn't make out the words. The office door slid open. Pallit's aide, red-faced, stood in the opening.

"Admiral," she said helplessly, "I tried to stop them, but they wouldn't listen—"

Two more people stepped in past him before he could finish speaking. The first was a tall man in a jacket of crimson velvet. The gold in the buttons would have paid the admiral's aide for a month. He carried a blaster loosely in one hand. The second man Pallit recognized immediately as Ser Hafrey, the Domina's armsmaster.

The man in the crimson jacket began speaking in the same language Pallit had heard before. Without the office door to block noise, the admiral had little trouble recognizing the words as Gyfferan.

"You," said the man. "Are you the commanding officer of the Fleet?"

Ser Hafrey echoed him in gently spoken Entiboran. "You. Are you the—"

Pallit held up his hand. "Please," he said in Gyfferan. "I speak this man's language well enough to understand his question. Yes, I command here. And you are under arrest."

"Wrong," said the man. He raised his blaster and pointed it at Pallit. "My name is Jos Metadi. I'm the General of the Armies of Entibor, and as of now you work for me." The blaster didn't waver. "Tell me quickly—what are you doing right now to take the war to the Mages?"

Pallit glanced over at Ser Hafrey, then back at the man in the crimson jacket. "Right now," he said, "we are defending ourselves whenever the Mages attack. Given the constraints of our resources, that is all we can do."

"In that case," said Metadi, "I accept your resignation."

He turned to Pallit's aide. "Mark down the admiral as 'retired,' and take me to the next person in the chain of command."

Before Pallit could raise his voice in protest, the Gyfferan had turned away and was striding down the hall, leaving Ser Hafrey to translate the last order in a hasty whisper for the aide's benefit. The aide looked startled and hurried after Metadi; Hafrey followed at a more leisurely pace.

After an instant of stunned silence, Pallit went after them. He arrived at the office of Admiral Tallyn, his second-in-command, just as Hafrey was translating again for General Metadi: " 'Mark down the admiral as retired. Take me to the next person in the chain of command.' "

The group swept out of the office, and went on to the office of Admiral Leivogen. Feeling at wits' end, Pallit followed—as did several of the other people who had been in Tallyn's outer office, including a handful of junior officers who almost seemed to be smirking at the sudden changes in the upper staff.

Metadi was a quick study. By the time he'd cleared the third office along the main hallway, he no longer needed a translator. He'd already learned how to say, "Mark down the admiral as retired," in passable—if strongly accented— Entiboran.

* * *

"Well," Tres Brehant said, in the resolutely cheerful tones of someone who has decided to look on the positive side of things even if it kills him, "at least we're in Fleet detention and not some wretched civilian holding pen."

"At least," agreed Gala wearily.

The room they were in now, somewhere in the depths of Central Command's main headquarters building, wasn't quite a cell—it had two chairs and a desk, and even a separate 'fresher cubicle—but it was plainly the last stop before the brig. For one thing, the ID plate was on the other side of the door, and the door was locked.

Gala slumped in her seat and frowned at the toes of her highly polished boots. "Damn it, Tres—we got so close!"

"Yeah." Brehant's attempt at positive thinking appeared to have been short-lived. "The palace and everything. Who *was* the old guy, anyhow?"

"What he said. Armsmaster to House Rosselin."

"I know, I know—but what did he want to talk to us for?"

Gala sighed. "In theory, the armsmaster is supposed to do things like take care of the antiques in the palace gunroom and teach rapier-and-dagger fencing and other useless sports to whatever members of the Ruling House happen to show an interest. In practice . . ." She shrugged. "He's said to be very powerful, and to have the confidence of any number of people."

"And let me guess—Internal Security hates his guts."

"You noticed," said Gala. She clenched her fist and pounded it, almost absentmindedly, on the metal arm of her chair. "Damn them. *Both* of them, for dragging us back and forth like counters in their stupid political games, when the raiders could be hitting the outplanets this very minute."

Brehant's attempt at good humor vanished altogether. Even his mustache seemed to droop. "So what do we do?"

"Eventually the folks on the top floor will remember that Internal Security sent us over here," she said, "and order somebody to come around and write up the charges. When they show up, I'm going to demand a court-martial."

"Make them listen to us before they shoot us?"

"It's likely to be the only chance we'll get. And we knew it might come to this when we left Parezul."

"I know. The things we do for crown and country."

The conversation lagged. Gala went back to studying the toes of her boots. Tres chewed at the ends of his mustache. The only sound in the room was the faint whisper of circulating air in the environmental-control system.

Brehant stiffened. "Someone's coming."

He was right; there was noise in the hall outside the closed door. Feet, a whole crowd of them, and voices. Gala stood up and straightened her tunic.

The door slid open. The hall outside was full of Fleet uniforms. The man who came into the room, though, wasn't Fleet at all—not even an officer in mufti. His clothes were too gaudy, his hair too untrimmed, and his whole bearing too casual. But he carried a sidearm like a man accustomed; and Gala wondered, after taking in the Ogre Mark VI heavy-duty blaster, if the man had come on a specialized errand for the Minster of Internal Security.

Too many witnesses, she told herself. *Work like that gets done privately. And besides*—she looked again at the crowd of other faces, and recognized one that she had seen for the first time only that morning—*the armsmaster is with him.*

The man with the blaster was saying something in slow, badly accented Entiboran. "You. Who is senior here?"

"We're both under arrest," Gala said, "so I suppose neither one of us has any rank at the moment. But until this morning, I was senior."

Ser Hafrey spoke rapidly in an undertone—translating, Gala supposed. The man with the blaster listened, sharp hazel eyes fixed on Gala and Brehant. When Hafrey was done, the man spoke again, this time rapping out a question in a language Gala didn't recognize.

Again the armsmaster translated. "Tell me quickly: what have you done to take the war to the Mages?"

Gala heard Brehant's quick intake of breath, but she didn't dare turn around. The man with the blaster had chosen to emphasize Ser Hafrey's translation by raising the weapon and aiming it at her head. She looked at the hard line of his mouth and knew that he wasn't one of those people who would hesitate to fire.

Hell with it. Neither am I. He can have the truth, and if he doesn't like it he can choke on it.

"Until this morning," she said, "the two of us were working on getting ships for an expedition—and trying to find out whether Central has any idea about the location of the Mage home worlds."

On a hunch, she'd answered the man's question this time in rusty schoolgirl Galcenian. The Mark VI blaster was a free-spacer's weapon, and Standard Galcenian was the closest thing to a common tongue that you could find on the commercial spacelanes. The hunch paid off. The man's face broke into a wide grin and he slid the blaster back into its holster.

"Finally," he said. His Galcenian, she noted, was considerably better than her own. "I'm Jos Metadi, General of the Armies of Entibor, and you're the fleet admiral."

"Ah . . . no, sir. I'm Captain-of-Frigates Galaret Lachiel, commander of Fleet operations in the Parezulan sector."

"Not anymore. Admiral Pallit decided to take an early retirement, and you've been promoted to fill his position. I want your plan of operations on my desk by local noon tomorrow."

What is it the old grannies say—"be careful what you ask for; somebody may give it to you"?

"Yes, sir," Gala said.

"Good," said Metadi.

He turned and strode out, with Ser Hafrey at his heels. The crowd of Fleet personnel parted to let him pass. Soon there was nobody left in the room except for the two original occupants. Gala took a deep breath.

"All right," she said to Brehant. "For my first official act, I pardon you and make you my second-in-command. Come on."

Tres was staring at the open door. "Where do we go?"

"My new office," Gala said. "Somewhere on the top floor. If we're want to have an OpPlan by tomorrow, we're going to be working all night."

Perada Rosselin: Galcen
(Galcenian Dating 967 A.F.; Entiboran Regnal Year 31 Veratina)

PERADA STUFFED the last pullover tunic into her carrybag and sealed the bag shut. Then she shoved the carrybag underneath her bed. Nobody was going to expect her to be ready for hours and hours, not when she was supposed to be going home this time with Zusala Reeth. Zusala had never in her life finished packing on time, and she wasn't going to change because a friend was coming along with her.

After four years at Zeri Delaven's academy on Galcen, Perada had grown accustomed to spending the holidays with one schoolmate or another. There was always somebody, she had discovered, whose parents or guardians liked the idea of saying later that one of the Rosselins of Entibor had been their houseguest for Midsummer or Winterend. She'd even stayed once with Elli Oldigaard, though neither she nor Elli had enjoyed it much; she suspected that the whole thing had been arranged by the grown-ups for their own reasons.

"Politics," she said aloud.

Everything grown-ups did was politics of one kind or

another—Perada had figured that out as soon as she learned
the word in Gentlesir Carden's third-year history class. It
was politics that kept her stuck on Galcen during the long
holidays, when all the other off-planet students got to go
home, and it was politics that kept her from staying very often with schoolmates that she actually liked.

Some of them, like redheaded Vixy Dahl from Suivi
Point, where everybody lived under big pressurized domes
and never had summer or winter at all, weren't "suitable"
enough. Vixy had asked, more than once, and Perada had
sent pleading messages home to Entibor begging to be allowed, but the result had always been the same. And some
others *never* asked, like S'yeze Chastyn, who was Perada's
best friend on the girls' side of the school. S'yeze was a
scholarship student, Zeri Delaven had explained to Perada
one day in private, and her family couldn't afford a Rosselin
of Entibor for a houseguest.

Perada hadn't thought much of the reason at the time—a
Rosselin of Entibor didn't eat any more food than anybody
else—but most grown-up reasons didn't make sense if you
looked at them too hard anyway. So she spent her holidays
with people like Elli and Zusala and Gryl, and wished,
sometimes, that she wasn't a Rosselin of Entibor at all.

That wasn't a thing that she could change, though, and
she didn't let herself think about it too much. Now, with the
carrybag tucked away under her bed, she decided to go
downstairs and see if Garen Tarveet had finished packing
yet.

She crossed the room and reached out to brush her hand
across the lockplate on the door. The door opened before
she could touch it, and Zeri Delaven stood in the hall outside.

Perada took a step back. The last time Mistress Delaven
had come to her room before holidays started . . . she didn't
want to think about *that*, either.

"I'm all packed," she said. Her voice sounded faint and
croaky, like something that belonged to one of the prickly
brown dust-crickets in the Academy garden. "If Zusula's
ready—"

Mistress Delaven shook her head. "I'm afraid there's been a change of plans."

"Oh." Perada took another step backward, and another. The edge of her bed hit the back of her knees, and she sat down hard on the firm mattress. "What—"

Zeri Delaven's thin mouth turned upward for a moment in a not-unkindly smile. "It's all right, child. Nothing bad has happened this time."

Perada blinked her eyes hard to keep from crying for no reason. "Then why aren't I going home with Zusala?"

"Because you'll be spending the long holiday on Entibor this year," Zeri Delaven replied. "Your Great-Aunt Veratina has named you heir to the Iron Crown,,and the Armsmaster of House Rosselin has come to take you back to An-Jemayne for your formal investiture as Domina-in-Waiting."

XI. Galcenian Dating 974 a.f. Entiboran Regnal Year 38 Veratina/1 Perada

T HE STATIS-PRESERVED body of Veratina Rosselin had lain in state on the unlit pyre in the Grand Plaza since late afternoon. Ranks of Domestic Security personnel stood about the perimeter of the immense open area, keeping back the local citizens, the curious foreigners, and the holovid news crews from all over Entibor. A light wind stirred the petals on the funeral garlands draped across the pyre: fragrant flowers, relics of an era when not even a Domina of Entibor could rely on a statis field to keep away the final indignity of fleshly decay.

As soon as full darkness fell, the bronze doors of the Palace Major swung open and a double line of palace servants bearing torches filed down the marble steps into the open square. The smoky orange flame of the torches reflected off the darkened windows of the palace and cast disturbing shadows on the statues of long-dead heroes. When all the torchbearers were in place, a small figure in the white garments of mourning emerged from the palace and descended the steps at a stately pace, a taller, dark-clad figure walking behind her.

"The Domina Perada," murmured Gentlesir Festen Aringher from his place among the honored outworld guests. He spoke for the benefit of his companion Mistress Vasari, but also for a palm-sized holorecoder that had escaped the attention of Domestic Security. "And her Consort, General of the Armies Jos Metadi, late of Gyffer by way of Innish-Kyl."

The Domina stepped up to the funeral pyre and reached down into the blanket of garlands. The night breeze stiffened, blowing the flames of the torches sideways against the dark as she lifted the Iron Crown from Veratina's body and raised the dark tiara of twisted metal up into the firelight. The watching crowd fell silent.

A moment longer Perada held up the Iron Crown where everyone could see it. Then she lowered it onto her own head, and a cheer rose up that echoed off the palace walls.

"Metadi's come a long way in a short time," Mistress Vasari observed under cover of the noise. From experience, she pitched her voice to escape the holorecoder's audio pickup. "Consort and General, no less. I wonder what the lady's getting from him besides the obvious?"

"I have my theories," Aringher said. "Handsome young men are two for a credit on any planet you care to name, but successful privateers are a much rarer commodity."

He waved a hand at Vasari for silence as the cheering died, and spoke again for the benefit of the holorecorder. "The Domina Perada has just formally assumed the Iron Crown of Entibor. We'll be hearing the funeral elegies for Veratina shortly; after that, the lights will go on again in the Palace Major, where tables are laid for the formal reception that will mark the official beginning of Perada Rosselin's reign."

In the center of the square, one of the torchbearers stepped forward. A profound quiet descended over the crowd as Perada took the flambeau and touched it to the base of the flower-draped pyre. At first nothing happened; then there was a sound of rushing air as the oil-soaked wood ignited in a splash of orange-and-yellow flame. The delicate garlands shriveled in an instant, and the Grand

Plaza began to fill with the mingled odors of ceremonial incense and burning flesh.

" 'Take the war to the Mages,' the man said." Gala pressed her fingers against her forehead and sighed. Behind her, on the broad desk that had been Admiral Pallit's, the comp screen continued playing its simulation unheeded. "Maybe I should have kept my mouth shut and let them court-martial me instead."

"It could be worse," Brehant said. "You could be at the Domina's reception with all the rest of the brass."

"I could be snug in my own bunk, too," she told him. "If I knew where that was. Something tells me fleet admirals don't sleep in the visiting officers' quarters."

She turned back to the simulation and frowned. "This isn't telling us anything we didn't know already. We need to take and hold the Mageworlds before we can end the war, and we need the cooperation of at least one other space fleet before we can even stop losing. Two or more fleets if we're serious."

"Talk about things we don't have and can't get."

Gala switched off the simulation. "I'll be saying as much in the OpPlan when I deliver it." She picked up her stylus and made a check mark on her datapad. "That's one more document I can add to the stack I've got for our newly minted General. My letter of resignation. I can join Pallit in early retirement."

"Put the letter of resignation on the bottom of the pile," Tres advised. "And don't date it."

"All right," Gala said, assembling her documents. "No date. But it goes in. Saves everyone concerned some time and trouble if they've got it on file."

She slipped the collection of documents into a courier pack and summoned a messenger. "Deliver this to the office of the General of the Armies."

"What, no personal delivery?" Brehant said after the courier had departed.

"No—we're the high command, not a bunch of errand-runners. Besides, he might think we don't have enough to do."

"And do we?"

"You know it," she said. "Now that we've got our wish list finished, we need to review personnel records for the whole Fleet. I want to know who's loyal to whom, and why. And after *that*, I want you to gen up messages to my opposite numbers in all the fleets that have suffered Mage raids, plus the commanders of all the fleets that might someday suffer Mage raids, plus the commanders of any other fleets you think could be useful."

"Why not the Mages, too?"

"If I knew their address," said Gala, "I might."

Tres shook his head and made a note on his own datapad. "Notes to commanders. Got it. What then?"

"We wait for responses. Anybody who comes up friendly or even neutral gets offered everything we have on the location, capability, and intentions of the Mageworld raiders."

"No request to reciprocate?"

"No."

"You aren't even going to ask permission first?"

"It's in the OpPlan," Gala said. "Annex L. If the General doesn't like it, that's what the letter of resignation is for."

She pushed back her chair and stood up. "Oh, and one more thing: the officers who resigned or retired this morning while General Metadi was making his tour of headquarters. I want citations awarding them all the Legion of Merit."

"You're not serious."

"Serious as radiation burns," she assured him. "So get to work on it. In the meantime, if you want me, I'll be in my quarters—assuming I can find them."

On the other side of An-Jemayne, two men sat at a table in an outdoor café. The establishment's usual patrons were absent—watching the old Domina's public burning on their home holosets, most likely—and with the exception of a surly waiter and an even surlier cook, the pair had the place to themselves. They nursed their cha'a and watched night-flying insects blunder in and out of the glow of the lanterns. Finally one of them looked at his chronometer and said, "It's time."

They abandoned their table, leaving an octime tip, and wandered over to the café's outside wall, where someone had pasted up a large advertising poster full of sporting announcements. The first man looked at the calendar block for the twenty-third of the month.

"Heavy-grav wrestling in the Old Arena," he commented. Next to the announcement for the twenty-third was a tiny mark like an accidental smudge of ink. "We don't want to miss that."

"No," said the other.

They left the café and went on foot through the deserted streets of the working-class district, into an area of more prosperous homes. At the third house from the corner on a certain street, they went up the front walk. The first man palmed the lockplate beside the door.

The door slid open. The two men passed through the vestibule into a sitting room full of overstuffed furniture done in glossy fabrics. An out-of-season flame display flickered on the artificial hearth, casting its light on the man who sat in an armchair nearby.

"Were you followed?" he asked.

"No," said the man who had palmed the lockplate.

"Can you swear to it?"

The other newcomer frowned. "Do we have to go through this stuff every time?" he complained. "Nobody followed us. Nobody ever does."

"It's necessary," said the man in the armchair. He stood and led the way toward the back of the house, through an unused kitchen into a small room that might once have been a pantry. Now it was bare except for a row of pegs along one wall. Most of the pegs were empty, but long black robes hung from three of them, along with featureless black masks of molded plastic.

The three men moved quickly, shedding their street clothes and putting on the masks and the hooded robes. Black staves, hidden until now, hung from leather cords on the pegs where the robes had been: heavy rods of ironwood or ebony, each half again as long as a man's forearm. The men took these down also and slipped them underneath their belts.

When they were done, they went back out through the deserted kitchen to another doorway, this one opening onto a short flight of steps. The steps led down to a basement chamber hung on all sides with heavy curtains of black cloth. Floor and ceiling were also dead black, with the exception of a white circle some eight feet across painted on the floor in the center of the room. A thick candle on an iron stand cast its light on the figures who knelt around the circle's perimeter.

The leader spoke. "Tonight the young Domina takes the Iron Crown. Her luck is strong: already she dispels the fear that she might be another like Veratina, and she has named as her Consort one of our greatest enemies. We have to break her luck, and break it soon. But first—"

He paused and looked around the group. The flame of the candle was reflected in the shiny black of his mask as he swung his head to look at each one of the others in turn.

"First," he said again, "I have someone to show you."

The leader pulled aside one of the black curtains. It concealed an alcove that might once have held laundry equipment. Reaching down, he dragged out a bound and bleeding form.

"This man," he said, "works for the Minister of Internal Security. I found him spying on this house. I suppose he wanted to see what we do here. What do you say—shall we gratify his curiosity?"

"Damned sorcerers!" the prisoner choked out.

"Not really," the leader said, "but you can call us that if it makes you happy. It won't matter for long." He turned back to the others. "To break the Domina's luck will require all of our energy, and more: an effort this great requires a life. I stand ready in the Circle; is there anyone who will match me?"

No one moved. Then one of the kneeling figures stirred and rose. The leader shook his head.

"Your offer does us both honor; but no." He pointed at one of the two late arrivals, the man who had palmed the lockplate and been the first to enter. "You."

Fireworks lit up the night sky over An-Jemayne. Inside the Palace Major, the long, high-ceilinged banquet hall was almost as crowded as the Strip in Waycross. The new Domina sat in a chair of state at the far end of the room, with Jos Metadi standing behind her, while the people with important greetings for the new ruler came and went, making their brief speeches and fading again into the press.

Tillijen wished she hadn't come. She and Nannla had chosen to wear their best port-liberty clothes, sans visible weapons as a concession to court protocol. The leather and brocade and fine white spidersilk weren't like anything now fashionable in An-Jemayne, and she hoped that the extravagantly unusual outfits would keep people from remembering too much about her face. Her own memories—of features, of mannerisms, of all the gilded and jeweled trivia that filled this life—were coming up with too many matches for comfort.

"I was an idiot to agree to this," she muttered. She clutched her goblet of sparkling punch in a desperate hand and wished that the recipe—already not a drink for weaklings—had been made even stronger. "I should have stayed back on the 'Hammer and spent the evening polishing the tableware."

Nannla gave Tilly's free hand a reassuring squeeze. "Don't worry so much. Even if somebody does recognize you, what are they going to do? Challenge you to a duel right here in the middle of the Domina's inaugural bash?"

"Don't laugh. It could happen. I got into a lot of trouble back when I was a kid . . . you've never heard the half of it. Some people might still be mad at me."

"Angry?" Nannla snorted in disbelief. "At the new Consort's official nearest female sort-of-relative? Tell me another one."

"I hope you're right—Lords of Life!" Tilly blanched and pulled Nannla around into a quick one-hundred-eighty-degree course change. "That was Khrysil Gandeluc. If she'd recognized me . . . I should have gone to Ophel when I had the chance. I swear, if I hadn't promised Jos I'd stand by him I wouldn't be here at all."

Nannla tossed back the last of her punch and switched the empty goblet for a full one from the tray carried by a passing footman. "Well, *somebody* has to be the poor guy's family. I don't think he's got anyone else." She nodded toward the line of notables waiting to make their speeches of welcome to the new Domina. "Even Ferrda agrees. Take a look at him."

Tillijen followed the gesture with her eyes. The *'Hammer*'s engineer had decked himself out for the reception in a formal coat of metallic bronze body-paint. A line of solid gold and silver studs ornamented the crest that flared atop his rounded skull. He towered over the diplomats and hangers-on like one of the Great Trees of his home world, and appeared oblivious to the comment his presence was generating.

"What the hell does he think he's doing?" Tilly demanded.

"I don't know," said Nannla. "But it must be important to him or he wouldn't have spent all that time with the paint pot."

Errec Ransome caught sight of his reflection in one of the tall casement windows—an unexpected encounter, as he emerged from behind a thicket of ornamental bushes in gilded porcelain planters—and thought for a moment that he saw not himself, but another. The clothes he wore, plain black and white cut after the free-spacer's style, were not his own, but a gift of sorts from the Palace. A messenger in blue and silver livery had delivered them to the *'Hammer* without explanation that afternoon. Jos was probably the one responsible; the Domina had no way of knowing that Errec's clothes locker held mostly castoffs from the *'Hammer*'s slop chest.

Errec had come to the reception unarmed, as always. Jos would have a weapon on him somewhere—Jos was never

unarmed, even if you couldn't see what he was carrying—
but Errec knew for a fact that Tillijen and Nannla didn't
have anything on them more deadly than boot knives and
pocket stunners. Ferrdacorr had claws and fangs and his
own massive strength under all the body-paint; there
wouldn't be any need to worry about him. Errec didn't
bother asking himself why he should be worried in the first
place, or why the sudden glimpse of his own dark-clad mirror image should have affected him so much. For now, he
had other things to do: there were Mages at work in An-
Jemayne.

He moved back into the shadow of the indoor greenery.
He'd always had the knack of effacing himself when he
chose to do so, and he'd watched with sympathy Tillijen's
self-conscious efforts to remain unnoticed. People almost
never saw Errec unless he wanted them to; even in deep
space, in the safety of the *'Hammer'*s common room, he
found it difficult to relax his guard completely. When he desired, as now, to be invisible, nobody looked in his direction
at all.

Once he was safely out of the common view, he closed
his eyes and let his mind go free, seeking those knots and
distortions in the currents of Power which betrayed the
workings of the Mages. It didn't take him long to find them.

Yes. There. I can feel it begin. . . .

"A word with you, my lady?"

Tillijen glanced around in surprise. She'd only left
Nannla for a few minutes to search out the ladies' retiring
room, and hadn't expected anybody to take note of her comings and goings.

The speaker turned out to be Nivome do'Evaan, the big,
dark-browed Rolnian who served as Perada Rosselin's Minister of Internal Security. Jos Metadi had described Nivome,
with more charity than she'd expected, as a tough guy in a
thankless job. Errec Ransome, on the other hand, had called
him dangerous.

Right now, Tillijen felt inclined to agree. She looked at
Nivome without saying anything, hoping that the Rolnian

would take the hint and go away. She'd heard enough, in her occasional fleeting contacts with old acquaintances over the years, to know that anything more than casual involvement with the Minister of Internal Security would lead to more trouble than anyone really needed.

"Tillijen Chereeve," the minister continued in his rumbling voice. He paused. "Or should I say Lady Chereeve? Your presence at Her Dignity's accession is an unexpected pleasure."

"The pleasure is mine, I assure you," Tillijen said automatically. She scanned the throng of guests in the reception hall as she spoke. Where in the name of space and all the shining stars had Nannla gotten to?

"Not all of it, surely," Nivome said.

Again he paused. Tillijen decided that the minister used the silent spaces between his utterances for deliberate effect—the mind flinched away from what came next, like bruised flesh anticipating a second blow. And sure enough, here it came.

"Is your illustrious family aware of your return? Unless I'm mistaken, House Chereeve still pays its remittance to your bank account on Ophel, contingent on your agreement not to come back to Entibor or any of its colonies during your lifetime."

"Consider me as being here incognito," Tillijen said at last, after the silence had stretched out farther than she could stand. "House Chereeve doesn't need to concern itself with an Ophelan free-spacer who isn't related to them anymore."

"I understand," Nivome said. "Rest assured that your secret is safe with me—it would distress House Chereeve no end to learn that you'd come back."

He bowed, and left. Tillijen stood thinking, wondering exactly what the Rolnian had meant by his hints and veiled accusations. A threat? Almost certainly. Her last formal exchanges with House Chereeve, years ago now, hadn't been pleasant for anybody involved. Blackmail? Maybe. But he hadn't asked for anything; he'd just talked.

Or was Perada's Minister of Internal Security merely

amusing himself by playing dominance games with a wandering free-spacer who didn't have the power to send him away?

That, she thought as she spotted Nannla at last and hurried to join her, *sounds a lot more likely. But he's nobody to get mixed up with, all the same.*

In the black-draped room on the far side of An-Jemayne, two of the Circle-Mages rose to take hold of the man their leader had indicated. Their caution was unnecessary. The man made no attempt to flee. The leader spoke again.

"You were the Second of our Circle," he said. "But this person"—he gestured toward the bound man lying next to the curtains—"tells me that you have taken the coin of the agents of Internal Security. Now, as First, I call on you to make repayment. Offer your life to break the Domina and keep the Circle one."

"My lord," said the Second. He took a step away from the two who were holding him, moving into the center of the painted circle on the floor. "I am at your service. But what if it's not my life that gets taken?"

"Then the working has my energy to strengthen it, and you have the Circle to do with as you will." The First raised his staff in a quick salute. "Until, of course, some other member comes forward to challenge you for it."

"Of course," echoed the Second. If he was afraid, it didn't show in his voice—and behind the black mask, his expression could have shown anything at all. He raised his staff in his right hand, bringing it up to the vertical in front of his face. At the same time he took a step backward and bent his knees. "And so, we begin."

The First moved closer, his staff held loosely in his right hand, its tip pointing toward the floor. The Second pivoted, keeping his own staff vertical. The First took another step inward—and the Second lunged, sweeping down with his staff at the First's unprotected skull.

But the First was no longer standing where he had been. Black robe swirling with the movement, he pivoted and punched out with his staff, knocking the blow aside. Before the other man could recover, the First struck again, slamming his staff backhanded into the Second's mask, smashing broken plastic into the man's eyes—crushing, also, the bone underneath. There was no outcry, but the staff in the Second's hand clattered to the floor. The air around the two men began to glow first a dull purple, then a clear violet, and at last a brilliant blue.

The First took another step forward to stand behind his blinded opponent. He slipped his staff across the Second's throat and reached across to seize the free end with his left hand, so that his arms formed a scissors behind the other's neck. Then he began to pull up and backward, pressing his staff against the Second's windpipe until bone and cartilage cracked beneath the assault.

The Second dangled there helpless, his body limned in tongues of blue flame and his breath stopped in his ruined throat. Then he stiffened, his back arching and his feet kicking out in a last convulsion. The blue light that surrounded him pulsed, then flared up into a cyan blaze as the First let his body drop into the center of the painted circle.

"It's done," said the First. "Our working is finished."

He lowered his staff and turned to the outsider in the Circle, the bound and bleeding man who had come spying for the Minister of Internal Security. He brought his staff up again so that the man could see how it glowed all along its length.

"Have you seen enough?" he asked. "Or would you like to see more? Come, we have much to show you."

"How extraordinary!"

Mistress Vasari's voice was light as always, but the slim fingers that had rested with perfect formality on Aringher's coat sleeve moved downward to take his hand. He looked over at her curiously.

"What's extraordinary, my dear?"

"That painted personage looming over the rest of the reception line," she said. While she spoke, her fingers tightened and released in the rhythms of the pulse-code: *The man standing by the windows. The one in black. I know him.*

"A Selvaur," said Aringher. "From Maraghai. A Lord among the Forest Lords, or so I hear."

Unobtrusively, he squeezed her hand in return. *I hadn't noticed him until you pointed him out. Dare I ask where you know him from?*

"Someone told me they all call themselves that," Vasari said. "The Selvaurs, I mean. Bigger snobs than the Khesatans."

There was more tension in Vasari's long fingers than could be accounted for by the presence of a nonhuman ambassador to planetary royalty. *Where do you think I know him from?*

"Yes, but they say this one really means it," Aringher replied, while in pulse-code he said, *Maybe he's supposed to be here. You can't be the only one with an interest.*

"I wonder what he wants to say to the Domina." Vasari's tension hadn't eased; Aringher, who had always thought her imperturbable, found this curiosity disturbing. Her fingers, cold against his own, said, *You don't understand.*

"It doesn't matter what our scaly friend tells Her Dignity," Aringher said; and in the pulse-code, *What don't I understand?* Aloud, in counterpoint, he added, "What matters is that the Selvaurs haven't sent so much as an unofficial envoy to anyplace in years."

Vasari's hand lay motionless in his. "They say he's a friend of the Consort."

"I *knew* it had to be more than the good captain's looks that Her Dignity was interested in," said Aringher, and pressed the code-rhythms urgently into Vasari's palm a second time: *What is it that I don't understand?*

"Not that there's anything wrong with Metadi's looks, mind you," Vasari said. Her hand trembled as she answered: *That man died four years ago.*

Tillijen glanced uneasily about the reception hall. Khrysil Gandeluc wasn't anywhere in sight, thank fortune—*Maybe she got bored and went home; she wouldn't have stuck out a party this dead for fifteen minutes back in the old days*— but Nivome do'Evaan was still there, and she'd felt his dark eyes following her more than once, making her feel more than ever like an alien masquerader amid familiar surroundings.

She wondered if the rest of the *'Hammer*'s crew felt anything like the same way she did. Nannla didn't, obviously; the number-one gunner was on her third glass of punch, and her dashing costume was drawing admiring looks from even the most staid of court matrons. As for the flaming youth of An-Jemayne, they'd be wearing ruffles and leather before the week was out.

Ferrda was another one who took stares for granted, and seemed to enjoy them. He'd made his speech to the Domina—not bowing, which caused a delighted, scandalized murmur to run through the banqueting hall—and now he stood to one side watching the crowd. Once in a while he would look over at where Jos Metadi stood behind the Domina's chair of state, and his jewel-studded crest would spread itself higher for an instant in the true Selvauran expression of amusement.

Tillijen didn't know if Metadi noticed the Selvaur's reaction or not. The captain—*the General, now; I'll have to remember that*—was wearing his best don't-scare-the-dirtsiders outfit, something plain black and expensive cut in the conservative Entiboran style. The notables who came to offer their greetings to the Domina sometimes spoke with him and sometimes ignored him; he maintained the same politely impassive demeanor in either case.

That left only one member of *Warhammer*'s regular crew unaccounted for. Tillijen tapped Nannla on the arm. "Have you seen Errec lately?"

"I spotted him a while back," her partner said. "Right about the time you took one look at that woman in the feathers and seed pearls and tried to hide behind the curtains."

"I told you, if she remembered me there could be big trouble ... but where is Errec right now?"

"Who knows? You know how he can fade out like a bad comm signal when he doesn't want anyone to find him."

"I know," she said. "But—"

A glaring light from the plaza cut her objection short. Tillijen spun toward the disturbance in time to see something big and heavy come smashing through the tall windows with a high-pitched crash of breaking glass.

Hovercar, observed the same inner voice that spoke to her when she was working the *'Hammer'*s number-two gun. *Decelerating.*

The hovercar settled to the floor in the middle of the banqueting hall amid a cacophony of screams, shouts, and hysterical babbling. Security operatives were everywhere, as if they'd spontaneously generated from the floor underfoot, sprinting to cover the windows and doors with blasters and energy lances. Tillijen saw without surprise that Jos had produced a small but deadly hand-blaster from inside the plain black coat and was standing in front of Perada. One of the security agents caught sight of it and started toward him, then visibly thought better of the idea. Tillijen looked down at the knife that had somehow made its way into her own hand, and tucked it back into its sheath.

Nannla had her by the other hand now, urging her forward toward the edge of the crowd that had begun to gather around the open-topped hovercar. There was a man inside—perhaps a man. Not enough of it remained whole for Tillijen to decide. The body had been broken almost to jelly by multiple blows; the head was an oozing, pulpy mass. Appallingly, it still breathed.

Somebody was shouting for a medic. Nannla clucked her tongue disapprovingly. "Do they think anyone is going to thank them for saving his life? I've seen chopped meat patties that had a better chance for a normal life after reconstructive surgery than that poor son-of-a-bitch."

Tillijen didn't answer. She was looking at Jos Metadi—who was, in turn, looking at the grounded hovercar. Another moment, and he was moving, pushing the Domina onto the floor and flinging himself on top of her.

"Down!" he shouted. "Get *down!*"

Tillijen didn't wait. Jos never used that tone of voice without reason. Instant obedience, on those occasions when he did use it, had saved her life more than once already, and had gone a long way toward making her a rich woman besides. She flung herself down onto the polished wooden floor of the reception hall. A second later, the hovercar exploded with a ground-shaking roar. Flesh and metal flew in all directions, and a dusty plaster rainfall came down from the ceiling and pattered onto her back and shoulders.

As soon as the noise of the explosion died away, she rose unsteadily to her feet, her ears ringing. She looked first for Nannla, and felt a wave of relief when she saw that her partner was already standing. One side of Nannla's face was plastered with blood and bits of raw meat, but she wasn't acting like somebody who ought to be in pain.

"Are you hurt?" Tillijen asked.

"No." Nannla pulled out a handkerchief and ran it over her cheek and jaw. She pulled it away and grimaced at the formerly-white cloth. "But messy. Very messy."

The hall was full of noise and movement—screams and sobs, the clangor and hooting of alarms, the sound of running feet as emergency crews poured into the room through every available entrance. One team, clad in the bright orange jumpsuits of Fire and Rescue, was shooting a cloud of white powder at smoldering curtains around a blown-out window. Others worked over the injured. And Perada was on her feet again, her face set and angry.

"You," she said, and Tillijen saw that she had fixed the armsmaster, Ser Hafrey, with a sharp blue gaze. "And you." This time she spoke to the Minister of Internal Security, and Tillijen had the pleasure of seeing Nivome do'Evaan look like a man who—if it were not for the dignity of his office—would have winced under that penetrating regard.

And he damned well should, Tillijen thought. *He's the one who's supposed to keep stuff like this from happening.*

"Come with me, gentles," the Domina said to Hafrey and Nivome. Her voice was icy. "Now."

She turned away in the direction of a side-chamber—not much more than a large alcove—that opened off the reception hall. The curtains that had screened it from the main room had been blown to tatters by the explosion, but it was, at least symbolically, private. The armsmaster and the Minister of Internal Security followed Perada; so, without waiting for an invitation, did Jos Metadi, his blaster still in his hand.

The captain isn't trusting anybody right now, Tillijen thought. Then he glanced over at her and Nannla, and jerked his head in a "come-along" gesture. *Nobody he hasn't shipped with, at least.*

Tillijen and Nannla joined the group in the side-chamber—a sheltered nook that had apparently been devoted more to politics than to flirtation, since it held a table and a desk comp and what looked like the ruins of a shielded comm setup. To Tillijen's expert eye, it looked like comp and comms were a dead loss; part of the blast from the hovercar had ripped through the curtained entrance and out through the high arched window, leaving the electronics slagged and smoking.

Perada already stood with Jos Metadi at her back, facing down the two men—armsmaster and Interior Minister—who should have seen that her accession went smoothly and stayed free of deeds of ill omen. Nothing remained, as far as Tillijen could see, of the mischievous schoolgirl who'd sung "Bindweed and Blossom" at a shipboard party, then gotten tipsy on aqua vitae and dragged the captain off to bed.

"Very well, gentles." The Domina's voice was clear and unwavering. "What, exactly, is the meaning of this debâcle?"

What Nivome or Ser Hafrey might have said, in excuse or self-justification, Tillijen never knew. Errec Ransome stepped forward—she hadn't seen him join the group in the private alcove, but that wasn't surprising; Errec came and went almost invisibly even under normal circumstances, which these definitely weren't. She suspected that he'd been with them the whole time, choosing his own moment to fade back into view.

He met the Domina's gaze directly.

"Mages," Errec Ransome said. "You have Mages on Entibor. And this means that they will break you, or die in the attempt."

Errec Ransome: Ilarna
(Galcenian Dating 970 a.f.; Entiboran Regnal Year 34 Veratina)

A COLD blue light filled the sky over Amalind Grange: the glow of heavy-duty nullgravs running at max power. One by one, the wing-shaped raiding ships lowered themselves noiselessly to the ground. Errec Ransome watched, as frozen as the snow-covered fields outside the window, while the lead ship in the first wave settled itself on the spot where a spreading bitterwood tree had stood a moment before. The massive tree—as tall as the uppermost windows of the Grange itself, and almost as ancient—crumpled and vanished underneath the raider's unrelenting mass.

The silence of it terrified him. He'd been a spacer once; he knew how nullgravs worked, and how much sound they made doing it. He knew how closely Ilarna patrolled its planetary space, as well. This many ships should not have come through the defenses unopposed, without raising a single alarm. And now the bay doors of the black ships swung open, spilling out blue-white light, and the ships began disgorging soldiers—dark, anonymous figures in light blast-armor, carrying energy weapons both large and small.

Magecraft.

The Adepts on Galcen had spoken of such things, of alien, unnatural twistings of the universal Power, brought into the civilized galaxy by the raiders from beyond the interstellar gap. Errec Ransome had not quite believed them. But only Magecraft could silence nullgravs, and hide an invasion fleet, and keep all the Adepts in the Ilarnan Guildhouse fast asleep while their doom came at them through the falling snow.

All of them but me.

With the thought, the sorcery that held him motionless seemed to break. He stumbled backward through the curtains into the darkened hallway and began shouting and pounding on the closed doors.

"Wake up! Raiders! Wake up!"

No one responded. He pulled the next door open and ran into the room, crossing in two strides to the bed and grabbing Mistress Sandevan by her shoulder.

"Raiders! Wake up!"

He jerked Allorie onto her back. She flopped over limply, her breathing slowed and her body relaxed in a slumber too deep to be natural. He shook her, but she only yawned and mumbled in her sleep. Cursing, he let her drop back onto the pillow.

A quick stride took him to the window of the bedchamber. He yanked the curtain aside and looked out. The Guildhouse was surrounded by the dark, wing-shaped spacecraft, wave on wave of them landing after the first. Another instant, and the entire perimeter of the Grange came alive with multicolored light—the armored raiders were charging forward through the snow.

One of the outbuildings exploded in a flash of lurid red. Errec choked back a cry.

The apprentices' dormitory—gone.

Another flash of red washed across the night. The old stable, now a home for the Guildhouse's collection of hovercars and speederbikes, broke up in a sheet of orange flame mixed with thick black smoke. Secondary explosions rocked the Guildhouse as the vehicles themselves perished.

No chance of escape there—anyone trying to get away would have to go on foot, or not at all.

Nothing is coincidence, Errec thought. *Nothing is chance.* The ancient scrap of accepted wisdom had always comforted him before; now he felt as if a good knife had turned and cut his hand. *The raiders came tonight on purpose— they're counting on the cold and snow to take care of anybody who tries to run.*

He let the curtain fall and made for the stairs. At least he had his boots on, and a warm night-robe over his shirt and trousers. His wakefulness earlier had served him there. And he wasn't unarmed, not while he had his staff and his training in the disciplines. If he could make it out of the Guildhouse and slip through the raiders' lines, he had a chance.

Efface myself until morning, then see if anyone else got out alive.

The sounds from outside came through clearly. He heard them as he ran down the carpeted staircase: the staccato popping of projectile weapons, the whine of blasters and the heavier crump of large-scale energy guns, the crackling of flames.

What are they shooting at? Errec wondered. *No one's awake and moving but me.*

But that wasn't quite true. Coming up the stairs, his staff ablaze with blue-white fire, strode Master Guislen.

"Errec!" he called. "Where's everyone else?"

"The whole upper dormitory is asleep like the dead," Errec replied. "Sorcery ... Magecraft ... I don't know why it didn't get me as well."

"That doesn't matter right now," Guislen said. "Come on—we need you. Hurry!"

The senior Master turned and hurried back down the stairs, turning to the right and through a small passage leading to a side door near the kitchens. Errec followed, his staff at the ready. Guislen reached the door first and pulled it open.

Errec ducked through the gap and out into the snow-covered yard. The flames from the burning outbuildings lit up a semicircle of troopers in blast armor.

Not so many—we can break through if we hit them hard.
He brought up his staff to strike down the nearest one, calling in Power to make his weapon into a bar of flame.

"Raiders!" he shouted at Guislen. "Take them!"

But no fellow-Adept ran forward, staff ablaze, to stand beside Errec Ransome in the fight. *Betrayed!* he had time to think, in the fearful instant before Guislen's blow crashed into his head from behind.

A white light burst in front of his eyes, and he fell.

XII. Galcenian Dating 976 A.F.
Entiboran Regnal Year 3 Perada

THE SUMMER Palace of House Rosselin looked out over the Nechelan Mountain Intervals, half a continent away from the noise and press of An-Jemayne. Perada wished that the intrigues and rivalries of An-Jemayne could be left behind as easily.

If that were so, she thought with weary humor, *I'd move the court here for good.*

She knew that such a maneuver wouldn't work, though, no matter how tempting it felt. She'd come to the Summer Palace for the childbirth, done in the old-fashioned manner according to House tradition, and had stayed on because the palace's isolated luxury made it a good place in which to recover. She'd stretched that recovery as long as she could, buying time with another old custom that deferred formal court life until the baby was weaned—*I can't stretch it out much longer*, she thought regretfully; *not with the teeth he's growing*—but her efforts had proved useless just the same. She was the Domina, and where she went, the intrigue and rivalry followed.

Informal court life, and the day-to-day decisions that only

the Domina could make, continued. Today she was trying, as gracefully and inconspicuously as she could, to avoid the Minister of Internal Security. She couldn't refuse him admittance, not without also dismissing him from his post, and his connections to the merchant houses and the banking interests were too strong for that. Veratina hadn't made him her Consort—even in her declining years she hadn't been that stupid—but she'd given him almost everything else.

He caught up with Perada in the High Walk, in the room where ruby windows caught the light and reflected it over the suspended pathways above a stony gorge.

"Good morning, my lady," he said, with a full bow of respect. "How are you feeling?"

She made a noncommittal gesture with one hand. "Well enough. Tired, sometimes."

The statement wasn't entirely a lie, she reflected, though her fatigue was mental, not physical, and it was the thought of going back to the Palace Major that brought it on. Eleven years under Zeri Delaven's tutelage hadn't prepared her for life in a museum display of architecture and etiquette. Nivome do'Evaan of Rolny, though, wasn't one of the people to whom she was prepared to admit the problem.

Let him think I'm still recovering. House Rosselin's traditional insistence on the old low-tech birthing customs would make the idea believable. *My physicians won't talk—unless he's suborned them. Has he suborned them?*

She looked more closely at the Minister of Internal Security. His face and bearing told her nothing beyond what she already knew, that he was an ambitious man and an aggressive one. *I'll have to ask Hafrey about the physicians,* she thought with resignation. More and more often, of late, there were times when she felt like nothing more than the prize—or sometimes the battlefield—in an ongoing struggle between Nivome and the armsmaster.

"I'm sorry to hear that Your Dignity remains unwell," the Rolnian said. "Your people are understandably concerned."

"Without reason," she said sharply. "As I trust you'll make clear to anyone who asks."

"I do my best," he said. "But as the minister in charge of

internal security on this world, I have to report honestly on what people say and what they believe."

"And what *are* they saying?"

Nivome's features arranged themselves into an expression of solemn concern. "They remember Veratina, Your Dignity—who birthed a placeholder child the year after her coming-of-age, and gave them nothing else for the next five decades."

Perada smiled sweetly at the Minister of Internal Security. "Tell your informants that they don't need to worry. Veratina's placeholder was early-born and never strong afterward—ask them if they remember *that* as well!—but young Ari, thank fortune, is full of absolutely appalling good health."

"But a placeholder, not an heir."

"All in time, Gentlesir Nivome," she said, laughing. "The good people of Entibor won't have to wait five decades, I promise you—but give me a while to work on other things!"

"As you wish." Nivome bowed slightly, as one who concedes a single point out of a match still being played. "I'd hoped that you would remember the service I gave you before."

"I haven't forgotten." She looked out through the ruby-tinted windows at the precipitous walls of the gorge below. The sun was going down, and her body—an efficient clock in such matters—was beginning to insist that she cut the conversation short in favor of finding Ari and giving the young placeholder his next meal. Her breasts felt heavy with milk; if she waited much longer they would begin to ache. "If that's all . . ."

"More or less," he said. "I merely wanted to let you know that the offer remains open."

"I'm honored. But I'm served well enough, thank you."

"That's another matter I wanted to discuss," Nivome said.

Perada's head began to ache. She wished she could afford to insult Nivome by closing her eyes and massaging away the tension. *Go away,* she thought. *Go back to An-Jemayne and leave me alone!* But thinking it didn't do any good; he was still there. She suppressed a sigh and said aloud, "What is it?"

"I do not think," he said, "that your General is suitable."

"And why not?"

"What do you know of him?"

Perada smiled, more because she knew it would annoy Nivome than because she felt amused. "Sufficient," she said.

"Tell me then," Nivome said, "how do you think he obtained that fancy ship of his—*Warhammer*, is it?"

She didn't need to look at Nivome's face to know that the question had been aimed, like a dart, straight at a vulnerable spot. Ser Hafrey's reports on Captain Jos Metadi hadn't contained that information, either, and nobody on board the *'Hammer* had ever spoken of it. There were some things, as Nannla the gunner had said, that polite people didn't ask.

"In the usual way men of his profession acquire starships, I suppose," she said. "I never bothered to inquire."

"Perhaps you should have, Your Dignity."

This time Perada did sigh aloud. "Tell me, then, since you seem determined to make me ask the question: how *did* my General of the Armies obtain his ship?"

"Your Dignity, I'm sorry, but I do not know."

"Lords of Life!" she exclaimed. It was one of Jos Metadi's milder oaths, and she hoped that Nivome appreciated the fact. "Then what is the point of all this—this digression? It's late, and I have pressing business to take care of; say what you have to say and get done with it."

"Very well, Your Dignity," Nivome said. "In brief: no one can—or no one *will*—say for certain how Jos Metadi first obtained his ship. But certain facts are known: when the ship left port, its crew was complete, experienced, and competent. When it appeared again—and not at its expected destination, my lady—there was only one crew member aboard. That one was your Gyfferan. He took the ship by survivor's right, changed its name, collected a crew of disreputable individuals, and turned at once to piracy."

"Privateering," Perada corrected absently. "What, exactly, do you expect me to do with all this information—if you want to dignify a collection of unsubstantiated rumors with such an honorable name?"

"Nothing, Domina." He smiled. "It *is* only a rumor, after all."

Errec Ransome stood near the mess table in *Warhammer*'s common room, watching Tillijen and Nannla playing at cards and following the back-and-forth of the game.

"You know," said Nannla, pulling a card from her hand and laying it faceup on the common-room table, "this planetary royalty business isn't all it's cracked up to be. I'm surprised our little 'Rada hasn't gone mad with boredom."

Tillijen looked at the card, then at her own hand, and shook her head. "What about poor Jos?"

"Jos has the whole Entiboran Fleet to keep him occupied," Errec said. "He may complain some, but don't let that fool you. He's having the time of his life."

"Good for him," said Nannla. "But Ferrda's already taken his cut of the loot and gone back home to Maraghai—how much longer are the rest of us going to wait before we retire from the trade and open up a dirtside cha'a shop?"

"Not on Entibor, thank you," Tillijen said. "I think I'll stick with the *'Hammer* for a while longer. Unless you're serious about quitting space for good."

Nannla laughed. "Don't worry. I'm not *that* desperate for entertainment." She tilted her head to look up sidelong at Errec. "What about you?"

"What Jos is doing right now is important," Errec said. "And sooner or later, he'll need somebody to find Mages for him. I can wait."

The entry alarm from the top of *Warhammer*'s ramp broke into the conversation with a loud buzz. Nannla glanced up again at Errec. "See who it is, will you? And if it's the Free-Spacer's Protective Agency collecting for their charity fund, tell them we gave on Innish-Kyl."

Errec laughed under his breath and headed for the *'Hammer*'s main hatch. The ramp was down, as befitted a ship grounded for a prolonged stay in a friendly port, but the force field was up. Even through the blurring effect of the field, however, the visitor's face was familiar.

Errec halted a few steps away from the opening. "Anije Vasari," he said. He drew a careful breath and let it out again slowly. "*Mistress* Vasari, I should say."

"Master Ransome," said the slim woman on the other side of the force field. "Errec—may I come aboard? I need to talk with you."

He stood for a few seconds longer without moving, then gave a sigh and hit the button to lower the field. "Come on, then. There's cha'a in the galley, if you want some."

"Gracious as ever," she said with a brief smile. "I'd say you hadn't changed a bit, but I'd be lying and you'd know it."

He didn't bother denying the charge, only shrugged and led the way back into the common room. Nannla and Tillijen were still playing cards; Nannla looked from him to Anije Vasari as they entered, and gathered up the cards from the table.

"I think we'd better move the game down to Engineering," she said. "Come on, Tilly. . . . Errec, give a yell if you need us for anything."

"Don't worry," he said. "I'll be all right."

The two gunners headed aft. Errec found a couple of mugs in the galley, filled them both with cha'a, and gave one to Vasari. He gestured her to a chair at the common-room table and sat down opposite her with the other mug of cha'a.

"Now we can talk," he said. "What brings you down to the port quarter, Anije?"

"Looking for you." She gazed into the depths of her cha'a. "Everybody thought you'd died on Ilarna, you know."

He suppressed a shudder, remembering. "I'm not surprised."

"They wanted to mark you on the rolls as dead, but Master Otenu wouldn't let them."

"I remember Otenu. He always did see more than he let on."

"If you say so." She pushed the mug away from her and laid her hands flat on the table. "This time he says I'm supposed to bring you back home to Galcen."

" 'Home'?" Errec shook his head. "I was never at home there, and Otenu knows it. *This* is home."

"A grounded starship? I don't believe it."

"Believe it," he said. "If I'd wanted to go to Galcen, I could have shown up on Otenu's doorstep any time during the past four years."

"But you were busy," she finished for him. "Fighting Mages with Jos Metadi. Who isn't fighting the Mages anymore."

"He will be. When the time comes."

She looked at him, and he could sense her assessing the weight of his statement. Anije Vasari was another of those who had always seen more than they let on.

"And when the time comes," she said slowly, "can you guarantee that he'll be able to find them? Space is big, Errec; it takes a lot of work to find anyone out there. A lot of work, or an Adept who can tell the pilot where the target will be. Your Captain Metadi is General Metadi now, and he's putting together a fleet—how many Adepts will he need when he's finished? Somebody has to train them and make them ready, somebody who's actually fought the Mages and knows how the job is done."

"Meaning me," he said, feeling suddenly tired. He'd seen her argument coming as soon as she began to speak, but that didn't help much. Not when he knew that she was right.

Jos Metadi had discovered at an early age that life was full of unexpected lessons, and he'd made up his mind to appreciate the fact. Nevertheless, he hadn't expected to find out that planetary royalty, living in a palace that was bigger than some landing fields he'd grounded the *'Hammer* in, had fewer opportunities to be alone than the average free-spacer between ports of call. The nursery wing of the Summer Palace was one of the Domina's few places of refuge: when she was there, the household staff would deny admittance to official visitors calling on routine matters of state, and provide a formal escort even for known members of her inner circle.

As far as Jos knew, besides the palace staff there were only two people for whom the high-security lockplates on the heavy doors would automatically open. One of them was Perada herself. It gave Jos a surprising amount of pleasure to know that he was the other—surprising, because he'd never figured himself to be a likely candidate for domesticity, even on such a grand level as this.

Today Perada was sitting in a high-backed wing chair by the tall windows, her feet propped up on a cushioned hassock, feeding young Ari his late-afternoon meal. The baby's wispy dark curls looked like faint sable brushstrokes against the white skin of her breast. The boy had a robust appetite—he'd been born large, and showed all signs of continuing that way—and he had what everybody assured Jos was a calm and good-natured disposition. Jos wasn't sure how they could tell.

"I'm going to have to go back to the Palace Major sometime within the next month or so." Perada was leaning her head back against the chair cushions. Her eyes were closed, and her voice sounded weary. "There's no help for it."

"Who's making you?" Jos inquired. He was sitting in a matching wing chair a little more than comfortable conversation distance away. He'd more than once tried moving the heavy chair a foot or so closer to its partner, but when on each succeeding visit he found the chair carefully replaced in its customary position, he'd finally given up. "Is there some part of running Entibor that you can only do in an overdecorated warehouse?"

"Unfortunately, yes. It's been over a year since I've held a formal court—"

Jos frowned. "You mean to tell me that spending every other Fifth-Day down in the Great Hall listening to anybody who wants to come in and bend your ear with a long-winded complaint isn't the same as holding court?"

"No. Those are informal audiences."

"If you say so." Jos was silent for a while, thinking about the prospect of changing residences. "Moving back won't make things any harder for me—easier, maybe, since Fleet Central HQ isn't all that far from An-Jemayne—but you shouldn't have to put up with living someplace you don't like. Didn't your mother's branch of the family have a town house in the capital or something?"

Perada nodded without opening her eyes. "And a manor in Felshang, and a winter retreat in the Immering Isles and a country cottage in Yestery Lea. But whenever I'm in one of those places, I'm plain Perada Rosselin, and I can't speak or act as the Domina at all." She sighed. "Living here is as close to that life as I can get without bringing the whole government to a screeching halt, and I've indulged myself outrageously by staying this long."

"Somebody's been going on at you about it." Jos felt a momentary flash of anger, mixed with a by now familiar sense of frustration at the lack of a target. Palace routine and royal custom couldn't be argued with; he'd learned that much early on. He couldn't help adding, "If you want me to tell whoever it is to back off a bit, I'll be happy to play the bad-mannered Gyfferan for as long as it takes to get the message across."

She opened her eyes—checking out his expression, Jos supposed, to gauge whether he was serious or not—and smiled. "It's kind of you to offer, and if it were somebody like Lord Gelerec talking I might even take you up on it. Gelerec goes on forever and stays in the same place. But Nivome do'Evaan is another matter."

Jos had to admit, reluctantly, that she was right. Reluctantly, because he didn't much care for the big, heavyset Rolnian who was Entibor's Minister of Internal Security—the man radiated ambition so strongly he probably glowed in the dark, which wasn't necessarily a bad thing except that nobody in the Fleet cared for Nivome very much either, and Perada herself seemed edgy whenever he was around. He was some kind of legacy from Domina Veratina, and he'd put his roots down too deep for the new ruler to pull him loose.

Errec doesn't like him either, Jos thought. *And Errec hasn't been wrong about anybody yet. Maybe he and I*

should put our heads together about our buddy Nivome . . .
see if we can work something out.

"What else did Nivome have to say?" he asked.

"Not much. He tried to sound me out about insuring the succession—"

"Having another kid, you mean."

"An heir." She looked down at Ari, where the baby had fallen asleep against her breast. "If House tradition didn't rule out a quick trip to a good biolab, I could stop that sort of questioning. But custom is custom."

The hell with custom, Jos wanted to say, but he knew better. He wished he knew what murky historical precedent kept the head of the Ruling House of Entibor from making use of the same technology as an ordinary citizen. Someday, he decided, he'd have to get Tilly drunk and ask her for the real story.

"So what did you tell Nivome?" he asked.

"Not to rush things, more or less. But that's another reason for going back to the Palace Major, if I can't legitimately plead family matters any longer. And fond as I am of this little one—" She smiled down at the sleeping baby. "—I'm not *quite* ready to go through all that again. We have plenty of time."

Fleet Admiral Galaret Lachiel still hadn't gotten used to her new office. She'd had all of Pallit's awards and memorabilia packed up and sent to his retirement address in Cazdel Province, and the newly promoted captain-of-frigates who was running the show these days in the Parezulan sector had shipped Gala's own stuff to Entibor via courier, but even after almost two years her life at Central seemed unreal. Something about "easy come, easy go," maybe, as if a part of her remained waiting in that bottom-floor holding room.

She stood now by the holochart of Entiboran space, talking to the man who had thrown the job of fleet admiral at her with no more warning than she'd have gotten in a game of twiddleball. Jos Metadi dressed these days like a respectable Gyfferan merchant-spacer, except for the blaster and the boots. He still stood out like a marker beacon among the glittering nobility—some of the restive young sprigs, the ones with Centrist leanings, had taken to imitating his style—but she doubted if he cared, or if he even noticed.

The gossips at court might believe that Perada had brought Metadi home to Entibor for his good looks, but nobody in the Fleet had been that foolish for quite a while now. Gala had seen to it that the intelligence reports on Metadi's earlier privateering raids made it into the open files. Most of the eager young junior officers, she suspected, would have given up a year's pay and a chance at promotion to have been along for any one of them.

She touched the controls for the holochart, changing the diagram of Entibor's sphere of influence to a display graphing the war's progress in terms of known losses both to the raiders and to the fleet.

"You see how it's going," she said. "We're losing ships; they're losing ships. What good it's all doing I can't begin to tell you—but I *do* know that sooner or later we're going to run out of ships."

"That's not good," said Metadi. "Admiral, you've worked with these people longer than I have—is there some reason I'm not aware of why we're not building more ships?"

"Lord Pelencath was in here this morning," Gala said. "I'm sure you recall the man—ties to the bankers, ties to the sillyweed cartel, ties to everyone. He spent a stimulating two hours explaining to me in some detail how an increase in shipbuilding would ruin the economy."

Metadi shook his head. "And Mage raids don't? That does it; I'll never make it as an economist."

"Neither will I, if it's any consolation. Actually, I think it's Pelencath's own private economy he's worried about." She grimaced. "Unfortunately for us, the man deeply and sincerely believes that whatever's good for him has to be good for Entibor."

"There's nothing like befuddled self-interest, is there?" Metadi paced from one side of the office to the other, then halted abruptly and turned to face her. "Stop me if I'm wrong," he said, "but it all belongs to the Dominą anyway, right? If she decides that from now on all the bread will be brancakes, then that's the way it is."

"In theory, yes," said Gala. "Until someone produces a new heir with some claim to the Iron Crown, and there's another succession crisis, in which case absolutely nothing gets done for five or six years while the Great Houses concentrate on poisoning each other's cha'a in the mornings."

"We can't have that. The raiders would be all over us."

Gala nodded. "Pelencath wasn't crude enough to suggest anything directly, as far as disputing the succession goes—but he made implications."

"Damn." Metadi made another restless circuit of the office. "*Is* there anybody else who's up to making a claim?"

"Not that I've noticed," she said. "But I'll be frank with you, General. I joined the fleet to stay out of court politics. Someone from Internal Security would know more about stuff like that than I would—and rumor even at my level says that the minister is not well received at court. . . ."

She allowed her voice to trail off. Judging by Metadi's expression, he hadn't thought about that aspect of the problem before now, and he wasn't much liking it. After a while, though, he seemed to put the succession problem aside, and turned back to the holochart.

"I'll let Perada worry about how she handles the dandified hangers-on," he said. "You tell me about the Mages."

"They're out there," Gala said. "I've noticed a slight decrease in the frequency of their raids."

"That's good."

"Well, yes . . . except that it's counterbalanced by an increase in Mage activity in sectors not belonging to Entibor. The raiders may have done nothing more than switch their area of operations, and they may have done even that for reasons which have nothing to do with anything we've tried so far."

"Short of asking 'em in person, there's no way to tell." Metadi frowned at the graph currently filling the holodisplay. "Do we have anything on where they've been working lately?"

"Only from confidential agents—no one besides us would

show enough weakness to broadcast their troubles." Gala touched the chart controls again, bringing up a star map to replace the graph and illuminating the key points in bright red. "But what data we have puts the Mages working near Utagriet, mostly, with side trips to Artha and Bexevan."

"Artha belongs to Khesat, and Bexevan is a Miosan holding, right?" Metadi used the controls to add more colors to the map—blue for points in the Khesatan hegemony and yellow for the Miosan worlds. Then he added a third set of colored lights, this time bright green. "And all the volume around Utagriet—"

"—is claimed by Maraghai. Right." Gala studied the pattern the colors had revealed. It wasn't encouraging. "You know, General—I suppose I ought to be glad we've shoved off Entibor's Mage problem onto somebody else, but somehow I'm not."

Metadi grinned briefly. "If you don't watch it, the newsreaders are going to start calling you a Centrist. Speaking of which, are we offering information and assistance to other Mage targets?"

"Backdoored through Suivi Point in the case of Miosa," she said, "but yes, we're offering. And the responses range from none, to an accusation of complicity with the Mages, to twelve pages of tiny script in the most frivolous language imaginable, to the effect of 'no.' "

"That was Khesat, right?"

"Right. It came"—Gala shuddered—"with a musical score."

"I'm glad to see they're keeping amused over there. Did you remind them what happened to Sapne?"

Gala nodded. "Miosa accused us of starting the plagues ourselves and making it look like the Mages. And Khesat—in their reply, Khesat rhymed 'Sapne' with 'winemelon.' "

"But 'Sapne' and 'winemelon' don't rhyme."

"Apparently in Khesatan they do."

Metadi was silent for a while, looking at the star map. Gala couldn't tell what he was thinking, but she didn't believe he was pondering the oddities of Khesatan musical theater. Finally he said, "You haven't mentioned Maraghai. Is that the world which didn't respond?"

"Yes—but that's no surprise. Those people don't respond to anyone."

"The Selvaurs? They wouldn't." He paused and glanced at her sharply. "You didn't happen to imply that this was a problem they couldn't handle by themselves, did you?"

"I don't think that I did."

"If you did we're buggered. They're sensitive about their honor. Still—" Metadi looked thoughtfully at the green lights in the star map, and began to smile. "I have an idea. Let's take a trip to Maraghai. I want to have the Selvaurs tell me face-to-face that they won't go into a mutual defense pact."

"They won't talk to you."

"I think they will," he said. "Come on, Admiral. I've been stuck on-planet for months. Let's go."

Jos Metadi: Sapne
(Galcenian Dating 966 a.f.; Entiboran Regnal
Year 30 Veratina)

Emana Market on Sapne had never been a good port for free-spacers. The powerful merchant combines that handled most of the off-world trade preferred to deal with the shipping lines running out of Gyffer or Mandeyn. Independent carriers like *Meritorious Reward*—whose pilot/apprentice was a hazel-eyed youth giving his name, truthfully, as Jos Metadi and his age, somewhat less truthfully, as twenty years Galcenian—had to make do with onetime deals, mostly stuff either too small or too irregular for the big firms to handle.

Sometimes, if rarely, an independent could make a high profit carrying material that was risky to work with or that needed emergency delivery. The *Merry* had picked up one such cargo on Kiin-Aloq, a load of self-replicating antiviral agents in sealed metal crates, each crate stenciled with a fearsome list of handling instructions and a warning: IF NOT USED BY—a Kiin-Aloqan date in the perilously near future— DESTROY UNOPENED. To *Meritorious Reward*'s captain and crew, the bonus paid for a successful delivery in half the usual time more than offset the danger involved in making a high-speed run with hazardous cargo.

Not until the *Merry* set down at Emana market did anyone learn the truth of the situation: there was plague in the spaceport, fast-acting and deadly, and the shipping firms out of Mandeyn, Gyffer, and Cronn no longer stopped there at all.

"Pulled out and gone home," said the *Merry*'s captain to the members of the crew. "No reps left in port. The Red Shift Line lost a dozen crew members off one ship the last time they came in here, and that was all it took. Nobody's coming to Emana Market now but the little guys—and once the word gets out, they won't be showing up either."

He took a long drink of his cha'a. "*I* certainly won't be."

"That's all right for next time," said the *Merry*'s first mate. "But what do we do about the cargo?"

Silence fell over the mess table. The sealed metal cargo crates in the main hold suddenly took on an ominous, if invisible, presence at the meal. Jos Metadi paused in eating his reconstituted water-grain frumenty and tried to convert Kiin-Aloqan dates into the Galcenian ones used on the *Merry*.

"Two and a half ship-days," he said aloud when he'd done.

The others stared at him.

"Until the cargo turns bad," he explained. "That's all we've got."

The first mate looked at the captain. "The kid's right. And Sapne runs point-seven-five ship-days to one planetary. If we don't off-load those crates before close of local business hours, the buyer is likely to refuse delivery. And there goes our bonus. Hell, there goes our pay."

"It's consigned to Sapne Health and Ecology. I've been trying to raise them for an hour now," the captain said. "Nobody answers at the local office. I'm going to try the branches next. Meanwhile—" He turned to Lenar Covain, the *Merry*'s purser. "—you start talking to bankers on another comm line. I want the bonus transferred to our account as soon as those crates touch dirt."

"We can't lift without fuel, Cap'n," the chief engineer said. "Not and get anywhere useful after. This high-speed run took more than I liked."

"Sapne doesn't take off-world credit," the purser said. "Says so in the port guide. Until we get that bonus we can't pay for anything."

"Order it anyway," the captain said. "We'll pay 'em when we get paid. Now you all have jobs to do. Do 'em."

It was two hours, ship-time, before any response came in from Sapne H-and-Eco. *Meritorious Reward* remained ramp-up and lock-sealed. Jos occupied himself down in the main hold, helping to lash the heavy crates onto nullgrav cargo sleds and steer them into position near the loading doors. As the *Merry*'s pilot/apprentice he didn't have to work cargo, but sitting still and doing nothing had never been his idea of a good time.

Besides, the view from the pilothouse had spooked him. The grainy flatscreen monitors up there relayed images from the port outside, and the prospect wasn't encouraging: no atmospheric-craft activity in the open sky above Emana Market, no ground or low-level vehicles, no dockworkers. He'd seen ships, though, too many ships in port for the landing area to seem so dead. Time wasted dirtside was money lost, and the spacecraft on the landing field should have bustled with furious activity. Instead they were silent, ramps up and dark.

An hour before five-time, local, the captain and the loadmaster came down to the hold looking worried.

"All right," the loadmaster said. "We've got some people from H-and-Eco coming over to make pickup. They want those crates out on the field and ready when they get here, so get moving."

The crew swung into action. The loading gang took their places, two to a crate, and Jos hit the switch that opened the cargo doors. The multiply layered metal wall that was the hull of *Meritorious Reward* split and came gaping open. The stark blue sky and glaring sunlight of equatorial Sapne blazed into the shadowed hold, and the first of the cargo sleds began its rumbling progress forward.

A pod of high-speed cargo haulers from H-and-Eco roared onto the field as the last of the sleds cleared the hold. A driver and a freight handler—both wearing full protective gear, all the way down to masks, spats, and gloves—jumped out of the lead cab and started wrestling the crates into the back of their hauler.

"Come on!" the driver yelled at the *Merry*'s master rigger, a big Casheline named Treece. "Wind's gonna change. We better be gone before the dust starts blowin' or none of this stuff's gonna do any good."

"Then why the hell couldn't you be ready when we set down?" demanded the rigger.

"Nobody's left in the office here. We're from the next district over; came soon's we got word."

Treece swore aloud and turned to the other members of the cargo team. "All right!" he shouted. "You heard the man. The wind's gonna change—I want this job finished."

As each hauler was loaded it headed off to the east. The last of the crates went into place not quite a ship's hour later. Off to the west, a line of red, like a moving cliff, appeared—a dust storm, a big one, heading down. The last cargo hauler pulled away from the field so fast that its nullgravs howled under the strain.

"Seal her up!" Treece shouted, and Jos hit the button to bring the doors of the hold groaning shut.

The wind hit them before the hold could close and seal completely. To Jos, standing by the doors, it seemed as if an ocher curtain swept across the sky in a single instant, blocking out the sun. The red dust that the wind carried blew into the hold with enough force to scour metal. For a few seconds the entire cargo space was full of swirling, stinging grit; then the doors slammed and the plates interlocked and the wind died.

For a moment there was silence in the hold. Then somebody—Jos never remembered later exactly who—said, "You know, this is going to be a bitch to clean up."

Jos had to agree. Red sand lay drifted everywhere in lines and curls and whorls, like a message written in some exotic script. They could get rid of the stuff on deck without too much trouble using push brooms and vacuum hoses, but the grains that had worked their way into the cracks and joints of the cargo machinery would have to be gotten rid of the hard way, with hours of hand labor after the captain lifted ship.

But the *Merry* didn't leave port. At the mess table that night, Jos learned why.

"No money yet," said Covain the purser succinctly. "They can't put the chit through until local noon tomorrow, earliest."

"Why the hell not?" the first mate wanted to know.

The purser shrugged. "Most of the banks on Sapne are only working quarter-days. They say there's not enough staff left to keep them open any longer than that."

"Where'd they go?"

The purser took a sip of his cha'a. "Well, the way I understand it—they're all dead."

XIII.

DROPOUT. NOW."

Jos pulled back on *Warhammer*'s hyper-space engines and brought up the realspace engines in the same move. The grey quasi mist of hyper vanished like a morning fog under the sun, replaced by a deep blackness studded with stars. The '*Hammer*'s navicomp chittered and bleeped. Jos leaned back in the pilot's seat and stretched. "We're out."

"I noticed." Fleet Admiral Galaret Lachiel was sitting in the copilot's place more out of courtesy than as a practical matter—though Jos had to admit that she'd handled her share of the work capably enough to hold down a free-spacing berth if she ever wanted one.

Jos bent his attention to the switches on the main console, bringing them into the proper configurations for realspace running: life support, power, control. All the relays and monitors appeared satisfactory; he flipped on the intraship comms to check on the rest of the crew. "How's everything?"

"Looking good ventral," Tilly said over the link, followed by Nannla saying, "Clear dorsal. No targets."

"This is Maraghai," Jos said. "In this system there are no targets, except on my direct command."

He heard Nannla's faint alto chuckle. "Roger that, Cap'n. No vessels in sight or on the scopes."

"Good. Engineering?"

"All satisfactory, Captain," Errec replied.

"Very well."

It sounded odd, Jos reflected, to have Errec's voice coming up from engineering, instead of the familiar growling roar—but somebody had to take Ferrda's place now that the Selvaur had gone home. Jos thought again about getting another round of ship's-memory upgrades and adding some automation to the engineering spaces. He didn't trust machines as a rule, but he'd like to be able to fly *Warhammer* single-handed if he needed to. Even stripped to the bone, the ship needed at least three to lift, and from five to seven in the crew to make any kind of distance in safety, let alone comfort.

Fleet Admiral Lachiel stirred restlessly in the copilot's seat. "Where exactly is Maraghai?" she asked.

Jos tapped the Position Plotting Indicator screen where the navicomp data was being displayed. "Out there. Beyond sensor range. The navigational instructions for Maraghai are explicit. They don't want unannounced drop-ins."

"The way things are these days, I don't blame them."

"Neither do I—but everybody I've ever talked to says the Selvaurs were like this even before the Mages showed up." He touched the intraship comms again—"Stand by for braking"—then hit the lateral jets to spin *Warhammer* around her vertical axis. "Braking, now."

The engines fired again: a low rumble and a steady pressure, while Metadi watched the readouts on the panel.

"And . . . cut." He pulled the throttle levers to their closed positions. "Steady in space via maneuvering jets."

"Engines zeroed," came Errec's voice over the intraship comm. "Request permission to secure."

"Secure engines. Gunners, zero and secure your guns."

"Zeroed," Nannla said, and Tilly echoed her a moment later.

"Very well. I'll see you all in the common room in a few."

He clocked off the internal comm link and glanced over at Lachiel. The admiral looked back at him curiously.

"You know," she said, "I've read the instructions for Maraghai. You're going a long way beyond what they require."

"I'm playing this based on what I know about Selvaurs. I'm letting them know that I've come in peace, that I trust them completely, and that I expect us to be treated as their guests."

" 'Guests'?" The admiral laughed. "That's optimistic."

"Maybe. And maybe they'll leave our offer lying on the table, but if they take it up . . . Ready."

He picked up the external comm link. "Maraghai control," he said, speaking not in the Galcenian he and the admiral used for Fleet business, but in his native Gyfferan. "Maraghai control, this is Freetrader *Warhammer*."

A static-distorted roaring burst out of the external comms, making Lachiel flinch back. "What was *that*?"

"That was their reply," Jos said in Galcenian. He keyed the link again and switched back to Gyfferan. "Roger, Maraghai Control. Six humans on board. Request transit to the surface."

Another burst of noise filled the cockpit. Lachiel winced. "You can understand all that?"

"Yeah," he said. "They're testing me. Selvaurs trust their own kind first, people who speak their language second, people who understand their language third, and everyone else a distant fourth."

"So you're all the way up to third?"

"That's right. Near as I can figure it, they think that anyone who's learned to understand the Forest Speech has spent a lot of time around a Selvaur without getting killed, and that means they don't have to kill you out of hand as a bit of unfinished business."

Lachiel shook her head. "And the Mages attacked *these* planets too?"

"Looks like," he said. "Maybe the Mages want to keep us guessing about their intentions, or maybe they just don't know any better. . . ." He let his voice trail off.

"You forgot the other possibility," Lachiel said. "Maybe the Mages really are that strong."

"If I'd forgotten it, Admiral, we wouldn't be here." The external comm link came alive again before he could say anything more. After the noise stopped, he keyed open the link. "This is *Warhammer*. Roger, out."

He clipped the handset out of the way on the overhead and flipped on the *'Hammer*'s main beacon. Then he unstrapped himself from the safety webbing and stood up.

"Now what?" Lachiel asked.

"Now we go have some cha'a. We won't have to do anything for a little while. Not until they get around to sending a shuttle out for us."

"We won't be landing?"

Jos shook his head. "No one goes to Maraghai itself except in a Selvauran ship. If we were trading, we'd be on our way to one of their other worlds or moons. On Maraghai— there's nothing there but Selvaurs. They like to keep things simple."

"I thought there were some people living there too."

"Humans, you mean," Jos said. "The Selvaurs *are* people. In fact, if you ask one of them, he'll tell you that the Forest Lords are the *only* people. If he hasn't already ripped your face off for asking."

Lachiel smiled briefly. "With tempers like that, they must be a trial to the local authorities on other planets."

"Not really. Selvaurs never start fights."

At a drop-point near Entibor, the infinitely thin interface between reality and hyper rippled and spread apart. Sleek dark warships entered realspace one by one in good order, took their places in a cylindrical formation, and set course inward toward the planet.

Their arrival did not go unnoticed. The interceptor vessels

that circled Entibor in high orbit moved without delay into gun and missile range. More ships headed in to join them from waiting stations throughout the system. The surface of the planet bloomed with a myriad small fires as yet more Entiboran warships lifted to form a shield around the planet and its orbiting web of power generators, communications repeaters, and industrial platforms.

High above Entibor's south pole, the first vessels of the local defense forces came within range of the newly arrived ships. The Entiboran commander on-scene, Captain-of-Corvettes Orisa Graene, sent out a signal, blanketing all frequencies: "Stop and identify yourselves."

The reply came back in heavily accented Entiboran: "This is a diplomatic mission from Galcen. We wish to land."

"Maintain your position relative to Entibor," Graene ordered. Then she passed the word to her own gathering flotilla: "If even one of those ships gets any closer to the surface, shoot without warning."

Captain-of-Corvettes Graene used a low-security cipher for her second message, to make sure that the Galcenians had the chance to read it. Entiboran intelligence workers had long since broken all of Galcen's low-level material, and Galcen had undoubtedly returned the favor with interest. At least these days Entiboran Central Headquarters was giving its frontline people part of the overall picture, rather than none at all—the flow of information had picked up since the accession of the new Domina and the sudden retirement of an entire echelon of senior officers. Fleet gossip wasn't clear on what had happened that day; and Graene, who came from a respectable middle-class family on the colony world of Ghan Jobai, didn't have enough connections at Central or at court to get the real story.

She directed a grateful thought toward whoever or whatever had been responsible for the change, and got ready to send out a third message, this time to the planet's surface. She wasn't sure who would be making the decisions on the receiving end. Fleet Admiral Lachiel was absent from the planet, gone off on some sort of mission with the General of the Armies. Lachiel's second, Trestig Brehant, was currently inspecting the frontier defenses out beyond Parezul, a long way by courier from Entibor. Graene didn't know which officer at Central was third in line—but she hoped whoever it was hadn't left the office for a leisurely dinner.

She looked down at the datapad on which she had been enciphering her request for instructions. *If this is a diplomatic mission,* she thought unhappily, *leaving an ambassador to cool her heels on the doorstep might not be a good idea.*

"They can only shoot me once," she said aloud, and cleared the datapad. Quickly, before her nerve failed her, she wrote out a new signal: "Unless otherwise directed, I intend to escort the Galcenian ambassador to the surface."

Then she turned to her aide. "Get in touch with the Galcenians. Tell them that they can bring one ship to the surface, the one with their ambassador. Then make a signal to, let's see, *Gladheart* and *Bright Prospect.* Tell them to escort the ambassador's ship to the field at—" She paused, then shrugged. "Wippeldon is as good a place as any. If the ship deviates from its assigned path of approach, tell *Gladheart* and the *Prospect* to use their best judgment."

The aide raised his eyebrows, but said nothing. Graene caught his change of expression and gave him a rueful smile in return.

"And here we thought garrison duty was going to be dull and boring," she said. "By this time tomorrow, we'll probably wish that it had been."

Still feeling a bit bemused by their reception in Selvauran space, Fleet Admiral Lachiel followed General Metadi into the *'Hammer*'s common room. One of the gunners was already there—the Entiboran, Tillijen, whose family name Gala had yet to hear—sipping at a cup of cha'a.

"There's more fresh in the pot," she said as they came in. She spoke in Galcenian, but something about the faint underlying accent convinced the fleet admiral that Tillijen's Entiboran would be as proper as her own, or better. "Might as well grab a mug and get ready for the wait."

"It's not as if we've got a choice," Metadi said, heading for the galley. Over his shoulder, he added, "Time to pack a carrybag if you haven't already. We could be away from here for quite a while."

Gala nodded, but didn't leave the common room. She'd been living out of a carrybag since the 'Hammer lifted from Entibor, and packing up again would be a simple matter of sealing the closure. In the meanwhile, she could drink her cha'a and watch the rest of the crew drifting in from their stations: the dark-haired topside gunner who was Tillijen's partner, and Errec Ransome, copilot and acting engineer. Ransome had barely spoken to anyone during the voyage—he was not so much taciturn as invisible—but as far as Gala could tell, for him this was normal behavior. At least, the others never mentioned it.

After a while the silent waiting began to pall. Nobody seemed to feel like making idle conversation. The Entiboran gunner was closemouthed whenever Gala was around, and her partner followed her lead, while Errec Ransome was monosyllabic even at the best of times. Eventually Tillijen flipped on the holoviewer, but that didn't help either—there were no local signals. She turned the set off again.

Metadi drank his cha'a, keeping one eye on the bulkhead panel where local repeaters echoed the sensor readouts from the main console in the cockpit. Finally he set the empty mug aside and disappeared into his cabin. He didn't come out for some time—not until a steady beeping from the repeater showed a vessel inbound. Gala checked her chronometer, and noted with surprise that most of the apparent delay had been subjective. The Selvaurs hadn't taken long after all.

The cabin door opened and Metadi reappeared, carrybag in hand. Gala saw that he'd put aside his respectable Gyfferan outfit in favor of the clothes he'd been wearing on the day he first showed up at Central Headquarters—gold buttons and all. She realized that she wasn't looking now at the Consort, or even at the General of the Armies of Entibor; she was looking at Captain Jos Metadi, the noted—and notorious—privateer.

She raised her eyebrows. "The Selvaurs do know this is a diplomatic mission, don't they?"

"No, they don't," said Metadi. "Not officially. I didn't want to give them the chance to say no before I got there."

"So instead, we're giving them the opportunity to say no from right up close."

Metadi grinned briefly. "Something like that."

One of the readouts on the bulkhead panel changed from green to flashing red. At the same moment, a metallic sound from above told Gala that another vessel had mated with them at the 'Hammer's dorsal transfer ring.

"Right," said Metadi. "Let's go."

Gala and the members of the 'Hammer's crew picked up their carrybags and followed him to the transfer port. After that came the familiar and tedious business of cycling through the two vessels' mated airlocks; then, at last, a door that opened into the body of the Selvauran ship.

They were in a long compartment, high and metallic, with an arching, groin-vaulted ceiling like that of some antique great hall on Entibor. Along the walls, in between the metal ribs that rose and fanned out above, Gala saw body-sized patches of what looked like white foam. She didn't feel like asking questions aloud in an unfamiliar setting—no telling who might be listening in, or why—but she managed to catch the eye of Tillijen the gunner and project an air of curious inquiry.

"Passenger pods," said Tillijen. "Not much fun if you're used to watching what goes on, but it's the way they do things around here."

While she was speaking, Metadi had gone over to the nearest pod. He stepped backward into it, and the foam closed over him. Gala contemplated without enthusiasm the prospect of doing likewise. She'd never cared for being blindfolded and helpless, and the Selvauran pods came too close for both for comfort.

Come on, she told herself. *Are you going to be the last one in?*

Quickly, before her nerve could fail her, she picked out a pod and backed into it. The foam was body-warm and yielding; it flowed into place before she could close her eyes. She felt no irritation and no interference with her breathing. There was only a white fog in front of her face, and lukewarm, faintly synthetic-smelling air in her nose and lungs. She concentrated on the familiar sensations of acceleration and deceleration that were her only contact with what was going on outside.

Finally the cushioning foam broke away from her face and she was able to step free, clutching her carrybag in one hand. The door of the long chamber was open again, this time leading to a corridor walled on both sides with some unfamiliar substance cast into the semblance of great, overarching trees.

"Welcome to Maraghai," said General Metadi. "The next step is getting in touch with Ferrda. If we're lucky, he's got enough standing these days to help us connect with the people who run things around here."

"And if he doesn't?" Gala asked.

"Then we might as well turn around and head back home," Metadi said. "Because there's no chance they're going to talk to a bunch of thin-skins otherwise."

Festen Aringher sat on the veranda of the Mount Kelpen Lodge, drinking redroot tea spiked with Felshang brandy and feeling pleased with the galaxy. The mountains, bright and gaudy in their autumnal foliage, rose up behind the lodge; and from his position on the front veranda, he could look downward and out across the plain to the spaceport at Wippeldon. From time to time, between sips of tea, he lifted his binoculars to scan the landing field and the sky above it.

His vigilance—he'd been lounging purposefully on the veranda for several hours today alone—was rewarded. About midmorning, he recognized the distinctive profile of a Fleet messenger unit from Galcen, with a pair of Entiboran heavy surface-to-system fighters flying beside it on its approach. "*Bardalft*-class," he murmured under his breath, and was surprised when a voice behind him on the veranda said, "You have good eyes. What else have you seen?"

Aringher lowered his binoculars and turned his head to

see who had spoken. The new arrival was a tall young man of otherwise nondescript appearance, wearing the livery of the vintners' guild. He could have been waiting for half an hour, or a few seconds; his bland features revealed nothing, neither impatience nor boredom.

"Whom do I have the honor of addressing?" Aringher had his suspicions, but on occasions like this it always paid to observe the formalities.

The other didn't make a direct reply. "May I sit?"

"Of course."

The young man folded himself into one of the cushioned lounge chairs with a sigh of relief. "The time has come for you to take your proper role here—the one which Crannach delivered to you."

Aringher felt the flash of satisfaction that comes from seeing a theory confirmed. It was indeed possible that the newcomer worked for the vintners' guild—it was a nice respectable job, excellent cover—but this was one of the Galcenian agents whom he had been warned to expect when the day came. The civilized galaxy's politicians might not be Centrists, or anyway not enough of them were, but it was inevitable that sooner or later some planetary government would figure out the advantages of unity over local sovereignty. Nobody had expected the world to be prickly, custom-ridden Entibor; but one did one's best with the material at hand.

Aringher thought for a moment; under the circumstances it was best to say something significant and, at the same time, noncommittal. "There have been a number of new arrivals today," he said. "There weren't any for quite a while, but there've been at least five since I've been sitting here. After spending much time on-planet, one comes to anticipate them eagerly."

The younger man seemed to relax. "Is there a chance you could order up another cup of tea? I'd like to sit and watch the comings and goings at the field myself."

"I was just leaving," Aringher replied. "But you can walk along with me if you like. I was planning to go down to the port and check the boards for departures. I think it might be time for me to move on."

"I'd be honored to go with you," the other man said. "Maybe I can pick your brains on the way. I'm new here myself and I don't have a guidebook. Are there any decent stage plays in town?"

Nivome do'Evaan of Rolny, Minister of Internal Security for the Domina of Entibor, left his desk and turned to the window overlooking the inner courtyard. He frowned at the time-polished flagstone and the marble fountain as if he considered them responsible for his current dissatisfaction.

Moving the Domina's household back to the Palace Major had not improved matters as much as he had hoped. Perada remained unwilling to speak with him on anything other than business—as far as he could tell, she had no quarrel with his handling of state security, which meant that her reluctance was personal rather than professional.

His frown deepened. When it came to professional matters, he wished the Domina would pay more attention to some of the things he was telling her. There was, for example, the matter of an heir. He'd already warned her more than once of possible trouble if she didn't produce one soon. That was true enough. Under the crust, Entibor was far more volatile than he thought the Domina realized.

He also knew that Perada would want a new gene-sire for her next attempt. A man who had already produced a male would be unlikely to get a second chance—not unless he was able to bring the Domina something else of value besides the needful amount of fertile seed.

"My lord," said a messenger, breaking into his thoughts. Nivome turned. "Yes?"

"A ship is arriving. A Galcenian ambassador."

"The Galcenians already have an ambassador," said Nivome, frowning. "And this is a highly informal way of getting the news."

"We got an intercept of the report," the messenger said. "Central was going to bring the ship in—it's probably landing right now."

Central. Nivome wished, not for the first time, that Jos Metadi had left the Fleet headquarters alone. *Things were a lot easier back when the High Command couldn't blow their own noses without having a week of meetings first.*

"Where did you intercept the news?" he asked.

"Our trace on Ser Hafrey's communications."

Nivome ground his teeth. The old armsmaster had his hooks set in far too many fishes for a man with only a minor position in the Domina's household. Someday . . . He put the thought aside. "Hafrey has been spying on Central?"

"No. Someone there thought to pass the news direct."

"Ah. I see. Do nothing to Hafrey for now—but can you tell me who reported to him?"

The messenger shook his head. "I don't know. It came from within Central, we're certain of that much."

"That much isn't enough. I want to know who's feeding information to Hafrey before it reaches me. Find that person. But do it discreetly."

"Discreetly, my lord." The messenger bowed and stepped backward to leave. "I understand."

Nivome held up a hand to stop him. "One thing more— where is this new ambassador arriving?"

"At Wippeldon, my lord."

"Very well. Go."

The messenger left. As soon as the door had slid closed behind him, Nivome leaned forward to touch the comm link on his desk. He wondered if Ser Hafrey was listening to the Interior Ministry's communications, as he was listening to Hafrey's.

"Send my ground transport," he said as soon as the link clicked open. "And a note to the Galcenian ambassador. Tell him that I will meet him in his office in ten minutes."

Then Nivome straightened his considerable shoulders and walked from the room.

It had been a while since Jos Metadi had last gone dirtside on Maraghai—the previous visit had been part of a trading trip, made in order to dispose of some pieces of looted Mageworlds gear that the regular market couldn't handle—and he was glad to see that nothing had changed so far. Not surprising, really, since the Selvaurs weren't in the habit of making decisions in a hurry. With their long life spans, they could afford patience.

Not for very much longer, Jos thought as he and the rest of the 'Hammer's crew reached the end of the decontamination corridor. As usual, the decon procedures, whatever they were, had been subtle; the Selvaurs liked their mechanical devices unobtrusive to the point of invisibility. *The Mages have noticed this part of the galaxy; and I think the Mages are working faster than anyone suspects.*

Fleet Admiral Lachiel was looking about with a dubious expression. "This is all it takes to get on-planet?" she asked. "There are more checkpoints and paperwork to get from Felshang to Yestery back on Entibor."

"Don't let it fool you," Jos said. "We wouldn't have gotten this far if the Selvaurs didn't know who we were, and hadn't already decided to let us in."

"I see," said Lachiel. "So what do we do now?"

"We go where we're taken."

As Jos spoke, the doors at the far end of the long chamber opened up for them, revealing a vista of towering, forested mountains and one blessedly familiar Selvaur. Ferrda had cleaned off the metallic body-paint—it had been a formal outfit in honor of Perada's accession to the Iron Crown—but he was wearing the gold and silver studs in his crest. A little bit of privateering display, Jos suspected, kept up for the benefit of the folks at home.

Ferrda raised a scaly green arm in salute. *Ho, Jos!*

"Ho, Ferrda," Jos replied. "It's been a while."

You're not kidding. I thought you'd given up on the traveling life.

"Not exactly. I've got something in mind that could work out well for both of us."

Ferrda hooted derisively. *I should have known it wasn't pure friendship that brought you out this far.*

"You think I make deals with my enemies?" Jos contrived an expression on injured innocence to go along with his protest, and Ferrda *hoo-hoo*ed with genuine mirth.

You'd make a deal with Death's grandmother if you thought there was a profit in it, the Selvaur told him.
Which is the way it should be, among respectable freetraders like us. Come along—I have an aircar waiting.

The aircar was a big one, built to Selvauran scale, and it held all the *'Hammer*'s current crew, and Fleet Admiral Lachiel, in easy comfort back in the passenger compartment. At a gesture from Ferrda, Jos slid into the copilot's seat. Ferrda engaged the nullgravs to lift the car from the holding pad, then fed in power. The aircar rose to its cruising altitude, and the mountain slopes diminished to gentle folds of green velvet far below. Jos watched the landscape unroll beneath them for some time, waiting for Ferrda to start the conversation. No good had ever come of hurrying a Selvaur—the saurians did things in their own way, and thin-skins already had a bad enough name for rushing matters.

So tell me, said Ferrda, after sufficient time had passed that Jos was startled by the sudden vocalization. *Are you still standing at stud to the Domina, or have you come back to the hunting trail?*

Jos laughed and decided that it was a good thing Fleet Admiral Lachiel couldn't understand the Forest Speech. The soundproofing between the pilot's compartment and the rest of the aircar wasn't much to speak of, and he doubted that Lachiel would have appreciated the joke. He hoped that Nannla didn't take it into her head to provide the admiral with a translation.

"Some of both, these days," he said. "How about you?"

Hunting, mostly ... I got a big fanghorn this morning, and the skull ought to make an impressive courting-gift once I start looking around. I'm going to be roasting him tonight—would you like to come to the party?

"Wouldn't miss it for half the worlds in the galaxy," Jos said, and meant it. He had pleasant, if blurry, memories of the only other Selvauran party he'd attended; and if Ferrda was making ready to look for a wife in earnest, the guest list this time wouldn't be limited to the unmated hunters of the dirtside community. "How about the rest of the crew?"

Bring 'em all, just like last time. Even the skinny one in the fancy uniform.

"That's the fleet admiral," Jos said. "And don't let looks fool you; she's a hunter. She wouldn't be with me if she wasn't."

Errec Ransome: Captivity
(Galcenian Dating 970 a.f.; Entiboran Regnal Year 34 Veratina)

Errec woke slowly. His head ached and his mouth tasted foul. With a painful effort, he forced his eyelids open, then half-rolled, half-staggered to his feet. His knees felt weak; he braced himself against the metal bulkhead for support and took stock of his surroundings as best he could.

He was in a windowless, unfurnished room behind a closed door. His clothes had been taken away from him—the loose garments that covered him weren't his own. His staff was gone, and so were his boots.

The sound of air recirculating, and the faint vibration of the metal deckplates beneath the bare soles of his feet, told him that he was aboard a spacecraft. The lights above were too bright; he squeezed his eyes shut against them. They were the wrong color, too, the spectrum of a different sun from the one he was used to.

The gravity wasn't right, either. He suspected that he was on board one of the raiding ships.

Errec shook his head, trying to clear it. *A prisoner of the*

Mages. That was another wrongness. He ought to be dead; everybody else was.

His skull throbbed. In spite of the pain, he tried to reach out as he had been taught, letting his mind ride on the currents of Power to see what it could bring home.

Space surrounded him . . . deep space, the empty no-time no-place that meant the raider had already made its jump into hyper. He knew those echoing silences; he had brought ships through them and had enjoyed the work, in the days before he came to join the Guild. He searched farther and deeper, moving in and out of the flow like a glider on the air, looking . . . who was near?

The pain inside his head grew stronger. He wasn't alone on the starship; but the others, the living ones whose presence he could feel if he reached out far enough, all thought in strange patterns and odd symbol-sets. He couldn't understand them, and they made his head hurt in a way that had nothing to do with physical harm.

Then, abruptly, his will and his energy both failed him. His knees buckled and he slid down the bulkhead until he was sitting propped against it, his arms clasped around his updrawn legs.

Exhaustion claimed him; his head dropped forward and he slept. When he opened his eyes again, he found that the light, while still alien, was not so painful. He stood up, moving more easily this time, and walked around the perimeter of his cell—exploring, as best he could, the limits of his confinement.

The room had two obvious doors. One was locked. The other led to a waste-reclamation site and water source: a refresher cubicle, though not designed as he was accustomed. He caught some of the flowing water in his cupped hands and drank as much as he thought his uncertain stomach would tolerate.

The side of his head was tender where Master Guislen had struck him down. He put his head under the cold water, and ran his fingers through his hair to loosen the clumps of dried blood. When he was done, he returned to the other room.

Where the cell had been empty, now a tray of food rested on the floor. The tray was made of something light and soft: even broken, it wouldn't take an edge, and it wasn't heavy enough to be used as a bludgeon. Out of hunger, Errec tried the food. It didn't taste bad, and it didn't poison him. When the tray was empty, he lay back on the deck and fell asleep.

How long things went on in this manner, Errec couldn't be sure. The room didn't change in any way, not even by dividing the time into periods of light and dark. He was certain that he was being spied upon, both by electronic devices and by less physical means. The trained defenses in his mind felt a tickling probe of contact from time to time, whenever someone attempted to find out what he was thinking.

But he wasn't weak. Not that way. He resisted. And he watched—searching the currents of Power for the workings of those other minds, memorizing the traces that their workings left behind.

Meanwhile, the food continued to come at irregular intervals. It only arrived when he was in the second, smaller room, the one with the water. Once he stayed awake in the main room until his throat was parched and he began to hallucinate from dehydration and lack of sleep. Not until he lost the last fragments of his resolve and stumbled to take a drink—he was only gone a moment—did a new tray of food arrive.

When his strength returned after the failed experiment, he went back to searching the minds around him. The structure of their thoughts was alien at first, very alien. But he had been taught how to deal with that. He hadn't liked what he had learned from the Adepts on Galcen—he'd stayed with it only because the masters at Amalind had thought that his skills might someday be needed—but now, in his captivity, he made that training serve his own need.

He remained in the outer darkness, gathering impressions, determining how the minds around him thought and what the alien symbols portrayed. Then he pushed in deeper, and deeper again.

He was an interrogator. He would ask them the question. Sooner or later, they would answer.

XIV. Galcenian Dating 976 a.f.
Entiboran Regnal Year 3 Perada

AFTER SEEING what passed for a spaceport on Maraghai, Gala wasn't sure what to expect by way of domestic architecture. The aircar had been commonplace enough—a bit outsized in its dimensions and unfamiliar in its outlines, but nothing more unsettling than that. At length the craft settled down in what seemed to be nothing more than a forest clearing. Immense trees, their gnarled and furrowed trunks each one bigger around than the joined hands of the *'Hammer'*s crew could have encircled, thrust upward on all sides.

It took Gala several minutes to realize that not all the massive pillars in the shadow of the forest canopy were living trees. Some of them were the columns and corner posts of a house built on the same towering scale as everything else on-planet. From the air it had been invisible, its shapes and colors blending seamlessly into the tree-covered mountainside.

There didn't appear to be any sort of hangar for the aircar. Gala wondered if the Selvaurs had designed the vehicle on purpose to stay out in all weathers.

I'll have to take a closer look, she decided. *If that's the case, maybe we can learn a few things from these people even if they are green and scaly and never start fights.*

She picked up her carrybag and left the passenger compartment with the rest of the *'Hammer*'s crew. General Metadi and the Selvaur were talking about something. She heard the Selvaur, Ferrda or whatever his name was, make one of his hooting noises and saw him point toward a small tree on the edge of the clearing.

A second glance, and she saw that the tree wasn't a tree at all, but a wooden framework from which hung the bloody and gutted body of a monstrous beast. Stretched out so, with its forelimbs dangling downward, it was almost twice as long as Gala was tall—not counting the head, which lay on the ground nearby, propped up so that the sweeping, serrated horns wouldn't fall against anything and break.

Metadi caught her gazing at the barbaric display and gave a cheerful grin. "Fanghorn," he said. "Herbivore, believe it or not—they come down from the upper slopes to browse in the wetlands at dawn and dusk."

"Herbivore," said Gala thoughtfully. She moved in for a closer examination of the rack of horns, each flat tine edged like a tiny saw. "What do the predators around here look like?"

The General jerked a thumb at Ferrda. "Him."

"Oh."

"Don't worry. I told him you were a hunter too."

"I do my best," said Gala, "but I never brought home anything like that."

This time Metadi chuckled. "Mage warships will do just as well. Only drawback is, you can't cook 'em. That fanghorn, on the other hand, is going to be the guest of honor at this evening's party. Put on your fancy clothes, if you brought any; we're all invited."

"I'll stick with the uniform," Gala said. "It's the fanciest thing I've got."

Several hours later, as the evening worked its way toward its height, she was beginning to regret her decision. The great atrium of the house under the trees was full of Selvaurs in garish body paint, some of them with crested skulls and some without, and all of them growling and roaring in animated conversation. The handful of humans in the crowd—honored members of the thin-skinned community on Maraghai, or so the General had said—looked small and fragile in a setting built to the huge saurians' own scale.

Some of the guests were dancing, singly or in small groups. The music, mostly drums and horns, came from two or three sides of the atrium at once, and none of the musicians appeared to pay any attention to what the others were playing. The confusion of tunes and rhythms didn't appear to bother the dancers at all, or anyone else either. A few of the guests were singing songs in languages that Gala didn't recognize.

An open fire burned high in the stone-lined pit at the center of the atrium, and tables loaded with food flanked the pit on either side. It was the food, especially, that was causing Gala to have second thoughts about her dress uniform. She'd always considered herself to have a fairly cosmopolitan appetite—she'd eaten hedgeprickles baked in clay at a barbecue on Tanpaleyn, and she knew how to take apart an Immering Isle tree-crab without needing to use either the tweezers or the mallet—but this was the first time she'd ever had to confront an appetizer that seemed determined to crawl off her plate before she could eat it.

"Is it going to offend our host if I don't eat some of this?" she asked Tillijen under her breath.

"It depends," the gunner said unhelpfully. "If he caught all of those flybynights himself instead of trading for them, he might be a bit put out to have them ignored."

Gala swallowed hard and reached for the bone-handled knife that had come with her plate—a courtesy to thin-skins, Metadi had said, because they lacked anything serviceable by way of fangs and claws. The flybynight scrabbled ineffectually in its pool of sauce.

Now or never, she thought.

"It's not really alive," said Errec Ransome's quiet voice

in her other ear. "Not anymore. It just doesn't have a nervous system that's bright enough to get the message."

"I suppose it's wiggling around out of habit?"

"Well, yes." After a brief pause, he added, "Put the knife in right behind the head. That'll discourage it. And you might try washing it down with something."

"Stick to water," Tillijen said. She refilled her mug as she spoke—she was drinking something red and foamy that came in wooden kegs. "Unless you've trained to drink like a spacer."

The last sentence came out in accentless, if slightly tipsy, Court Entiboran. Gala looked at the other woman for a moment, then speared the flybynight behind the head with one jab of her knife and bit it in half. It kicked a little going down, but not much.

"I'll show you a spacer," she said, also in Court Entiboran, and took a long swallow of the liquid in her own mug. It was pale brown and sharp-flavored, with a serious kick to it. "I've spent more hours in hyper than you have alive."

The other gunner—the dark-haired one who came from who-knew-where—chortled with delight. "Oh, a challenge!"

She picked up a stone jug and a couple of turned-wood goblets from the table and poured out two equal tots of a thick green liquid. It had an oily sheen to it, and a bitter, medicinal smell. "Here you go—let's see which of you gets to high orbit first."

"You're on," Gala said, and picked up a goblet.

Festen Aringher and the young man from the vintners' guild made a leisurely progress through the colonnaded lobby of the Mount Kelpen Lodge and thence to the main garage. Aringher kept up a stream of chatter about the salubrious quality of the mountain air, the early onset of this year's autumn, and the probable quality of the brittlestem harvest, and the young man responded in kind. Not until they were in Aringher's hovercar and speeding down through the foothills toward the Wippeldon plain did another subject arise.

"I must admit," the vintner said as they drew near the outskirts of the city, "that I have a favor to ask of you."

"I'm all ears," said Aringher. "Well, actually not ... it would look distinctly odd if I were ... but I'm always glad to help out a fellow-creature in distress. Within the limits of my abilities, of course."

"Of course." The hovercar swung around a curve and past a landscaped shopping arcade before the young man spoke again. "I understand that you've met the Domina."

Aringher was silent for a few moments in his turn. "On a couple of occasions," he said finally. "I doubt she'd remember me, though—one face at a reception is much like another."

"I suppose you're right. But the other occasion was much less formal, or so my sources tell me." The vintner looked amused. "I'm sure that Her Dignity will remember the curtain cords, for instance."

"I'm sure. Though why you think that experience would encourage her to listen to whatever message I'm supposed to carry, I can't imagine."

The vintner didn't reply. Aringher steered the hovercar across traffic and into the sprawling lot of the shopping arcade.

"There's a travel office here that I always recommend highly," he said as the car sank to a halt. He opened his door and got out, leaving the vintner no choice but to do likewise. "They have a direct linkup with the port."

"I'll keep that in mind." The young man didn't say anything more until they were both walking through the crowded arcade. Then he said, "You're a part of the Domina's social circle—"

"You exaggerate, I'm afraid."

"Maybe. But if you ask at the palace for an audience, they aren't going to show you around to the servants' entrance."

"I suppose not." Aringher paused at a news kiosk and put a half-octime coin in the slot for a quick printout of the hour's top stories. The presence of a Galcenian ship at the

Wippeldon landing field hadn't yet made it onto the nets, but it was only a matter of time—of minutes, by now, rather than hours—before the word got out. "But if you want to send the Domina a message, there's a public comm link right here. If you need change for an octime . . ."

"This isn't a matter for jesting," said the vintner. "You are well known at home, and have the complete trust of a number of people. They believe in both your discretion and your reliability."

"Such touching faith," Aringher said.

"Nevertheless, you come highly recommended."

"I suppose I ought to be flattered. What exactly do our friends at home think that I'm suited to do?"

"Merely this: take a place in the court of Entibor, where speaking directly to the Domina is possible, and await instructions."

"My, my. That's all?"

The vintner didn't smile. "It's quite enough, I think."

"Well then," said Aringher. "In what form will the instructions come?"

"With this." The vintner passed over a flat package. "A textcomm. With a personal key, and the highest security."

Aringher tucked the package into the inside pocket of his coat. "If I recall correctly, this toy only works with a direct line of sight to a relay source."

"Don't worry. Such sources will be in-system soon."

"Quite. Thank you for telling me, and for telling the Minister of Internal Security. He'll have a transcript of this conversation within the half hour, if he doesn't already have it—and the minister, I have no doubt, will report it to the Domina. His loyalty, like mine, is complete."

As he spoke, he could see belated realization spreading across the features of the young man from the vintners' guild like an embarrassing puddle. With a smile, Aringher handed over his folded newsprint, entertainment section uppermost. "In the meantime, I'd suggest you take in this revival of *The Uncouth Stratagem* at the Festival Playhouse. I think you'll find it . . . appropriate."

* * *

Errec Ransome wasn't surprised when Tillijen and Fleet Admiral Lachiel embarked on what looked like being an epic contest. The two women had been regarding each other uneasily ever since *Warhammer* left Entibor, and the tension was bound to come to a head somehow—better Nannla's way than some other. At a Selvauran party, nobody was going to care.

The process was likely to take a while, however. Galaret Lachiel had tipped back her goblet of *urraggh* like a pro, and already a small crowd of spectators, human and Selvauran alike, was gathering around that end of the buffet table. Errec effaced himself and moved away. He liked Selvaurs, finding their thoughts admirably self-contained and unobtrusive, but their physical presence could be overwhelming. As for Tilly and Lachiel, with the green fire of the *urraggh* running through them their minds were wide-open enough to feel almost indecent.

The table on the other side of the fire pit was all but deserted, and Errec found a fresh platter of roasted barkbeetles going nearly untouched. He picked out a good-looking one and stripped off its legs—Ferrda claimed the legs were the best part, but as far as Errec was concerned they had too much shell and not enough substance—then popped the beetle into his mouth. A burst of hot liquid filled his mouth as the carapace cracked under his teeth.

He picked up another beetle and started to work on it, considering as he did so whether or not to have another mug of the Selvauran ale. Regretfully, he decided against the idea. Ale and *urraggh* might work to dim unwanted perceptions, but in this convivial crowd they were likely to relax him first, and he couldn't afford what might happen then.

He ate another barkbeetle and tried not to wonder too hard about what might be going on at the far end of the atrium. Jos Metadi and a handful of Selvaurs sat in a close group at the edge of the firelight, all of them laughing uproariously and eating as if a ten-year famine had been announced for tomorrow at 0900 Galcen Standard time. Errec had never tried to look into Jos's mind—there were some things he had promised himself he would never do—but the temptation was growing stronger. Whenever he swatted the thought away, it came circling back again like a persistent insect.

To distract himself, he went over to where the skinned and dressed-out fanghorn was hanging above the open flames, close enough to roast the carcass on one side but far enough away that part of the flesh remained blood-raw. Selvaurs liked their meat both ways, and a good host would see to it that the cooking, or lack of it, suited all tastes. Errec used his banqueting-knife to pull off a strip from the half-roasted portion, then ladled some of the herbs-and-blood dipping sauce into a small bowl.

Sauce in one hand and rasher of fanghorn in the other, he went out onto the wide porch that ran all around Ferrda's immense, sprawling house. Maraghai's moon—a twin planet, really, streaked with bands of vaporous color—was up and filling an enormous portion of the night sky. The clearing where Ferrda had landed the aircar was full of thin, watery light, and the shadows under the great trees were almost blue-black in their intensity.

Out of sight of the crowd, and insulated by distance from its perils, Errec was able to relax. He sat down on the porch railing, with his back against one of the fat wooden posts that supported the overhanging roof, and settled in to eat his share of Ferrda's roasted fanghorn in peace and solitude.

He'd finished the meat, and was sitting quietly in the darkness doing nothing in particular, when the door to the atrium swung open. A burst of noise spilled out onto the night air and a human figure stood backlit for a moment by the firelight before the door closed again. Galaret Lachiel, moving like someone with a profound need for fresh air, crossed the porch and leaned on the broad railing.

While Errec watched, the fleet admiral groped unhandily for something in the pocket of her uniform. He heard the faint ripping sound of a foil packet being torn open, and a muffled curse as Lachiel almost dropped the contents onto the floor of the porch. Then there was only a brief swallowing noise, and then silence.

Soberup pills, thought Errec, with a certain amount of sympathy—he'd been in the admiral's position himself a time or two. *The spacer's friend.*

He waited for a minute or two longer and then let himself become noticeable again. Lachiel turned her head slowly in his direction.

"Oh. It's you. Ransome."

"Yes." He didn't say anything more for a while. The shadows under the trees moved and shifted as the night wind freshened and grew colder. "Who won the contest?"

"Damned if I know." There was another long pause. "About the time we started singing the winebottle song, we lost count."

Errec laughed faintly. "I've heard that one a time or two. It's enough to make almost anybody lose count." He let the conversation lapse again into silence for a while—companionable silence, this time—and then said, "How's the rest of the party going?"

"Pretty well."

"Is Jos still talking with Ferrda and that crowd?"

"The last I looked." Lachiel shifted position in the darkness; Errec could sense curiosity stirring amid the fumes of *urraggh* that swirled in her brain. "You know him. What's he doing?"

Errec shrugged. "I'm not sure. Ferrda was a member of the crew during his young-wandering-time—"

"His what?"

"It's a Selvauran thing," he said. "Once they're full-grown, the elders kick them off-world—they can live on the other planets in-system, or on the Selvauran colony worlds, but they aren't allowed to settle down and raise a family on Maraghai itself until the elders say that they're ready."

"Tough luck if the elders don't like you, then."

"I suppose. But it keeps the home planet empty and primitive, and that's how they like it. The ones who want to come back—they spend the next three or four decades trying to get themselves killed."

"Really?"

"It works out that way in practice," he said. "The idea is to gain so much fame that the elders haven't got any choice but to let you in."

"And your Ferrda did that—how?"

"By being associated with Jos. Jos has some serious fame."

"I see," said Lachiel thoughtfully. "These elders ... the ones who make all the decisions ... they wouldn't be a bunch of Selvaurs whose hides have gone all grey and wrinkly, would they?"

"Like the Selvaurs Jos is drinking with? Yes."

Nivome strode into the office of the Galcenian ambassador without waiting for the receptionist to announce his arrival. If the ambassador was displeased by the interruption, the man hid it well. Palace rumor said that the Minister of Internal Security was not one whom it was a good idea to offend, and Nivome took pains to make certain the rumor spread.

"My lord Nivome," the ambassador said, rising and coming forward from behind his desk. "To what do I owe this unaccustomed pleasure?"

"Then you haven't heard?"

The ambassador looked blank. "My lord?"

"That you're going to be replaced."

"I'm afraid not, my lord." The ambassador had moved to extend his hand to the Interior Minister; now he let it fall, and his expression grew wary. "I shall query my government by the next available Galcenian courier—"

"The next available courier is landing in Wippeldon right now," Nivome said brutally, "and the new ambassador is on it."

"Your news is certainly ... interesting," the Galcenian said, his voice suddenly formal and cold. "May I beg my lord's indulgence?"

"Of course," said Nivome. His parting bow was deep but not especially respectful. "Of course."

Outside the ambassador's office, he walked down the velvet-hung corridor to the reception area, then out beneath the portico, where his hovercar and driver waited.

"Where to, my lord?" the driver asked.

"Take me to—no, take me to the Palace Major," Nivome said. "Call ahead and request an audience with the Domina."

"Yes, my lord."

Nivome got into the rear compartment of the hovercar. The vehicle rose and started off through the streets of the Embassy Quarter—an elegant, well-groomed district built up outside the boundaries of the city proper, in deference to the long-standing tradition that no power but Entibor had a seat in An-Jemayne. They had not gone far before the speaker from the front seat clicked on.

"My lord," came the driver's voice, "I am unable to reach the Palace Major."

"Why not?"

"There seems to be a communications breakdown." The driver paused a moment. "Consistent with jamming."

"Jamming?" Nivome checked his chronometer. The Palace Major was fifteen minutes away, assuming no traffic disasters along the route. He made a quick calculation. "Take me to Fleet Local Command. Do it now, do it fast."

"My lord." The interior comm clicked off. The hovercar accelerated sharply, taking its next corner at a speed that had it heeling sideways, and sped off on a new course.

The ride seemed interminable, but it was less than five minutes by the minister's chronometer before the gate of the Local Command Headquarters flashed past the windows of the hovercar. The driver pulled up outside the main building, and Nivome leaped from the passenger compartment before the car had settled to the pavement.

He dashed into the building through the closest entrance, where a low-level officer was standing guard. Nivome pulled out his palace credential and brandished it in the youngster's face.

"Where's the duty officer?" Nivome said, speaking loudly

but distinctly. "There's a problem at the palace. I want loyal troops there. I want them there *now*."

The party seemed to go on forever.

Gala's impressions melted into a confused blur of drums and music and an endlessly replenished supply of food and drink. She remembered Tillijen shooting an empty goblet off of Nannla's head with a full-power blaster burn, to the enthusiastic roarings and applause of an audience of Selvaurs, and she remembered joining with the gunner and her partner in teaching the winebottle song to the crowd gathered around the last of the ale barrels. And she remembered watching Jos Metadi and his friend Ferrda talking to one set of wrinkleskinned Selvaurs after another, all night long.

The moon had gone down and the first pale light of morning was filtering down into the atrium when Metadi left the Selvaurs and came over to join his bleary-eyed crew.

"Made it," he said.

Gala blinked. In spite of the soberup pills she'd taken, her head felt as if she'd stuffed it with some of the cushioning foam from one of the Selvaurs' landing pods. "Made it how?"

"The Selvaurs—the elders—they've agreed to cast in with Entibor." Metadi's tired features broke into a brief, feral grin. "We're going to take the war to the Mages and show those bastards what a real fight is like."

Ships, thought Gala, grinning back at him. *Trained engineers, the best in the galaxy* . . . "How soon can we get with their people to work on the details?"

"Not for a little while yet," Metadi said. "We have to go back to Entibor first."

"So how soon do we leave?"

"As soon as possible," Metadi said. "We have to get back home and arrange things to formalize the relationship between the two worlds."

Something in his voice made Gala uneasy. "Arrange what sort of . . . things?"

"Ambassadors. Port privileges. Giving them my firstborn son as a foster child."

"*What?*"

"It has to happen that way," he said. "Family to family. It's how Selvaurs do things."

There was a moment of profound silence.

"Oh, dear," said Tillijen at last. "The Domina will not be pleased. That isn't how Entiborans do things. Not at all."

Jos Metadi: Sapne
(Galcenian Dating 966 a.f.; Entiboran Regnal Year 30 Veratina)

MERITORIOUS REWARD didn't lift from Sapne Market on the next day, or on the day after. The red wind that had come howling into the open cargo hold, or perhaps the pod of cargo carriers from Sapne H-and-Eco, had carried the plague with it.

Treece, the master rigger, was the first to show symptoms. He complained at dinner that the sand from the windblast had made his skin itch—and indeed, the rigger's face and hands looked red. He seemed to have no relish for his meal, and left the mess table moving as if his joints and muscles pained him. An hour later, Jos found him collapsed on the deckplates outside crew berthing: still conscious, but too weak from pain to move, with drops of blood running from his nose and mouth and oozing out from beneath his tight-shut eyelids.

Jos hit the bulkhead button for intraship comms. The *Merry* didn't have a real physician on board—only the big shipping lines could afford a luxury touch like that—but the purser had basic training, a full kit, and all the medical data that ship's memory could hold. For most shipboard problems, that was enough. Jos punched in the purser's comm code.

"Treece is sick," he said as soon as the link clicked on. "He looks real bad."

"He's not going to be the only one," the purser said. "I just got through processing a slug of messages from over on *Wandering Star*. This thing's been hitting their crew too. It's fast and nasty. . . . Is Treece bleeding?"

Joe swallowed. "You got that one right."

"Damn. Looks like our luck's run out. Get him into his bunk and I'll be down as soon as I can get the kit together."

Jos half-carried, half-dragged the rigger to his quarters in crew berthing, a four-person cabin Treece shared with three other men from the senior crew. The purser showed up a few minutes later, looking worried.

"Whatever this is," he said, "it's new. There's nothing coded for it in the standard kit, and I can't find it in the on-ship data bases."

"Do the dirtsiders know anything about it?" Jos asked.

He couldn't help staring at Treece. The red flush on the rigger's face had worsened. He was burning with fever, and his skin had begun to peel and split. Blood oozed from his cracked flesh, and sweat mixed with blood stained his clothing and the sheets.

"I don't think so. It's spreading too fast for them to get a grip on it. In fact—" The purser selected an ampule from the medical kit, frowned at it with a dubious expression, and pressed it against Treece's arm. "—I'd say those pharmaceuticals from Kiin-Aloq were somebody's best guess at a solution. And offhand, I don't think they're going to work."

The purser was justified in his pessimism. Nothing in the *Merry*'s medical kit turned out to be of any use. Neither did the captain's attempts to reach somebody—anybody—from dirtside medical. Treece's fever climbed higher, his muscles cramped until he screamed, and shortly after ship's-midnight he vomited black blood and died.

By that time, three other members of the cargo-handling team had collapsed. By morning, two of those three were dead.

Jos still hadn't fallen ill. And since he was alive, he was detailed to help the purser—and when the purser himself fell sick, the first mate—take care of the rest of the crew.

It was a hellish time. One by one, the men and women aboard *Meritorious Reward* collapsed, bled, screamed in pain and delirium, and died. A few of those who were ill recovered, including the purser; and two or three people, like Jos, stayed unaffected, but those were the exceptions. The *Merry*'s first mate was one of the dead; a few hours later, the *Merry*'s captain was another.

But the time came at last when the sickness, if it hadn't yet ended, seemed at least to abate. When a full ship's day had passed without any fatalities or anyone new falling sick, the purser—as senior surviving officer—called a meeting of the handful of people who remained on their feet.

The surviving crew members of *Meritorious Reward* sat at one end of the long mess table; there were no longer enough of them to fill the seats around it. To Jos, they looked like a convocation of skeletons. He swallowed a mouthful of the high-energy rehydrating drink that the *Merry*'s medical data base had not very helpfully suggested for all hands, and tried to fix his weary attention on what was going on around him.

"What it all comes down to," the purser said, "is that there's not enough of us alive to lift ship even if we had the fuel. Our pilot's on the sick list. Maybe he'll get better, and at least we have his apprentice, but there's no way we can muster enough hands to cover everything else."

Jos knew that what the purser said was true. The *Merry* was a big ship for an independent merch, with enormous cargo space coupled to a massive power plant, and she needed her full complement to run. They could have worked it, maybe, for long enough to reach a safe port, if anyone from engineering had remained alive. But without the crew members who kept the *Merry*'s engines running on the good side of uncontrolled disaster, lift-off was impossible.

"So what do we do?" one of the other crew members asked finally. "Stuck in a plague port with a ship we can't lift—"

"We do the best we can under the circumstances," the purser said. "I've been talking to *Wandering Star*—"

"They're still here?"

The purser nodded. "Still here, still on the air. Same problem as us. Not enough hands. They've got an engineer—well, he signed aboard off a little short-hopper when his partner died, so I guess he's one of theirs now—but no pilot or navigator. We've got a pilot"—he nodded at Jos—"so they're willing to take us on as well."

Jos let the unexpected promotion pass without comment. If he could handle the work, getting his papers changed to make him a full pilot wouldn't be any trouble. And at the moment, he had other things to worry about.

"Why not take *Wandering Star*'s people on board with us?" he asked. "She's a *Libra*-class—it's going to be a tight squeeze if we go over there."

"Their engineer isn't qualified for work on anything bigger than a short-hopper like the one he came off of. He can handle a *Libra*'s power plant—just barely—but that's about the best he's good for." The purser shrugged. "Sorry. I've been all over this, and it's *Wandering Star* or nothing."

"What do we do about the *Merry*?" asked another of the surviving crew members.

"Leave her," said the purser. "Post a message for the bank to transfer our pay and the delivery bonus over to *Wandering Star*'s account—we can sort out who owns what shares later—but if it comes to a choice between getting paid and getting off this planet alive . . . well, I know which one I want to take."

XV. Galcenian Dating 976 A.F.
Entiboran Regnal Year 3 Perada

PERADA SAT in the informal reception room of the Palace Major, listening to the gentle plashing of the indoor fountain and the uncertain soprano voices of the An-Jemayne Children's Choir. Her mother's branch of House Rosselin had long been one of the choir's traditional sponsors, and the choir had customarily repaid the family's patronage with a private performance each year at the manor house in Felshang. Now that Perada was Domina of Entibor, the yearly recital had moved to the palace, and the young singers were so overawed by their surroundings that they could hardly keep on key.

Gentlelady Wherret and the Delaven Academy Glee Club, Perada reflected, could have done better any day of the week—they'd worked on most of the same pieces, in fact, and Perada knew the descant line of the *Lightbearer Canon* considerably better than the current singers did. But it wasn't done for the choir's patron to say as much; and if she broke from custom and did anything as radical as opening her mouth and singing along with the music, the choir director would die of mortification on the spot.

A quick flash of red light alerted Perada· to a message coming up on her infoscreen—a discreet panel set into the wall of the reception room at an angle not visible except from the chair of state. She turned her attention from the recital and watched the words forming out of the background mist:

HAFREY SENDS. NEW DEVELOPMENTS. NEW AMBASSADOR FROM GALCEN. YOU SHOULD MEET HIM PRIVATELY/INCOGNITO BEFORE ANY FORMAL PRESENTATION.

The time-tick on the infoscreen—and a quick glance at the elegantly calligraphed program in her lap—told her that the recital had at least an hour yet to run. Arranging her features into a regretful expression, she rose and made the demi-bow that even a Domina could give to art. Then she left the room by the side door that led to her private apartments.

Ser Hafrey was waiting for her by the doorway to her sitting room. "My lady," he said, with a bow of full respect. "I'm honored that you could come."

Perada returned his courtesy with a brisk nod. "Your warnings and suggestions have proved their worth more than once already. . . . You said something about an ambassador?"

"Yes, my lady," he replied. "Though in truth we do not know anything for a certainty, except that a ship approaches with someone identified as such on board."

Finally, she thought with a thrill of excitement. *A response from Galcen!*

"What do you think they want?" she wondered aloud, taking care to keep the emotion from showing on her face or in her voice. An arch-conservative like the armsmaster was unlikely to approve of her plans—her hopes, really; "plans" was too definite a word—for a permanent alliance of all the worlds threatened by the raiders.

"It's no secret that you've been seeking a mutual defense pact with Galcen, my lady," the armsmaster said. "And their current ambassador is not a man I, for one, would entrust with negotiations for anything more vital than a dinner engagement."

Perada smiled in spite of herself. "He does that much well enough, from the look of him."

"Indeed," said Hafrey. "But I suspect that he will find himself put out of his office by this new arrival—and that you will find yourself facing someone with both the authority and the skills to negotiate with you."

She recognized the warning for what it was, and nodded acknowledgement. "So. And why can't this person be presented to me here, like an other ambassador?"

"Incognito has its advantages, my lady. What the Domina says is law. What some minor aristo says is gossip."

"And a simple tourist isn't any ambassador, either. It cuts both ways. But I do like the idea of getting out of the palace. I assume you've already arranged—"

The door at the other end of the passageway slid open. Perada schooled herself not to show annoyance.

My private apartments are about as private as a shopping arcade. . . . I don't think there's one single lockplate in the whole palace that has my ID on it and nobody else's.

Her irritation faded slightly when she saw that the newcomer wore a Fleet uniform. "You have news?"

"From Central," said the messenger. "A report of a ship from Galcen landing on the field at Wippeldon."

He handed over a folded piece of stiff paper sealed with a wafer of gold foil. The Fleet might use voicelinks and printout flimsy to handle its internal communications, but when word went out to the Domina, only the best would do. If the best was slower, as it so often was, custom didn't allow a ruler to complain about the honor.

Perada broke the seal with her thumbnail. The contents of the message proved to be much the same as the news Ser Hafrey had brought, with the addition that the Fleet was going to put up the new ambassador in the Orgilan Guesthouse.

She passed over the message to Hafrey. "Where exactly is the Orgilan? I have to admit I don't know An-Jemayne as well as I ought to."

"It isn't far, if memory serves," the armsmaster replied. "I'm sure we can find it without undue trouble."

"Very well, then." She quit trying to hide her enthusiasm

any longer. Let Hafrey and the messenger think it was eagerness for a brief adventure—they'd be half right, anyway. "Let's go."

"You'll need an incognito, my lady," Hafrey reminded her.

"I hadn't forgotten," she said. "Will this do?"

As she spoke, Perada pulled off the Iron Crown and handed it to the Fleet messenger. She shook her head, and the half-dozen braids that had supported the black metal tiara, freed from their formal arrangement, fell onto her shoulders. The messenger was staring at her as if he'd never in his life seen a grown woman with her braids down—living in the Fleet, maybe he hadn't.

She took off her baldric of state and handed it to him as well.

"Keep these until I get back," she said. She turned again to the armsmaster. "I'm ready." .

Garen Tarveet—once a citizen of Pleyver, and now, he supposed, a citizen of nowhere at all—wasn't feeling as happy as he ought. The Palace Major was open to him, as the Summer Palace had been, but he wasn't deluded into thinking he was a person of any significance at the Domina's court. The rooms he had been given were comfortable, at least by the standards he'd grown used to at school, but the wing of the palace they occupied was clearly reserved for pensioned-off palace servants and the Domina's indigent relatives. For the former heir to all of Tarveet Holdings, it was a lowering experience.

He'd had more than enough leisure time to contemplate his declining fortunes. At least while the Domina and her entourage . . . he *hated* being thought of as part of somebody's entourage! . . . at least while the Domina's household was in residence at the Summer Palace, he'd been able to talk with 'Rada' once in a while. Nobody else on Entibor seemed to have a proper appreciation for galactic politics; as far as most of them were concerned, the universe ended at the edge of the planet's atmosphere. As for Captain Metadi . . . *General* Metadi, thanks to 'Rada! . . . if the man couldn't carry a thing off and sell it he probably didn't believe it was real.

Here in An-Jemayne, though, Garen never got a chance to discuss things with 'Rada at all. Every hour of the Domina's working day was filled with formal audiences and informal receptions and traditional presentations of everything from dramatic performances to giant wheels of cheese. The long-range plans they'd talked about so often and worked out so carefully seemed to have been forgotten altogether.

He spent his time, most days, as he did today: reading translations of what passed for political philosophy here on Entibor and nibbling on the small hard biscuits that people in An-Jemayne liked to serve alongside their wine. He didn't care for the wine, but the dry pastries had a brittle, dusty flavor that suited his prevailing mood.

Trash and drivel, he thought, scowling at the text reader in his lap. The book it displayed was supposedly written by the foremost political philosopher Entibor had ever produced. Garen was not impressed. *The author should have given thanks that breathing is controlled by the autonomic nervous system—if he had to think about respiration in order to do it, he would have turned blue and died.*

He didn't hear his door slide open, and didn't look up until a familiar but unexpected voice broke into his concentration. "Garen! Come on—I think I need you!"

It was Perada. With her long hair hanging down in half a dozen braids and her eyes lit up with excitement, she looked like a schoolgirl on a spree. Hafrey the armsmaster stood a little behind her, looking grave and reserved as usual. Garen thumbed off the text reader and put it aside.

" 'Come on'? Where are we going?"

Perada grinned at him—a most unroyal expression, and one that Hafrey obviously didn't approve of. "To see the Galcenian ambassador," she said.

Garen sneered, more or less as a reflex. "*Him?* Whatever for?"

"I think our chance has finally shown up," she said. "These are new envoys, just arrived from Galcen. I need you to listen while I talk—help me find out what's on their minds. You've studied this a lot more than I have. You can tell me if what they're saying makes sense or not."

"My lady," said the armsmaster. Not impatiently; Hafrey was never impatient, any more than a ticking bomb was impatient.

She waved a hand at the older man. "Yes, yes—are you coming or not, Garen?"

"I'm coming," he said.

He followed her out of the room and down through the backstairs portions of the Palace Major, with the armsmaster a watchful shadow at their heels. Somewhere in the basement depths, they came to a tunnel of arched stone where a hovercar was waiting. Once they were settled into the hovercar and on their way, Garen turned to Perada.

"This is unusual," he said. "There's already one Galcenian ambassador here in An-Jemayne—why send out another one?"

"I don't know why," Perada said. "That's what I want to find out, and I want you to help me. In fact, I want you to do the talking."

Garen felt his ears turning red. "It won't work."

"Why not?"

"I'm an outlander. I don't have any status in your court. And I'm a terrible liar. If I tried . . . he'd see through me in a moment."

"Oh." She paused, looking at him for a moment with sharp blue eyes. Then she turned to Hafrey.

"Witness me," she said to the armsmaster. "I am creating this man a citizen of Entibor. I am creating him Lord Meteun."

She turned back to Garen.

"You are now the lord of one of the districts in the northern hemisphere, including a seaport and a spaceport, and open lands adjacent to the royal park surrounding the Palace Minor. Your duties include advising me on economic and interstellar matters."

The Domina relaxed again in her seat. "So now you don't have to lie."

Lord Meteun. Garen contemplated the name uneasily.

"Wouldn't there already be a noble by the name of Meteun? How is he going to feel about having his title coopted?"

"I am the Domina," Perada said. "And there isn't a Lord Meteun anymore. The last one was in Veratina's day, and the family line ended with him—no females in that generation."

"My lady," said the armsmaster. He was looking out of the heavily reflective window of the hovercar, and something about his voice and expression made Garen nervous.

Perada followed Hafrey's gaze. "Yes—what is it?"

"We're going too slowly." Almost before the armsmaster had finished the sentence, he was working the latch on the hovercar's passenger-compartment door. He kicked the door up and open with both feet. "Get out! Assassination! Jump! Move, move, move!"

Long skirts and yellow braids flew wildly as Perada flung herself out the open door. Garen recognized the tuck and spin; they'd practiced it three days out of every week in gymnastics class at the Delaven Academy. He'd never been very good at it.

He didn't have the chance to hesitate. Hard fingers caught him by the upper arm, and the armsmaster half-pulled and half-slung him out the door after Perada. More of the academy's gymnastics lessons had stuck with him than he'd expected; in spite of the awkward exit, he hit the ground in a creditable if bone-jarring roll. A few seconds later, Hafrey joined him, and they dashed toward the public comm-link kiosk where Perada had taken cover.

In the street behind them, the hovercar exploded.

Garen saw a blaster in the armsmaster's hand, and wondered where it had come from—but not for long, as an instant later bolts of red and green fire started coming down at them from the roofline on both sides of the street. Hafrey began firing back. Garen couldn't tell if he was hitting anything or not, but the fire from above slackened.

The armsmaster fired a single bolt at the wall ahead, where a closed door blocked the way to safety. The door swung open. Garen saw Perada throwing herself into the dark interior. A moment later—without ever having a very clear memory of how he traversed the open ground to get there—Garen was inside the building also, with the armsmaster close behind him.

Perada was breathing hard and the color was high in her cheeks. "Are they likely to come after us?"

"Not immediately," said Hafrey. "Once the targets are out of the killing ground, most ambushes are useless. But we may be dealing with optimists; pending arrival of security troops, I suggest we relocate ourselves."

"Very well," Perada said.

Garen, for his part, was happy to defer to the armsmaster's expertise in the matter. They were in the downstairs vestibule of what looked like a low-rent office block. A flatvid notice display filled the back wall with a list of suites and occupants. There was a set of lift doors on one side of the vestibule and another door on the opposite side with a label on it in Entiboran block letters. Judging by the graphic posted next to the label, the door opened onto the emergency stairs.

The armsmaster gestured in that direction. "Up," he said. "And back."

They headed up the narrow stairway. Another emergency door opened onto the second-floor landing; Hafrey pushed the door open and they went out into an empty corridor. Perada spoke for the first time since they had left the downstairs lobby.

"Who knew where we were going?"

She had her breath back, and her face was set and pale. Her voice had an edge to it that Garen had never heard her use before. He realized, with a sense of shock, that Perada was no longer a schoolgirl excited by her close escape, or even a young and frightened woman. She was the absolute ruler of a planet and all its colonies, and she was angry.

"Who knew?" she demanded again.

The armsmaster remained calm. "I knew," he said. "The driver knew. Anybody who was eavesdropping on our private communications also knew."

"And somebody tried to kill me. Do you think it was done out of general discontent with me and my policies, or do you think there was a specific cause?"

Hafrey remained unruffled. He was palming lockplates and rattling doors on either side of the corridor—looking, Garen guessed, for a door that would open and let them through.

"It could be either one, my lady. But if you're asking me for a professional opinion, I'd say it was specific, and designed to prevent you from meeting with this new Galcenian."

"Who does that leave us with?"

Hafrey shrugged. "Anyone who knows or can guess at the Galcenian's mission. Nor can we leave out the possibility that the Galcenians themselves sent this ambassador, for no other reason than to draw you away from the palace without a guard."

"I see," said Perada. "You will provide me with a list of suspects, in order of likelihood. And include on your list yourself, with a convincing reason why it couldn't be you who arranged this affair."

"My lady—" Hafrey began.

Perada ignored his protest. "After all, Ser Hafrey, I'm certain that the Minster of Internal Security will be eager to provide me with a convincing reason as to why you *could*."

Nivome do'Evaan didn't wait to see if the officer at Fleet headquarters obeyed his order. Later, if the man failed him, there would be time for making the entire Fleet regret the oversight—but right now there was too much else to do. Instead, the Minister of Internal Security turned and strode back to his hovercar.

"Get me to my office," he told the driver. "The one in the old Executive building—*not* the palace. Stay well clear of the palace."

The hovercar rose and surged forward through the city streets with a flagrant disregard for safety and traffic regulations. The driver had worked for Nivome long enough to know that the wrath of the Interior Minister was more to be feared than any slight problem with the officers of Domestic Security.

Nivome spent the time during the ride drumming on his

thigh with his fingers. Once inside the Executive building, he snapped to the receptionist, "Get all the department heads in my office. Immediately."

By the time he'd taken the lift to his top-floor suite, the department heads—who hadn't needed to come as far—were all assembled in the outer waiting room.

"Right," he began at once, not bothering to move on into the inner office. "Who has a location on the Domina?"

"She left the palace a few minutes ago in an unmarked hovercar," said the head of Royal Intelligence. "She was with Hafrey and that friend of hers from Pleyver. Garen somebody."

"I didn't ask where she isn't," Nivome snapped. "I want to know where she is."

The head of Royal Intelligence flushed and pulled out his pocketlink. "One moment."

Nivome cut him off with a chopping gesture. "No electronic discussions. Face-to-face only."

The head of Royal Intelligence left, and Nivome turned back to the others. "All right, the rest of you. I am issuing arrest warrants for Hafrey the armsmaster and for the Galcenian ambassador—both Galcenian ambassadors—hell, any damned Galcenian you can find. I want to know what happened to communications with the palace, and I want to know who in this office is leaking information to Hafrey and the Fleet."

"All of that without using electronic comms?" said the chief of staff.

"All without electronic comms. Now get to work!"

The department heads scattered like leaves before the wind. The head of Royal Intelligence, returning, had to fight his way through the crush at the office door. Nivome regarded him impatiently.

"Well?"

The other man caught his breath. "Her Dignity's hovercar has been located at the intersection of Fairing Street and Mercers' Row. The car is on fire and the Domina herself has not been located."

"Locate her. Wait. You and I are going to locate her. But first—"

Nivome stepped into his inner office. There was a safe on one wall, disguised as a framed scrap of late-Diffusionist tapestry. He hit the safe's ID plate with one hand and reached inside with the other as soon as the door slid open, bringing out a heavy blaster on a dark leather gunbelt. He strapped on the belt, then reached into the safe again to pull out another, smaller weapon.

"Here," he said to the head of Royal Intelligence. "Take this. We're going to the intersection of Fairing and Mercers'."

"What am I to do with my wretched reputation?" Festen Arlingher asked himself. The open countryside blurring at high speed past the windows of the railcar obstinately refused to supply him with an answer.

Even to him, his decision to buy a ticket on the first available pod-rail leaving Wippeldon for An-Jemayne looked like he was going to break his long personal rule against getting involved with politics.

"Imagine. To be thought reliable. By politicians."

He shook his head and told himself not to be so hasty. Not every plan launched by the Galcenian Council came to fruition. They prepared for potential events as much as for real ones. The chances were that no call would ever arrive on that little machine now packed among the socks in his carrybag.

"A philosopher. I should be more of a philosopher," he said at last, as the railcar slid into its berth at the An-Jemayne Transit Hub.

He left the hub pod-rail station and ambled through the main concourse like a man with nothing in particular on his mind. Behind the façade, he chewed frantically over the questions of where to go and whom to speak with in order to gain an audience—informal and private—with the Domina. He could hint at great knowledge. He could strike up an acquaintance with a familiar and attempt to worm his way in that manner. He could disguise himself as a lady's maid and go to the employment office. . . .

This wasn't getting him anywhere. With an effort, he

forced his wayward mind into more sober channels. By the time he reached the front entrance of the concourse, he had something that passed for an idea. He summoned a hovercab and requested transit to the Palace Major. By the time the cab was halfway to the palace, he had worked up the idea into a definite plan—thanks in part to the young man from the vintners' guild. He rummaged for a moment in his carrybag, looking underneath the textcomm and the extra change of clothes to pull out a folded piece of black velvet.

I knew this would come in handy.

Aringher smiled a little to himself as he drew one of his personal cards from his jacket pocket and wrote a note on the back: "One whom you helped to tie up with curtain cords requests the honor of your ear for five minutes' time."

He tucked the note inside the folded cloth. Now to see if the young Domina in fact had the mischievous sense of humor he thought he'd glimpsed in her that night in Waycross. He'd been wrong about people's characters before, but not often—with luck, he hadn't lost the knack.

The hovercab bumped to a stop and settled to the ground. Aringher rapped with his knuckles on the panel separating him from the driver.

"What's going on?" he demanded.

"Don't know. Traffic's stopped."

Aringher craned his neck to look beyond the grounded cabs and buses lined up ahead of them. He didn't like what he saw. From the direction of the Palace Major, itself out of sight beyond the tall buildings close by, something that looked like a column of smoke was drifting lazily skyward.

He popped open the hovercab door and stood on the mounting step for a better view. It was smoke, all right—and unless he'd lost his eye for distance completely, the bottom of the cloud was somewhere close to the palace itself.

Then he heard on the wind, from somewhere off to the right, the sound of blasters firing.

"What do you know," he muttered. "My mother did raise a fool."

He stripped off a twelve-octime note and tossed it to the driver, and sprinted toward the sound of the guns.

Perada Rosselin: Entiboran Crown Courier
Crystal World
(Galcenian Dating 967 a.f.; Entiboran Regnal
Year 31 Veratina)

T HE ARMSMASTER, Ser Hafrey, was an elderly
man—almost as old as Zeri Delaven. Perada
hadn't met him before. She supposed that Felshang Province hadn't been important enough for someone from the
Palace to bother with. *She* hadn't been important enough,
not until now.

The library at school had genealogies and tables of succession for every planetary monarchy in the civilized galaxy. In
the years between her mother's death and now, Perada had
studied the ones for Entibor over and over again. House Rosselin . . . House Chereeve . . . House Lachiel . . . Whenever
somebody died, the pattern changed. But she'd never expected to find herself Domina-in-Waiting; there were too
many people left alive to get in the way.

Something must have happened, she thought. *But what?*

As soon as the courier ship reached hyperspace and the
"danger" light over her stateroom door quit flashing red, she
went in search of Ser Hafrey to ask him questions.

The armsmaster wasn't in any of the staterooms, nor in
the dining salon, nor on the observation deck, where curv-

ing walls of armor-glass made windows onto a field of stars. A year or two ago, Perada would have thought the stars were real; now she was old enough to know better. There wasn't anything visible in hyper—"just funny-looking grey stuff all over the place," Garen had said—so the view of deep space outside the glass walls of the observation deck must be a holovid.

An iron staircase led in a tight spiral down from the observation deck to the deck below. Keeping a firm hold on the railing, she descended. There was a force field at the bottom of the staircase, probably to keep idle passengers from disturbing *Crystal World*'s crew. An abstract holovid that looked like a colored waterfall hid whatever parts of the ship lay beyond that point.

Perada halted on the second step from the bottom. "Ser Hafrey?"

"A moment, my lady," came the armsmaster's voice from beyond the shifting colors of the holovid. "If you will be so good as to wait for me on the observation deck . . ."

Perada felt disappointed—she'd hoped for a chance to see what the working part of a starship looked like—but she said, "Yes, Armsmaster," and went back up the steps. She sat and watched the imitation starfield until the sound of footsteps on metal told her that Ser Hafrey was coming up the iron stair.

He came onto the observation deck and bowed to her, a very deep bow, the way the majordomo at home had always bowed to her mother. Perada wasn't certain she liked it. Nobody at school bowed to anybody else; it was one of Zeri Delaven's rules, like always packing your own bags.

"You wished to speak with me, my lady?"

"Yes," she said. "Ser Hafrey, why am I the Domina-in-Waiting?"

"It pleased the Domina Veratina to make you so," the armsmaster said. "She has the right to name whomever she chooses, since she has no heir of her body."

"I know about *that*," Perada said impatiently. "They even talked about it at school."

Ser Hafrey looked disapproving. "The matter is scarcely fit gossip for schoolgirls, my lady."

"It wasn't me," she said. "It was a class in the upper division. 'The Entiboran Succession Crisis,' they called it. Because people kept dying."

Mother too, she thought, but didn't say. *And Dadda. And the baby.*

She'd figured that much out for herself already, from listening to the upper-division students and from reading the archived newsfiles and holos in the school library. Zeri Delaven had never spoken to Perada of how her family had died, but the newsfiles had told her more than enough. Maybe aircars did explode by accident sometimes—but Perada didn't think so.

"Exactly, my lady," said Ser Hafrey. "The Domina named you as the heir to put a stop to talk like that."

Perada frowned. The armsmaster was being stupid, not understanding what she was trying to say politely, the way Zeri Delaven said that people should talk. And she didn't think the armsmaster was a stupid man, which meant that he was doing it on purpose. *I don't like that,* she thought, and decided not to bother with being polite anymore.

"She wanted to stop people killing each other, didn't she?"

Hafrey looked at her for a moment, up and down. She couldn't tell what he was thinking.

"Yes, my lady," he said. "When quarrels among the Great Houses disturb the citizens and become casual gossip in schoolrooms across the galaxy, a Domina must take action."

"But why did Great-Aunt 'Tina pick *me*?" she demanded. "There's *lots* of other people she could have named instead."

"None of the others are Shaja Rosselin's child."

As answers went, it was no answer, and Perada knew it. She also knew—the charts at school had made a lot of things clear to her—that she was the only candidate with no family, except for Veratina, living.

So she doesn't have to worry about Mother, or Dadda, or little Beka. Only about me.

Perada nodded. Let Ser Hafrey think she was agreeing with him; she was really agreeing with herself.

"But what if the other people don't want me to be Domina-in-Waiting?" she asked. "Won't they try to kill me, too?"

The armsmaster smiled faintly, for the first time.

."No, my lady," he said. "I am charged with your safety. Regardless of what the rivals among the Great Houses might wish, none of them are likely to dare an attempt."

XVI. Galcenian Dating 976 A.F.
Entiboran Regnal Year 3 Perada

My lady! My lady!"

The words had a strong Galcenian accent, the kind that made the syllables sound like they'd been measured out evenly and cut to length with scissors. Perada stopped and turned, frowning a little as Ser Hafrey moved to place himself between her and the speaker. She craned her neck a little for a clear view and saw a well-dressed man of middle years trotting up the street toward them. He held a scrap of black cloth in one hand.

"My lady," the man repeated as he came nearer, "I believe you dropped this."

"'Rada, do you know this person?" Garen muttered in her ear.

"We've met once or twice," she said.

Once, at least. She clearly recalled seeing the man lying trussed with curtain cords on the floor of the Double Moon. And the scrap of cloth he was holding was the half-mask she'd worn as part of her incognito on Innish-Kyl, for a tête-a-tête that had ended with blast beams in a darkened alley. Another day of blaster fire, and here he was again.

Garen took the mask and handed it to her. She glanced at it. Masks were anonymous by definition, but this one was thick velvet lined with satin, as hers had been, with double-sewn tabs and a stiff interlining to give it shape—good quality, and either her own mask or its near-twin. A square of white pasteboard slid out from between the folds.

There was writing on he back on the card, in Galcenian script: *"One whom you helped to tie up with curtain cords requests the honor of your ear for five minutes' time."*

She tucked the card into the pocket of her gown, then lifted the mask to put it on. Hafrey looked dubious.

"My lady, I'm not certain it's safe. You don't know this man—"

"Oh, but I do. And I'd like to know him a good deal better. In fact, I think I want to know everything about him." Masked now, she turned back to smile at the man from the Double Moon. "Absolutely everything."

The man lost none of his aplomb. "I blush to admit," he said, "that our previous meeting was both informal and hurried. How should I address your ladyship today?"

Perada strove to match his air of unconcern—a hard thing to do, with her pulse still racing from the ambush, but she managed. "I am Gentlelady Wherret of Arenvel, and this"— she nodded toward Garen—"is Lord Meteun."

The man made a quick bow after the Galcenian manner. "Your servant, my lady. I am Festen Aringher, late of Galcen, sometime of Suivi Point, and now a roving philosopher."

"I see." Perada considered him for a moment. "Gentlesir Aringher, you are most convenient in your arrival. As it happens, we're on our way to pay a call on one of your fellow-citizens . . . if you would be so good as to come with us?"

Ser Hafrey had been listening to the conversation with a growing air of extreme disapproval. "Gentlelady," he said in his most severe tones, "we must proceed before the opportunity is lost. Surely you can issue this gentlesir an invitation to attend you later, at court?" .

"No, I can't," Perada said. "After our last meeting I lost

track of him, and I don't want to misplace him a second
time."

Garen was frowning at Aringher. "Weren't you at the
formal reception after the old Domina's public burning?" he
asked. "You had a holorecorder, and I thought you were
some kind of news collector."

"Holovids?" Perada wrinkled her nose, grateful for the
mask that hid her involuntary grimace. "Did you make one
the other time, too?"

"Unfortunately," said the Galcenian, "no. I had no inti-
mation that the spectacle to come would be so entertaining."

"Indeed? Then there are limits to your philosophy."

"Gentlelady," Hafrey said again, "this is neither the time
nor the place for miscellaneous pleasantries. We must bid
the gentlesir a good day, and be about our business."

"Lead on, then," she told him. "But Gentlesir Aringher
comes with us."

Hafrey sighed. "As you will, my lady. As you will."

They walked on in silence for another block. Hafrey set
a quick pace; Aringher for his part kept up without trouble,
and seemed unaffected by either the armsmaster's suspicion
or Garen Tarveet's hostility. Perada found the lack of conversation oppressive—but since the situation was at least
partly her doing she didn't feel she had the right to complain.

Garen spoke first, which wasn't surprising. Ser Hafrey
was capable of remaining silent forever if he wanted to, and
Gentlesir Festen Aringher appeared serenely unaware of the
chilly atmosphere.

"There aren't a lot of people on the street," Garen said.

Perada glanced about. She saw one or two other people,
well off in the middle distance, but not the crowds she
would have expected on a midday street near the center of
An-Jemayne.

"You're right," she said. "There aren't. Maybe the explosion and the shooting scared them off."

"I don't think so. By now we should have people coming
out to see what the commotion was all about."

Gentlesir Aringher cleared his throat. "If you'll look over

to the left," he said diffidently, "you can see something that looks like smoke rising from the palace. Perhaps the crowds are there."

"We have to hurry," Ser Hafrey said. "If there's trouble at the palace we don't have much time."

They hastened their footsteps.

"I'm not familiar with this part of the city," Perada said. "How much farther do we need to go?"

"The Orgilan Guesthouse isn't far," Hafrey said. "Once we're there, you can transact your business and be done."

Aringher regarded him with curiosity. "We haven't been introduced," he said. "But if I may be so bold as to ask—what exactly is your function in the government of this planet?"

"I have no function in the government," said Hafrey. "I am the armsmaster. I teach the use of weapons to members of the Ruling House, and maintain their collections of armaments."

"How fascinating."

"It is that," Hafrey said. "For example, I recently completed the restoration of a tabletop agonizer dating from the reign of Marfa the Second. Perhaps you'd like to see it put to use?"

"I'd be delighted," Aringher said. "My days are spent in the pursuit of knowledge."

"Days like the ones you spent recently at the Mount Kelpen Lodge overlooking the Wippeldon spaceport—until the very moment a Galcenian courier landed there, whereupon you departed for An-Jemayne as rapidly as transport could be bought?"

Aringher raised his eyebrows. "My goodness—you certainly are observant."

"Like you, I'm a student of human nature."

"Gentles," Perada said, "I hate to interrupt such a pleasant conversation, but the street is emptier than it was a few minutes ago. If this goes on, I'm going to start feeling conspicuous."

"It doesn't matter," said Hafrey. "We have arrived."

The Orgilan Guesthouse was a brick building with marble

steps and an ornamented pediment, after the style of a previous century. Perada started up the steps. Garen followed; but before Aringher could do likewise the armsmaster stepped in front of him.

"Gentlesir, I must insist that you remain outside."

The Galcenian shrugged and fell back.

Perada said, "No. Gentlesir Aringher comes with us."

"Gentlelady," Hafrey said, "this is most improper."

"You forget yourself, Armsmaster," she told him. "I'm the one who says what's proper and what isn't. It's not for you to decide."

Hafrey bowed. "I serve," he said, and she thought she heard him sigh. He stepped out of Aringher's way, and the four of them entered the building together.

Inside, the Orgilan was sedate but luxurious. Heavy curtains in the downstairs windows blocked out the noises and distractions of the city outside, and thick carpet hushed their footsteps. The walls, paneled in slabs of cut stone in swirling patterns of green and grey and shimmering metal, reminded Perada of the visual artifacts that filled the Pleyveran Web. The memory unsettled her—there had been people shooting at her that day, too.

I wish Jos were here, she thought. *This is Fleet territory, and he knows how to talk to the Fleet.*

They climbed the stairs in silence to the second floor. A single officer waited outside the closed door of one of the rooms. At a word from Ser Hafrey, he touched the lockplate and the door slid open. Perada let the armsmaster go first over the threshold, according to custom, and entered the room herself when he gave the nod. Garen Tarveet and Gentlesir Aringher trailed along behind.

The room was a sitting room like any one of a hundred others in An-Jemayne: chairs, a settee, a low table, autumnal flowers in porcelain vases, an old-style fireplace retrofitted with a ceramic heat-bar. A vaguely familiar man in clothing of Galcenian style and cut rose from one of the chairs and bowed politely as she came into the room.

"Greeting, Gentlelady," he said in fluent, if accented,

Entiboran. "I am Vannell Oldigaard, empowered to speak for the Galcenian Council."

Oldigaard, Perada thought. *That explains why he looks like somebody I ought to know—he's one of Elli's uncles or cousins or whatever.*

"Be welcome, Gentlesir Oldigaard," she replied in Galcenian. "I am Gentlelady Wherret. The Domina sends her greetings, and asks me to make you acquainted with Ser Hafrey, a member of her household, and with Lord Meteun, her economic advisor."

Oldigaard bowed again. "Ser Hafrey, Lord Meteun."

"They have the Domina's ear," Perada said. "And if I may speak for a moment on my own behalf—please greet, also, a compatriot of yours, Gentlesir Festen Aringher."

The Galcenian envoy favored Aringher with a stiff nod and turned to Perada. "If I may introduce my own associate—"

"Please do." Perada became aware, somewhat belatedly, of another man standing behind Gentlesir Oldigaard. *Where was he a moment ago?* she wondered. *How could he do that?*

Then she took in the man's austere black trousers and tunic, and the long staff of polished wood that he carried in his right hand. Her question was answered: Vannell Oldigaard had brought an Adept with him from Galcen.

"My advisor on matters of strategy and security," Oldigaard was saying. "Master Guislen."

Fleet Admiral Galaret Lachiel woke up with a pounding headache. She opened one eye and winced at the yellow sunlight that poured down through the row of windows high up along one wall. From where she lay, she had a view of rough-hewn wooden roof beams and part of a massive doorframe. The posts of the door were stripped and polished tree trunks, half again the height of a tall man, and the skull of something large and carnivorous grinned down at her from the rustic lintel.

We're still on Maraghai.

She closed both eyes again, feeling relieved in spite of

the physical discomfort. Selvauran parties weren't easy on the thin-skinned guests, and she was glad General Metadi hadn't taken literally his determination to leave as soon as possible. Even with the help of soberups, she hadn't been fit to lift ship when the celebration ended, and neither had anyone else in the *'Hammer*'s crew.

She had a vague memory of Ferrda showing them to the guest wing of his big, rambling house—lots of porches and covered walkways and rooms that seemed half open to the outside air—and telling them that they could den up with him for as long as they needed to. She didn't know enough about the length of Maraghai's days and nights to judge how long she'd slept.

Long enough, I think. We need to go back home and make certain everything's in order there. There'll be time to talk ships and guns with these people after the papers are signed.

And after we bring back the kid.

Gala flopped over and buried her head in the pillow with a groan. She'd forgotten, for a moment, about Metadi's bargain.

Her Dignity isn't going to like it one little bit.

She groaned again, then pushed herself out of bed and began dressing. Her carrybag had made it into the bedroom somehow; maybe she'd carried it in herself after all the drinking and singing had faded into the grey of early morning. At least she had a clean uniform to put on. She wanted a turn under the sonics to shake the sweat out of her pores and the sleep-fuzz out of her brain, but she didn't think she was likely to get one. The Selvaurs acted like people who thought it was more fun to stand underneath a freezing waterfall.

Worse than that, she thought as she struggled to pull on her boots. *They act like people who'd* build *a freezing waterfall if the place they lived in didn't come by one naturally.*

She sealed the fasteners on her tunic and ran a brush through her hair. Then—because the habit of years remained strong—she made up the long, wide bed and put her wrinkled clothes away in her carrybag before pushing open the door and stepping out onto the wide veranda.

The pungent, bitter aroma of fresh-brewed cha'a told her that someone else was awake. She let the smell guide her along the veranda and down a covered walkway to an open-sided dining shelter—little more than a shingled roof over a table and benches. A self-powered galley urn stood on the table, surrounded by empty mugs and flanked by platters of fruit and cold meat. *Warhammer*'s two gunners were already there, and so was Errec Ransome; she didn't see Ferrda or Jos Metadi.

Gala filled a mug with cha'a and drank it without speaking while she waited for the stimulating effect of the drink to click in. She eyed the breakfast table suspiciously, but the smoked sausages and slices of cured meat lay quiet and behaved with proper circumspection.

She poured more cha'a into her empty mug. "Where's the General this morning?

Tillijen and Nannla looked at each other and then at Errec Ransome. The Ilarnan shrugged. "With Ferrda, I think. Doing sworn-brotherhood stuff."

Gala reached for a slice of the cold meat, then thought better of it and opted for a segment of pink-fleshed melon instead. The sweet, slightly acid taste washed away the lingering residue of booze and soberups. She ate it all, then took a second piece and nibbled on it between sips of cha'a.

"Does it have to do with that deal of his?" she asked.

"I think so," Ransome said. "Getting him tied in to all Ferrda's connections and obligations, making him family—Selvaurs are very concerned about family."

"So are Entiborans," said Gala. "Unfortunately."

Tillijen nodded. "You've got that right."

Nannla picked up a blue ovoid from the fruit tray and began peeling the skin away in strips. The pulp inside was bright yellow-green.

"Tell me something," she said. Her manner was casual, but her voice and eyes were not. "How much trouble is Jos going to get into over this?"

"A lot," said Tillijen.

"Maybe," said Gala. "We're dealing with a placeholder, not the heir. Nothing says treaties can't be made that way."

"By people who have the right. Jos doesn't."

"We'll be fine as long as Perada doesn't repudiate the alliance," Gala said. "Or name a new Consort. Metadi's the one who lit a fire under Central Command when nobody else could; if she ditches him now, we're dead meat."

"Hell with the alliance," Nannla cut in. "What about Jos? He's too sentimental for his own good anyway—if Her Dignity throws him out, it's going to take somebody else a long time to patch him back together again."

In the upstairs sitting room of the Orgilan Guesthouse, Gentlesir Vannell Oldigaard had at last worked his way around to talking business. Perada hadn't learned yet whether the envoy was a Galcenian councillor himself, or simply authorized to speak in the Council's name—not that it mattered, since any promises he made beyond his original instructions would have to be ratified in Council later. She wondered if Oldigaard knew she realized as much, and decided that he didn't.

The new *Domina's just a schoolgirl,"* somebody probably told him. *"Make all the concessions you have to; we can always repudiate them later."* It's a good thing this schoolgirl stayed awake in Gentlesir Carden's history class.

"It is the Council's belief," Oldigaard was saying, "that a joint effort to drive the raiders from those areas of space claimed by us and by our trading partners would best be carried out under a unified command, with the backing of a unified political unit. To this end, we believe that it would be best for Entibor to place its fleet under—"

The tramping of heavy boots drowned out the rest of the sentence. Perada heard the voice of the Fleet officer outside the door raised briefly in futile expostulation. Then the door of the sitting room slid open and Nivome do'Evaan came stalking in with half a dozen Internal Security guards at his back.

"Arrest them," he said to the guards. "Him, him, him"—pointing as he spoke—"him, and him."

The guards pushed into the room and started putting binders on everybody insight—even Master Guislen. Nivome turned to Perada. "Gentlelady, will you accompany me?"

She made no move to rise. "Call your people off. This is a private conference and under my protection."

"As an incognita, you have no protection to give. Let me speak with you privately."

"Very well," Perada said. She stood up. "In the meantime, treat these others with respect."

She headed for the door. Nivome nodded to the guards in a "you heard the lady" gesture, and followed her out into the hall. The Fleet officer who'd stood guard at the doorway was gone—Perada hoped that the guards hadn't arrested him, too, in an excess of patriotic enthusiasm—and the corridor was empty. She walked a little farther, to make sure of being out of the Galcenians' earshot, and turned to face the Minister of Internal Security.

"Gentlesir Nivome," she said, and took off the mask. "You had something to say to me?"

"Do I speak to the Domina?"

"For simplicity's sake—yes."

"Then you should know, Your Dignity, that the Palace Major has come under assault."

The smoke, she thought. *It wasn't just the hovercar.*

"Who did it? Was it—" She remembered the reception after Veratina's burning, and the hovercar that had come crashing through the windows with its fearful cargo. "—was it the Mages?"

"No, Your Dignity, it was not."

"Then who?"

"The members of the group appear to comprise a number of officers from your military forces." He glanced back at the room they had left. "And the Galcenians have chosen today to start new machinations of their own. The coincidence has not escaped me."

She drew a deep breath. Her hands were shaking; she couldn't tell if it was from anger or from fear. "And because of this . . . this *coincidence* . . . you decided to break into my private negotiations with an extraplanetary ambassador? Gentlesir Nivome, I have entrusted the security of my palace and my government to you. I do not, however, recall appointing you to my diplomatic staff."

Nivome bowed his head briefly, accepting the rebuke. "Your Dignity, may I speak plainly?"

"I thought you had been." She sighed. "Oh, go ahead."

"Thank you, Your Dignity. Bear with me, then. Your policies have not met with universal approval among the merchants and the aristocracy. To be frank, they suspect you of harboring Centrist leanings."

"Because I tell them we can't defeat the Mages alone any more than Galcen can, or Khesat, or Maraghai? That's not Centrism, that's the truth."

"And it's thinking so that makes you a Centrist," Nivome said. "At least, to certain of your subjects. And as long as you have no direct heir, those subjects will find excuses to plot against you. Your only guarantee of safety—"

"—is to provide myself with a daughter. Rest assured, I shall endeavor to do so."

"Your Dignity," he said, "you are, at this moment, both nongravid and fertile. With all respect, the carpet on the floor here is quite soft."

She felt an angry rush of blood to her cheeks. "If you want to be gene-sire to the Domina-in-Waiting, you have strange ideas about the best way to advance your cause."

This time he did not back down, but met her eyes squarely. "I am, as you have reason to know, fertile. Is your Consort? If so, he has shown little evidence."

"And *you* produce males!" Perada snapped back. "Don't deny it—just last month, Karil Estisk registered you as gene-sire to her son. No. I will not risk it."

"Then find someone more to your liking, only do not delay."

Perada drew a deep breath. Sometime during the argument her hands had clenched into fists, and she could feel the fingernails digging into her palms like knives. She forced her fingers to uncurl, then spoke to the Interior Minister with all the calm civility she could muster.

"The subject, Gentlesir Nivome, is closed. As for the attack on the Palace Major—"

"Your Dignity need not concern yourself. I took the matter in hand before proceeding here."

"In that case," she said, "we have nothing more to discuss."

She put on the velvet mask, then stepped past the Minister of Internal Security and went back to the sitting room. Between the Galcenians, the guards, and her own entourage, the elegant chamber had become uncomfortably crowded.

"Gentles," she said, "I apologize on the Domina's behalf for any inconvenience you may have suffered. Gentlesir Nivome do'Evaan of Rolny is the Domina's Minister of Internal Security, and his zeal for her service sometimes outweighs his wisdom."

She paused for a moment, and watched as the guards unfastened the binders with which they had confined Ser Hafrey and the others. Garen was pale with suppressed indignation, and kept rubbing his wrists as if he had bruised them. When all the men were free, she continued.

"The Domina has further informed me that henceforth the seat of government and the official residence of the Ruling House shall be the Summer Palace. Gentlesir Nivome will see to your transportation."

Oldigaard looked flustered. "Your Dign—Gentlelady Wherret, this is most irregular. I'll need to contact my ship."

"Your message will be carried," Nivome said. "In the meantime, since the Domina has ordered it—" He paused and looked at Perada. "—transport awaits."

"Excellent," she said. She glanced over at Garen. "Lord Meteun—please continue your discussion with Ambassador Oldigaard during the journey."

Oldigaard harrumphed. "Strictly speaking, Gentlelady, I'm not yet the ambassador, since I haven't presented my credentials."

"You can present them at the Summer Palace," she said. "I'm sure Her Dignity will forgive any small irregularities."

* * *

Captain-of-Corvettes Graene watched the status board on the bridge of her ship and tried not to make matters worse by drumming her fingers on the edge of the comp console. *Gladheart* and *Bright Prospect* had escorted the new ambassador's vessel safely dirtside, but the other Galcenian ships were still out there: numerous, uninvited, and armed.

She hoped that the courier she'd sent out looking for Trestig Brehant found him before too long. She wasn't senior enough to handle a sensitive development like this, and she didn't like having to do it. Even less did she like the fact that nobody at Central had assumed command as soon as she made her report.

What's the problem? Did everybody down there get paralysis of the brain as soon as the General and the fleet admiral had to leave the system?

The status board blinked into life. She leaned over the comp-console officer's shoulder to interpret the signals, and swore under her breath. More dropouts, coming fast and thick—"Somebody must love me. Whoever those guys are, they aren't us and they aren't Galcenian either."

"I'll tell you who they are," said the comp-console officer. "I saw ID signatures like that once before, off Parezul. Those are Mages."

Graene straightened her shoulders. She wasn't senior enough to handle a development like this one, either, but it looked like she was stuck with it. She forced a deliberate lightness into her voice.

"Galcenians at our back. Mages in system space. Who *invited* all these tacky people?" As soon as the burst of nervous laughter from the crew had died, she continued. "Report to Central, then get me an intercept course on those dropouts."

She turned to the crewmember on comms. "Make a signal to the Fleet. 'Mage ships entering the system. Attack and report.' Send to all units, inserting the coordinates and all other data we have."

"What about the Galcenians?" the comp-console officer inquired.

"We'll send them a thank-you note when this is over. It's

because of them that we're as ready as we are—if they hadn't shown up looking big, bad, and dangerous, we'd still be scattered all over local space."

Graene frowned. Having the fast, heavily armed Galcenians frighten the Home Fleet into readiness was a good thing; having them available to throw against the incoming Mages would be even better. She wished she had the authority. . . .

"Patch me through to Central and ask—no."

Central had been sitting on its collective hands ever since this mess started. Once the Mageships made contact, she couldn't afford to wait while crucial messages lay unattended on somebody's desk. Better to explain at her court-martial why it was that she'd bypassed Central than how she'd managed to lose the battle. She started over.

"*Inform* Central of the situation. Then get me the senior Galcenian commander. Tell him the Entiboran commander desires a face-to-face conference on the subject of unified command."

Jos Metadi: Sapne
(Galcenian Dating 966 a.f.; Entiboran Regnal
Year 30 Veratina)

THE PURSER was the last one off *Meritorious Re-*
ward. He turned at the sealed hatch, and, with
the help of two of the junior cargo clerks, put a stencil
across the metal: THIS SHIP IS NOT TO BE CONSIDERED ABAN-
DONED PROPERTY, SALVAGE, OR WRECK. FORWARD ALL MONIES
DUE FOR CARGO TO ACCOUNT 4816576, MERCHANTS' COOPERA-
TIVE CREDIT UNION, SUIVI POINT, IN NAME OF FT WANDERING
STAR. LENAR COVAIN, CAPTAIN, ACTING, MERITORIOUS REWARD;
FOR, SMYTT AND TRUBRUK, OWNERS.

"Right, then," he said. "That's the last paperwork I'll do
on the *Merry*, I think. Let's go."

The little party—less than a third of the *Merry*'s original
muster roll, counting those on stretchers—made their way
across the field to where *Wandering Star* stood on her landing legs under the crisp sky. As Jos walked across the field,
he saw drifts of the red sand around the legs and fins of
other ships, and, beside one ship with an open ramp, a half-
fleshed skeleton facedown on the hardpack.

A woman, black hair streaked with grey pulled back from
her face, met them at the top of *Wandering Star*'s ramp.

"Captain Covain?" she said, her outplanets accent making the vowels sound twice as long as they should. "I am Captain Maert. Please to come aboard, you and yours."

Maert's clothing was far more informal than anything worn by the party from *Meritorious Reward*. Rather than the customary merchanter's gear of unicolored coveralls with a ship's emblem on the sleeve, she wore a velvet waistcoat, a spidersilk shirt, and a scarlet cummerbund over trousers tucked into high boots. Jos had seen her kind around the ports—hard drinking, free spending—the small independents who ran fast, worked armed, and died young.

"I think we should be leaving soon." she said, her sibilants drawn out into long hisses by the unfamiliar accent. She led the party forward through work-scarred passageways to a vaguely circular common room—mess hall, recreation area, and overflow bunk space all in one, with a miniature galley in a closet-sized nook off to the side.

"Do you have acceleration pads for everyone?" Covain asked.

"No, but we do our best, eh? Sick men get pads. Those with no pads, stand against aft bulkheads and hold on tight. Where is your pilot?"

"Here," Covain said, indicating the stretcher with Jos standing beside it.

"Him? Can he fly?"

"Not the sick one. The boy."

"Aye. Well, go you both forward. I see you there soon."

Jos went forward, strapping the master pilot into one seat behind the forward windows and himself into the other. He looked at the command console. Someone had used red plas-tape to relabel all the controls in a script he couldn't recognize, but the layout looked standard, if old-fashioned, and the basic functions—throttle, course, turn—were plain. He picked up the clipboard with the launch checklist he had carried over from the *Merry* and began running it down.

"Rated/certified pilot in command seat, check," he said, looking to his left, where the master pilot lay strapped, eyes squeezed shut, lips moving in a constant, soundless muttering. Jos went down the list. "Engines on-line. Engineering reports ready to reply to all orders. Check."

Captain Maert walked into the bridge, and began strapping herself into the remaining seat. "Are you ready?" she asked.

"Ready, Captain. Where are we going?"

"We figure that out after we make orbit."

"Oh." He paused and glanced at her over his shoulder. "Captain, if I may be so bold, why aren't you flying yourself?"

"Until last week, I was gunner. First time up here."

"Right," Jos said. "Last step on the checklist. Contact inspace, Captain."

"Do so."

Jos reached forward and pulled the handset for the exterior comms out of its clip. He keyed on the link.

"Sapne Inspace Control, Sapne Inspace Control, this is Freetrader *Wandering Star*. Request permission to lift ship. Over."

No answer came back—only the howl of an open carrier frequency. The master pilot cried out as if the noise hurt him, and Jos hastily keyed the link off again.

"They give permission," Captain Maert said. "Make orbit, pilot."

Jos looked for the nullgrav switch. Found it, and pressed. The *Star*'s nose came up hard.

"Stand by, everyone," he said, and pressed the throttles forward to what he hoped was escape position. The engines fired hard, their response far quicker than what Jos was used to aboard the *Merry* with her greater mass and greater inertia. Acceleration pushed him back against the cushions of the copilot's seat. Then the glow of superheated air cleared, the sky darkened, and the stars came out.

"Make orbit," Maert said. "When you do, come back to the common room. There is much to discuss."

But before the discussion could take place, there was another detail that needed attention. Three more crew members on the sick list had died during lift-off, the *Merry*'s master pilot among them. The dead were cycled out of *Wandering Star*'s airlock, and their personal effects were put under seal in number-one cargo bay.

XVII. Galcenian Dating 976 A.F.
Entiboran Regnal Year 3 Perada

FROM THE window of her twentieth-floor apartment in the Celadon Towers housing block, Mistress Anije Vasari could see smoke rising from the Palace Major.

She stood and watched for some minutes as aircars and gyroflits circled the palace complex. At first the majority of them bore the insignia of the Ministry of Internal Security; then the white and grey of the IS craft gave way to the brighter hues of Fleet On-Planet units. Had this been an ordinary disaster—a kitchen fire gone out of control, say—she'd have expected Domestic Security and Emergency Response instead.

"I wonder if our pals in the black robes had a hand in this?" she wondered aloud.

The local newsreaders hadn't been much help. Vasari could recognize a security-imposed blackout when she saw one. A few hours ago she'd caught a brief flurry of stories about a Galcenian ship landing at Wippeldon under Fleet escort—and after that, nothing. The holovids, for their part, barely acknowledged the existence of trouble at the palace;

their reporting, done at a discreet distance from the Security lines, would have served equally well for a pod-rail crash or an explosion in a fuel refinery.

She turned away from the window and went back to her desk comp, where she'd been drafting an interim report for Master Otenu when the first news stories began to break. A copy of the unencrypted plaintext filled the main screen.

> ... I haven't yet convinced Errec Ransome to sever his ties with Jos Metadi and return to the Guild, but I believe that I've planted the idea in his mind. I'll keep working on it whenever the opportunity presents itself, but there's a limit to what I can do. Even if the idea of coming back isn't, strictly speaking, his own, the decision will have to be.

She contemplated the final paragraph for a moment, then sat down at the desk and added a few more lines.

> There currently appears to be a civil disturbance in progress at the Palace Major. I don't know who is responsible—possibly the situation is nothing more than Entiboran politics as usual, which is to say, vicious—but considering the level of known Mage activity on this planet, I think a bit of personal investigation is in order.
>
> I'll encrypt this and send it before I leave my apartment. If all goes well I should be able to send a follow-up within the next three local days.

A few more commands to the desk comp, and the encrypted message began its journey through the mail nodes to the commercial data-transport service that would carry it to Galcen. Vasari wiped all traces of the plaintext and set the comp to cycling the apartment through a looped facsimile of its daily routine. With her absence hidden at least from casual snoopers, she left the Celadon Towers and started out on foot for the Grand Plaza and the Palace Major.

* * *

At the far edge of the home system, a courier ship blipped out of hyper into Entiboran space. The vessel began driving in toward Entibor, transmitting Ophelan identification signals continuously as it went. Before it could cross the orbital plane of the sixth planet, however, the Entiboran warship *Songwind* ripped an energy bolt across the courier's bow, lit the vessel up with fire control, and locked all guns and missiles on the target.

"Ophelan vessel," came the message—all frequencies, in the clear—"start braking now."

"This is CS-Ophel-178," the courier ship transmitted in reply. "We are carrying urgent messages for Entiboran Fleet Central Command."

"Come dead in space and transfer your message packets to us. We will see the messages delivered from this point."

"Braking now."

The Ophelan's pilot wasted no time. On "now," the vessel performed a skew-flip and lit off its main realspace engines—a fast and showy way of dumping velocity, and one that *Songwind* was hard put to match in time. A podlike minishuttle detached from the Ophelan ship, to be pulled across the space between the two larger craft by *Songwind*'s tractor beam before docking at the Entiboran's access hatch.

The airlock cycled, then opened to let out three officers in Entiboran Fleet uniforms. *Songwind*'s junior officer of the watch, who'd expected to log aboard folders of unaccompanied hardcopy, stared for a few seconds and then recovered himself enough to salute.

"You've got the messages?" he asked as soon as the formalities were done with.

"We *are* the messages," said the senior officer, a lieutenant-of-ships with a Ghan Jobain accent. "There was a Mage attack on Tanpaleyn. We made it out to Ophel, and asked for the courtesy of a courier to help us bring the word home."

"Your own ship—"

"Shot up," the lieutenant-of-ships said. "And too slow even if it wasn't"

"Bad news?" asked the JOOW, though he had a hard time imagining what could be worse than a Mageworlds attack.

"The raiders have changed their tactics. They took out the comm relays first—and then they went for captures instead of kills. They were sacrificing their own ships if it meant they could take undamaged Fleet units."

The JOOW whistled. "The captain's got to hear about this."

"*Central* had better hear about this," said the lieutenant-of-ships. "From now on, we'll have to assume that the raiders have all of the Fleet's crypto and recognition signals—and anything that looks like one of ours could just as well be one of theirs."

Mistress Vasari made her way through the crowded streets toward the Palace Major. She listened as she went to the voices and the undervoices of the nervous people she saw around her. The local newsreaders might not be talking much about the events at the palace, but the populace had no such scruples.

"It's the inheritance wars all over again," said one overheard citizen. . . . "It was a setup by Internal Security," said another, "so the minister could put down a coup and get back in favor." . . . "Galcenians," said a third. "My sister works at the spaceport, and she says the Galcenians have landed and taken over."

Vasari, when she heard the last, suppressed the urge to break into un-Adeptlike snickers. If Galcenians—herself included, oh, yes!—were even half as devious and omnicompetent as Entiboran prejudices gave them credit for, they'd be running the galaxy already and the Mages would be licking their wounds at home.

The narrow street opened into the wide expanse of the Grand Plaza, and she saw the high, ornamented façade of the Palace Major looming up ahead. Much closer, and a more immediate problem, were the security lines that held back the gawking crowd. Whatever had happened at the palace was still going on. Flames licked intermittently at windows and doorways, and red and green bolts of blaster fire sliced back and forth across the open space between the Internal Security barricades and the building proper.

Vasari contemplated the prospect without enthusiasm. Then, with a sigh of resignation, she effaced herself to the best of her ability and continued forward. She was taking a risk, she knew that—stray blaster bolts didn't have eyes and minds that she could influence and turn aside as she could the eyes and minds of the crowd—but she had work to do.

She crossed the Plaza, her shoulder blades tingling with the moment-to-moment expectation of a blaster bolt, and found entry to the palace at one of the lesser doors. Once inside she could relax her guard a little, though not completely, and devote a portion of her attention to other things. Magework, for one—she didn't have the infallible knack for sensing it that Errec Ransome was said to have, but she could follow a bad smell when the dirty rag was shoved close enough to her face.

She extended her senses, tracing the paths of all those who had gone in and out of the palace in the recent hours. And there it was, under the stink of blasters and explosives, beneath the smell of blood and pain. She traced it, following first one path and then another, seeking along each one for the distinctive touch of Magery.

Most of the trails she followed ended in death ... but then, in an undamaged corridor, she found a servant in the palace livery, hurrying along like a man with an important errand. Vasari felt the hair on her neck rise up. This was the one: the taint of Magework was strong upon him.

She kept herself out of his mind and sight. Coming up behind him as he walked, she reached around his neck and applied a choke hold. The man collapsed, his legs no longer able to support him as the lack of oxygen affected his brain and rendered him temporarily unconscious. Vasari put her arms under his shoulders and began dragging him off backward, his heels rucking up the carpet as she tugged him along.

Subtle and discreet as a roadway flare, she thought. *What can I possibly say if Domestic Security or an IS trooper finds me?—"Oh, dear, I'm afraid that my friend has taken ill?"—I don't think so.*

She didn't have to go far. There was an empty room with a closed door a little farther along the corridor. She bumped the lockplate with her shoulder. The door stayed closed. She exerted her will and pushed against the lockplate again.

This time the door opened. She dragged her liveried burden into the room and dropped him onto the floor as the door closed behind her. The man lay on the flowered carpet, breathing wheezily. She stood over him, waiting, until his eyes came open and focused on her face.

"All right," she said to him. "I'm not as good at this as some, but I'm better at it than anyone else *you'll* ever meet."

She knelt beside him and touched one finger, delicately, to the center of his forehead. "I am an interrogator, my friend, and you're going to tell me everything you know."

The senior fleet officer on duty at Entiboran Central Command Headquarters was not a happy man. The day had begun badly and had grown steadily worse.

The Galcenians had been trouble enough. In spite of their unannounced arrival, Captain-of-Corvettes Graene had seen fit to pass them through to the surface—along with their refusal to call upon the current ambassador for accommodation, and the resulting need to house them in the Orgilan Guesthouse at Fleet expense. A few days cooling their heels in high orbit would have done wonders to put them in a less demanding frame of mind . . . but the Galcenians had only been the beginning. For the same day to see an attack on the Palace major was, in the senior fleet officer's opinion, intolerable.

The Fleet's Quick Reaction Team had arrived on-scene adequately fast, if not in time to keep the Interior Ministry from taking over the situation on the ground. Domestic Security had gotten stuck with the dirty job in this case, working with Fire and Emergency to bring out the dead and injured: palace servants, stray members of the nobility, and a bunch of kids from a choral group who'd been singing madrigals in the informal reception room where the first explosions had hit. .

The senior fleet officer rubbed his forehead. At least the choir members, both living and dead, matched up properly with existing records. Some of the other, adult bodies didn't—the likeness was superficial only—which had implications that the senior fleet officer didn't want to think about. He'd been hearing rumors for months now that the raiders from the Mageworlds had other weapons besides their black ships and their black-masked sorcerers, weapons founded in a technology that could engineer plagues and duplicate human bodies at will.

If anybody we meet could be working for the enemy . . .
He shuddered. .

But if the Mages were behind at least part of the attack on the Palace Major, that made the rest of the story look even worse. Based on the scanty reports Domestic Security was allowing to leak out, at least part of the planning had been executed right here in Central Headquarters, by former Fleet Admiral Pallit. Word was that a number of former officers who'd been part of Pallit's personal clique were even now in the basement of the Internal Security building—and the senior fleet officer knew what *that* meant.

He thanked Fortune that he'd always had the good sense to keep his head low and his mouth shut. *Better them than me*, he thought, and picked up the sheet of message flimsy that had caused his current headache.

Mage raiders on Tanpaleyn, he thought. *How hard did they get hit, if our people had to beg a ride on an Ophelan courier to bring the news here fast enough?* He tried to imagine what the attack had been like, and failed. *But the Mages were going after whole ships. Were taking them. Which means that anything we've got, they've got, too.*

It was damned suspicious, all of this stuff going down while the Consort and the fleet admiral were off doing the diplomatic on Maraghai, and Tres Brehant was inspecting Fleet defenses at the opposite edge of Entiboran space from Tanpaleyn. The Mages couldn't have been any luckier if they'd planned the schedules themselves.

Maybe they had. Another thought to be avoided.

So far, though, the Mage ships that had been spotted in the home system were still hanging out beyond the orbital sphere of the farthest planet, and there weren't too many of them. Which left open the question of why they weren't trying to press an attack—typically, the raiders hit fast and hit hard.

He pressed the button for the comm link on his desk. "Any word yet from the couriers?"

That was one thing he'd known right away that he had to do: send out high-speed Fleet couriers looking for Lachiel and Brehant. As soon as one or both of them came back— with or without the Consort, he didn't care—then everything, Mages and conspirators and Galcenians alike, would once again be somebody else's problem.

"No reports from the couriers, sir."

Damn. "Thank you."

He clicked off the link and rubbed his aching forehead yet again. More and more, he felt himself in sympathy with the officers who'd resigned their commissions after the Consort brought in Galaret Lachiel and made her fleet admiral over their heads in despite of custom. Maybe they'd seen what was coming, and made the right decision.

"Your Dignity," said the Minister of Internal Security, looking up from the textcomm in his lap, "the majordomo at the Summer Palace reports that everything is in readiness. Your son, and the nursery staff from the Palace Major, arrived safely less than an hour ago."

"Thank you, Gentlesir Nivome."

Perada let the acknowledgment rest without amplification, and went back to watching the clouds outside her window. She wished that House Rosselin's Summer Palace were either a longer or a shorter journey by aircar from An-Jemayne: longer, and she could have chosen with plausible grace to darken her side of the passenger compartment and close her eyes in feigned sleep; shorter, and she would not have been forced to cope with Nivome do'Evaan at such excruciating length.

Better yet, if Nivome had chosen to take the pilot's seat—
she knew that the Rolnian had the necessary skill, and presumably the appropriate licenses—she'd have had the
compartment to herself, and could fret and worry in peace.
But she supposed it was beneath the dignity of the Minister
of Internal Security to handle his own aircar. If Nivome's
position entitled him to a pilot, he would make a point of
employing one.

Not like Jos, she thought, and smiled in spite of the day's
troubles. The Consort had startled people at first with his insistence on doing his own flying; later, Perada had watched
with amusement as the wilder offspring of the fashionable
nobility took up the practice themselves in imitation. A few
of the less idle-minded ones had even gone so far as to join
the Fleet, a move that had been out of vogue at court for
some decades. She smiled again. *Give Jos another five or
ten years, and the Fleet will be his from top to bottom.*

On the other side of the passenger compartment, Nivome
cleared his throat discreetly. Perada braced herself for another round of helpful news reports and strong implications
that she could do worse for a new Consort than the minister
who labored so tirelessly on her behalf.

Tireless, yes. On my *behalf . . . I doubt it.*

She felt a moment's envy for Garen Tarveet, also en route
to the Summer Palace but in much more stimulating company. She'd have preferred to travel with Hafrey and the
Galcenians herself—even with the unexplained and enig-
matic Master Guislen—but Nivome would have insisted on
accompanying her, and Garen deserved a chance to talk
with the not-yet-accredited ambassador. Her former schoolmate had a knack for judging profit and loss, and for spot-
ting the traps and pitfalls in a blandly worded proposition;
she needed Garen's insight if she was going to come out of
the impending negotiations with Entibor's honor and sovereignty intact.

Nivome cleared his throat again. "Your Dignity."

"Yes, gentlesir?"

"You will be gratified to learn that the pilot transporting

Lord Meteun and the Galcenian ambassador has landed safely at the field below the Summer Palace."

"Excellent. I trust that they've been provided with suitable accommodations and a chance to refresh themselves after this afternoon's brief unpleasantness."

She turned back to the window. *Galcenians. Great-Aunt 'Tina always said that they'd steal your petticoats if you let them. But I don't think she'd ever met a Galcenian in her life who wasn't bowing to her in formal court.*

They want a partnership, with Galcen as the senior member. That's nothing to be surprised at—I'd try to get the same thing for Entibor, if I were asking Galcen's Council for help against the raiders. The only crime here will be mine, if I give them everything they ask for and forget that they were the ones who chose to come begging to *me.*

She was finding it harder and harder to ignore Nivome; the man's ambition had an intensity that was almost palpable. It made him seem to take up much more room in the small passenger compartment than his physical presence implied, and it pressed upon her awareness whether she looked at him or not. She knew what was on his mind. He wanted to be gene-sire to the Domina-in-Waiting; well, so might any man. But Nivome hinted at more. He spoke of being both gene-sire and Consort.

He does worse than just want it, she thought. The insight wasn't a new one, but it was the first time it had affected her with such a sense of urgency. *He thinks he deserves it.*

The corners of her mouth turned up briefly. Perhaps it was time for her to take a bit of the minister's advice after all, for the sake of public morale and her own peace of mind.

As soon as Jos gets back from Maraghai.

In Entiboran nearspace, Captain-of-Corvettes Graene was on the verge of shuttling across to the Galcenians' flagship when a comms runner brought her the message from Central. She accepted the slip of flimsy and read it, frowning slightly—Central had proved remarkably unhelpful so far in today's crisis, and she didn't have much confidence in their

ability to make useful suggestions, much less orders that she
would have to obey.

All units, crypto compromised, she read. *Use plaintext
only. Institute field-expedient recognition signals.*

"Are you sure this message came from Central?" she
asked the messenger when she was done.

"The communications officer verified it himself," the
messenger said.

Graene wondered where Central had gotten the word
from. There was no point in asking the messenger; he
wouldn't know. Neither would the comms officer. Central
knew—at least, she hoped Central knew the source of its
own information. With Mage ships spotted in-system, Central Command had better not be acting on yet another of the
vaguely worded bits of information, more hint then help,
passed along by Internal Security or by one of the factions
at court.

Sometimes she thought that General Metadi and Fleet
Admiral Lachiel hadn't gone far enough when they purged
Headquarters. Their sweeping reforms had flat-out missed
all those officers who'd made safe careers out of keeping
their heads down when the trouble started. It was her own
bad luck, and Entibor's, that put one of them in charge at
Central on this day of all days.

She gave a mental shrug. At least the message hadn't
contained orders to break off contact with the Galcenians. In
fact, the orders to transmit all messages in plaintext and to
devise recognition signals as necessary would make liaison
easier if her proposal was accepted. And so far the
Galcenians hadn't refused to discuss the idea of a unified
command, which was damned decent of them. But since the
Galcenians, as a group, weren't especially decent, that left
the question of where the fishhook was hiding in their easy
agreement.

I suppose I'll find that out soon enough.

She tucked the folded slip of flimsy into her tunic pocket
and hit the plate to open the airlock to the shuttle.

"Well," she said to the messenger, "it's time for me to go
practice my Galcenian. Wish me luck."

* * *

Mistress Vasari sat back on her heels and looked at the man whom she had been, after the Adepts' fashion, interrogating. He lay sprawled supine on the thick carpet, a nondescript man in the palace livery of dark blue and dull silver. His chest rose and fell with his regular breathing, and his eyes were open.

He should have seen Vasari watching him, and after what she had done to him the sight should have made every muscle in his body recoil. But—to Vasari's intense frustration, since she hadn't finished questioning him—the man had nothing left in him to react with; his mind was as blank as his face. She'd had him on the verge of total revelation when he snapped, cutting off his mind from every physical contact so instantly and completely that it had to be a trained last-ditch defense.

Nobody home in there anymore, she thought, with a touch of unwilling respect for her adversary's thoroughness. *Wherever he's gone, he isn't coming back.*

She wished she'd learned either less or more before the defensive reaction took over. As it was, she had only partial information, the vague shape and outline of treachery without the names and times and places that would make it useful. That, and her now-certain awareness that the Mages on Entibor had not forgotten the promise they'd made to the Domina Perada on the night of her accession.

Vasari regarded the man for a moment longer, then reached out and put her hand lightly over his nose and mouth. A faint green light played around her fingers for a few seconds. The man shuddered once all over and then was dead. Vasari stood, dusted off her clothing where she had knelt, and left the room without looking back. The door locked itself behind her.

She left the palace, taking care to stay unseen by agents of both Internal and Domestic Security, and made her way back to her apartment in the Celadon Towers. Once there, she contemplated the blank screen of her desk comp and tried to decide to whom, if anyone, she should tell what she had learned.

Too much . . . she knew too much and not enough. Some people on Entibor were entirely too fond of hunting for spies and traitors. The Internal Security Minister, in particular, had a reputation she didn't like—Adepts had run afoul of such men before, on one world or another over the centuries. On the other hand, there really *were* spies and traitors at work in An-Jemayne, and for all she knew, the Entiboran Adepts were numbered among them. She'd held aloof from them, avoiding their company and their Guildhouses, for just that reason.

She activated the screen of the desk comp. *I ought to send the follow-up to Master Otenu and let* him *decide.*

But her hands remained motionless on the keys, and the screen stayed blank. She felt a vast if wordless reluctance to pass along to Galcen any of her most recent discoveries, and she had been trained to pay attention to such things. Such feelings as those had kept Adepts from harm in the past: the journey not taken, the door unentered, the hesitation with the cup of poison at the lip.

Not Galcen, she thought, and turned the screen off again. *But who, then? The Domina is right about one thing. No one can fight the Mages alone.*

There was only one person she could think of who knew Mages, and who was free of political ties. And—it pleased her to think that, true to her training, she could make one action serve many ends—she already needed a good reason to make contact with Errec Ransome again.

The aircar set down on the landing field of the Summer Palace in early evening. The mountains rising beyond the grassy plain had darkened to blue-black shadows with the descent of the sun; and the palace itself, a long white building high among the foothills, seemed to float against the dark background like a pale cloud. A hovercar waited on the field to take the Domina and her Minister of Internal Security up the long slope to the palace gate.

Perada made the ride in silence, keeping her gaze fixed on the dark outside the hovercar's armor-glass windows. She had no desire to catch Nivome's eye and trap herself

into once again recognizing his presence. The journey from
An-Jemayne had been hard enough to endure already.

The majordomo of the Summer Palace had done well, in
spite of the abrupt and out-of-season descent of a double-
handful of assorted notables. Perada saw no white-shrouded
furniture, and no blank spaces where valuables had been put
into storage while she was in residence elsewhere. She let
the majordomo escort her at once to the nursery wing—no
doubt the way by which he chose to take her avoided those
parts of the palace his frantic cleaning crews had not yet
reached. Nivome followed her; she thought of dismissing
him, but decided, reluctantly, that doing so would be unfair.

Little Ari was already playing contentedly on the thick
rug of the main nursery, under the eyes of a veritable pla-
toon of nursemaids. She picked him up—*oof*ing slightly as
she did so; he was still big for his age, and growing heavier
every day—and hugged him. He caught one of her braids
and began to chew on it thoughtfully. She laughed.

"Mamma's little placeholder's not so little anymore," she
said. He was the lucky one, though, she reflected wistfully—nobody ever bothered to kill placeholders.

An unfamiliar footfall made her turn. The Galcenian who
called himself Festen Aringher stood in the door of the
nursery, smiling pleasantly and seeming oblivious to the
suspicious glances of Nivome and the battery of nursemaids. He held a textcomm in one hand.

"Your Dignity," he said. "I have some news that may interest you."

"Really?" She tried to maintain a proper hauteur, but it
was hard to do with Ari pulling on the braid he had captured earlier. "My Minister of Internal Security has been
keeping me up to date with the reports from An-Jemayne."

"This news comes from system space, Your Dignity. By
way of my—personal connections, shall we say." He
paused. "Connections not necessarily available to the Galcenian ambassador and his strategic advisor."

"Ah. You begin to interest me."

She heard Nivome exhale heavily, like some large and
barely tame animal. "Your Dignity, this man—"

"Has something to say to me. Speak on, Gentlesir Aringher."

The Galcenian bowed. "My thanks. The word I have is that all Galcenian forces now present inside Entiboran space have agreed to place themselves temporarily under the command of the Fleet officer in charge of in-system defense, with the stated goal of resisting an imminent Mage attack."

ERREC RANSOME: CAPTIVITY
(GALCENIAN DATING 970 A.F.; ENTIBORAN REGNAL
YEAR 34 VERATINA)

ALONE IN his cell, Errec Ransome woke and slept and woke again. He had lost track of time, but that didn't matter. His careful investigation of the minds around him—Mages, almost certainly—went on unhindered by the lack of physical routine.

The journey ended before he could learn what he wanted to know. There was a moment, in one of the intervals between food and sleep, when he recognized the distinct internal sideslip, a sensation half of body and half of mind, that signaled a dropout from hyperspace. Not long after, he felt the rocking and buffeting of a descent through atmosphere. With a sigh of hydraulics and a clank of metal, the ship grounded and settled onto its landing legs. Then came silence. The hum of the air system stopped. Once again he grew tired and drowsy, his mind fogging in spite of his efforts to stay awake. Against his will, he slept.

When he awoke, he was in another place.

He lay on a low, wide bed, with a pillow underneath his head and a blanket drawn up over his torso against the faint chill of the air. He was naked under the blanket, and the stubble of beard that had grown during his time aboard the starship was gone—he found it a disturbing thought, that someone had undressed him and cared for him while he lay asleep.

He pushed himself up on one elbow and looked around. This time, the room that held him had pale translucent walls that let the light from outside filter through. Strips of dark wood kept the panels together and cast intricate shadows on the floor. Except for the bed and a half-dozen black and white floor pillows stacked in one corner, the room was as bare of furniture as his cell aboard the raiding ship had been.

The loose garments that his captors had given him lay folded across the foot of his bed. He got up and put them on, and began once more to inspect the limits of his prison.

Some of the latticed panels that made up the patterned walls slid aside in their tracks like doors. The first one he found led to a refresher cubicle of the same design as the one aboard the ship. The second opened out into the world.

He stood on the threshold and looked down a short flight of irregularly shaped stone steps into a tree-shaded garden. The dappled green of the foliage was not any of the multiple greens of Ilarna, nor of Galcen, and the sky overhead was a different blue than either. And he was alone. The others continued to watch him—he could sense them, when he reached out into the currents of Power and felt the pull and twist of their workings—but there was nobody near at hand.

He ventured out into the open air. Short, feathery stems of grass tickled against the insteps of his bare feet like dense green plush. Tall trees, their spreading crowns heavy with leaves, provided comfortable havens of shade against the bright sunlight; smaller trees offered low branches laden with sweet-smelling flowers and brightly colored fruit. And the entire area was surrounded by a force field that he could not break.

Magework, he thought. *It has to be.*

Nothing else could have stopped him. Even when he was very young, force fields and related devices had shown a tendency to break down without warning whenever they blocked the way to someplace he wanted to go. Later on, after he found the Guild, he had learned to be more subtle, and even stronger—but the force field on his garden cell had stopped him utterly.

Maybe I'm unconscious someplace, and hallucinating all this.

He shook his head. He knew the logic and imagery of dreams, and this was different, too intense and too consistent in its details. He was a prisoner among the Mages—so far as he knew, the only prisoner they had taken from the destruction of Amalind Grange—and the Mages had brought him for their own reasons to this place of almost luxurious comfort.

He didn't like it. His imprisonment was yet another wrongness, added to the wrongness of being alive at all. He had seen for himself how the Mages dealt with Adepts on Ilarna, and he had never heard of them taking prisoners on the other worlds they had raided. Why, then, had they taken him, and what was it that brought them to care for him so tenderly?

He reached out in search of a mind that would give him the answer, and found that all those within the range of his touch were guards: unsophisticated, untrained minds that gave him nothing because they knew nothing, except that their prisoner was to be maintained alive and comfortable at all costs.

Errec returned to the cell the Mages had built for him—a snug and cleanly designed prison, as pleasant to look at as any garden bungalow—and set about the work he had learned on Galcen how to do. He ate, and slept, and walked about on the footpaths under the trees, but all the while the greater part of his mind was bent toward the seduction of those who guarded him.

Eventually—it took some weeks, but Errec had patience, and all the time he could have asked for—one of his guards called on a superior to make a visit of inspection, in order to confirm that the cherished prisoner was being treated according to instructions.

The Mage who arrived in response to the guard's invitation came no closer to Errec than did the guards themselves; he was a felt presence rather than a visible one. But the excitement of the occasion made Errec's work easier, rendering the minds of the guards even more labile and amenable to suggestion. It took almost no work at all, only a delicate nudge to an impulse that had formed already, for one of the guards to say, "I don't understand what we're doing here on Cracanth, my lord. Why are we keeping this one alive, when all the others are dead?"

"Because," the Magelord replied, "this one is our luck."

Errec withdrew, puzzled, from the minds of his captors. The symbols and thought-patterns that surrounded the Mages' idea of luck were not the same as his own; he'd given up believing in a capricious fortune when he joined the Guild. It took him careful probing, over the next several days, to determine what was intended—but eventually he understood.

The Mages had their seers and truthspeakers, just as the Adepts had those who could watch the flow of the universe and predict the eddies and currents of the time ahead. And the word that the truthspeakers gave to the Magelords was simple: their efforts would prosper, so long as Errec Ransome lived.

That night marked the first time he attempted suicide.

XVIII. Galcenian Dating 976 A.F.
Entiboran Regnal Year 3 Perada

Jos Metadi had been poor company on the journey back to Entibor from Maraghai, and he
knew it. He wasn't used to going anywhere on-planet and
calling it home. From the day he left Gyffer until he took on
the work of remaking Perada's Fleet, home had been the
ship, and dirtside only a place you went to do business or
get drunk. It was a thing to leave behind you as soon as
possible. The idea of deliberately returning somewhere, of
going back to friends and work that were waiting for you,
was new, and Jos wasn't sure he was ready for it.

He wouldn't have admitted as much to anyone—not even
to Errec, who'd never betrayed a secret in all the time Jos
had known him—but the thought of explaining his deal with
Ferrda had kept him staring at the overhead in his cabin in
the muted light of ship's night, and pacing the deckplates all
day. So much depended on the deal going through, and if
somebody chose to take it wrong . . .

He gave up thinking about it, or tried to, on their last day
in hyperspace, and went to fill up his favorite blue mug
with fresh cha'a. Fleet Admiral Lachiel was in the common

room already, eating freeze-dried winemelon slices for breakfast like a true spacer, without bothering to rehydrate them first.

"Decent rations," she said. "Better than Fleet issue, if you want to know the truth."

"Remarquaine. Ferrda picked them up the last time we were there. The Fleet could probably cut some sort of deal with the factory if they tried."

"I don't think so—the rules for procurement discourage off-planet purchases. 'Buy Entiboran' and all that."

He looked at the depths of his cha'a, and the pale steam rising in faint attenuated curls. "It's a good idea, I suppose, as long as Entibor has what you're after. But winemelon grows on Remarque."

"And ships grow on Gyffer and Maraghai." Lachiel put down her last, half-eaten slice of melon. "My lord general, may I speak freely?"

Jos grimaced. "I'm not anybody's lord—we didn't do things that way back where I grew up. Hell, unless we're both in uniform you don't need to bother with the 'General' part."

" 'Jos,' then. Were you drunk?"

"Several times in my life, yes. But if you mean at the moment I made the deal with Ferrda, no."

"There's no way to back out if you have to?"

"No." He tried to explain. "Ferrda and I shook hands on the deal. I'm a free-spacer, and my word and a handshake are all that I've got. If those are no good, then I might as well go dirtside and become one of those melon farmers."

"Some people," she said, "might say that the General of the Armies of Entibor isn't a free-spacer anymore."

"They'd better not say that where I can hear it."

"I'll make certain the warning gets around." She picked up the partial slice of freeze-dried melon and started crumbling bits off the ragged edge with her fingers. "I don't suppose the Selvaurs would keep up their end of the alliance if you didn't deliver the kid?"

Jos shook his head. "Not a chance. And I wouldn't blame them, either."

"Damn." There was nothing left of Lachiel's melon now but confetti-sized fragments and a brittle strip of rind. "We've got to keep the Selvaurs—if we lose them, there goes our chance of pulling in anybody else. Damn."

She pushed the plate away and looked him in the eye. "All right, Jos. I'll back you."

"How far?"

"As far as it has to go."

A buzzer sounded, rough-edged and strident.

"Dropout warning," said Jos. He felt the nervous tension of the past few days changing into the anticipation that came before action. The time for wondering how to do it was over; from now on, what was done was how it would be. "Time to get to the bridge."

The buzzer kept sounding as they hurried to the cockpit and strapped in. Jos hit the Off switch to silence it, then picked up the link for the intraship comms.

"Places, everyone. Gunners, to your stations."

Lachiel made a startled noise. "We're coming into Entibor," she protested. "There's no need for—"

"There's always need for guns."

"You didn't have them up at Maraghai."

"I was trying to make a point at Maraghai," he said. "And it worked. But don't think I wasn't sweating the whole time."

Lachiel shrugged under her safety webbing. "It's your call. I make it dropout in plus five, counting."

"Understand dropout in five. Switching to manual control."

Jos toggled the switch, and the two of them sat watching the navicomp clicking down. The grey, wavering non-stuff of hyperspace swirled outside the armor-glass viewscreens like puddles of oil on top of milky water.

"Three, two, one, mark," Lachiel said.

Stars burned through the grey in a dazzle of light as normal vacuum replaced the hyperspacial resonance effect. Jos let out a sigh of satisfaction.

"Let's see how close we got," he said.

The navicomp clicked on and began to struggle with beacons and angles and star maps. A field spiked, and the navicomp chittered as it tried to correlate an unexpected radiant source with its tentative conclusions.

"What the hell—!" Jos exclaimed.

"Energy flare in system space."

Jos worked the controls for *Warhammer*'s sensors and for the ship's electronic-countermeasures apparatus. A pattering of signal came over the cockpit's audio—fire-control readings.

"Someone's shooting," he called out over the intraship link. "Condition red, weapons tight."

"Got 'em, Captain," Nannla replied from the number-one gun bubble. "No targets."

"Stay passive," Jos said. "Errec, what's power look like?"

"Rated max available," Errec reported from the engine room.

A loud rush of sound cascaded from the console speakers, almost wiping out intraship comms. Jos adjusted the sensors again to bring down the noise.

"That guy's close," he said to Lachiel. "And he's looking for us."

"Then let's get going."

"Wait a minute, wait a minute, I'm getting a weapons signature on that flare . . . a Mod Pandemonium."

"That's a Galcenian setup!" Lachiel started furiously working the settings for the external comms. "I'd like to go active and see if someone will report to me."

"Let's find out what's happening first," he said. "We might not want to let on that the fleet admiral and the General of the Armies are out here without any protection."

"I'm picking up some ship-to-ship comms already," Lachiel said. Her voice hardened. "And what's going on is a Mage attack in progress."

"We knew it had to happen sometime. Where do the Galcenians fit in?"

"Damned if I know. But they're here."

"Captain," said Tillijen over the link from number-two gun bubble. "I have a target showing on the indicator. If I can see them, they can see me. Looks like we're detected."

"Hell." He turned to Lachiel. "Admiral, you have crypto to contact Fleet? Get a message together. Tell them we're going to be arriving in high orbit and proceeding directly to the surface, at—" He looked at a chrono. "—sixteen sixty-eight, plus or minus ten, and not to shoot at us."

She nodded. "Tomorrow?"

"No, today."

He saw Lachiel's eyebrows go up in disbelief. "It's not possible. Not in this ship."

"Make the signal," Jos said. "Let me worry about getting there."

He waited a few seconds for Lachiel to begin sending the encrypted message, then keyed on the intraship comm and called down to engineering.

"Errec," he said. "We're heading in at a run. I need you to go take a look at the main engineering control board."

"I can see the board from here, Captain."

"All right. You should be staring at a row of switches labeled 'auxiliary heat dispersal.' "

"I've got them in view."

"Flip 'em on."

"Got it." A pause. "All the redlines have moved to the right. If I didn't know better, I'd say we just got another fifty percent rated power."

"Good," said Jos. He reached up and flipped two switches on the overhead panel. "Now take the safeties off line."

"Right." Another pause. "Safeties off."

"Now I'm going to give it throttle. I want you to balance the loads, and I want 'em balanced at twenty percent over redline."

"If you say so." Errec sounded dubious. "But remember, I'm not really an engineer."

"After this run," Jos promised him, "you will be."

"Captain," Nannla's voice cut in. "Target inbound, locked on with fire control, signature looks Mage."

"Weapons free," Jos said. He twisted ship to present a narrower profile, and to put the target inside the covered arc of both the dorsal and ventral guns. The 'Hammer started firing, a steady pounding that made itself known in the vibration of the freighter's strength members and in the wavering power readouts on the main console.

"Two—one—boost," Jos chanted, and pushed the throttle levers forward. Acceleration shoved him back against the cushions . . . but it wasn't so bad that he couldn't reach out and push the levers forward a little bit more.

Rain beat steadily against the windows of the Orgilan Guesthouse. The day was a grey and chilly one—late autumn had never been An-Jemayne's best time of year—and the heat-bar in the sitting-room fireplace glowed faintly as it warded off the cold. Ambassador Oldigaard sat at a graceful antique desk close by the hearth, watching incoming message traffic on a shielded textcomm.

The screen of the textcomm currently displayed reports sent in by the flotilla that had accompanied him to Entibor. He found them uneasy reading. Already, in the reaches of space beyond Entibor, Galcenian ships fought side by side with Entiboran vessels against the Mages.

"I don't like it," he said aloud.

The room's other occupant turned at the sound of his voice. Master Guislen, a quiet presence in formal black, had been standing at the tall window and looking out at the rain-lashed street. Now he faced the ambassador and said, "What is it, exactly, that you dislike?"

"The Domina," Oldigaard said. "We should have had her agreement to the proposals by now. Instead, she only smiles and gives excuses for why she has decided absolutely nothing—while my escort ships are fighting the Mages under local command!"

Guislen left his place by the window to stand nearer the hearth. "If that idea worries you," he said, "then why not direct our ships to withdraw?"

"If I'd had the chance to forbid them in the first place—but I didn't expect to be trapped in an aircar halfway between here and the Summer Palace at the point when the question came up. Withdrawing now would be a disaster. We'd lose whatever goodwill our ships have earned for us.

Our own fleet personnel wouldn't understand the political necessity."

"True. Some other kind of pressure, then." Guislen looked thoughtful. "Her economic advisor, Lord Meteun . . . she depends on his analyses, I think. Can something be done to break him away from her, or to divert his attention?"

Oldigaard nodded slowly. "You have a point. He's from Pleyver; something may be possible there. But that's in the future. We need to apply the pressure now."

"She's young," said Guislen. "Perhaps her husband—"

"Consort. The head of Entibor's Ruling House doesn't marry; she names consorts at her pleasure, and dismisses them at will. The old Domina—Veratina—went through hers like some women go through clean underwear, for all the good it ever did."

Guislen accepted the correction with a look of faint amusement. "Perhaps the young woman's consort, then, provides a weak point that can be suitably exploited."

"Metadi?" Oldigaard snorted. "The man's not an opportunity, he's a menace!"

"If you say so," murmured Guislen. "But his political views can't be popular. He's Gyfferan, which means he's probably egalitarian and possibly a Centrist, neither of which is likely to sit well with the local conservative element."

"As far as our sources can tell, the man has no political views. What he does have, unfortunately, is a damnable amount of charisma—the fire-eaters in our own fleet already admire him too much for comfort."

"Then take what advantage you can of his absence; it won't last forever."

"I have been—"

The textcomm flashed its warning light, and Oldigaard turned his attention back to the flickering screen. He read the message, then thumbed the screen dark again.

"Metadi!" he said. "Even when he doesn't plan it that way, the man's timing is impeccable."

"I take it the Consort has returned."

"Yes. And if convincing Her Dignity to commit to an alliance on our terms was difficult before . . ."

Guislen smiled. "I wouldn't worry. The pressure on the Domina will continue regardless."

Oldigaard regarded the Adept narrowly. "What do you mean?"

"Entiborans—the common mass of them—are a superstitious lot," said Guislen. "If the autumn harvests are troubled with blight and crop failure, the people will remember that Perada has as yet no heir, and she will be pushed toward a second attempt well before she apparently desires to make one."

"Entiborans are also stubborn. And I'm not fool enough to count on blights and droughts showing up when they're needed."

"Maybe you can't trust Entiborans—or Entiboran weather—but I think you can trust the Mages."

"What do you mean?"

"Their biochemical knowledge is legendary in the outplanets," said Guislen. Again he smiled. "If unaided nature fails to bring about a useful state of terror, the Mages will assist things until it does."

The main landing field of An-Jemayne Spaceport was strictly out-of-bounds for unauthorized personnel. Skipsleds scooted back and forth at speed between the ships and the pallets of cargo, throwing up plumes of water from the rain-slicked pavement as they went; heavy machinery—loading cranes, repair booms, catchcradles—worked without regard for spectators. Mistress Vasari had no business being there, standing well inside the safety lines and watching the spaceport traffic.

There was a lot of traffic to watch, even with the Fleet and the Mages skirmishing on a daily basis in the outer system. The field was forested with ships, small and medium-sized ones mostly, though from the vantage point of a person on foot they loomed like giants. The truly big ships never landed at all, but were built in orbit and spent their working lifetimes far beyond any planetary atmosphere. An-

Jemayne's ground facility had enough business without them: couriers and other small Fleet craft, deadly and bright with blue and silver trim; midsize freighters in the colors of the big shipping lines, or in a patchwork of independent hues; light orbit-to-atmosphere shuttles taking off and landing, the flame of their jets making dots of orange against the low grey clouds.

And not far from where Vasari watched, the ship was landing that she had come this far to see.

Warhammer came down in a roar of engines and a tooth-rattling drone of heavy-duty nullgravs. The nullgravs slowed the last stages of the descent, and kept the starship from grounding until the pilot had maneuvered the ship's bulk into the proper orientation and extended the landing legs. Then—slowly, a delicate balancing of three systems at once—the engines fell silent, the nullgravs faded out, and the hydraulics in the landing legs groaned and took the strain.

Gracefully, for all her awkward shape and size, the *'Hammer* settled into position. Vasari waited. A few seconds later, a skipsled arrowed out onto the field from somewhere in the heart of Fleet territory. No cargo rode on the sled for this trip—the load platform held a group of uniformed types, hanging on to the safety railing while the sled's driver fired it up to unprecedented speed.

They must really want to talk to him, Vasari thought.

Someone aboard the *'Hammer* must have been watching the monitors. The ramp went down; the main hatch opened. Figures emerged: Metadi, in mufti—plain shirt and trousers, boots, black velvet long-coat with silver buttons; a tall woman in Fleet uniform who had to be Admiral Lachiel; two more women in free-spacers' rig; and last, an unobtrusive figure in a mechanic's coverall. Errec Ransome.

It only took Vasari a few seconds to realize that nobody else was noticing Ransome at all. She wasn't surprised when he failed to join Metadi and the others on the crowded skipsled. Instead, he moved off at an angle, threading his way in between the puddles of rainwater and the crates and stacks of cargo, on what errand she couldn't tell.

Vasari smiled. She'd done her homework before coming out to the field; she knew where the nearest civilian gate lay in relation to *Warhammer*'s berth. If she headed straight there, instead of trying to shadow a powerful Adept who already had a head start . . .

Her gamble paid off. When Errec Ransome, still unnoticed by untrained eyes, had finished making his circuitous way to the civilian gate, Mistress Vasari was able to step out of the shadows into his path.

"Going somewhere?" she asked.

He gave a vague shrug. "No place in particular."

"Fine," she said. He was probably lying, or at least telling a bit less than the truth, but it didn't matter. "Because I want to talk to you. Have you been thinking about that discussion we had?"

"Yes. I can't go back. Not yet."

"Good."

Errec looked amused—or as amused as he ever seemed to look these days, more like a man remembering an emotion than like someone feeling it—and said, "I thought this was going to be another one of those interviews where you try to talk me back into the fold."

"Later. Right now I need your help."

"What kind of help?" His voice and eyes were both wary—*Nothing remembered about that emotion,* Vasari thought; *it's all there and all genuine.*

"The Mages are active again on Entibor," she said. "I need you to help me find them."

"And what then?"

The rain had started up again while they spoke, soaking both Vasari's working blacks and Ransome's frayed coverall. Vasari didn't care; she could tell by the look on Ransome's face that she had him now.

"After we find them, we pump them dry." She smiled at him sweetly. "And after *that*, Errec dear, you can do whatever your bloodthirsty little heart desires."

The winds of late autumn blew around the Summer Palace of House Rosselin, making the big, airy building un-

pleasantly chill and damp. The Summer Palace, with its
high ceilings and ample cross-drafts, had never been meant
for keeping warm, and unlike the Palace Major it had never
been retrofitted with advanced environmental controls.
Perada wore a half-cape these days when she went for an
afternoon's walk along the graveled paths of the formal
garden.

Today she'd kidnapped baby Ari from the nursery staff—
dedicated professionals all, whose respectful demeanor almost concealed their unspoken opinion of the Domina as an
untrained dilettante—and carried him off to the garden. Ari
was toddling now; it amused her to contemplate the grave
concentration with which he made his slow, careful progress
from one point of interest to the next. He was a quiet child,
even-tempered and not given to crying, who seldom wanted
anything that she could not provide. For that alone she
would have loved him, after hours each day spent talking
with diplomats and government ministers and petitioners
from this district or that guild, all of them needing her to do
the impossible.

This morning's report by the Minister of Agriculture had
distressed even Ser Hafrey, who normally paid no heed to
the work of the various ministries. Sometime during the
course of the last few weeks of fighting, a Mageworlds task
unit had reached the outer fringes of the atmosphere before
being detected and destroyed. Not soon enough, apparently;
the ministry reported a subsequent withering of food grains
in areas free of drought or natural disease.

"We are looking," the Minister had said, "at the possibility—indeed, at the probability—of a biological attack."

Perada shivered, not so much from the autumn wind as
from the memory of the pictures that had accompanied the
minister's report: bare swaths of muddy, rainwashed ground;
fruits and vegetables crumbling into loathsome dust; acres
of brown leaves on brittle stalks, in a district where the
grain should have rippled like a golden carpet from horizon
to horizon. And the blight was growing, following the prevailing winds. The minister had brought a list of recom-
mendations with him—strict quarantines, interruption of

on-planet and off-planet movement, stockpiling—but not even his most optimistic projections had contained any assurance of success. The name of Sapne had not yet been spoken aloud, but the plague world was close to the front of everybody's mind.

Nobody thought that a whole planet could go down so fast, Perada thought. She took away a lump of gravel that Ari had decided to chew on, and let him use her long skirt to pull himself back up to a standing position. *Everybody thought the disasters on Sapne were natural until it was too late.*

And now it's happening to us.

She heard footsteps crunching on the gravel behind her, and turned to see who it was that approached. Her heart leapt—*An absurd term,* she thought, *but how else to describe the sensation?*—when she saw that it was Jos Metadi who stood there, hatless as always, with the tails of his black long-coat catching and lifting on the rising wind.

" 'adda!"

Ari didn't have many words, but that was one of them. He let go of Perada's skirt and ran toward Metadi. Jos caught the boy before he could overbalance, and lifted him up to sit in the crook of one arm. Perada came forward more slowly, extending her hand and letting him take it in his free one.

"I'm sorry I couldn't welcome you properly inside," she said. "But I didn't know—"

"Didn't anyone at Central bother to tell you the *'Hammer* was landed? They snatched me off to a briefing the moment I arrived," Jos said; "surely they had time." Ari was pulling at the buttons of his coat, but he didn't seem to notice.

"Central rations its electronic messages these days," she said. "Out of caution, I suppose—the Mages are probably listening to everything they can pick up." She gave a nervous laugh. "I'm sure that the letter announcing your arrival will get to me in a day or two."

He didn't smile. The hand gripping hers tightened for a moment. "Let me announce myself, then. I'm back."

"I'm glad." The wind gusted, whipping her skirts around

her ankles and tugging at the hem of her cape. "It's getting cold—let's go inside, and you can tell me how things went on Maraghai."

"If that's what you want to hear."

There was an edge to his voice. She could tell he was tense about something, but he didn't speak further.

They walked to the palace in silence and entered through the terrace door. An armed trooper straightened to attention and presented his ceremonial pike as they passed. A modern energy lance, slung from his back with the power cells inserted, showed that the antique weapon wasn't his major defense.

One of the nursemaids met them just inside the door. She reclaimed Ari so deftly that the baby was on his way upstairs to the nursery before Perada could raise a protest—it was Metadi's presence that had done it, she decided. The staff had their doubts about her, maybe, but they had absolutely no doubts whatever about Jos.

Still saying nothing, they passed through the antechamber into the private reception area known—from the tall, narrow windows that lined it on both sides—as the hall of light. The afternoon sun slanted through diamond-shaped panes to fall onto the polished floorboards. Except for a table and chairs of pierced fruitwood that had stood in the hall since the day the first Rosselin heir had assumed the Iron Crown, the room had no furniture; it had all been taken to augment the display in the public rooms.

Finally Perada couldn't put off asking the question any longer. "Did the mission go well?"

"We got what we went for," Jos said. "The Selvaurs are willing to make an alliance."

The wave of relief that washed over her was so strong that she had to sit down in one of the delicate carved chairs. She hadn't realized until now how much she had wanted—how much she had needed—to hear that Entibor was not alone.

"Thank fortune," she said. "And thank *you*. You couldn't have brought me a better gift if you'd ransacked half the galaxy for it."

Jos didn't smile back at her. His expression—his whole bearing—was tense and edgy. "It looks like you haven't done too badly in that line yourself."

"You're talking about the Galcenians?"

He gave a curt nod. "They were all over system space when we came in. The briefing at Central was long on speculation but short on facts. My commanders insisted on calling them our 'allies.'"

"I wouldn't really call them allies," she said. "They want something a bit more permanent than that."

"You could do worse."

"It's hard to see how," she said. "Strip away the fine words, and Galcen wants to make Entibor into a client world—a colony, is more like it. At least the Mages are honest about what they're after."

"The Galcenians are good fighters, though. Better to have them on your side than not."

"I suppose." She looked at him. He stood near the foot of the carved table, too far away for their hands to touch, and his face had not lost its lines of tension. She licked suddenly dry lips and went on. "But I want them with us on our terms, not theirs. This alliance you've brought back from Maraghai sounds like enough to tilt the balance."

"I hope so. It's an arrangement between equals—Selvaurs don't make any other kind."

"Under whose command?" she asked. "Ours or theirs?"

He gave a quick, tight shrug. "We haven't settled that."

"I want you to run it. I've said so from the beginning."

"I could." It was a statement of fact, not a boast. He wasn't looking at her at all; instead, he was gazing with intense concentration at the patterns of light and shadow cast onto the tabletop by the leaded window-glass. "But it won't work unless the Entiborans and the Selvaurs come to the same conclusion on their own."

"I can speak for Entibor," she said. "As for the Selvaurs . . . you know them, Jos. Knew Ferrdacorr, anyway. Will they accept a—a thin-skin leading them?"

"I hope so. Under certain circumstances."

He still wasn't looking at her. Perada felt a strange, unexpected chill. "What kind of ... circumstances ... are you talking about?"

Jos lifted his head to meet her gaze, and she saw that his face was pale and set. "I've promised to give them Ari as a foster child."

"What?" She stood up so fast that her chair fell backward and hit the floor with a clatter. "You had *no right*—!"

"Do you want an alliance?" His voice had an edge to it like a knife. "If you want the Selvaurs to fight on our side, that's their price: family bond with me and mine."

She felt like she was choking. "Family? You think a bunch of scaly, green, bad-tempered—"

"Ari will be safe with Ferrda's people. Can you promise me that much if he stays on Entibor? I had to shoot my way in, and I suppose that in order to take him to safety on Maraghai I'll have to shoot my way back out."

Perada had to grip the edge of the table with both hands. The rush of anger was so strong it was making her dizzy. She drew her breath in through her teeth to keep from screaming.

"You had no right," she said again. "If the Selvaurs want your blood kin, you'll have to look some place besides here."

His face was like a carving out of ice. "What do you mean?"

"You are the Consort," she said. "Ari is your son by law, and by my command. But your gene-child, he is not."

Jos Metadi: Deep Space
(Galcenian Dating 966 a.f.; Entiboran Regnal
Year 30 Veratina)

THINGS WEREN'T good aboard *Wandering Star*. The combined crews worked together as well as could be expected, but the sick ones continued to die at an astounding rate. Two days in orbit over Sapne saw four more cycled out the airlock. During those two days, Jos and Maert and Covain worked over the manuals for the navi-comp—a model far different from the one Jos had used on *Meritorious Reward*—and discussed where they should go.

"We can't bring plague to a civilized world," Covain insisted. "That wouldn't be right."

"I'm not planning to, but there are places," Maert said. "And maybe by when no one else is sick, no one is infectious."

"Maybe," Covain said, but he didn't sound convinced.

"How about Yasp?" Jos said, looking up from the text-files in the *Merchanter's Guide*. "It says here they've got orbiting reception areas, including quarantine berthing."

"You don't feel up to a ground landing?"

"I can do it," he said. "But I think maybe Captain Covain has a point."

"I'm the captain," Maert said. "On my ship there is no other." She paused for a moment. "You will make course for Yasp. Seek the quarantine berthing."

Jos did the calculations, once with the navicomp, then again using ship's memory as a check. Later that day, Maert called the crew to acceleration stations, they made the run to jump, and Jos took *Wandering Star* into hyperspace.

When the stars had flared and died outside the bridge windows—actual armor-glass, not viewscreen projections— and the view had changed to the grey pseudosubstance of hyper, Maert leaned forward and handed him a piece of paper. It was a full pilot's license, with the name of the last holder masked off and Jos' own name lettered in its place.

"Here," she said. "You're an accredited, certified pilot now."

Jos looked at it.

"You wonder if other ships will take this? Look." Maert pointed to the bottom, where one signature had been crossed out and another added. "That's my chop. Everyone knows me. Anyone doubts it has to fight me. No one will dare."

"Two weeks to Yasp," Jos said.

That ship's-night on the midwatch, Sedver—one of the supply clerks from the *Merry*, who'd contracted a mild case of the plague and then had seemed to recover—relapsed. He fell to the deck, blood running from every orifice, and died before his shipmates could carry him to a bunk.

Number-two cargo bay was pumped clear of air, taken down to freezing, and turned into a temporary morgue until they got to realspace and a chance to use the airlocks. Sedver was only the first occupant. Before the night was over, Berud—the engineer off the hopper, whom so far the plague had spared—came down with the fever, cramps, and rash that marked the first stages. In four days he was dead, screaming in pain. The *Star*'s medical locker had expended all its painkillers.

By then Covain and three crew members from *Wandering Star* had relapsed too, and died. The ones who remained— there wasn't any shortage of berthing spaces now—gathered around the mess table, their faces haggard, and wondered which one of them would be next. That night Captain Maert opened the grog locker, and they held a noisy, drunken freespacer's wake for those who had died already, and for themselves.

The plague walked through the ship, and this time mortality was complete. Jos used the engineering skills he'd picked up in his short turn aboard *Quorum*, and everything that he'd learned since, to keep the freighter's engines running. They weren't too different from *Quorum*'s, though far simpler than *Meritorious Reward*'s. Between checking the course—the autopilot was old and cranky—and checking the engines, he barely had time to eat, and what sleep he got he took in the pilot's chair or on the spare acceleration couch down in the engine room.

He knew that the number of the ship's crew was steadily diminishing, but not until Captain Maert stopped him as he made his endless cycle from the bridge to engineering and back to the bridge again did he realize how far it had gone.

"Come, young Jos," Maert said, laying a hand on his arm. She opened the door to the captain's cabin—the only single on the little ship, to starboard off the common room—and gestured him inside. In the better light of the cabin, Jos saw that Maert's eyes were fever bright, and the plague's telltale rash had started on her forehead and her hands.

She lay back on the bunk. From the way she moved, he could tell how much the effort of rising from it and fetching him had cost her. "It is only the two of us now," she said, "and soon it will not be me." She pointed to the cabin's fold-down desk. "All the account numbers are there. Now I give this ship to you. It is yours. You are captain."

She held up her hand. "Now you shake my hand. I say 'Done?' and you say 'Done.' That's how it is among freespacers. Come now."

Jos took her hand. It was hot and dry, but her grip was still firm. "Done?" she said, and, "Done," Jos replied.

"Now, Captain, I ask you to leave me," Maert said. "You have your ship to fly."

Two days later, Jos put Maert's body into the morgue.

While he was securing it to the deck, the navigation alarm buzzed in the headset of his pressure-suit. He made his way to the bridge, and was ready in time for dropout from hyper. When he checked the navicomp readouts, he saw that he was near the Yasp system, but not yet in it and not yet in communications range. He set course for the star, clicked on the autopilot, pulled off the helmet of his p-suit, and went back to the galley for a cup of cha'a.

As he reached for the cup, the muscles in his arm throbbed. He felt lightheaded. The room swam before him. "Too tired," he muttered. "Only me left." He reached up to rub his eyes, and his hand came away with a smear of blood. His hand was showing the beginnings of a crimson rash.

"Only me. Not even me."

He went forward again and picked up his pilot's license, the one Maert had given him. He unsealed his p-suit, put his license into the internal pocket, and sealed up the suit again. Then he picked up the external comms. Setting the link to automatic repeat, he spoke one word, "Plague," and began transmission.

That done, he made his way back to the captain's cabin, strapped himself into the acceleration couch, and sealed the faceplate of his p-suit. The suit's air would give out in less than the two to four days it usually took for the plague to run its course, but—considering how all the others had died—perhaps that would be a mercy.

The fever came over him, and he shook, and sweated, and the nightmares came. At one point in his delirium, he saw the door open, and a man came into the cabin. Jos would have thought he was a ghost, except that none of the many dead, on Sapne or in space, had looked like him: pale and dark-haired, and dressed in plain black.

The stranger carried a polished wooden staff in one hand, and when he saw that, Jos knew his visitor was an Adept, a member of the powerful and mysterious Guild. Rumors of the Adepts and their powers were all over dockside, and once or twice back on Gyffer Jos had even seen Adepts, quiet black-clad figures going about whatever business such people had to do.

"Don't worry," the Adept said. "I'm here now, and I'll take care of you."

"There's no one on the ship but me."

"You're right," said the other. "But don't worry. I can handle it."

"What are you doing here?"

The Adept smiled—somewhat ruefully, it seemed to Jos. "I owe you a debt, I suppose. I don't really remember. But it doesn't matter. You rest, and I'll take care of the ship."

Jos gave up and closed his eyes.

When he opened them again, he wasn't in the *Star*'s forward cabin anymore. He was in a brighter, larger, whiter space, lying on a soft bed. He felt weak, but his head was clear.

"Good morning," said an older man in a pale blue uniform. "Glad to see you with us."

"Where am I?" Jos asked.

"Infirmary Three, Yasp Reception," the man said. "And you've been very ill—you spent a week in the isolation pod before we could be sure we weren't going to lose you." He produced a clip-pad from some place Jos couldn't see. "Now, if you don't mind, there are a couple of points to clear up. You had some papers on you which gave the name Jos Metadi?"

"That's right. I'm Metadi."

"Ah. And who are you, Gentlesir Metadi? And what is the name of the ship you were on? I'm afraid the log was incomplete, and the registry here doesn't list a vessel of her description."

"Warhammer," Jos said—a name out of Gyfferan legend, and maybe better luck for the old ship than its former name had been. And definitely not on anybody's list of ships that had ever touched dirt on plague-ridden Sapne. "My ship is called *Warhammer*, and I'm her captain."

XIX. Galcenian Dating 976 A.F.
Entiboran Regnal Year 3 Perada

Have you found what you're looking for?"

Mistress Vasari couldn't keep the relief out of her voice. She and Errec Ransome had been walking in the rain and mist for some hours, ever since leaving the gate at the landing field. She wasn't lost, in the general sense—she'd lived in the capital long enough by now to have some feel for the local geography—but she had no idea where they were going. Errec had chosen the route, without bothering to explain how or why, and she had gone with him.

They'd come at last to a grubby business and light-manufacturing district, somewhere in the outskirts of greater An-Jemayne. Business hours had ended, but full dark was still almost an hour away. Already, though, everything looked drab and greyed out. The streetlamps hadn't yet flicked on, and buildings on all sides blocked most of the light. And here Errec Ransome had, finally, stopped.

"There are Mages here," he said.

"There are Mages all *over* An-Jemayne, Errec. That's the problem. As far as I can tell, they've got all the local talent either totally hoodwinked or completely subverted—the

Guild hasn't gotten anything useful out of Entibor in decades—and not even the Ministry of Internal Security has managed to catch them at work. I was hoping you could help with that."

"I've found them for you," he said. "You'll have to ask your own questions."

"I'd rather you did the interrogation, to be honest. You're better at it than I am—the only Mage I ever got close enough to, destroyed himself while I was working on him."

He shook his head. "I don't do that sort of thing anymore." She waited for an explanation, but he didn't give her one. Instead, he pointed to a doorway in the brick wall of the nearest office building. "Behind there. Up a flight of stairs. If you want them, come on."

He walked over the twisted the mechanical fastener on the door. The metal broke. He applied his shoulder. The door squealed open on rusty hinges.

"Remember," she said, "these people also carry blasters."

Errec glanced back at her. "I know."

She followed him up a narrow staircase to the second floor, and down an unlit corridor to a closed door. This one opened quietly. Inside, a circle of black-robed figures knelt facing inward, heads bowed. Vasari felt a thrill of recognition: for the first time, she was actually watching the enemy at work.

The privateers were right. Errec's turned into one hell of a Mage-finder. These guys were so warded and guarded that I couldn't spot them at all.

Errec stepped over the threshold of the room and into the center of the kneeling Circle. For several seconds, nothing happened at all. Then the air in the darkened room began to glow with a greenish light—faint and sourceless at first, then concentrating on Errec. The members of the Circle had not moved, but Vasari could feel a struggle going on nevertheless.

The green light grew brighter. Errec closed his eyes and brought his hands up, empty, as if they held a staff. The light collected in his hands—*Power,* thought Vasari, *he's calling in more Power than he can hold*—and increased in intensity until she had to shield her face. The silence in the room grew louder and louder, until the absence of sound reached a point where her ears hurt from it.

"Ask them your questions," Errec said. His voice was oddly normal and conversational, as if he were not keeping in balance more of the substance of reality than any one person ought to hold. "They won't break away."

Vasari hesitated a moment, then stepped forward and laid her hand on the shoulder of the nearest Mage. As Errec had promised, the mind within lay open and unresisting.

"Interesting," she said. "A minor Circle, but part of a larger work. Hold them as long as you can, Errec—this is going to take quite a while."

The private rooms of House Rosselin's Summer Palace had the same high-ceilinged, many-windowed architecture as the public chambers. The design factors that made for coolness and light during the long summer days of these higher latitudes had a less fortunate effect during the autumn evenings. All along the dim unheated corridors, the night outside made the windowpanes into black and chilly squares.

Jos Metadi had been prowling restlessly through the palace ever since leaving Perada in the hall of light. The dinner hour had passed long ago, and he had ignored it; he didn't have an appetite. Nor did he have the faintest idea what he was going to do next.

He didn't even know if the deal with Ferrda was still good. *Mine by law and custom—I don't know if that's enough or not. I don't know if Perada ...* He stopped the thought before it could finish. He didn't want to think at all about Perada right now if he could help it. Later, maybe. After he'd figured out what he was supposed to do.

He wished he were out in space somewhere. Fighting Mages was easy, and he suspected that at the moment he would enjoy hunting down something dangerous and blowing it to pieces.

The servants were nowhere in sight; he hadn't encountered a warm body in palace livery since the nursemaid took

Ari upstairs. *They're probably all lying low,* he thought. *They can tell there's bad stuff happening, and they want to stay out of it. Smart people.* He decided that he envied them.

Jos halted. His wanderings, prompted by who-knew-what unconscious impulses, had brought him to the doors of the nursery wing. On an impulse—*Ari's a good kid; he doesn't need to get jerked around by all of this*—he put his hand on the lockplate.

The door didn't open.

For a while he stood there, not thinking, only looking at the door. After a few seconds, a single realization struggled into the foreground of his mind: they had changed the ID codes for the nursery locks.

Changed them to keep him away from Ari.

He drew in a sharp breath and turned away. This time his strides were fast and purposeful, taking him from the nursery wing to the Domina's private apartments. Those lockplates had always answered to his ID as well.

They still did. The door slid open at his touch, and he stepped into the bedchamber of the Domina of Entibor: a big, airy room, with casement windows stretching from floor to ceiling all along one wall. Curtains—thin, summery things—framed a vista long since taken over and obliterated by the night. The panes gave back nothing but reflections, and beyond the reflections, darkness.

The floor of polished parquetry was meant to be cool and slick against bare feet on high-summer nights and mornings. Jos remembered the feel of it, as he remembered not caring whether the flimsy curtains were drawn or not, and forced himself to push the memories away. He couldn't afford to think about those things right now.

Perada sat in one of the cushioned bentwood chairs on the opposite side of the room from the bed. The back of the chair was taller than she was—she wasn't a big woman; Ari was going to dwarf her before he was half-grown—and she had her feet on a cushioned footstool. She wore a quilted night-robe, and her hair hung down in two long, shimmering braids.

Jos couldn't think of what to say. She could have made it easier by speaking first, but she just looked at him, her eyes bright and blue, like the heart of a flame. Finally he mastered himself enough to speak.

"Why have the lockplates been changed in the nursery wing?" He knew as soon as he'd spoken that it was a disastrously wrong thing to say. But words couldn't be called back any more than could a blaster bolt, and he couldn't do anything but stand there waiting.

Perada's eyes went cold, and her voice had nothing behind it that wasn't iron. "I suppose that the locks were changed at the order of the Minister of Internal Security."

"Nivome do'Evaan." He pronounced the Minister's name with distaste. There was a clammy suspicion in the back of his head, and he wasn't going to think about it, especially not now. Later, after all this was straightened out . . . later there would be time to speculate about Ari Rosselin's genesire.

"Yes," Perada said. "Nivome."

"Did you tell him to do it?"

Her lips thinned briefly. "The Minister of Internal Security is responsible for the protection of House Rosselin. And my lord Nivome takes his duties seriously."

"I'll bet he does."

"He would be no use to me or to Entibor, otherwise."

Jos drew a deep breath. "Then I wish you joy of him." It was all painful now, whatever he might decide to do or say; better to deal the worst hurt himself than to wait for the blade to strike home. "Maybe you ought to take *him* for Consort, if he's so damned devoted."

Perada went stiff and pale. Red patches burned on her cheekbones like rouge or fever. "It wouldn't do at all, I'm afraid. Nivome has his undoubted talents, but commanding a warfleet isn't among them."

"So you're keeping me around for the military stuff, is that it?"

"Well . . . fleet command *is* one of *your* undoubted talents."

"Fine." Jos's head was pounding and his shoulders hurt.

"I'll run your warfleet for you as long as you need one. You want anything else, get someone else to do it. I'm done."

The Silver Slipper was a fairly decent place. Not quite on-base, it stood near Central HQ in that area which formed An-Jemayne's version of a portside strip. After too long on ship's rations and Selvauran cookery, Tillijen and Nannla had chosen to dine there for their first night in port.

Tillijen went back up to the buffet, leaving Nannla behind to sip warm mezcla from a silver-fitted thimble-cup. Tilly wanted to refill her own plate with another assortment of Entiboran dainties—things that bore no resemblance to whatever they had once been while running the woods, swimming the seas, or growing in the fields. Only now that she was tasting the flavors of home again, after so many years away, did she realize how much she had missed them.

"My lady Chereeve?"

She started, and turned—half-expecting to see Nivome do'Evaan, the only man on Entibor to address her by that name. But the speaker was a smallish, muscular man with thick red hair, dressed in plain dirtsider clothes, and his accent was respectable middle-class Entiboran. Tillijen shook her head. "Never heard of her."

"Tillijen Chereeve," he said. "Oldest daughter in your generation to the head of House Chereeve."

"I told you, there's nobody by that name left alive. I signed the papers and declared myself dead, the way they wanted me to, and that was it." Her voice was low.

"For someone who's dead to House and homeworld," the man said, "the Minister of Internal Security is certainly spending a great deal of trouble to find you."

"Ooh, that was nasty," Tillijen said, with genuine admiration. "I suppose he's hoping to find out what happened on Maraghai—if you're one of Gentlesir Nivome's enemies, I'm almost tempted to give it to you for free, just to disoblige him."

The man looked as if he might have been amused, if he hadn't been too well-mannered to indulge himself at her expense. "We would appreciate knowing it, that's true—"

"We?"

"—but that isn't why I'm here. My lady—"

"Tillijen."

"My lady, you are alone, and Internal Security has agents everywhere. Please come with me. You do not dare fall into the minister's hands."

"Why?"

"In brief—one Tillijen Chereeve, were she alive, would be a female of childbearing years, and closely enough related to House Rosselin that a child of her body would be difficult to disprove as one of the Domina's by genetic means—should both the Domina and the lady Chereeve be dead. Especially if half the genetic material for the child was provided by my lord Nivome, and he swears that the Domina selected him for her honor."

Tillijen kept her face calm and her voice equally low. "No one can possibly think of getting away with that."

"An officer of the Interior Ministry is in this building right now, looking for you. At this very moment he's talking with your companion. She may or may not direct him this way. You must go at once, and not return to any of your usual haunts."

Out of here, to the port, and see if someone can fetch me out of a sealed gun bubble, Tilly thought. Then, *No. All they'd have to do, if they knew where I was, would be to put Nannla in danger, and offer to trade my life for hers. Damn them all. Just when you think you can't make things any worse . . .*

"I can give you escort to a place of safety," the man said, "until such time as the danger is past. Should the Domina again become gravid, you will be safe. Until then . . . the ministry's agents are charged with the task of finding you and ensuring your cooperation. You cannot return to your ship without hazarding your life—and the lives of your shipmates."

"How do I know you aren't one of those agents yourself?"

The man looked apologetic. "Some things you have to take on faith, I'm afraid, at least for now." He made a formal bow and extended his hand. "My lady, will you come?"

If he isn't Nivome's man, she thought, *he's probably a friend, at least for the moment, and I can trust him. And if he's lying, and he is Nivome's man . . . I still have my blaster.*

"What the hell," she said. "Lead the way."

Jos couldn't sleep. Instead, he paced the corridors of the Summer Palace all through the rest of the night. The anger that had caused him to turn his back on Perada and leave her apartments faded soon enough, leaving behind only a flat weariness. He might have gone back—he didn't think that he was so stupid-proud he couldn't admit to saying everything wrong that could possibly be said—but going back wouldn't help get Ari to Maraghai, not when the boy's mother was dead set against the idea.

It had to be done, though. Jos had given his hand on it. Besides, he'd seen the reports at Central—the withered crops after the Mage raiding ships had passed—and he knew what they meant. The Magelords had decided to treat Entibor as they had treated Sapne, and nobody on-planet would be safe.

Ferrda will take the kid; Ari's mine by law, anyhow, and if that's good enough for me it'll have to be good enough for the Selvaurs. Then Perada will have her alliance, and Ari will be as safe as anyone's going to get . . . and I can go fight Mages, since that's all that anyone seems to think I'm good for.

The decision didn't make him any happier, but at least it gave a direction and a sense of purpose to his thoughts. The main problem was the lockplate, and beyond the lockplate the phalanx of nursemaid-bodyguards. Shooting the lock open would take care of the first step, and he supposed he could always stun any member of the nursery staff who chose to interfere—but anything violent was likely to draw instant attention, and it was a long way from the nursery wing to the landing field.

What I need, he thought, relieved to confront a practical

problem for a change, *is an ally. Somebody who's willing to act in the Domina's best interest whether she knows what her best interest is or not—and someone who's willing to take on Gentlesir Nivome do'Evaan.*

Put that way, the choice was obvious.

Jos found Ser Hafrey sitting in the morning room, a graceful chamber overlooking a vista of gentle, forested hills. The rising sun filled the room with warm golden light.

"Good morning, General." The armsmaster came to his feet as Jos entered—he might almost, Jos thought, have been waiting for him to arrive.

"I suppose so," Jos said. "Ser Hafrey, I need your help."

The armsmaster didn't look surprised. "In what fashion?"

"The child, Ari . . ."

"Her Dignity's placeholder. A fine boy."

"I want to get him off-planet."

"To seal your agreement with the Selvaurs. Yes."

"Dammit," said Jos. "Does the whole Summer Palace know about that treaty by now?"

"There are no secrets, I'm afraid. One picks things up, here and there."

"I suppose so. But it's not just the treaty I'm worried about. The war is going to heat up real soon now, and no one on Entibor is going to be safe."

Hafrey looked faintly amused. "I thought making it safe was your responsibility, General."

"Yeah—but things are going to get a lot worse before I can make them any better. I've seen what happens when the Mages decide to get mad at a place, and believe me, getting away from it is the only thing to do."

"You think Maraghai will be immune to such tactics?"

"No. But when the plagues come, they'll be set up for Selvauran biochemistry, not human."

"Don't you mean 'if the plagues come'?"

"I prefer not to bet on that sort of thing," Jos said. He paused and looked out the window. A red bird was darting from branch to branch in the trees nearby, making a crimson flash of movement like a blaster bolt in a dark alley. After a while he said, "I thought for a while yesterday that I might be able to take 'Rada into space with me. . . ."

"It wouldn't have worked," Hafrey said. The note of sympathy in his voice was, as far as Jos could tell, perfectly genuine. "No reigning Domina has ever left the planet, and—because this is Entibor—habit has become custom, and custom has taken on the force of law. To leave the homeworld would be to abdicate all power. And she will not do that."

"I guess not. It doesn't matter anyway."

The armsmaster looked thoughtful. "You're not a man with a strong attachment to any one world, General—no free-spacer can afford to be—so perhaps you don't understand how deeply such things are felt on Entibor. Did you know, for instance, that in certain stock phrases and legal documents, the words for 'death' and 'exile' are considered as equivalent? A Domina is bound by that tradition, no matter what her own desires may be."

"Well, that explains why 'Rada decided to fly all over half of space before she came here." Jos was silent for a moment. "Will you help me, then?"

"Her Dignity will not be pleased."

Jos let out his breath in a long sigh. "Thanks anyway. I'll do the best I can on my own."

He turned to go.

The armsmaster held up a hand to stop him. "Timing is everything, General. If you were to wait here alone for, let us say, fifteen minutes, and then pay a visit to the nursery, you might very well find that no one is there except your son."

"My son . . . fifteen minutes, you said?"

"That should be long enough. Further I cannot go, and still maintain my oaths to the Domina and to House Rosselin." The armsmaster bowed to him—the full bow of profound respect. "Good day to you, General. And good luck."

Jos waited for fifteen minutes by his chrono, then left the morning room and set out at an unhurried pace for the palace nursery. The lockplate answered to his ID at the first touch, and the door slid open.

Inside, everything was silent and empty. Jos wondered what Hafrey had done to achieve this sudden depopulation, then thought better of wondering. The armsmaster's reputation wasn't a sinister one, exactly, but people sometimes got an uneasy look on their faces when they spoke of him. Even 'Rada, back on Pleyver—*"He's always been loyal to the House. Veratina trusted him"*—better not to think about 'Rada, either.

Jos moved through the deserted nursery until he reached the dayroom. Ari was there, awake and warmly dressed, sitting in a pool of sunshine from a low window, playing with bright-colored blocks. As Hafrey had promised, the child was alone, although a packed and sealed carrybag waiting conspicuously on the table nearby hinted that he hadn't been left that way for long.

When Jos walked into the room, the boy looked at him and threw his arms in the air. " 'adda! Uppie!"

"All right, kid, here's an uppie for you," Jos said.

He slung the carrybag over his shoulder, then picked up Ari and left the day room by the door that led to the outside. Nobody was in sight there, either. He didn't meet anyone on the walk to the hovercar, or on the long drive to the landing field on the grassy meadow below the palace.

He'd expected to find the landing field empty as well, except for the small aircar he'd flown up from Central HQ— but the armsmaster was as thorough as he was resourceful. As Jos drew near the perimeter he heard the deep rumbling noise of a Fleet suborbital courier coming down on jets.

The vessel had hardly settled on its landing legs before a hatch opened in the passenger section and a ramp swung out.

"Looks like our ride," Jos said. In the infant-seat beside him, Ari sat wide-eyed and silent. Not even the hasty transfer to the courier, or the noise and pressure of the takeoff, caused him to do more than fret briefly.

Another fifteen minutes—a few more than thirty, all told, since Jos had left Hafrey in the morning room—and the courier was landing at the field in An-Jemayne, where *Warhammer* was berthed. A quick walk across the hardpack, and Jos stood beneath the battered, familiar hull of his own ship. A Fleet officer wearing the lace and braid of somebody's flag lieutenant stood by the *'Hammer*'s main ramp.

It took Jos a moment to recall where he knew this one from—she'd been in the reception area the day he'd taken command at Central HQ. She gave him a snappy salute as he came up.

"Ready to lift, Captain."

"This ship takes three to lift, minimum," Jos said. "And five is better. I'll need to call in my crew."

"Ship," said Ari, quite distinctly. "Uppie!"

"I have navigator, engineer, and gunners qualified with antique spacecraft standing by," the lieutenant said. "Your duty officer gave them permission to enter."

"Antique," said Jos, bemused. *Hafrey must have connections all over the planet, to pull something like this together on short notice.* "I like that."

Another young officer—one of the Fleet-happy pups from House Kiel—came dashing up before he had finished speaking. The pilot from the courier, Jos supposed.

"Here's the last," the lieutenant said. "He'll need to leave the planet as well."

Jos looked hard at them both. "Does the fleet admiral know what you're doing?"

The lieutenant and the courier pilot glanced at each other, and the lieutenant said, "She didn't ask any questions, sir."

"I see," said Jos. *I guess Lachiel meant it when she said that she'd back me.* "Just as well. Come aboard, both of you. Let's go."

Errec Ransome: Captivity
(Galcenian Dating 970 a.f.; Entiboran Regnal Year 34 Veratina)

Errec Ransome awoke feeling lethargic and oddly detached from reality. The light of morning shone in through the translucent walls of the snug prison house where the Mages kept him in such unwanted comfort. He sat up and stretched, wondering why he felt so fuzzy, and tried to pull the events of the night before out of the fog of memory.

Then he recalled. He had tried to hang himself, using strips torn from the tunic the Mages had given him.

Looking down, he saw that the clothing he wore was whole and unaltered. If he had ever torn up any garment at all, it wasn't this one. He raised a hand to the side of his neck. No rope burns marred the flesh underneath his fingers.

But I remember. I remember it now.

He stood and walked outside. The tree he had climbed to make his attempt was there, but nothing about it spoke of what he had tried to do. The stout branch overhung the gravel path as it had always done, but his makeshift rope, if it had ever existed, was gone. He wondered again if he had dreamed the attempt, or hallucinated it.

I am insane, he thought.

Then he shook his head violently, though the movement brought on a brief whirl of vertigo. *No. What I know I did is what really happened.*

He remembered it all—the pain in his throat as the noose drew tight, the burning as his lungs fought for air, the black tide rising behind his eyes as he lost consciousness.

Why am I still alive?

His knees felt weak underneath him. He let himself sink down onto a sun-warmed stone bench at the edge of the path, and dropped his head into his hands. He hadn't understood, before, how closely his captors were watching him.

He had been intercepted. He had made a mistake. He had worried that a longer drop would break the improvised rope rather than breaking his neck. And the Mages had come. They had come, and they had saved him.

Anywhere else, that would be an admirable act. Not here. He could not accept it here.

He could no longer climb the tree. Even from where he sat, he could detect the force field around its upper trunk and branches. He stood and walked back to the little house where he lived. Lived. They were intent that he should live.

Well, then, he would live. For the moment. He went inside, lay down on the bed—as always, anonymous hands had made it up, silently and invisibly, while he was out of sight in the garden—and allowed his mind to wander. The Mages had not learned how to imprison that, had they?

Alone with the currents of Power in the universe, he stretched forth his senses along those pathways that the Adepts of Galcen had shown to their students, looking for the guards that kept and tended him.

New minds were there, not the simple uncomplicated ones he had corrupted to his will before. These guards were stronger; they understood Power in their own terms. Ransome waited in the shadows of their thoughts, touching first one, then the other—gently, gently, fleeing farther into the dark at the slightest hint that the watchers might be aware of his presence.

Much that he found in their minds he did not understand.

Some things, such as their willingness to use the currents of Power as tools, like physical objects, he found disgusting. That the Mages could even contemplate doing so . . . it was hideous, to disturb the natural order and make the universe respond to small, imperfect creatures like them. Like him.

He recoiled. Then he drew nearer again. If he was to escape, it must be through these men. He would test them. He would trap them.

He took a shard of rock he had found on the gravel path, a sliver of flint with a point to it. After dark, when the air had cooled, he lay on his pallet with the stone tooth in his right hand, watching the vague shadows cast by the trees outside against the translucent walls. With a sudden movement he flung his right arm across, jabbing the shard of flint into his left wrist, reaching for the artery.

Pain blossomed along his arm. Blood came, making the flint slippery in his grip—but not enough blood, not yet. He sawed the flint back and forth, making the wound deeper. His breath came in ragged, sobbing gasps. At last the blood spurted up around his fingers, lukewarm to the touch and smelling sickly-sweet, and he let the flint slide out of his grip.

The blood kept on flowing, soaking the sheets beneath and above him. Errec felt his body sink into a deadly lassitude. He made no effort to fight it, but lay back against the pillow and let his mind go free. His breathing slowed, his heart slowed, his body cooled. But his masters on Ilarna—and on Galcen—had taught him well. This time he would not lose consciousness. He would watch.

Before long, the translucent wall panel that masked the door into the garden slid open. Two Mages entered, black-robed and black-masked like those who had destroyed the Guildhouse at Amalind Grange. One of them began at once to work on Errec's mangled wrist, applying a glob of reddish jelly and smoothing it into the wound.

The second Mage stripped off one of his black gloves and placed a hand on Errec's forehead. The technique was a familiar one, even allowing for the twisted nature of the Mages' beliefs. The man was touching a dying body, searching for the spirit within and striving to hold it in place while a physician did the necessary work—a dangerous technique, even among friends, and a mark of how important Errec Ransome was to his enemies, that they should risk it to keep him alive.

No hint of triumph colored Errec's apparent passivity. His mind was far away, and very quiet, waiting. . . . The Mage opened himself and reached out farther, touching the fleeting spirit and bringing it home.

Now, Errec thought. He let his mind follow the path of their physical contact, arcing across the infinitesimal gap between skin and skin, racing along the pathways of the Mage's arm and body to inhabit him utterly.

If the Mage working over Errec's lacerated wrist noticed that his companion had stiffened briefly, he gave no indication of it. Without looking up, he said only, "I think I've got him patched up again. Want me to change his clothes?"

The one touching Ransome's forehead didn't respond. Behind the man's plastic mask, his face was beaded with sweat.

"Hey," said his partner after a moment. "Are you all right?"

The Mage took his hand away. "Everything's fine here. Let's get moving; he'll come around before too long."

The two men did the rest of their work in silence: cleaning up the blood that had soaked their prisoner's sheets and mattress, putting fresh clothing on him, and departing as quietly as they had come. In the morning, Errec woke up between new, unwrinkled sheets. He looked at his wrist. Once again, the flesh had healed without a scar.

He smiled. This time it didn't matter. He'd made the necessary beginning, and everything else would follow.

He only had to wait.

XX. Galcenian Dating 977 A.F.
Entiboran Regnal Year 3 Perada

GAREN TARVEET'S quarters at the Summer Palace were considerably better than those he'd occupied in An-Jemayne—the result, he supposed, of his newly enhanced status. As the disinherited son of an off-world mercantile family, he might have been tucked away somewhere among the upper servants, but as Lord Meteun, who'd been with Perada when she escaped the abortive coup, he rated as a personal friend of the Ruling House.

The suite of rooms he occupied had excellent comp and communications links, and the quiet elegance of the furnishings made his family's estate on Pleyver look overdone. Just the same, bedrooms positioned to catch morning and evening breezes in the summertime proved clammy and hard to heat in the autumn. Today, as on most days, Garen awakened early, as soon as the morning chill penetrated into his bedchamber.

He lay for a while beneath the down comforter, taking stock of his surroundings and going over his plans. This was going to be a day for keeping alert. Last night, neither the Domina nor the Consort had come to dinner, and he and

Gentlesir Festen Aringher—whose presence Garen had yet to account for—had been reduced to making stilted conversation about Galcenian folk music for the benefit of the hushed and edgy servants.

Something is changing, Garen thought. *A balance is shifting ... but which way?*

He got out of bed and put on a loose purple dressing gown. The lacquered wood secretary in the opposite corner of the room concealed a desk comp. He sent the comp's morning routines out to grab fresh news and the latest agricultural reports, then sat down to run the sims. His own personalized simulations, these were—he'd been the best, at the Delaven Academy, at making and running them.

The desk comp spat out a sheet of flimsy. Garen looked it over and adjusted the sim parameters slightly: *assume crop failures are first move in Mage biochem attack, then replay.*

The sim took longer to run this time. Somewhere in the distance he heard the rumbling of jets, and frowned at the disturbance. Another sheet of flimsy curled out onto the desk. He checked the results and nodded. As he'd expected, the predictions came out much worse under the new conditions.

It was possible, perhaps, to import from off-world the food required to support Entibor, on a short-term basis at least—but the money would have to come from House Rosselin's private fortune if it came from anywhere at all. The public treasury was already pledged to more ships for the Fleet, and the cash that he and Perada had "diverted" from Tarveet Holdings was currently bankrolling half the privateers in Innish-Kyl.

Turning a nice profit, too ... but the hidden account on Suivi Point was sacred, a key part of his long-term plan. If anything could induce his family to reinstate him, it would be coming home from the war with more money than he'd left with.

He drew a line or two on the printout and considered the result. An alliance with Galcen or Artha might keep Entibor going long enough for the Fleet's new ships to make a difference. Then to return to Pleyver, and take it, with a fleet at his back to enforce his claim . . .

A sudden clamor outside his room—shouts, running feet, a babble of voices—broke into his concentration. The noise sounded like it was coming from the end of the corridor, where the nursery wing connected to the rest of the private apartments. Garen abandoned his sims and stepped into the hallway far enough to grab the arm of a hurrying maidservant in palace livery.

"What's going on?" he demanded.

"Oh, my lord Meteun!" The maidservant looked grateful for his appearance. "You'll tell the Domina, won't you, please?"

"Tell her what?"

"That the Consort has gone—and he's taken the baby with him!"

Now that it was too late to change her mind, Tillijen wondered if she'd done the right thing. She'd spent the night in a furnished room on the outskirts of An-Jemayne, watching news reports on the holoset—nothing so far about *Warhammer*'s return, which probably meant that Internal Security was sitting on the story, and not much about the presence of Mage warships in-system, either. Crop failures in the grain-producing provinces of Cazdel and Elicond did make the news, although the reports blamed the problem on unseasonable weather rather than on what Tillijen suspected was a Mageworlds attack.

Not that I blame them, she thought. *The last thing we need is for somebody to mention Sapne in public.*

She hadn't found anyone to share her opinions with, unfortunately. The redheaded man who had escorted her out of the Silver Slipper had gone off again on his own business after taking her to the furnished room. He had also locked the door behind him from the outside, which irritated Tillijen but didn't surprise her very much. She'd strayed into the shadowy world of spies and security agents, that much was clear. Whether she would get out again, and how, was anybody's guess.

Shortly after dawn the redheaded man came back, looking worried. Tillijen stood up from the couch where she'd dozed off during the late-night financial commentary.

"My lady," he said. "Please excuse my earlier informality. My name is Meinuxet. I serve a servant of the Domina, with what faith and honor I am able to give."

"And this servant of the Domina is——?"

"You'll meet him shortly," Meinuxet said. "In the meantime, because the Rolny has taken an interest in you, my master has sent me to look to your safety."

"Just what I needed," Tillijen said; "to come to the attention of people in high places."

"Inevitable when you travel in the company of Her Dignity," Meinuxet said. "But we have to go. Now."

"Go where?"

The man didn't answer, except to say "Please hurry" and turn off the holoset. She shrugged and followed him out of the room. A hovercar waited outside—the same one that Meinuxet had driven last night—and Tillijen once more found herself gestured toward the passenger seat.

She obeyed, feeling more curiosity than apprehension. There'd been ample time during the night for Meinuxet or his associates to dispose of her, if such was their intent, but she had remained undisturbed. Moreover, she still had both her blaster and the knife inside her boot. Whatever was going on, she didn't think that murder was part of it.

The streets of An-Jemayne were crowded with workday-morning traffic. Meinuxet navigated the crush at a speed just slow enough to avoid the attention of Domestic Security—though still faster than Tillijen would have liked—and took the hovercar out through the suburbs to a small airfield.

"If you're taking me back to the *'Hammer*,'" she said, "I have to tell you that this is the long way around."

"I'm sorry, my lady," the man said. "But it isn't possible at present for me to return you to your ship."

"Ah. Where *are* we going, then?"

The man didn't answer. He led the way to one of the aircars, and a few minutes later they were flying north and

west of the capital, into the highland forests. Tillijen gave
up her attempts at conversation—the man was obviously too
worried and abstracted to appreciate idle banter—and
waited until the aircar settled to earth again a couple of
hours later.

She looked out the passenger-seat window at the grassy
field on which they'd landed. "Is this it?"

"For now, yes. Come."

The morning air outside was crisper than it had been in
An-Jemayne, and smelled cleaner. Tillijen sniffed apprecia-
tively. "Nice," she said—truly fresh air was an impossibility
on shipboard, and most spaceports didn't have anything better. If Meinuxet was planning to stash her out here in the
countryside for safekeeping, things could be worse.

"Her Dignity will be glad to know you approve," the man
said—the first nonessential remark he'd made all morning,
and something about the tone of his voice made Tillijen pull
herself together and look around.

Then she saw it, a long, pale structure that seemed to
float against the hillside above the landing field like a low-
lying cloud: the Summer Palace of House Rosselin.

"What's up?" she asked. "Why are we here?"

"I'm putting you in a hiding place where no one can drag
you out: under the Domina's personal protection."

Jos didn't like having *Warhammer* full of strangers in uniform, even if they did all salute him and call him "sir," but
he didn't think he had much choice. Without the Fleet personnel, he'd be too shorthanded to lift. Of the *'Hammer*'s
regular crew, only Nannla had been aboard when he arrived
at the military landing field, and the number-one gunner
was near-frantic with worry over Tilly, who seemed to have
vanished during the night. Jos considered giving Nannla
leave to stay behind and look for her partner, then thought
better of it. If he had to shoot his way—and Ari's—out of
the system, he wanted at least one of *Warhammer*'s own
gunners on the job.

He turned to the young Fleet officer in the copilot's seat.
"You know what orders you're working under, or at least I

hope you do. So tell me—if we leave here without request-ing permission, are people going to shoot at us?"

"Yes." After a few seconds, the officer added, "But they're supposed to miss."

"Supposed," said Jos. He regarded his temporary copilot with a thoughtful expression. "Do you trust your friends?"

"Enough."

"I suppose that'll have to do." Jos keyed on the ship's in-ternal comms. "Engineering, report."

A stranger's voice came on over the cockpit audio. "I can't make any sense of this blasted power plant. Sir."

"Not surprising. Don't worry about it—just watch for redlines, and treat 'em as they happen. Our plan is a straight run-to-jump, with minimum time maneuvering. Got 'em heated?"

"Heating now."

"Good. Seal and strap, everyone. We're leaving."

"Ready," came the ragged chorus of unfamiliar voices.

Jos reached out for the controls, then hesitated a moment. "How's the kid?"

He'd strapped Ari into the bunk in number-two crew berthing, with the young pilot from the Fleet suborbital cou-rier to keep him company. Now the courier pilot replied over the link from the cabin, "The kid's okay, but I don't think he's real happy about all this."

"Tell him that makes two of us. But he'll like it on Maraghai. . . . How are the engines doing?"

"Engines ready," said the stranger in engineering.

"Ready to launch," said Jos. "Go."

The nullgravs tilted them back and they were off. They hadn't yet escaped the pull of Entibor's gravity when Jos spotted the first flicker on the sensor readouts.

"Somebody's locked on and tracking," he said, as the 'Hammer bounced and shook in the stress of launch. "You're sure they're going to miss?"

"Yes."

A flare of purple light washed over the armor-glass of the viewscreens. Jos glanced over at the copilot. "By how much?"

"Enough."

Then the acceleration eased, and a few seconds later they were free of the atmosphere, out in the clean black of space. The copilot leaned forward for a closer look at the sensor readouts.

"What's that up ahead?"

"Looks like trouble," said Jos. He glanced over the readouts with an experienced eye. "Entiboran Fleet destroyer, closing fast."

"We have a signal coming in from the Entiboran ship," said the copilot. "Voice comms."

"Put it on audio," Jos said. "But don't answer."

The link crackled briefly, and a tinny voice came over the cockpit audio: "General Metadi, I have received orders from Central HQ to prevent you from leaving the system."

Jos let the external comm link go untouched, and tapped the screen of the 'Hammer's navicomp with one fingernail. "Numbers, baby," he muttered. "Give me numbers."

"General," came the audio from the destroyer, "you are ordered not to take a course of five-seven-two from your current location, as that would put you on the arc to Maraghai."

Jos frowned at the navicomp. The red Working light was still flashing—no numbers yet. But five-seven-two wasn't impossible. Metadi tweaked the 'Hammer over toward that direction. The destroyer turned with him, running parallel to the new course.

The link crackled again. "General—I am ordered to take you alongside with tractors and transfer your crew to this ship. If you begin accelerating to jump speed now, I will be unable to lock on. Therefore, you are ordered not to accelerate."

Jos keyed on the internal comms. "Engineering, watch the redlines. I'm going to feed her power."

The 'Hammer accelerated in response to his touch on the controls. A few seconds later, the armor-glass viewscreens lit up with the faint aurora of distant energy fire, and the sensor readouts began to dance wildly.

"What the hell was that?" Jos demanded.

"It looks like another Entiboran vessel has taken the destroyer under fire with guns," the copilot said.

Jos remembered the Fleet briefing he'd attended not quite a day ago—the one he'd been in such a hurry to get away from, to get back to the Summer Palace. "That's not an Entiboran vessel," he said. "Not anymore. It's one of those ships the Mages captured at Tanpaleyn. They've refitted it as one of theirs, to run under a false signature."

Once again the external link came on. "*Warhammer,* I am unable to supply escort," said the talker for the Entiboran destroyer. The warship peeled away, abandoning its parallel course and bringing its energy guns to bear on the Mage attacker. "Good luck, General."

"And good luck to you, too," Jos said, after the link had clicked off. He checked the position plotting indicator. "More trouble. Someone's on our jump point."

"That won't be any of ours," said the copilot.

"Good." Jos clicked on the internal comm link again. "In the gun bubbles. Clear the way with fire."

"My pleasure, Captain," Nannla said from number-one gun. "Nothing beats a little death and destruction if you want to start the day off right."

The guns in the dorsal and ventral bubbles began to spit out jets of slow light, silent in the vacuum of space. The Mage ship on their jump point was out of range, but that wouldn't last forever.

"Someone coming in from up top, boss," said Nannla, over the link. "Switching aim."

"Negat," Jos said. "Take forward. The sensor readings look Galcenian, and those guys are supposed to be on our side, more or less."

"The Mage ship is moving," the copilot said. "Abandoning position on our jump point. The Galcenian is engaging her."

"Good," said Jos. "Let's all think nice thoughts about Galcen for a little while. Jump point locked in. Jump speed. Stand by. *Now.*"

* * *

"This proves my point, you know," Vasari said.

She and Errec Ransome were going down the stairway toward the street. It was morning now; the air was chilly in the unheated building, and she could see a patch of yellow sunlight coming in through the broken door at the bottom of the stairs. She was tired; sifting the minds of the Circle-Mages had taken all night, though she hadn't fully realized how much time had elapsed until the end.

Errec looked even more exhausted than Vasari felt. She had done the interrogation, but Errec had held the Mages for her the whole time. They'd died, of course, when he released them; all the Power he'd been balancing flowed out and into them at once, and burned them from within. Vasari felt no particular remorse—she had touched their minds, and knew them.

She did, however, feel some concern for Errec. He was looking shadowed around the eyes and white around the mouth. Exhaustion, maybe; she wasn't sure. His voice, when he spoke, sounded distant and weary.

"Proves which point?"

"That you need to come back to Galcen and teach the Guild how you do this stuff. Holding an entire Circle that way—"

"No," he said. "This is nothing an apprentice should be asked to learn. I wouldn't teach it to a Master."

"But—"

"No!" He came to a stop, a few steps above the bottom, and turned to face her. In a calmer voice, he said, "I'll help you hunt for Mages on Entibor all you like. But nothing else."

Vasari shrugged. She was a pragmatist; she took what she could get, and wasn't such a fool as to think she could best Errec in a contest of wills. She was also patient, and willing to try more than one approach. The Guild would have Errec Ransome in the long run, if not the short.

"Suit yourself," she said. "I can't make you."

They went on out into the dazzle of morning sunlight reflected off the windows of tall buildings all around. A minute or two later she said, "Considering what I picked up from this crowd, we've got our work cut out for us, anyway."

"What do you mean?"

"The Circle here wasn't an important one. The members weren't Mageworlders at all; they were mostly native-born Entiborans. One or two of them might have had enough talent to make it in the local Guild. The rest . . ." She shrugged. "Weak. But they were only one Circle out of I don't know how many, all working toward the same goal."

"Did you find out what it was?" he asked.

"They weren't sure themselves. They were only supposed to call up their energies and pass them on—but they'd been assured that the working was important. And urgent; this was something new and unexpected, not part of their support for the ongoing effort."

"That's not much to go on."

"Not when you consider how much it could be. There's the attack on the Palace Major. A Mage warfleet in-system, and Galcenians in-system too. They could be working on one of those things, on all of them, or on something else entirely."

"Maraghai," said Errec.

The alteration in his voice made Vasari glance over at him again. Whatever the name of the Selvauran homeworld meant to him, it wasn't good.

"You sound like you know what they were up to," she said.

He nodded. "Jos—the Consort—just came back from Maraghai. He's made a treaty with the Selvaurs for ships and mutual defense. But the Domina has to confirm it first."

"You think they were working to stop that?"

"I think they could have been. But I don't know of any way to counter such a massive working, short of killing every Mage in every Circle on Entibor."

"By the time we got to all of them, the treaty would have failed anyway." Vasari looked thoughtful. "But there *is* at least one person who can keep them from achieving success. Can you pilot an aircar?"

"Yes, of course, but—"

"A pod-rail or a commercial hop would be too slow. You're going to fly to the Summer Palace and have a friendly talk with the Domina."

The late-morning sun, bright and harsh, came through the diamond-shaped windowpanes of the hall of light with a glitter like the edges of knives. Tillijen stood to one side of the long room, next to Meinuxet. She felt awkward and out of place. She wasn't dressed for a visit to the private residence of the Ruling House—and the clothes she *was* wearing, she'd slept in. But Meinuxet had insisted.

Perada Rosselin sat alone at the head of the table, and Nivome do'Evaan of Rolny stood beside her. Tillijen needed only one look to know that the Domina was cold-to-the-bone furious, and that the target of her anger was the slight, grey-haired man who stood at the foot of the table.

The armsmaster, Tillijen thought. She understood now what Meinuxet had meant about serving one of the Domina's servants.

"Ser Hafrey," Perada said, "you have overreached yourself."

The armsmaster's calm demeanor did not alter. "In what way, my lady?"

"Do you deny that you assisted Jos—assisted the Consort in taking away my son, House Rosselin's placeholder?"

Tillijen closed her eyes. *"Assisted in taking away"* . . . *they must already be gone. I should have stayed with the ship. Poor Jos. Poor 'Rada.*

"I gave advice when it was asked," the armsmaster said. "So may anyone, with no blame attached to it."

"You did more than give advice, old man."

Nivome's voice held as much satisfaction as it did anger—perhaps more. The Minister of Internal Security turned to Perada and continued, "We've already heard the nursery staff tell us how they were hoodwinked. And that's not all—Your Dignity, look at these."

He brought out a handful of printout flimsies. "Messages arranging fast transportation and safe escort for Metadi on his way out of the system, all of them bearing the arms-master's personal verification."

The Domina took the flimsies and looked through them one by one. Her face, already pale and cold, seemed to grow even colder. She looked at the armsmaster, and her eyes were like frost over blue steel.

"Ser Hafrey. Do you admit to sending these messages?"

"Denial would be pointless, my lady," said the armsmaster. "I acted, as ever, for the good of Entibor and of your House."

Perada's mouth tightened. "You forgot one thing. It is not for you to set your judgment above mine."

"He has done so before, Your Dignity."

This time, the light in Nivome's eyes was unmistakably triumphant. Perada raised her eyebrows in an expression that was almost a mockery of curiosity.

"How so, Gentlesir Nivome?"

"Do you recall the circumstances under which you left Innish-Kyl—a door that should not have been locked, a pursuit that failed? Who do you think made those arrangements, if it wasn't your own armsmaster?"

From the look on the Domina's face, Tillijen thought, Perada remembered the circumstances very well indeed. She wasn't going to admit it, though—her voice was as cool as ever when she asked, "For what reason do you contend that he did this thing?"

"To persuade Your Dignity into an unwise alliance," said Nivome. "One which you might otherwise have thought better of."

Perada nodded. "I see. Is that so, Ser Hafrey?"

The expression that passed over the armsmaster's face might have been the faintest and briefest of smiles. "Only in part, my lady. It was not *your* reluctance that I sought to counter."

Nivome's face darkened with anger. "Your Dignity, this servant of yours has endangered your person and betrayed your trust. He no longer deserves a place in your household."

"Is that your final opinion on the matter, Gentlesir Nivome?"

• "Your Dignity, it is."

The Domina turned to Ser Hafrey. "And you, Armsmaster. Do you have anything further to say for yourself?"

The armsmaster said nothing—*He's too damned proud,* Tillijen thought. But Meinuxet took her by the arm and stepped forward to stand at the table beside Ser Hafrey, so that she had no choice but to come with him willingly or be dragged along.

"Your Dignity," the armsmaster's agent said, "the Minister of Internal Security is not one who should accuse others of a betrayal of trust."

He nodded to Nivome. "You might inquire as to when exactly the minister learned of the agreement between the Consort and the Selvaurs. I think you will find that he had placed a snoop on your own person, and, while you and the General were talking, he was listening. See . . ."

Meinuxet reached forward and plucked a speck from the edge of Perada's cuff, and continued speaking.

". . . even now he records your words, and the words of those who speak with you, for purposes of his own."

The redheaded man ground the speck under his fingernail; it sparked, and a tiny puff of smoke, visible only as it passed through a ray of sunlight, rose from it.

Perada turned to Nivome. "What is the meaning of this?"

"It's the business of my office, Your Dignity." Nivome was unapologetic. "Where there are secrets that can harm your person and your House, I and those who work for me must find them out however we can."

"Maybe so," the Domina said. "But do not expect it to endear your person to me when you have finished."

The Minister of Internal Security bowed, undaunted. "I only ask to serve."

"So I am told by all my servants," said Perada. "Ser Hafrey!"

"My lady."

"I have heard the accusations and your defense. This is my word on the matter: You are no longer armsmaster to my House, you are no longer living to Entibor. You are dead. Go where you please and trouble me no longer."

The Domina paused. "However. I would not leave the House without an armsmaster; it would run against all custom. Tillijen—are you willing to enter my service?"

Even through her own shock, Tillijen heard Nivome's furious intake of breath. "Your Dignity, this person is—"

"—is my choice for armsmaster, and it's not your place to speak against her. I've dismissed one servant today for placing his judgment above mine; be careful that I don't dismiss a second!" The Domina's voice had risen slightly. She paused, then repeated, in a calmer tone, "Tillijen—what do you say?"

Tillijen chose her words carefully, trying to talk at once to the Domina of Entibor and to the schoolgirl who'd bunked in the captain's cabin. "I think that Gentlesir Meinuxet here is more suited to the work than I am, and I know that if my ship comes back for me I'll be off without a backward glance; but if you still want me until then and under those terms—Your Dignity, I'd be honored."

Errec Ransome: Captivity
(Galcenian Dating 970 a.f.; Entiboran Regnal Year 34 Veratina)

THE GUARDS had changed again. Errec Ransome sat on the stone bench outside his prison house and watched them at a distance. His eyes were closed, as if he were enjoying the warm sun after a long night, but with his inward vision he sought the presence of his adversaries in the tangles of Power.

The Mage who had touched him earlier was going somewhere, and Errec was going with him, his consciousness hidden in the shadows that bordered the other's mind. He had reached out and inserted himself there, using a technique that his instructors on Galcen had spoken of, but that they had considered too dangerous to practice among friends.

An enemy, Errec presumed, was different.

So he watched and waited. After a while he realized that the man in whose mind he rode was going to a meeting with others of his kind. Perhaps, Errec reflected, he himself would become the first Adept ever to watch the Mages at work—or at least, the first to do so and remain faithful to the Guild. He supposed that Master Guislen had seen the

Mages' rituals, and perhaps even participated in them, before he betrayed the Guildhouse at Amalind Grange.

Errec suppressed the stirring of anger that followed upon that thought. Now was not the time for emotions that might draw attention to his presence. Later, if all went well, he could pay back Guislen's treachery as it deserved.

For now, Errec could only hope that his understanding of the Mages' beliefs and practices was good enough, snatched as it had been from stray thoughts as they moved through the unguarded minds of his captors. The man whose mind he occupied had reached the meeting place, and the time had come to put his captured knowledge to the test.

The Mages—eight of them—stood together in candlelit darkness, in a room where the stone floor had a circle inlaid with white marble in its center. And Errec made his move, turning the Mage's mind under his own, forcing the man's consciousness into those shadows where he himself had lurked, and pushing himself out, to look through the other's eyes, to hear with his ears, to speak with his tongue. This was nothing he had learned on Galcen, but it flowed from those lessons nevertheless: what, after all, was the interrogator's craft, but making another mind yield up its secrets unwillingly?

His attack was swift, and reached swift success. After that, his concentration went to maintaining the masquerade. It would not be long now. Only a small part of his strength was being used to keep his host's mind in the darkness.

The leader of the group of Mages began to speak. It didn't take Errec long to recognize the words as a ritual invocation marking the start of that day's workings. As soon as the man had finished, Errec stepped forward. He formed his thoughts into the proper shapes, then released enough of the mind he had captured to put those shapes into words that the Mages would understand.

"My lord," he said through his captive's mouth, and pointed at the leader with his captive's hand. "My lord, I challenge you for this Circle."

He couldn't see the other's face—a mask of black plastic

obscured it completely—but the Magelord's surprise was evident none the less.

"This is not proper," the man said. "There is a time—"

"I challenge you," Errec said again.

This was the crucial moment. If he had misread what his guards' minds had told him, if the leader of the Circle refused the challenge, all his efforts would have to be undone before they left any traces. Let the Mages suspect for even a moment that he could enter and subvert their minds so easily, and he'd never have another chance.

He thought he heard the First of the Circle give a faint sigh. "Very well, if you insist. Power honorably wagered and honorably lost will strengthen us all. So be it."

"So be it," Errec let the body he occupied make answer, and the First stepped forward to meet him inside the white marble circle.

The Magelord raised his ebony staff in a brief salute— and then, almost in the same movement, lashed out in a blow that came close to striking home. Errec struggled to keep control of his borrowed body; he needed its reflexes and skills to keep alive, and to make at least a creditable showing with the unfamiliar fighting style.

The staff that hung at his side was shorter than those he had trained with, meant for use in one hand, not in two. He let the body he occupied bring it up into a clumsy blow. The First deflected it, parried it and went into another attack. This time the blow struck home. Darkness cascaded from it, and Errec felt the body around him begin to die.

He sent his mind arcing across the moment of physical contact as he had done before. Practice had made the transfer easier; between one heartbeat and another the First was his.

The Magelord had opened himself to receive the influx of power from the dying man, and Errec was able to possess him utterly. The man whose body he had occupied only a second before crumpled to the floor in a puddle of black robes, and Errec lifted up the staff that had killed him.

Then he reached out further with his mind. He could feel the presence of the others in the Circle, touching what they thought was the mind of their leader, their minds linked in purpose and ready for whatever single directed effort he should desire. Behind the black mask, Ransome smiled.

He was an Adept, trained to work alone and trained to channel the flow of Power. He drew that energy into him now from the ambient universe—more energy than he could possibly hold without being consumed—and let it flow out along the threads that linked the Circle into one unit of mind and will.

Green light flared in the darkness, sparks and auroras and tongues of flame, as the Circle-Mages fought against the Power that flowed into them. They were too weak to hold it, too untrained to channel it, and Errec fed them more and more of it as their bodies convulsed and their minds burned up in fire.

In the end, no one remained alive but him. And the man whose body he had possessed, of course, but that would not matter for long. Errec left the dead where they lay, and let his borrowed body walk away from the darkened room.

He found a comm link—the design was unfamiliar, but the Magelord whose body he occupied understood it, and knew the proper codes for Errec's purpose. The link buzzed its alarm at the other end of the connection, and Errec spoke through the Magelord's mouth to the one who answered.

"Release the prisoner."

"My lord?" The guard sounded confused. "Is that right?"

"It is my command," Errec said. "I have seen that it is necessary."

"But—our luck?"

"The universe changes, and luck changes with it."

Errec forced out the words with an effort. The Magelord was strong, and he was fighting back from the shadows where Errec had pushed him. Errec turned more of his concentration to keeping the Mage from regaining control of his own body.

The pause must have been noticeable even at the other end of the comm link. "My lord! Are you well?"

"Yes," said Errec. "Lower the force field. Let the prisoner go."

"It shall be done."

Errec closed down the link without saying more. The man whose body he inhabited owned a hovercar, or at least a vehicle similar to one. Errec went there, and collapsed his borrowed limbs onto the cushioned seats.

Then, quite deliberately, he forced the Magelord's body to swallow its own tongue.

He remained with the body until it had stopped convulsing, then went back to his proper self, sitting on the stone bench in his prison compound. The warm sun of midmorning beat down on his face. He opened his eyes and saw that he wasn't alone any longer. Shadowy figures stood all around him, silent and insubstantial: the Circle he had broken, linked to him still.

"Will you be with me long?" he asked aloud. He stood and shrugged. "No matter."

Errec walked over to where the force field had marked the boundary of his garden, and found that it was gone. He stepped across the invisible line that had held him captive for so long, and began walking. He knew that he had to be well away from his former prison before he could pause to eat or sleep.

Already he knew that the next time he did sleep, the dreams would be bad.

XXI. Galcenian Dating 977 A.F.
Entiboran Regnal Year 3 Perada

PERADA SAT motionless as Hafrey departed from the hall of light. Tillijen and Meinuxet followed him, leaving her alone with Nivome do'Evaan. She hurt all over—a physical ache in her back and shoulders, the legacy of adrenaline summoned up by anger and left unspent—and felt in no mood to cope all over again with the Minister of Internal Security. She had already reprimanded him as strongly as she dared, but nothing in his face and bearing suggested that he had accepted the defeat. He looked more like a man who had cleared away one more obstacle to the ultimate victory.

I wish I knew how much of this disaster he set up on purpose, she thought. *If he hadn't taken it on himself to change those locks ...*

But he was there, and he had to be dealt with. Perada summoned up what remained of her resolve.

"Gentlesir Nivome, I gave you leave to go."

He made a formal bow. "And I am Your Dignity's servant in all things. But there are matters which we must discuss."

"Forgive me, Gentlesir—but the day so far has been a tiring one. I'm in no mood to hear about conspiracies and crop failures."

"Nevertheless," he said, "I beg the favor of Your Dignity's attention for a moment longer."

She saw how he stood there, solid and unmovable, and she had to concede defeat. "Go on."

"Your Dignity, I know you are reluctant to take active measures at this time, but the question of an heir to the Iron Crown becomes even more pressing now that House Rosselin's placeholder is lost."

"Not lost," she said—feeling a perverse urge to defend Jos Metadi's actions if Nivome do'Evaan was going to condemn them. "Off-planet. Which is nothing against custom—*I* went to school on Galcen, as you recall."

"I recall it, Your Dignity. And so, I'm afraid, do Your Dignity's subjects.

"What do you mean?" Perada had the sinking feeling that she'd lost a trick in the recent exchange. Dealing with Nivome was like that, always—too much like playing a cutthroat game of cards. She would have enjoyed it, in the same way that a good starpilot might enjoy a tricky bit of realspace running, if she hadn't known exactly what prize the Minister of Internal Security was playing for.

"People talk," Nivome said. "And the talk about Your Dignity is that your late mother made a serious mistake in sending you away from Entibor for your education."

Anger flared, the hot rush of it flooding her nerves and making her skin feel tight. She kept her face and hands motionless, and felt her muscles knot with the effort.

"My mother did it to keep me safe, Gentlesir Nivome. If she'd kept me with her on Entibor, I'd be dead."

And I never wondered until now, she thought, *whether or not the choice was a hard one for Mamma to make. If I'd had more time to think . . . if I hadn't been so angry . . . would I have come to do the same thing for Ari?*

Nivome remained implacable. "Unfortunately, Your Dignity, the only thing that most of your subjects understand is that the present Domina of Entibor spent over ten years on

Galcen, picking up who knows what sort of dangerous off-planet ideas."

"Such as?"

"Such as your disregard for the necessity of a proper heir, produced in good time."

She looked at him as coldly as she could manage. "I've heard this tune before, Gentlesir Nivome. It bores me."

"This time, Your Dignity, you *will* hear me out to the end!" Nivome's voice was almost a shout; it rattled the windowpanes in their diamond-shaped leadings. He pushed on without waiting for her to reply. "Until now the populace could forgive your eccentricities—given your age and good health, and the visible presence of a consort and a well-formed and vigorous placeholder—but the time for that is past. Crops are failing in the provinces; your placeholder has vanished; the Consort—if he still is the Consort!—has fled in disgrace; and *still* Your Dignity refuses to do your duty by the planet and people of Entibor and give them an heir to the Iron Crown!"

He stopped, but the words seemed to keep on vibrating in the silence that followed.

I've misjudged him, Perada thought. *Not all of this is ambition. Most of it, but not all.*

"I see," she said. "What, exactly, do you suggest that I do about the problem?"

"Dismiss the Consort," he told her. "Take another, more suited to the needs of the time. And allow yourself to become impregnated, so that the people will have reassurance that you are at least attempting to follow proper custom."

Perada looked at the Minister of Internal Security and tried to consider him with an objective eye. A big man—strong, intelligent, and by his own lights, loyal—and extremely male.

Veratina liked him, everyone says. Liked him a lot.
But even Veratina never made him Consort.

"Am I to understand," she said, "that you are offering yourself as a candidate for both endeavors?"

"You know from your own experience that I am capable."

"So would be almost any man on Entibor. The talent isn't unique."

"Almost any man on-planet might be capable," he said. "But perhaps not willing, once it becomes known that the Ministry of Internal Security has taken an interest in the proceedings."

"Do you make threats, Gentlesir?"

"Never, Your Dignity . . . but the ministry cannot escape its reputation."

"I understand."

For what felt like a long time, nobody spoke. Perada didn't look again at Nivome; she watched the dust motes drifting in the sunlight over the polished tabletop, and wished that she were anyplace else but Entibor. Pleyver maybe, or back at school on Galcen. Or in the captain's cabin on *Warhammer*, with no obligations to bind her and the galaxy to play in. Finally she let out her breath in a long sigh.

"Very well," she said. "Come back tomorrow morning, Gentlesir Nivome, and I will give you my answer at the hour of public audience."

Galaret Lachiel had an office at Central HQ—a suite of rooms that she'd inherited from Admiral Pallit—but she spent as little time there as possible. She preferred the familiar cramped office aboard her flagship, the Entiboran dreadnought *Diamond Verity*, where her old friend and ally from the Parezulan sector, Trestig Brehant, was flag captain. Gala remembered how little she'd cared for dirtside admirals back when she'd been a sector commander—and these days, with a shooting war going on in-system, establishing a shipboard presence was essential.

For that reason she had breakfasted, conspicuously, in the officers' mess aboard the *Diamond*, and was now sitting with Tres Brehant in her pocket-sized shipboard office, drinking cha'a and catching up on the political gossip. Considering everything that had happened in the past few hours, Gala was faintly surprised that she remained fleet admiral. So far, however, nobody from the palace or from Internal

Security had bothered to check on her involvement in *Warhammer*'s informal departure. The Fleet was regarded as politically conservative—an impression, according to Tres, that had been reinforced by Pallit's attempted coup—and Gala intended to keep the dirtside factions thinking that way as long as possible.

"I don't play politics" is the most potent political game of all, she thought. *General Metadi played it for as long as he possibly could, and General Metadi is a very smart man.*

Aloud, she said, "So the General's away, and with any kind of luck the Selvaurs will keep their end of the agreement."

"With any kind of luck." Brehant's eyes gleamed. "Enough good, heavy ships to seriously chew up a Mage armada . . . that's how they've gotten away with murder for so long, you know, by having more ships in any one place than the people they're attacking. They've left Gyffer strictly alone, and they've barely touched Galcen."

"That may not last," Gala said, "if those Galcenian ships in-system make the Mages angry enough. Count on it, Tres—one strike at the home planet, and our allies are gone before the news gets out."

The buzzer on the office door broke into the conversation, and the door opened to admit a messenger with a clipboard full of printout flimsies. "Situation reports from the outer system, Admiral. And the morning news summary from Central HQ."

Gala took the clipboard and started reading through the stack of flimsies. Brehant waited until after the messenger had left and she'd reached the bottom of the stack before asking, "What's the news?"

She put the clipboard down on her desk, next to the holocube of her family's beach hut in the Immering Isles. "Reports from all over the system have the Mages pulling away from Entibor."

"Well, that's something good, at least."

"No, it isn't."

"No?"

"Take a look at this." She pulled out the last flimsy in the stack and passed it over for him to read. "Six plague deaths in Elicond Province this morning. That's according to the public files. The analyst at Central HQ puts the actual death count at more than sixty."

"I see that," he said. "Do you buy it?"

"Put it together with the crop failures, Tres. Sudden, catastrophic . . . we're looking at something that was engineered. Like Sapne."

"Lords of Life, I hope not." Brehant chewed his mustache thoughtfully. "Everybody always claims it was Mageworlds sorcery that brought the plagues to Sapne—"

"Not sorcery. Damned good biochem. Better than ours."

"All right, biochem. Bad stuff whichever way you look at it. But I never did understand what the Mages got out of the whole deal."

"An example," she said. "Think about it. After Sapne, most of the single-world polities quit putting up any resistance—whenever the raiders hit, they'd just try to absorb the losses as best they could. Ilarna was building up its fleet and starting to look for alliances, and Ilarna got hit hard and ripped open while their warships were still blueprints in a shipyard comp file. And now it's Entibor's turn."

Gala watched as Brehant absorbed the implications of her statement. She could tell when the full impact hit him—he turned as pale as his dark skin would permit.

"So you think that the Mage ships are leaving—"

"—because there isn't any work left here for them to do. Entibor's going to be the example that convinces Galcen and Gyffer and Maraghai."

Brehant's shoulder's slumped. "You know, people are going to ask why we bothered to fight the Mages in the first place."

"Because we're the only fleet that's even come close to hurting the bastards, dammit!"

"I know, I know. But if the homeworld's a write-off, what are we going to do?"

I wish I knew, thought Gala. She picked up the holocube of the beach hut and put it down again. *I thought I was in luck the day Jos Metadi pulled me out of detention and gave me the whole ball of string to play with. Maybe I'd have been better off if he'd left me there.*

"We fight the Mages wherever we can find them," she said at last. "And we keep the plague out of the Fleet."

Brehant nodded. "I understand. Your orders, Admiral?"

"Lift all ships. No personnel transfer between vessels, effective immediately. The Fleet will operate out of Parezul for the duration, and anybody who's dirtside at noon tomorrow headquarters time, stays on-planet for good."

Perada waited until Nivome had left the hall of light before she buried her face in her hands. She wished she had the energy left to howl and scream and pull her hair out of its braids. *Tomorrow. I have to give him the answer tomorrow. And there's only one answer left to give.*

"Don't do it."

The voice was a familiar one. Perada jerked up her head and stared. Errec Ransome was only a few feet away, plainly visible in the sun-filled room.

Warhammer's copilot had changed since the last time she'd seen him, when he'd paid a brief, restrained visit to the palace shortly after Ari's birth. Today he wore a plain black tunic and trousers instead of his usual coverall, and for the first time since she'd met him on Innish-Kyl, he carried an Adept's staff—no makeshift this time, but a length of polished wood tall enough for him to lean on as he stood. Belatedly, she realized that he had entered the palace without disturbing any guards, human or electronic.

"Errec," she said. "How long have you been standing there listening?"

The half-accusation didn't seem to disturb him. "Long enough," he said. "The Minister of Internal Security is trying to force your hand. Don't let him."

She gave a bitter laugh. "It's not my hand that he's trying to force. And if you've been standing there for that long, you know that he's already succeeded."

"Listen to me, 'Rada," he said. "If you dismiss your consort and repudiate the treaty with Maraghai, the Mages have won. Not just Entibor, but everything."

Perada saw that he meant it—his voice had the certainty she'd heard before when Jos Metadi asked him about the beacons in the Pleyveran Web. She looked down at the tabletop.

"What Jos did ... taking Ari away like that ... I was very angry with him."

"He knew that you would be. He was afraid of it, I think."

"I see." She was silent for a while, remembering how Jos had been when they met in the garden—tense and edgy, not triumphant as befitted someone bringing home an alliance that might see the Mages defeated for good—and she knew that Errec was right. "What's it like on Maraghai, Errec?"

"You probably wouldn't like it very much." He actually smiled a little. "But a child growing up ... Ari will be happy there, I think. And safe."

"I'm glad." She paused. "You know Jos. Do you think he's going to come back?"

"Yes." Again that note of flat certainty. "But not soon."

"Then it's no good. I can't put off Nivome do'Evaan any longer."

Errec said nothing.

Perada looked at him standing there, and thought about how he had walked in past the guards without triggering an alarm, and how he had waited unnoticed until she was alone. Jos's copilot had always been quiet and gently-spoken around her, with none of Nivome do'Evaan's over-bearing presence, and as far as she could tell he had no ambitions at all. And he was—she was morally certain—an Adept.

"Errec," she said. "Are you afraid of the Minister of Internal Security?"

"No."

"There was a story I heard on Galcen." Her voice took on the remembered rhythm of the storyteller at the heritage park, talking to a class of third-year students from the Delaven Academy. "A folktale, from up in the mountains. About a king who needed an heir, and asked his chief counselor, who was an Adept, what he should do about his wife's barrenness. And the Adept said, 'All will happen according to your desire.' And when the spring came, the king had an heir."

"There are stories like that on every planet."

"Yes. But are the stories true?"

One corner of Errec's mouth turned up in what might have been a fleeting smile. "You'd do better to find a reliable biolab."

"I can't," she said. "No Domina has ever done it that way—Veratina tried it once, and the people never forgave her. Besides," she added, "there isn't time."

"How long do you have?"

"You heard Nivome. I've promised to give him an answer tomorrow, at the public audience. If I can announce, instead, that I'm expecting a second child . . ."

There was another long silence. Perada couldn't tell what Errec was thinking. His eyes were shadowed and remote, as if he gazed at an inward vista that she could not comprehend.

"Yes," he said. "That way is open."

Perada exhaled carefully. "Attend me tonight in my chambers."

In the sitting room of the Orgilan Guesthouse, Master Guislen stood once more at the window, looking down onto the street. The rain that had lashed against the panes all the day before had stopped during the night, and the sky outside had the deep, clear-washed blue of autumn. A few feet away, at the desk, Ambassador Oldigaard frowned over his afternoon session with the textcomms.

"Bad news?" Guislen asked.

"Contradictory reports. Our ships quote Entiboran Fleet gossip as saying that Jos Metadi brought home an alliance with Maraghai; but our agent at the palace says that Metadi has fled Entibor in disgrace, and that Her Dignity will soon repudiate him altogether."

Guislen shook his head. "Excitement without letup. If the issue stands in doubt, it may be necessary for us to intervene."

"A Selvauran alliance would be fatal," Oldigaard said. "Given ships and engineers from Maraghai, Entibor would have no need for a treaty with Galcen."

"Let us be honest among ourselves, at least. There are no Centrists here; and what Galcen wants is no ordinary treaty. You'll need more than sweet words to make Entibor into one of your client worlds."

"Criticism is easy," said Oldigaard. "Do you have any practical suggestions?"

"As it happens, yes. Go to the Summer Palace at once, before Her Dignity makes a final decision on the matter. Remind her, subtly, that there are other sources of ships and pilots besides Maraghai—offer full cooperation without preconditions, if need be."

"The Council would never agree to it."

"The Council doesn't have to agree to it," Guislen said. "Once they are dependent on our fleet, Entibor will have no choice but to ally itself with Galcen on Galcen's terms."

Oldigaard thought about the possibilities. At last he smiled and nodded. "Excellent. We can charter an airhop at the port, and be there tonight."

The textcomm beeped to alert Oldigaard to incoming news. The ambassador broke off the conversation to read it—one eyebrow going up as he did so.

"New developments?" asked Guislen.

"Oh, yes," Oldigaard said. "The newsfiles report six unexplained deaths this morning in Elicond Province." He read aloud. "'Elicond Public Health denies emphatically that the so-called Sapnean Plague is the culprit, and says that there is no immediate cause for alarm.'"

Master Guislen smiled. "Didn't I tell you that we could trust the Mages to do our work for us?"

"I've done a lot of things for the greater good of the galaxy," Vasari said, "but this is a first."

"Just be ready at the landing field."

It was dusk at the Summer Palace, and the two Adepts stood in the shadows underneath the trees that bordered the formal garden. Vasari suppressed her amusement with some difficulty—it was barely possible, she conceded, that Errec Ransome didn't find the evening's proposed activities as humorous as he might have—and said, "How long should I wait?"

"If I'm not back by dawn—"

"—I should assume she's cut your throat and tossed your body into the nearest well?"

"More or less." Errec sounded serious. "Or that I've been taken away by the Interior Ministry."

"What should I do if that happens?"

Vasari wasn't afraid of Internal Security—but in her experience, getting mixed up with surveillance agencies was always a bad idea. They made unreliable friends and unpleasant enemies, and their outlook, as a rule, was deplorably parochial.

"Nothing," Errec said. "The Guild hasn't heard from me since Ilarna. And you never set eyes on me at all."

She nodded reluctant agreement. "That's probably best. I'll be waiting with the vehicle, then." She hesitated, not knowing quite what else to say to him under the circumstances, and settled for, "Take care."

"I will," he said, and faded off into the shadows.

She waited for several minutes, then turned and began the long hike downhill to the landing field and the rented aircar.

The field at the Summer Palace lacked most of the amenities of a commercial establishment. A small building camouflaged by a stand of ornamental whipgrass housed the landing beacons and other necessary equipment, and provided an out-of-the-weather spot where visitors could wait for the arrival of a hovercar from the palace. Vasari avoided the building's interior on general principles—there was no point in hanging around under bright lights where anybody who showed up could see her face—and found herself a seat on the shadowed ground outside.

For some time, she sat there undisturbed. Far off, at the edges of her awareness, she could sense what was going on at the palace—Errec Ransome's familiar, if elusive, presence, and, through him, the Domina like a bright blue flame. Vasari was not one of those Adepts who could trace the patterns of the universe and predict their change, but sometimes the currents flowed and eddied so strongly that anyone with the Adept's gift could see them.

If I know what's good for me, she thought, *when this is finished I'll forget that I was ever here.*

The night went on. Vasari quit thinking about the passage of time. A light breeze came up, rippling the plumes of whipgrass around the small building. Errec Ransome emerged from the shadows to stand beside her.

She rose to her feet. "Does the Domina have an heir?"

"The Mages on Entibor work against her," Errec said. "I saw the pattern clearly: as long as she stays on this planet, she'll never conceive a daughter."

"And the reigning Domina never leaves Entibor." Vasari sighed. The Selvauran alliance seemed to recede even further into the impossible distance. "So what do we do now?"

"Nothing," said Errec. "The Domina isn't carrying a girl—but she never asked for one, either. What she asked for was time, and now she has it."

"A boy, then."

"Yes."

"Will that be good enough?"

"For a while," said Errec. "That's all anyone can ask."

The rumble of an aircar's engines overrode his voice as he spoke. Vasari looked in the direction of the sound, and saw a midsized commercial charter craft coming in from the direction of An-Jemayne. The charter glided onto an approach course and settled down in a nullgrav-assisted landing. Instinctively, Vasari moved farther back into the shadows.

The last thing we need right now is for some late-night diplomatic flunky to spot us tiptoeing out the back door.

The passenger-compartment door of the aircar swung open and a ramp extended down to the field. Light streamed through the open door of the compartment and silhouetted the figures of two men coming out. Even from a distance, Vasari could see that one of the men carried an Adept's staff. The two men started across the field toward the building—most likely to wait for somebody at the palace to come down with a hovercar, since the distance on foot was a long one for anybody not more interested in discretion than in comfort.

She heard a sharp intake of breath from Errec Ransome. When he spoke, it was in a low tone scarcely distinguishable from the sound of the wind in the grass.

"Do you know those people, Vasari?"

"I don't think so," she said, in the same low tone. "The Adept's nobody I recognize."

"Just as well," said Errec. "Because what I'm about to do is for the good of the Guild. Don't try to stop me."

"Stop you from what?"

But Errec wasn't there to listen to her any longer. He was moving out of the shadows, stepping forward into the path of the two men and barring their way with his staff.

"Master Guislen," he said. "Do you remember me?"

"No," said the Adept. His voice held a courteous puzzlement, nothing more. "Should I?"

"You should," Errec said. "Because I remember you. And I remember Amalind Grange."

Vasari expected Guislen to say something—a denial, maybe, or a question—but instead he brought his staff up to guard. Red fire flowed around him like an aurora of blood.

Errec took a step forward. The staff in his hands began to glow—first a pale orange, then a blinding white as Guislen struck out at him and he blocked the blow. Errec brought the end of his staff up in a trail of white sparks. Guislen blocked, and the air flared up in red and yellow where the two staves met.

Vasari moved hastily out of range. She and Errec Ransome had never practiced fighting together, and now was not the time to start. Instead, she made a wide circle around the patch of ground where Guislen and Ransome attacked and parried and attacked again, so that she came up behind the third man, the unknown who'd come out of the aircar with Guislen.

He was portly and well dressed, after the fashion of a high public official or a substantial man of business. More to the point, as far as Vasari was concerned, he'd pulled out a pocket comm link and was about to key it on. She stepped forward and put her hand against the side of his throat.

"Don't move," she murmured in his ear. She let him feel the touch of Power against his mind, enough to keep him quiet and imply the possibility of worse things in the offing. "And don't say anything. You aren't seeing this."

The duel ended as she spoke. A staff thudded to the ground, and when she looked—still holding the man silent—Errec Ransome was standing over the fallen Guislen.

"Cry for mercy," he said.

"Mercy . . . I can explain. . . ."

"I'll give you the mercy you showed to us at Amalind. You don't deserve more."

Before Guislen could speak again, Errec brought the heel of his boot down hard on the other Adept's chest. Ribs broke with sudden sharp cracks. Guislen arched backward in a massive convulsion, and pink foamy blood spewed from his mouth. A second convulsion, and he was dead.

Vasari let go the man she was holding. The commands she had laid on him, of silence and forgetfulness, would keep him from summoning help for a few minutes, but no longer. And the pilot of the chartered aircar would have seen the whole thing.

"Come on," she said to Errec. "We've got to get you to a spaceport. After everything you've done tonight, this whole planet's going to be too hot for you."

ERREC RANSOME: ESCAPE
(GALCENIAN DATING 970 A.F.; ENTIBORAN REGNAL
YEAR 34 VERATINA)

IT TOOK Errec Ransome ten days to make the journey from his prison house to a working spaceport. He'd walked without a destination at first, seeking only to put as much distance behind him as possible. Then on the second night he saw, beyond the horizon, the rising fire-trail of a massive surface-to-orbit ship lifting off, and turned his face in that direction.

Next day the temperature dropped and it began to rain.

He kept on walking. The broken ground—full of precipitous downslopes, thorny tangles, and grotesque piles of tumbled rock—slowed his progress and often forced him to turn aside from the straight bearing to the port. Patches of fog rose up from every dip and hollow, so that a sudden drop-off or a leg-twisting jumble of stone seemed to hide wherever he looked. And always, at the edge of his vision, moved shadows not cast by any natural part of the desolate landscape, persistent reminders that the dead walked with him.

The rain fell all that day and into the evening. About midnight a cold wind sprang up; it caught at his sodden garments and slapped them against his body with stinging force, then pulled away the cloth to slap at him again. By daybreak he was chilled to the bone and shivering without letup. He pressed his fist against his mouth to keep from answering the voices that spoke to him out of the shadows. And he kept on walking.

The foul weather came close to killing him, but in the end it brought him a different gift. Late in the evening of the fourth day he spied a white light coming from the mist on the far side of the next hill. He didn't dare let his mind go forth to see what awaited. Heedless of what might lie ahead, he broke into a stumbling run.

What he found was a cut where a road passed under the shoulder of a hill. Rain had washed dirt and stone down into the road from the hillside above. A convoy of vehicles had stopped; men with shovels were working on the slide.

The convoy drivers had rigged strong white emergency lights to punch through the dark and fog. The glare, and the noise of the workers, reached up even to where Errec crouched, half-frozen and half-starved, under a tree near the crest line. He was close to half-mad as well—the circle of his dead pressed close around him and would not let him be—but he retained enough grip on sanity to understand that the trucks presented him with his only chance for survival.

Stumbling through the shadows, catching onto bushes and saplings for support, he made his way down into the confusion below. His clothing was no wetter than anyone else's in the downpour, and thanks to those who had imprisoned him, the garments were of local cut. He took a shovel, and—using what scraps of Power he could in his weakened state—persuaded those he moved among to see him as another member of their crew, someone whom they recognized but didn't know well enough to engage in conversation. He fell to shoveling with the rest, and let his labor push the shadows away.

The work warmed him, and when someone came by with hot drinks and paper-wrapped food packets he took both gratefully. He tore open his packet with teeth and fingernails and ate all the contents. The meal, scanty as it was, gave him enough energy to begin work on the next step: he pushed away the faces of the dead and began, instead, to reach out toward the minds of the living.

He sipped at the hot liquid in his thick paper cup and eavesdropped on the thoughts of the men around him, as he had eavesdropped earlier on the thoughts of his guards. This time it was easier, since the convoy workers weren't Mages or Magelords, only drivers and freight handlers. They were taking the string of unladen vehicles to the spaceport, there to fill them with goods from the cargo carriers that brought home loot from across the Gap Between.

At least one of the convoy workers, Iel Geiraed by name, had other plans. Errec followed Geiraed's thoughts even more carefully than he did those of the others—and was rewarded, in time, by learning that the man possessed the local equivalent of a free-spacer's license and ID papers. Errec swallowed the dregs of the hot liquid in his cup and began the process of invasion and compulsion that had served him so well before.

It took remarkably little effort to persuade Geiraed to come up and ask to take Errec's shovel and relieve him at the dirt slide. Geiraed reached for the shovel, and their hands made contact. A touch was enough. Errec made the leap, and sent his tired body to rest in the dry warmth of a truck's interior while his essential self found refuge in the dim recesses of Geiraed's mind.

And rode there, hidden, while the slide was cleared, and for the rest of the journey to the port. Errec wasn't striving, this time, to assert control. He ransacked his host's mind thoroughly, as he had learned on Galcen how to do, and took into himself the man's knowledge and mannerisms and language, until the would-be spacer scarcely had a thought unmirrored by his invisible doppelganger.

On the tenth day, the convoy reached its destination: a fenced landing field surrounded by an ugly jerrybuilt boom town. The red earth behind the fence, scraped flat by heavy machinery and baked hard by repeated takeoffs and landings, stretched out to the horizon. Ships big and small stood in rows on their landing legs: some of them black and wing-shaped like the ships that had broken the Guildhouse at Amalind Grange, others made of plain or painted metal in dozens of different configurations.

Errec slipped out of hiding when the convoy halted outside the gate of the field. His unwitting twin, Geiraed, had business in the town—a meeting with an employment agent, a local who specialized in matching out-of-work spacers with ships in need of a crew. The agency had its office in a prefabricated metal-sided building set up on stone blocks in a side street near the port fence. Errec found a sheltered corner out back near the trash bins, and let his body wait there while his mind-mate took them both inside.

The employment agent had good news this time: not just one ship in port wanting hands, but several.

"Lord syn-Taalen's raider *Knife-in-the-Morning*," the agent said. "That's good, if you don't mind a bit of risk. Or if you'd sooner work cargo, there's *Wild-Rippling-Water* and *Heart-of-the-Sun* both looking to take on crew."

But Errec, riding unseen in the back of Geiraed's mind and looking about the office through Geiraed's eyes, had spotted another name on the agency list. Errec leaned on his host a little, influencing without overt command.

Geiraed pointed at the notice board over the agent's desk. "What about that one with the funny name?"

"Oh. You mean *Tzeelig*?" The agent shook his head. "I don't know if that'd suit you. It's an outlander ship, come from Ophel, and they wouldn't be looking if one of theirs hadn't died on the way."

The part of Errec that had once been a free-spacer was inclined to agree with the agent. A death on a voyage was never good, and *Tzeelig* didn't sound like a happy ship. But she was going back to Ophel, and Ophel was—barely—a part of the civilized galaxy.

He leaned on Geiraed again. "I'll take that one."

The agent shrugged. "Your choice," he said, and brought out the paperwork.

When Geiraed left the office, he had an employment contract in his coat pocket along with his ID and license papers.

Not thinking about why he did so, he wandered around to the back of the prefab building, where a dirt alley ran along between the trash bins and the rows of empty packing crates.

Later that day, a dark-haired, dark-eyed man bearing the license and identity papers of Iel Geiraed presented himself to *Tzeelig*'s supercargo and signed as crew. And a host of shadows—one of them newer than the others—came aboard with him.

XXII. Galcenian Dating 978 A.F. Entiboran Regnal Year 3 Perada

IN HIGH summer, the formal audience chamber at the Summer Palace was supposed to be pleasant and airy. Perada didn't find it so. This late in her second pregnancy, even the coolest rooms in the palace felt stuffy and uncomfortable.

She would have gone back to the Palace Major, and up-to-date environmental engineering, except that nobody on Entibor was traveling anywhere these days. Strict control of population movement was the only measure that could keep the plagues from overwhelming everything—and if the average Entiboran couldn't get a permit to travel from the center of town to a nearby suburb, neither should the Domina.

Custom. She shifted her weight on the solid wooden throne. The cushion, a thin leather pad almost as old as the throne itself, felt like it was stuffed with gravel. *Another month, no longer, and I won't be able to plead custom anymore. And Nivome do'Evaan will come to me for an answer again.*

Errec Ransome had promised her that Jos would come

back ... "but not soon." More and more, she feared that "not soon" would slip into "not soon enough."

She straightened her shoulders and lifted up her head under the weight of the Iron Crown. The holocameras mounted on the walls of the audience chamber would pick up her image and broadcast it to the people of Entibor—for all she knew, the newsfeeds were sending it out to the entire civilized galaxy—and she owed it to her subjects to show a proud face.

"Gentles," she said to the handful of men and women in the audience chamber. She spoke slowly and clearly, so that the audio pickups on the holocameras wouldn't miss anything. Most of the people in the hall would already know everything she had to say. The real listeners were outside the walls of the Summer Palace, following the news and hoping to hear something good for a change.

Perada didn't have much to offer them, but she'd make the best of what she had. "We have word, at last, from the Fleet."

One or two people moved a little closer. Tillijen, who normally stood at her left side as befitted the armsmaster, was one. Like Perada herself, *Warhammer*'s former gunner waited for a partner's return—but no ship of the Fleet had landed on Entibor since the plague first struck.

"The captain isn't going to do it if the people he's working with aren't allowed to," Tillijen had said. But that had been a long time ago.

"Our ships have driven the Mages from our home system," Perada went on.

She knew that the statement was an exaggeration—that it came close to being a flat-out lie. The Mage ships had begun pulling away from Entibor as soon as the plagues began, but they'd left enough ships in-system to make punitive raids and harass any off-world vessels bold enough to attempt planetfall. Still, the assertion sounded well.

"Now, together with our Selvauran allies, the Fleet is preparing to bring the Mages to battle."

She drew a deep breath, trying not to let her expression change as the child inside her squirmed and kicked. *Time for the inspirational part of today's speech,* she thought. *For all the good it's going to do anyone.*

"Let us therefore remain undaunted. This war is far from over, but the end is now in sight, and victory will—must—be ours." She paused and glanced about the audience chamber. "Is there anyone here with further messages or petitions?"

She wasn't expecting an answer. The public audiences these days were performances for the holovids, rather than the working sessions they had been as recently as half a year ago. Today, however, the double doors at the rear of the audience chamber swung open, and the court annunciator called out, "Gralanann son of Granaghal!"

With a name like that, Perada knew, the messenger had to be a Selvaur. The saurian who strode into the audience hall was larger even than Ferrda had been. His body-paint was metallic gold, and his crest was studded with rows of faceted stones. The interpreter who accompanied him was hard put to keep up with his long steps.

Gralanann halted in front of the throne and gave the brief nod that sufficed among his people for respect. He growled a sentence or two in his native tongue. Perada caught what sounded like Ferrda's name among the hoots and rumbles, and leaned forward as best she could over her swollen belly, anticipating the translation.

"Greetings, She-who-rules-Entibor," the interpreter said. "I carry word from Ferrdacorr son of Rillikkikk that his fosterling grows and does well under the Great Trees."

"Convey my thanks to Gentlesir Ferrdacorr," she said. "His care for the placeholder of House Rosselin is a comfort to all of us in these hard times. But surely, Gentlesir Gralanann, you have not braved the troubled surface of Entibor only to pass along family messages."

Gralanann gave a quick *hoo-hoo* of Selvauran laughter, and a longer rumble of reply.

"Thin-skin ills are no danger to the Forest Lords," the interpreter translated. "I bring an offer to your people from the elders of Maraghai."

"Let us hear it, then, by all means."

More rumbles from Gralanann, and an accompanying patter of translation from the interpreter. "We have a world, one among our distant outplanets. Good for farming. Not many of our people want to go there—no fame in farming, and too much fame in hunting Mages. But you have farmers, and no crops."

"The Forest Lords are offering this planet to Entibor?"

A quick rumble of negation. "We open it to colonists, no more."

Perada hesitated only a moment. Selvaurs had little respect for thin-skin dithering; she knew that much from the stories Jos had told about his dealings with them. And, in truth, there was only one answer she felt able to give.

"Let it be done," she said. "The Minister of Agriculture, the Minister of Transport, and the Minister of Public Health will work with your people to do whatever is needed."

It isn't much of an offer, she thought. *But we'll need food, even after the war is over—if the war is ever over—and at least it's a way to safety for a few of us.*

"All right, gentle sirs and ladies," Jos said, "it's time to place our bets and spin the wheel."

The officers who crowded elbow-to-elbow in *Warhammer*'s tiny common room made noises of agreement. They were a mixed lot—Galaret Lachiel was there as Entibor's fleet admiral, along with representatives of local defense forces from the worlds of Perpayne and Infabede, as well as a number of privateers and a huge Selvaur in crimson body-paint.

Over by the ladder that led up to number-one gun bubble, Nannla watched the proceedings with an expression of controlled impatience. Ever since leaving Tillijen behind on Entibor, the gunner had resented any time not spent in deep space hunting Mages; she'd gotten as bad as Errec Ransome that way, and Jos didn't blame her.

He brought up a chart on the common-room holovid screen, pulling the data out of newly expanded main ship's memory. Being in charge of a fighting fleet in wartime did have one or two advantages—chief among them being that it was easier to talk a shipyard into doing extensive refitting and upgrading to an already nonstandard vessel.

"We've been picking up word of Mage scoutships nosing around outside the system for weeks now," he said. "If the old patterns hold true, that's their buildup to a big push. Which means that we ought to have a Mage warfleet assembling someplace nearby—relatively speaking, that is."

Using a pointer, he highlighted a section of the chart. "Most likely, here. The Mages know about the Web— they'll be expecting us to make a stand either out beyond it, where there's room to fight and room to jump away to safety, or somewhere in-system, where there's good comms and clear lines of sight."

He paused and looked around the common room. "Gentles, we aren't in the business of running for safety. We're going to be waiting for them within the Web itself, where nobody can get away until it's finished."

A mustachioed privateer captain in a long-coat of purple moiré spidersilk was the first to break the silence that followed. "How do we know they'll come in?"

"If they want to do anything inside the system," said the senior captain from Infabede, "the Web's the only way to get there. Either they come through, or they go somewhere else."

"And the Mages *will* want to get in, sooner or later," Jos added. "Pleyver's on the arc for a lot of places. They'll need to secure it before they move on to the Central Worlds."

"Too bad we don't have Pleyver's permission to use their system for a battlefield," remarked the Infabedan. "It's going to make things tricky afterward no matter who wins."

Jos ignored the comment. Instead, he pointed to a place near the top of the chart. "I want the ships from Maraghai and Perpayne to go out here as if on normal patrol. The Mages will have you outnumbered and outgunned—but you'll also be too large and important a force for them to ignore. When they give chase, you run. Stay out of their range; all you have to do is get them to follow you into the Web."

"And then?" the Infabedan asked.

"At the time marked on your schedules, everyone here will arrive at the coordinates listed, proceed at high local speed into the Web, and go hunting. The Infabedan ships will remain outside to pick off stragglers. Up to now, whenever they've taken hits, the Mages have jumped back to their own worlds. This time they won't be able to do that. I want their fleet to vanish like it never existed."

You figured out yet what we're going to do if we lose? asked the Selvauran captain.

Jos grinned at him, teeth showing. "We all *die*, that's what. But anyone who comes out of this alive is going to have enough fame to make the wrinkleskins back home choke on swallowing it. That good enough for you, Ramgha?"

The Selvauran's yodel of agreement didn't need translation.

"Good," said Jos. "People, you've got the best available maps and coursebooks for the Web, but coordinated action is still going to be difficult. If you get lost or lose comms: look for the Mages, and attack."

Lachiel's expression grew sober. "With respect, General, where will you be during all this?"

"Right in the middle of things. I'll let everybody know when it's time to go home."

Lachiel frowned. "Jos—is it wise ... ?"

"No," he said. "This isn't the time for wisdom. This is the time when we make the gamble and trust in our luck."

The privateer captain laughed aloud. "Trust in *your* luck, you mean. I was with you at the drop points off Ophel, Metadi; your luck is good enough for me."

In the heart of the Web, the stars might as well have been in a different universe. The drifts of glowing dust, the phosphorescent gas, and the uncanny pseudostructures that loomed and shifted among the Web's magnetic fields all worked to obscure everything except the brightest and nearest realspace objects. Jos Metadi checked *Warhammer*'s chronometer again.

We should have heard something by now.

The air in the cockpit was cold—he'd shut down most of the *'Hammer*'s nonessential systems to conserve energy, the way he always did when there was a fight in the offing— and he shivered a little under his quilted vest. Maybe the Mages hadn't taken the bait.

He shifted in his chair and looked at the chronometer again. In spite of his words at the briefing, he knew that a battle here and now would be his sole chance. He'd drawn on all the credit he had—with the Selvaurs, with the privateers of Innish-Kyl and the local defense forces of half a dozen worlds, with the officers of the Entiboran Fleet—to pull together a temporary alliance. If they lost . . . worse, if the Mages never came . . . he'd never be able to do it a second time.

He'd never get his old crew back together, either. Right now he had a Selvaur down in the engine room, but Wrann was a barely blooded youngling fresh off the home planet— good enough with engines, but mostly on board because his mother's cousin Ferrdacorr was looking after a fosterling on Maraghai. Tilly was stuck on quarantined Entibor, playing bodyguard to Her Dignity, and there was a pink-cheeked Fleet ensign working number-two gun in her place.

And then there was Errec Ransome. Jos looked over at the man in the copilot's seat. Errec wore Adept's black these days, and he had a staff tucked away in his locker in crew berthing. He never spoke about what had happened to him before he made it off Entibor on the last Fleet ship to lift—but Jos had seen the regular news reports from the Summer Palace, and he knew something of how 'Rada's mind worked.

"Errec," he said quietly. "Any Mages out there?"

"Not yet," Errec said. His voice was even quieter. "But they're close. I can feel them moving around, out on the fringes of the Web."

"Any idea whether they'll come in?"

"They don't know yet either. Caution . . . greed . . . they're afraid of your luck, you know."

"Think it's going to scare them away?"

"Maybe. Or maybe you're going to draw them in. The Magelord who breaks your luck can call himself a powerful man."

"I see." Jos watched the floating strands of light outside the viewscreens for a while. Green ... blue ... violet ... bright enough to believe in, but not real enough to steer by. *If my luck breaks, and I die here, I'll never know. ...*

"Errec," he said. "Whose kid is it?"

He heard Errec draw breath and let it out in a faint sigh. "An Entiboran would say, yours. By law and custom."

Jos didn't say anything. When he glanced over at the co-pilot, Errec had gone distant and remote again—searching inside his mind for Mages somewhere out beyond the Web.

That's all he's ever going to say about it, Jos realized. *And I suppose that's my answer.*

The poor son of a bitch.

"Boss?" It was Nannla, over the internal comms.

"Yeah?"

"Can you give me a bit of lateral? I think I'm getting something."

"How much?" Jos asked.

Errec came back from wherever his mind had gone. "Turn sensors to five-seven-one, high."

Jos touched the maneuvering jets. "Five-seven-one, high. How's that, Nannla?"

"Something's out there, all right. What do you have on your screens?"

"Not much, in this soup ... weapons burst, far."

"That'll be the Mages," said Errec. "They're coming in."

"Getting here was damned hard," said the First of the Mage-Circle to his Second. "The public safety restrictions—Internal Security might as well have labeled them aimed at us."

The Second pulled off his outer wrap—in Sardanis, one of the cities in Entibor's southern hemisphere, the winter wind was bitter cold. His voice was hoarse. "And start a panic—'Mages on Entibor'? I don't think so."

"I hope you coughed on a lot of people on your way over."

"And offered their despair to the working," said the Second. "Every little bit helps."

"I'm glad you still have a sense of humor about this. Now's when we find out who believes—truly believes—and who wanted to join a Circle because Mamma and Dadda would be shocked if they ever found out that sonny was a big bad Mage."

"And you don't think we'll have enough true believers?"

"In my darker moments, no. But don't worry," the First continued. "Just in case—I've offered up *my* despair for the working."

"There are times," the Second said, "when I wish we could be more rational about this."

"I was afraid you'd say that. There's no other way to become part of the working of the universe."

The Second pulled his black robe on over his head and reached for his mask. "The Adepts seem to think there is."

"Spectators at the banquet," the First said, "that's all they are. They try to pull us down to their level. And speaking of pulling things down to levels, it's time to see who else is here."

The two men finished putting on their robes and masks, and descended into the ritual chamber. The empty basement room had a circle chalked on the floor, with a bucket of water standing by to wipe it away. These days, no one dared keep a more permanent meditation room. The agents of Internal Security had been ruthless in tracking down anyone even suspected of Magery.

Only one other man waited in the white chalk circle. "Cold night out tonight," he said.

"That it is." The First looked around. "Are we all that's left of the Sardanis circle? The faithful few?"

"Felspath won't be here. The plague took him. He died well, and gave his power to us all."

"Not as well as if he'd died in the Circle," the Second said. "But I suppose we can't all be that lucky."

The First stepped into the circle of chalk. "Shall we begin, then? It's past the time. The others will already have started."

As he spoke, the silver cords of light that appeared in the corners of his eyes—their presence made clearer and more visible by the ritual mask—began to glow and shift. The First wondered if anyone else saw them. It was gratifying to know that his faith was the true one, and that every time there was a working, he could see the objective reality of the good that they had done.

He pulled his staff from the clip at his belt.

"Such workings as this are rare," he said aloud, holding up the staff. "We are called to great honor and great sacrifice. We go willingly, knowing that we will become the silver threads of power, not merely be their manipulators.

"One in being, one in thought, let it be now!"

He struck the man to his right, a friend he had known for years, and felt the power, willingly given, willingly taken, flow through his staff. The power of the whole universe filled the tiny room. His staff was glowing. The silver cords were shifting.

Then darkness crushed him, and he fell.

Jos squinted at the *'Hammer'*s cockpit chronometer. Seventy-seven hours since the last contact with a Mage ship. Longer than that since he'd eaten or slept—not since before heading into the Web. Nobody else on board was in any better shape than he was, either. They were all glassy-eyed with fatigue.

If I had enough energy to stand up, I'd probably fall over.

He glanced at Errec. "Time to get out of here, do you think?"

Errec closed his eyes briefly. There were lines on his face that hadn't been there before; for an instant, Jos thought he was seeing his copilot as Errec would look years from now, if he survived to grow old. Errec opened his eyes again.

"Yes. There's nothing more to find."

"Then it's fallback time," said Jos. "Out to Farpoint, and see who's left."

Errec laughed without humor. "If we can find Farpoint."

"Do you have a fix on our location?"

"Realspace somewhere."

"No kidding." Jos suppressed a yawn of exhaustion. "Get us out of the Web, then, if that's the best you can do. Once we're outside, we can get a fix."

"All right," said Errec. "Setting course, seven-one-two. Out of the Web."

Jos keyed on the intraship comms. "All hands, stand easy on station." He turned back to Errec. "Any beacons in sight?"

"That's a negative."

"Well, keep your eyes open, and we'll see if anything familiar shows up."

The 'Hammer proceeded steadily through the treacherous spacescape of the Web. Jos didn't touch the controls, even when the instruments showed his ship veering wildly in course and speed. He knew the feel of the 'Hammer at all speeds and in all maneuvers—regardless of what the instruments said, his ship wasn't corkscrewing all over the volume.

The internal comm link clicked on. "I make something, bearing six-two-five low," Nannla called from number-one gun bubble. Her voice was ragged with exhaustion.

"I'll take her down for a look," Jos said.

What they found was a spaceship, broken apart and twisted by energy fire. A thread of atmosphere leaked from a partly sealed interior compartment to make an incandescent plume against the darkness.

"Anyone still alive aboard that one?" Jos asked.

"Yes," Errec replied. "But they're Mages."

"Leave 'em, then," said Jos. He continued on course. The wreck, slowing spinning around its longitudinal axis, passed below the 'Hammer's ventral side.

"Beacon showing," Errec said a few minutes later. "Correlates with Poddit's Ledge."

"Recommend me a course and speed."

"Steer one-five-one, this speed is fine."

"Got it." Jos changed to the new course.

A call came up from engineering over the intraship comms. *How much longer are we going to be out here? We'll need to refuel soon.*

"We're on our way out," Jos called back.

Within half an hour, although it felt much longer, the first true stars showed through the drifting clouds of gas. *Warhammer* wasn't the first ship to the rendezvous point, but it was far from being the last. Reports were still coming in of battle actions completed or in progress—the mass of accumulated data was being compiled on the larger Perpaynard cruisers, with their ample ship's memory and up-to-date hardware.

"Not as bad as it could have been," Jos said a while later. Bone tired, he still was unable to sleep; instead, he was sitting up in the *'Hammer*'s common room with a cup of cha'a and a sheaf of reports.

The very young Fleet ensign who'd handled number-two gun smothered an involuntary yawn and asked, "Did we win?"

"Yeah," said Jos. "I guess so. We've got most of our ships back. And counting up the after-action reports . . . it looks like none of the Mages have come out."

"A victory?"

"I'd call it one." Jos put down the stack of reports he'd been reading and started drafting a message instead. "Contact the Fleet, tell them to get the couriers ready. Start by sending the word to Gyffer and Khesat and Suivi Point. Tell them we finally did it."

"Who's going to tell Entibor?" asked the ensign.

"I'm going to carry that message myself."

Jos stayed in Infirmary Three, Yasp Reception,
for three days after he regained consciousness.
On the third day, the medical staff judged him recovered
enough to let him access the infirmary's text readers and the
general comp files, and he found out what Yasp Quarantine
Berthing was charging *Wandering Star*—or *Warhammer*, as
he supposed the ship now was—in docking fees. That led
him to check on the charges against *Warhammer*'s account
for his own medical care. An hour later he was arguing with
the physician in charge.

"Am I contagious?" he demanded.

"Well . . ."

"If I were contagious you'd be talking to me from the
other side of an armor-glass window. And if I'm not contagious I want out of here."

"Captain Metadi, you're still convalescent. You're in no
shape to go anywhere."

"I can berth on my ship. As long as I have to pay docking fees for her, I might as well do it some place where I
can look for a cargo."

The physician continued to protest, but in the end he agreed that Jos could leave. Jos took his old clothes—now laundered and decontaminated to the point of being threadbare—and his pilot's license. Aside from a dubious claim to a spacecraft of unknown history and obsolete construction somewhere in the quarantine docks, he had no other possessions.

The clothing wasn't really his either except, like the license and the ship itself, by survival and inheritance. His coveralls from *Meritorious Reward* hadn't made it through quarantine; he supposed they were already recycled into bedsheets and deckwipes. The clothes the infirmary gave him came from *Warhammer*, and most likely from the locker in the captain's cabin: Jos assumed that the garments belonged to the man or woman who had been captain before Maert. Man, most likely; the clothes were cut for somebody Jos's size or larger.

But the fit wasn't too bad, if he belted the shirt tightly and stuffed the pants legs into his boots. The style and cut were a bit gaudy for a merchant-spacer, but Jos wasn't inclined to complain, since the same orderly who'd brought the clothes also brought him a Gyfferan Mark VI blaster in a sturdy holster. He'd never had the money to buy one of his own.

He checked himself out at the main desk of the infirmary. After he'd signed four or five slips of printout flimsy and the main-desk datapad, the clerk on duty handed him an envelope stuffed with all the loose change Yasp Quarantine Berthing had found aboard *Warhammer* when they decontaminated her. The folding stuff was a bit faded and limp from the decon procedures—only the metal bits in the hard cash actually looked better for the experience—but paper and hard together added up to a respectable amount of walking-around money. Not enough to get his ship out of hock, but more than enough to buy a good meal and a drink. Definitely a drink. Convalescent or not, Jos decided, he needed one.

First find the docks, he told himself. *There's always bars by the docks.*

He couldn't read the local alphabet—the physicians and the desk clerk had spoken to him in careful, accented Galcenian, and the paperwork had run Galcenian translations under everything that needed a signature—but the signs had enough pictures to make up for the lack. He followed the stylized spaceship icons for a while, then discovered that they led to the main station-to-surface shuttleport.

Not exactly what he wanted. He tried again, this time asking directions of anybody who looked knowledgeable. After several hours of not-quite-random searching, he located the docking area. The icon wasn't a spaceship after all, but a nullgrav skipsled.

And outside of orbital docking he spotted a bar, with a man in a black apron polishing glasses behind the counter. Jos took a seat at the bar and called for a cha'a and chaser.

The bartender fetched him the two drinks. The cha'a had its familiar stimulating tang; the other was something he hadn't seen before—local, apparently—that smelled like a combination of swamp water and cleaning fluid. He tasted that one. Even cold, it made a pleasant burning on his tongue.

He paid for his drinks and put the envelope of cash back inside his dark leather jacket; itself another legacy of the captain he had never met. It was only then, as he sipped alternately at the cha'a and the strong drink, that the real question came to him: even if he did pay his port fees, how was he going to fly *Wand*—fly *Warhammer*—without an engineer?

"You look like you know your way around the docks," he said to the bartender. "Where's the shipping office around here? I need to sign on a crew."

Jos had spoken very slowly in Galcenian. The bartender answered the same way.

"Shipping office is at mainside complex."

The term was one Jos hadn't heard before. "Mainside? Where's that?"

"Down below," the bartender explained. "On the dirt."

"Thanks," Jos said. He took an unhappy gulp of the strong drink. With the shipping office located dirtside, he'd have to spend more money riding the shuttle down and back, with the docking fees charging up for each minute he was away. All that just to find enough crew to lift.

If Yasp Quarantine Docking would let him go at all. He needed to check over those account cards that Captain Maert had left him. Those were what he needed to tell him if he'd have to sell his ship to pay his way out of quarantine. He needed to go aboard *Warhammer* to get those numbers, if for no other reason. While he was there, it was nobody's business if he decided to walk around the first ship that he could call his own.

Not bad, he thought, *for a kid not quite ten years out of the warrens on Gyffer. My own ship. Even if I don't turn out to have her for very long.*

He downed the last of his drink, paid the tab, and stood up as if to go. The bartender held up a hand to stop him.

"Wait a minute. You the captain of that armed merchant in Quarantine?"

Jos turned back to look at the bartender. "Maybe. Depends on why you're asking."

"Looking for a crew?"

Progress, Jos thought. *Maybe I won't have to go dirtside after all.* "I might be, yes. Why?"

"There's a lad here," said the bartender. "Needs a berth. His ship came in shot to pieces and couldn't be made spaceworthy—got sold for scrap to pay fees. You talk with him?"

Jos shrugged. "Talk's easy."

"I call him, he comes."

"Right," said Jos. He sat back down and ordered another drink. What came through the door of the bar a few minutes later wasn't anything Jos had expected. The "lad" the bartender had summoned was a big saurian type, almost a third again taller than Jos himself, with a scaly, grey-green hide and a bright green crest rising from the top of a rounded skull. The creature opened its mouth, revealing a formidable array of pointed teeth, and let out a bass-voiced bellow that rattled the glasses behind the bar.

"This here's Ferrdacorr," said the bartender, indicating

the scaly green one. "He says that he's pleased to meet you, and he's the best damned engineer that *you've* ever seen."

"Yeah?" Jos had never met a Selvaur before in the flesh, but he'd read the descriptions and heard the stories. Port gossip had it that Selvaurs were tough customers but good workers, if they could be convinced to work for you at all. Gossip also said that they didn't care much for weaklings and pushovers.

The Selvaur didn't say anything, just looked Jos up and down, like a customer eyeing the chops at a butcher's stall. Jos ignored him and spoke to the bartender.

"Tell your pal Ferrdacorr that he'd better be a good engineer," he said. "Because I plan to take my ship into some dangerous places."

The creature let out another roar.

"He says he understands you well enough," said the bartender. "But if you want him, you'd better take his partner too, the best damned hull technician in the galaxy."

"What's his partner? Another Selvaur?"

"No," said a voice by Jos's elbow. "*I'm* his partner."

Jos turned toward the speaker, and found that this time he was looking at a young woman of about his own age. She was wearing the same kind of flamboyant outfit that Captain Maert and the *Wandering Star*'s other crew members had worn, this time with ruffled cuffs and a vest embroidered in crimson glitterthread. She carried a blaster in a cross-draw holster and what looked like a knife in her boot.

"I'm Rak Barenslee," she said. "Hull technician. Also pilot in training, cargo appraiser, and gunner, late of the privateer ship *Strahn's Luck*. Are you the captain of the *Libra*-class that came in a couple of weeks ago? Because if you are, Ferrda and I can help you run her the way she wants to be run."

XXIII. Galcenian Dating 978 a.f. Entiboran Regnal Year 3 Perada

AMBASSADOR OLDIGAARD had returned to the Summer Palace. Now that the hot months had come to the lowlands around An-Jemayne, bearing famine and disease on the parching wind, the palace in the remote mountains was a very pleasant place to be.

Or it would have been pleasant, he reflected, if not for the fact that every time he came to speak to the Domina, he came as a beggar with his hat in his hand. That hadn't been what the Council had told him to expect, or what he'd expected for himself.

The Domina should have been at a disadvantage. She needed the strength of Galcen. But she delayed her decision, again and again. And as a result, he was stuck on a plague world, with precious little communication in or out, while the Galcenian fleet was allied for all practical purposes with the Entiborans.

And as long as Perada held out, saying neither yes nor no, the harder it would be to change that status quo. Not for the first time, Oldigaard regretted the loss of his Adept, the man who had promised that he could influence the Domina.

Oldigaard's restless pacing had taken him to the Fire Room, a high and drafty place which took its name from the ornamented hearths—now empty—along two walls. Small tables, surrounded by deep chairs, and rank after rank of books, each one a priceless antique, made the chamber look like a scholar's retreat rather than a ruler's semipublic waiting room.

Oldigaard sat in one of the chairs, his legs stretched out before him. He looked at his chrono. An hour remained before his latest appointment with the Domina. Today he would give the Council's ultimatum, and for better or worse he would act on the reply.

"Good morning," Festen Aringher said. "Since I find you alone, may I have a word with you?"

Oldigaard looked up. He'd seen his fellow Galcenian from time to time, both in the palace and in An-Jemayne, but he hadn't exchanged above a dozen words with him. He had supposed that the man was a translator on the Domina's staff.

"A word, no more."

"It will take a few words, but not many. To be brief: for the duration of this crisis, I am the ambassador plenipotentiary between Galcen and Entibor."

Oldigaard sat up sputtering.

"By whose authority?"

"The same who sent you to replace poor harmless Nepalat. When you get your next sheaf of instructions from home, you'll find that two things have happened: first, that the party which appointed you to the ambassadorship has left power, and second, that you have been recalled by their replacements."

"I'll wait until I see that message, if you don't mind."

"You'll only embarrass yourself and Galcen both if you deliver the overly dramatic ultimatum which you carry in your coat pocket. So, to make the transition easier, I suggest that you look for the message." Aringher glanced ostentatiously at his own chrono. "I'll wait."

"I'm afraid that I can do nothing until I return to the capital, after I've concluded my business here."

"As you say."

At that moment another figure joined them—a slender woman in black, with a long staff in one hand. "May I present my associate, Mistress Vasari?" Aringher said. "Like your late companion, an Adept from Galcen."

"We've met," the woman said. Her pleasant voice was unpleasantly familiar. "But I'm delighted to make your acquaintance again under less trying circumstances."

"Likewise, Mistress," Oldigaard said, his diplomatic training coming to his rescue. "You must understand that this is highly irregular."

"We must all bend before the wind," Vasari said. "This is an unconventional situation we find ourselves in. But you have a mission as important as ours."

"I haven't agreed that you have a mission at all," Oldigaard said. He was wondering if he could somehow dash from the room, seeking other people, even servants, to be around. The isolation he had looked for by coming to this room seemed now to be a trap.

"As may be," said Aringher. "We'll leave you now, for the time which remains before you present yourself. I'll see you again there. My advice would be to get your messages—read them—and use the private audience to introduce me as your replacement."

He bowed and retreated through one of the shadowy doorways. Mistress Vasari remained.

"Are you the threat that goes with the honeyed words?" Oldigaard asked.

"Not exactly," she said, and smiled. "There have been changes at home. One of them is that the Centrists now control the government. They plan for you to be the first Councillor from Galcen to the Republic which—if all goes smoothly—will form after the war has ended. Now I leave you to your textcomm."

Nivome do'Evaan looked at the sheaf of messages he'd received from his field agents. The raids against the suspected Mages had gone poorly. As far as he could tell, the only suspects who'd been scooped up were also the only ones he could be certain weren't actually guilty.

Nevertheless—there were still Mages on Entibor, and they still went about their workings. Nivome frowned in the direction of the Domina's apartments. The woman was proving more headstrong than he'd thought likely, even in his most pessimistic moods, and not at all amenable to influence. His efforts to locate the gene-sire of the unborn child, as a possible source of persuasion, had so far proved fruitless.

Well, if that was the way of it, he'd have to find a new Domina. The old one, Veratina, when she'd finally shown herself to be unreliable, had died, despite Hafrey's snooping. Now that Hafrey was gone, this latest Domina would follow her great-aunt. Perhaps a mishap at the birthing. After that, a struggle—no female heir was readily apparent. But with the Mages still active, and with the population greatly reduced by plague and forcible relocation off-planet, maybe the emergence of a strong Lord Protector would be possible. Why settle for Consort when more could be his?

He allowed himself a moment to contemplate the vision of a renewed and orderly Entibor, feared by its enemies and strong in the politics of the civilized galaxy. It could be done, if a man were willing to take the necessary steps. . . .

A messenger knocked on his door. "My lord minister, her Dignity requests that you attend her."

Nivome got to his feet. "Attend her. That I shall."

Mistress Vasari stood outside the door to the Fire Room. A feeling of something left undone oppressed her. The niggling memory of bad dreams, perhaps. She should have rejected the feeling, but was unable to do so. What was it?

Perhaps Magework. Errec Ransome had never had any problem finding Mages. And there had been the day of the coup at the Palace Major, when she'd found Mages herself. But there was no such odor here in the Summer Palace. Why not?

Best not to ignore dreams. She cast her mind back to the nightmare that had kept her tossing in her bed the night before. A dream of a dark place, lit on its horizon all the way around, by a light impossibly bright for the blackness that surrounded it. And there had been a voice, speaking to her in a language she didn't understand.

Time passed, and she looked up, surprised. Her aimless wanderings while deep in thought, puzzling over the mystery, had taken her to the Hall of Statues. Why could she find no Mages in the Summer Palace?

There *were* mages in the Summer Palace. That much seemed obvious. They had to be here, if they were anywhere. But these would be the strong ones, the ones with powerful wards, guards, and shields. The ones fighting in the shadows to bring about the victory.

"Nothing by chance," Vasari muttered, an article of faith among the Adepts. "Nothing by chance."

And the Mages insured that their victories were not by chance. She closed her eyes, and stretched out with her other senses. *Why am I here?* she asked. *Why am I in this room rather than some other?*

And the answer came back. *To find death.*

What had Errec said the Mages did? They created their power to alter the universe through the deaths of their members. The Mages on Entibor would welcome the plagues, the bombing raids. If they were killed by their own side, it added to the strength of their ultimate working.

A whiff of Magecraft made her wrinkle her nose. She opened her eyes again. Around her stood a group of black-robed and masked figures.

"Welcome," said one.

Vasari raised her staff before her.

"Let me pass," she said.

"No," said the one who had spoken before. "But you do have a choice. Will you fight me alone, or all of us together? There is more honor in a single combat. . . ."

Before he could finish speaking, Vasari swept out to the side with her staff, its butt spearing toward the belly of the Mage closest to her right. That one dropped his own shorter staff with a clatter and bent forward, retching sounds coming from behind his mask.

Vasari didn't watch him, or hesitate, but continued to
sweep her staff toward the man in front of her who had
been speaking. He blocked the blow with his staff, then
lifted it up and over to launch a counterblow toward her left
arm.

As she parried, Vasari opened herself to the Power of the
universe, and let it flow through her. Her staff blazed with
a blue light. But the staves of her opponents were blazing
too.

She didn't allow herself the luxury of thought, but instead
fought on, grimly and silently, as the Hall of Statues filled
with twisting shadows and the clatter of staves meeting and
springing apart.

Oldigaard was waiting outside the private audience chamber a minute before his appointment. He'd had the chance
to use his textcomm, and had found messages—brought by
courier from Galcen, undoubtedly, and sent to him during
the flight up to the provinces. The messages confirmed what
Aringher had told him. How the man had known . . . but of
course. If he was an ambassador, he had a textcomm of his
own.

Deep-cover ambassadors prepositioned on other planets.
Who would have thought it? But here came the man himself.

"Well," Oldigaard said, when Aringher had come within
speaking range, "I suppose I should offer you congratula-
tions; all I can muster, however, is sympathy."

"Thank you," Aringher replied.

The doors opened and both men walked in.

There was the Domina, sitting in her chair of state, her
mouth drawn tight. As this was a private audience, she wore
a loose gown instead of the heavy state robes. She looked
unwell, Oldigaard thought; the strenuous regime of immuni-
zations that attempted to ward off the rapidly mutating
plagues could not have been easy on a woman in her condition. Tillijen, the armsmaster, stood at the Domina's left
shoulder, one hand on her blaster.

Nivome, the Minister of Internal Security, stood on the

Domina's right. He, too, seemed unhappy. To Oldigaard it looked as if their arrival had interrupted an argument. Only Tillijen's face registered no expression.

"Your Dignity," Oldigaard began, "I believe you are acquainted with Gentlesir Aringher."

"I am," Perada said. "Surely you did not request this audience just to perform an introduction."

"Only in a sense," Oldigaard replied. "It is my honor to introduce him as the new ambassador from Galcen to Your Dignity's court."

With that, he bowed low, then stepped back to give a clear field to his replacement.

"Your Dignity," Aringher began, and got no further.

A clatter rose from behind them. The doors swung open, and a figure collapsed forward into the audience chamber, wooden staff falling to the floor with an echoing rattle. It was Mistress Vasari. Blood flowed freely from her body, and her clothes were torn and ragged.

Vasari raised herself on her hands, and turned her bruised face to Perada. "Mages," she said. "In the palace. A working. . . ."

Jos took the 'Hammer back to Entibor at speed. Reports of conditions on the home world hadn't been good—plagues and crop failures and repeated harassing attacks by the Mages—and word of a major victory in the Web was likely to be the first positive news people there had heard for months.

"First thing after we report," he promised Nannla, "we'll see about getting Tilly back on board."

It was late in the ship's night, midway through the hyperspace transit. The three remaining members of Warhammer's original crew were sitting around the mess table in the darkened common room, drinking purple aqua vitae by the pale blue light of the safety glows.

The number-one gunner downed her glass. "If she'll come."

"What do you mean?"

"The last word I got, Tilly was being armsmaster to Her Dignity. That's not the sort of job you walk away from."

"Don't worry about Tilly," Errec said. The copilot had been quieter even than usual for most of the evening, and this was the first time he'd spoken in some minutes. "She'll come back if you ask her to."

Nannla brightened. "You really think so?"

"Some predictions are easy."

Jos poured himself another shot of the aqua vitae and wished that the same could be said about his own reception on Entibor. He hoped that the news he carried would at least win him a fair hearing. The planet's current troubles had proved him right about taking Ari to Maraghai—but being right had never made anyone better loved.

"What *I* want," he said slowly, "is to take 'Rada off planet before the plagues get so out of control that nobody's safe."

"Won't work," Nannla said. "Tilly told me, once—the Domina never leaves Entibor. Custom."

"Hang custom."

"You'll never get a trueborn Entiboran to agree with you on that," Errec said. "Custom is life and death to them."

"We'll see," Jos said. "I'm going to try my best, anyway."

"What'll you do if it doesn't work?" Nannla asked.

"Then I'll stick to fighting the Mages," Jos said. He tossed back his shot of aqua vitae. "What about you guys?"

"I'm with you, boss. One of these days I'm going to retire and use my share of the loot to open up a tea shop in Sombrelír, but not just yet."

"Errec?"

The copilot shook his head. "I can't. I have to go back to Galcen."

"To the Guild, you mean," said Jos, unsurprised. He'd been expecting something like this for a while now—ever since Errec had taken to wearing Adept's blacks. "You don't have to do it if you don't want to, you know. They can't make you."

Ransome gave a faint laugh. "I know. They don't have to. But I know that I need to go."

"Whatever makes you happy," Jos said. "We've only got this run to finish first."

"Mages in the palace." Mistress Vasari's voice was only a thread of sound, and blood bubbled from her mouth when she breathed. "I found the Mages," she said. She choked, and more blood ran from her mouth, thick and dark. "I know what they're doing."

"Don't try to talk," said Perada. Somewhere behind her, she could hear Tillijen speaking urgently over one of the room's hidden comm links, trying to summon help. "Everything's going to be all right."

"No," Vasari said. She moved her head from side to side—a fraction of an inch, a visible agony of effort—and said, "They're trying to tear away the skin of the planet."

Perada's breath caught. She felt the child inside her kick, hard and low, as if the sudden surge of adrenaline had jolted it. "How—?"

"A working. Volcanoes. Mountains. The oceans boiling . . . the sky in flame. . . ."

"Massive geothermal upheavals," Perada heard Aringher murmur under his breath. "At a guess, they're aiming for total devastation in the shortest time possible."

"But they can't!" Perada protested. "They'll all die too!"

"They don't . . . care." Vasari was struggling to form the words. Her breath choked and gurgled. Another rush of blood came up, soaking the carpet under her mouth. "Mages gain strength . . . from death. The more who . . . die . . . the greater the . . ."

The Adept's voice stopped altogether. Perada looked away.

She's dead. We'll all be dead, soon.

Aringher was speaking in an undertone to Garen Tarveet and to Ambassador—to Gentlesir—Oldigaard. "Take an aircar to the nearest landing field with an operational courier ship. I need you to carry the word to Galcen. I intend to remain on Entibor and render what assistance I can in this extremity."

"Then I ought to stay here, too." Garen sounded terrified but stubborn. Perada knew the combination well from their days together at the Delaven Academy—nothing Aringher could say was going to persuade him.

She stood up, pushing herself awkwardly to her feet with her hands on the arms of the chair of state, and stood face-to-face with Garen. "You need to go," she said. "Somebody has to finish carrying out the plans we made, and I won't be able to."

"What do you mean?" Garen's question came out in a squeak.

"The Domina of Entibor doesn't leave the world of Entibor," Perada said. "And even if I wanted to break custom, I couldn't—I need to stay at work here for as long as possible, to start getting people away."

"Your Dignity," Nivome broke in, "Lord Meteun is right. You need to go. You can't save more than a handful—"

"Then I *will* save that handful!" Perada snapped. "Starting with you, Garen Tarveet. Take ship with Gentlesir Oldigaard, and do whatever it is that the new ambassador is asking you to do."

Jos Metadi: Suivi Point
(Galcenian Dating 970 a.f.; Entiboran Regnal
Year 34 Veratina)

*W*ARHAMMER HAD come into Suivi Point with a hold full of cargo, some of it honest trade goods but most of it seized under Gyfferan letters of marque. Jos Metadi hadn't taken long to reconcile himself to the privateering life. The *'Hammer* had the guns and the speed for taking prizes, and enough cargo space to stash the loot—and as Rak Barenslee said, anything they took off a Magebuilt ship probably belonged in the civilized galaxy anyway.

Jos had been making a name for himself of late, gaining a reputation both as a good captain and as a lucky one. At Rak's insistence, he'd taken to dressing the part: flashy velvets and spidersilks, heavy with gold braid and precious stones. All that unnecessary flamboyance made him uneasy, somewhere in the Gyfferan core of his soul; he told himself it was advertising, nothing more, and soothed his feelings by dressing like a proper man of business outside the port quarter.

Today, though, was a port-quarter day. They'd already off-loaded the cargo and found a buyer, rendering the *'Ham-*

mer's account at the Merchants' Cooperative even plumper than before, and Jos and Rak were making a tour of the Strip to celebrate. They'd had dinner together in a good restaurant just beyond the portside airlocks, then taken the main glidewalk through the entertainment district, heading for the docks and home.

They stopped along the way at the No-Name Lounge—advertising, again, to get word out among the free-spacers that Metadi's *Warhammer* was back in port from a lucky run—and sat up front near the bar, drinking fruit punch spiked with Ophelan rum and eating salted frillfruit out of the bowl in the middle of the table.

"Here's to the next cargo," said Jos. "It's out there waiting for us to find it."

Rak laughed and handed him a frillfruit. "No worries, then. You've got the knack—all we have to do to get rich is stick with you."

"Couldn't do it without a great crew. And you're the best."

"Don't you know it," said Rak, and Jos felt his ears reddening.

These days on *Warhammer*, they were sharing quarters. Nobody else in the crew seemed to care—not the gunners, who'd signed on as a team anyway, and certainly not Ferrda—and Jos himself found the setup highly educational. That didn't stop him from being embarrassed, though. He looked away briefly to hide his discomfiture, pretending a sudden interest in the free-spacers drinking at the No-Name's bar. Then he turned and looked again, with an interest no longer feigned.

"What's up?" Rak asked.

Jos nodded toward a dark-haired man in spacer's coveralls, sitting at the bar with the stiff formality of someone entirely drunk. "That guy. I've seen him before."

Rak followed his glance. "Longish black hair, plain outfit with no ships' patches on it? Soused as a bar rag? That one?"

"That's him."

She looked dubious. "Where do you know him from?"

"I don't know him. But I saw him once."

"He must have made quite an impression on you." Rak shook her head. "Sure doesn't look like much at the moment, though."

"Maybe not," said Jos slowly. He pushed back his chair and stood up. "But I think he saved my life. If he's down on his luck right now . . . well, I owe him a big one."

Rak sighed and got to her feet. "Messing with drunks is always a bad idea. I'll watch your back."

Jos wandered over to the bar, trying hard to look casual and nonthreatening. Rak trailed him, just out of arm's reach. When he came within speaking range of the stranger, he became, if anything, more confused than before. The man at the bar both was and wasn't like the Adept whom he'd seen in his plague-induced delirium. The dark hair was right, along with the pale coloring and the slight but muscular build, but this man's face was all hollows and angles, with weary purple smudges under the dark eyes that gazed so fixedly at the middle distance.

Undaunted, Jos persevered. "Hello. My name is Jos Metadi. Can I buy you something?"

The man ignored him.

"The thing is, I think I know you."

The man continued to ignore him.

"Jos," muttered Rak from behind him. "He's past noticing anything but the bottom of the bottle. Let's go."

"All right," said Jos, after a moment's pause. "Sorry to bother you, stranger. I thought I recognized you from somewhere, is all."

Reluctantly, he began to move away.

"You're real." The man's voice was barely above a whisper, but the articulaton was painstakingly clear.

Jos halted. "What?"

"You're leaving. You must be real. The ones who aren't real don't leave."

Rak tugged at his jacket sleeve. "Jos, he's not just drunk, he's crazy. You don't *need* trouble like that."

"He's not going to make any trouble. Not for me. any-

way." Jos sat down on the empty stool next to the stranger.
"You have a name I can call you by?"

"Errec," said the man after a long pause. He looked at Jos
for a moment, then seemed to make a decision to amplify
the statement. "Ransome."

"Thanks." Jos tried again. "Look, this is going to sound
like a strange question, but do you know me?"

"Not yet," Ransome said. "Someday. I think."

"Someday." Jos drew a deep breath and proceeded carefully. "Are you—did you ever belong to the Guild?"

"They burned the Guildhouse."

"They?"

"Mages," said Ransome. He looked at Jos again. This
time his dark eyes seemed to take in the gaudy clothing and
the heavy blaster, not to mention Rak Barenslee standing
equally armed and dangerous a few feet away. "You kill
Mages."

"I take their ships and seize their cargos," Jos said. "They
fight back, most of the time. So, yes—I kill Mages."

"I can find them for you."

Jos blinked. "What?"

"Their ships. I can find them."

"Jos," Rak said. "*Nobody* just 'finds' things out in
space."

"I don't know," Jos said. "Maybe this guy can."

He turned back to Ransome. "Are you saying you want
to sign aboard *Warhammer*?"

"Your ship? Yes."

"Jos, he's crazy. Don't do this."

"I told you," Jos said. "I owe him one. And besides—I
think he's telling the truth."

XXIV. GALCENIAN DATING 978 A.F.
ENTIBORAN REGNAL YEAR 3 PERADA

MEINUXET CHECKED the visual log from one of the spy-eyes that were scattered, like a trap-line, all around the Summer Palace. A week after the emergency evacuation had begun, so few people remained in residence that there wasn't much point in checking them—no point, if poor Vasari's dying revelations turned out to be true—but Ser Hafrey had set up the system, and Meinuxet would continue it.

Dutiful to the last, he thought, with a touch of amusement at his own predictability.

Still, he continued checking the logs. Even in this last extremity, there were mysteries to be uncovered, and tantalizing hints of things going on: shadows out of place, blurs and fuzz in the records. Possibly technical faults in the devices. Possibly . . .

This place, the Blue Room, a clutter of furniture and bric-a-brac, was a nexus of the anomalies. He hoped to find out what was going on. And so he waited, hoping that whatever was going on here didn't present more difficulties than he could deal with. Mistress Vasari had stumbled on one Mage

Circle within the palace walls . . . where there was one there might be two.

"Where do you eat?" he asked in a whisper. "Where do you drink? Why don't you leave footprints?"

With most of the palace maintenance staff gone, the floor of the Blue Room had not been swept in some time. Meinuxet could look back the way he had come, at the sun reflecting off the polished hardwood of the floor, and see the marks of his passage in the dust.

He loosened his blaster in its shoulder holster, silently pushed the safety to the off position, and stepped off the main path through the maze of standing curio cases.

Tapping the walls. At least I'll feel busy.

Then the sound of footsteps echoed in the room, and he froze. A man entered: Nivome do'Evaan, the Minister of Internal Security, Ser Hafrey's old enemy. The minister walked partway into the room and stopped.

"Come out," he said in a loud voice.

Meinuxet remained frozen. The Minister of Internal Security wasn't speaking to him, it seemed, but to a blank section of the palace wall.

"Come out," Nivome said again. "I know you're here. We need to talk."

The air seemed to warp and waver, and a dark figure stood before Nivome where a second before there had been only empty space. Black robes, black staff, featureless mask of hard black plastic: Meinuxet realized with an inward tremor that he was looking, for the first time, at one of the dreaded Mages. He didn't dare move; he hardly dared to draw breath.

"You are a dead man," the Mage said—*To Nivome,* Meinuxet told himself; *to Nivome, not to me.*

Nivome paid no apparent attention to the threat. "You'll never break the Domina," he told the Mage. "While she lives, while she is fruitful, this world is beyond your grasp."

"Perhaps. But you were told where to find us; you were given safe conduct. My brothers in An-Jemayne believe you have something of importance. Speak now, tell me what it is, and maybe you will walk away."

Nivome scowled. "I want to rule," he said. "But not over a lifeless hunk of rock. Call off your attack, and I can give you a peace treaty in this part of space. More than that—I can give you the gateway to the Central Worlds."

"You're offering us things that we already have."

"You'll get neither one of them if the Domina reigns. I've spoken with one of your seers—"

"We do not use that word."

"But you understand it. Hear me out. I have spoken with one of your seers, and he tells me what you all know—that while the Domina lives, you will never reach the Central Worlds. I can deliver her to you dead."

"Can you indeed?" The Mage's black mask hid any expression, but he seemed to pause and consider what he had heard. "Well. Because of what we have seen, we know that you speak part of the truth."

"I must rule over a living world," Nivome said. "Or I throw my lot in with the Domina, and thwart you all."

"A living world you asked for—a living world you shall have. Only deliver the Domina to us, that the luck may change."

There'll never be a better chance, Meinuxet thought. The weight of his blaster was heavy in his grip. *But the first movement will draw their attention.*

Which one to shoot first? The Mage or the traitor? Which one is the more dangerous?

Put that way, the choice was easy. *The traitor.*

Meinuxet raised his arm—and felt, before he could press the firing stud, the crushing pain of a blow coming down on him from behind.

Another Mage, he thought. His mind was still clear—it surprised him, really, the clarity of everything, even as his hand lost all strength and dropped the blaster, and his legs failed him, and he toppled to the floor. From a very great distance, he heard the first Mage speak to Nivome again.

"It seems that your secrets were not as well kept as you thought."

Meinuxet heard footsteps—coming close, jarring the wooden floor painfully underneath his head—and Nivome do'Evaan saying, "He'll be dead in a minute or two. I'm not worried."

"Please yourself," said the Mage. "Now, go. Carry out your side of our bargain while you still can."

Perada's back ached from sitting at the combined desk comp and communications rig in the sub-basement recesses of the Summer Palace, and her eyes felt hot and gritty from gazing at the comp screens. She'd had a bed and a chair-of-state moved down into the shielded chamber a week ago, as soon as she'd fully taken in the implications of Vasari's final words. A holocamera on the far wall, now inactive, was trained on the corner of the room that held the empty chair-of-state. The bed hadn't been slept in for over seventeen hours.

The sliding door of the room opened and Tillijen came in. "Domina, you should get some rest."

"Why should I bother?" Perada asked. "Any day now, I'll have all the time in the universe for resting. In the meantime, I'm busy."

"No surrender, then," said Tillijen.

"No," Perada said. "I don't know how much time we've got. But as long as we can still get ships, we'll keep moving people off-planet."

"What about the plague?"

Perada shrugged wearily. "I don't know. Let them stay in deep space until everybody's either dead or clean, I suppose. And don't *you* start telling me that it's never going to save everybody, or that it isn't even going to make a dent in the mortality rates, or anything like that. I don't want to hear about it."

She picked up a datapad from the table by the desk comp, checked it against the comp display, and wiped the pad with a stroke of the attached stylus. "The agricultural settlements on that Selvauran outplanet will have to take in more than just farmers, that's all. Now, let's see . . . if those merchant ships from Wrysten get here tonight or tomorrow . . . that's a few more we can save."

A beeping from the comm set broke through her words.

Tillijen leaned forward over her shoulder to look at the ID code on the incoming message.

"It's a Fleet override. This must be important."

It was. The ships that had dropped out of hyper on the edge of the system hadn't been merches from Wrysten after all; they were Mages, dreadnoughts and battleships to augment the small raiding and harassing craft that had remained in-system since the plagues began. Captain-of-Frigates Trestig Brehant, the commander of the system defense fleet, was warning all planetary installations to prepare for a serious attack.

Perada clicked off the comm set and turned to face Tillijen. "It's time to make one more broadcast, to show the people on the ships—and the ones who'll never make it to a ship—that their Domina hasn't taken herself to safety off-planet, that she's still working hard to bring her people luck." She rubbed her bulging belly with one hand as she spoke, trying to ease the itching, tight-stretched skin. "Let's fetch the Iron Crown for this broadcast, Tilly, since it'll probably be the last."

Tillijen nodded and moved toward the door. "Where should I go to look for the crown, Your Dignity?"

"The jewel chest in my private chambers," Perada said. "Not the Khesatan trinket case—I bought that one on Galcen, the year before I left school. The ugly square box with the arms of the House carved on the lid."

"Right, Your Dignity."

"Thank you, Tillijen. And hurry . . . we don't know how much time we have left."

The man who had once called himself Ser Hafrey sat at the light openwork table in the morning room of the Summer Palace. Outside the pointed arches of the windows, the sun was rising—an angry red-orange sphere seen through the haze on the eastern horizon. *Plague fires,* he thought, *somewhere between here and An-Jemayne*. There had been no reports from many of the provincial cities for a week now, a sure sign that the measures taken to control the spread of disease and famine had failed.

So far, the Summer Palace remained untouched. The trees outside the tall windows had all their summer green, not the premature withering of the blighted districts, and the flowers in the nearby shrubbery bloomed in shades of purple and blue that echoed the fruit in the cut-glass bowl on the table.

He raised a wineglass from the tray before him to his lips, and tasted the vintage. The wine was good, but it brought him no pleasure. He rose and paced for a moment, still holding the wineglass. The blackwood staff at his side swung with each pace. That too had remained hidden, a last remnant of what he had once been, but now the time was nearly past. He raised his glass toward the window, in a silent toast to those whom he knew were coming—to those who, in carrying out their own plans, were furthering his own.

If, he thought, *I am not wrong. If this garden has not gone too long untended.*

He had not dared give it the fullest attention of late. Too many eyes, too many ears, too many minds surrounded him, each one looking, listening, feeling for the slightest slip, the merest hint. But hint of what? None of them could guess.

"Don't flatter yourself," he muttered, turning away from the windows. "You aren't that subtle. And you make mistakes."

The passage of so many years could cause a man to falter, even one who had faced time on its own ground and forced it to relent. There was a time when he would never have let a power struggle with the likes of Nivome do'Evaan distract him from his proper work. But he grew tired, and he knew that he was old—and the help that he'd expected hadn't come. Perhaps he'd been wrong, and no one waited in the shadows of the future after all.

He sat down again and lifted a roseapple to his lips, then placed it back in the bowl untasted. Instead he refilled his glass from the decanter of amber fluid that sat beside the wineglasses, and leaned back in the delicately made chair.

The door behind him made a slight rattle as someone lifted the ring on the far side and pulled. Hafrey stood, turning to face the newcomer, taking his ebony staff from its clip.

The door swung open and a woman stepped through: Tillijen, the gunner from Metadi's ship, whom Perada had made armsmaster in his place. He smiled to himself, seeing now the appropriateness of it all.

"Greetings," he said. "So you were to be the one."

"But you've been exiled!" Tillijen exclaimed, then reddened, more than the ruddy light from the rising sun could have accounted for.

"A fate we all share, one day or another," he said.

An alarm began to shrill, high and insistent. Hafrey knew what it meant. The disaster long feared and long prepared for, a direct Mage attack on the Summer Palace, had finally come. He glanced out the window, over his shoulder. The clouds of morning had broken up; the sky was a clean blue.

"For some the day will arrive sooner than they expected," he added. "It has begun. Come with me."

He walked past her, through the door by which she had entered, into the receiving room. The dark wood floor and the paneled walls reflected lights set in high sconces. He went over to the fireplace at the far side of the room, its hearth tall enough for a man to walk into it without bending his head, and pointed with his staff to one of the stones in the back. The stone was smooth and polished, unlike the other, rougher, stones that formed the back of the hearth, and it was carved with the arms of House Rosselin and of Entibor.

"Look and remember," he said—talking to the past, now, and the shadowy future, as well as to the woman who stood before him. "All times and places meet where the power of the universe does not extend. Some have called me a traitor. Others may call you the same. But you and I, we will know the truth."

The alarm bell continued to clamor.

Tillijen pointed back in the direction of the Morning room. "Through this way," she said. "If that's the alert, we don't have much time."

"You must go your way," Ser Hafrey said. "And I, mine."

He bowed to her, the full bow of respect for what she was and for what she had been, and for the one whom she prefigured, and stepped aside into the shadows.

Ser Hafrey was gone. Tillijen couldn't tell where ... he simply wasn't there any longer. She turned back to the fireplace and pushed on the carved stone. The back of the hearth swung open.

A doorway, she thought. She'd heard stories of secret rooms, but had never encountered a real one before.

She had no time to think about this one—a flash of light brighter than anything she had ever seen before came into the chamber through the windows and through the open door leading back to the Morning Room. The light washed all the color out of the stones, and the reflected heat seared her face and hands.

Energy strike, she thought, and didn't wait for the light to fade. She leaped into the open passageway, set her back to the stone door, and pushed it shut. The latch clicked into place as the shock wave hit. The stone door vibrated against her back and shoulders. The explosion roared in her ears, and the foundations of the palace trembled under her feet.

She waited for her dazzled vision to return. Ser Hafrey—had he lived through the strike? Maybe, she thought; he was a clever one. But if he'd gone back to the morning room, he would have taken the full force of the blast. She put him from her mind. There was nothing she could do for him now.

Bit by bit, her vision returned. She stood in a small cubicle lit by a pale blue glowbulb in a rocky niche. At her feet a spiral stair led downward through the rock on which the Summer Palace stood. She took a step forward, drawing her blaster as she did so—not as a threat, or because she thought there would be a target, but for comfort's sake. With the fingertips of her other hand brushing the stone wall, she began her descent into the lower reaches.

The stairway opened out at the bottom into a passage—a tunnel, really, almost certainly below ground level. The air felt thick, and the hidden compressors of air-filtration systems throbbed against her eardrums. The available light was dim and tinged with crimson.

Emergency glows, thought Tillijen. *That's bad.*

Through the soles of her boots she felt another tremor in the earth. A second energy hit? Probably, she decided. She'd never been on a planet under serious Mage assault, but she'd been on a ship, *Rifter's Pride*, as it was disabled and destroyed by long-distance gunfire. The feeling was much the same.

The passage led forward about twenty paces before it branched into a four-way intersection. She took the right-hand path, and walked slowly forward, one hand brushing the wall and the other holding her weapon leveled at waist height. Doorways lined both sides of the passage; she tried all of them, and found them all locked.

She went on—looking for something, she didn't know what. Somebody to keep her company, maybe, for however long she had left. She'd thought, once, that she would be double-damned and dipped in bubble-sauce if she would let herself die on Entibor—now she'd be happy if she didn't have to die alone.

I wonder if Nannla will miss me. I'd like to have seen her again. . . .

She came to another intersection. Finally, she recognized familiar territory—a sub-basement corridor near the Domina's shielded chamber. Nor was she alone any longer. In the hallway ahead, a shadow was moving against the red-lit stone. The silhouette was unmistakable: Nivome do'Evaan of Rolny.

Tillijen gripped her blaster and followed.

She followed the Minister of Internal Security down the passage to the door of Perada's underground shelter. She saw that he was carrying something in the crook of his left arm—a square wooden box, large enough to contain an object the size of the Iron Crown. She'd never made it to the private chambers before the first energy strike hit; from the timing, Nivome must have gotten to them earlier than that. She wondered what had prompted him to fetch the crown.

He touched the lockplate outside the door of the shelter

room. It slid open, and he entered. Somebody else was already inside with the Domina; Tillijen caught the sound of voices before the door shut again. She hastened to press her own hand against the lockplate and get into the room as well.

Perada was sitting in the chair-of-state, looking stubborn. She had the box containing the Iron Crown open on her lap. Nivome was looming over her, his expression dark with frustration; and behind the chair of state, his appearance as blandly inoffensive as ever, was the new Galcenian ambassador, Festen Aringher.

"Gentlesir Nivome," Perada was saying, "Please believe that I appreciate your retrieval of the Iron Crown. But I don't intend to take it off-planet. I plan to make one final holovid broadcast, and then get back to the evacuation. Every ship that lifts is a blow against the Mages, and I want to strike them as many times as I can before they kill me."

"Your Dignity, there *are* no more ships that can lift!" Nivome said. "If we can make it to the field at An-Jemayne, we have a chance of making rendezvous with a courier landing from orbit. But only if we leave the palace now."

"Much as it pains me to admit it," Aringher cut in, "the minister is right. With a full-scale attack going on, no more carrier ships are going to enter the system. It's time for you to go."

"I can't, Ambassador Aringher. Custom forbids it. No Domina has ever left Entibor."

None of them had noticed Tillijen enter—they were too caught up in their fruitless argument. She moved closer, into Perada's line of sight, and said, "They're telling you the truth, 'Rada. You might as well order anybody who's still waiting dirtside to take on all the warm bodies they can, then lift ship and run like hell for a jump point. And as far as custom goes . . . I say cut your braids and get out. For the kid, if you can't think of another good reason."

Perada said nothing for a while. Aringher looked calm and unconcerned, but Nivome's heavy breathing was loud in the cramped room.

"Tilly," the Domina said at last, "give me your knife."

Tillijen pulled the knife out of her boot-top and handed it to Perada hilt-first. "Here you go, Your Dignity."

"Thank you," Perada said.

She took hold of a braid with one hand, pulled it taut, and began sawing at it with the knife. The ice-blond strands parted, leaving her with the braid still in her hand and a ragged clump of short hair on one side of her face. Working in silence, she cut off all the remaining braids as well, one at a time, until she had a handful of plaited yellow hair and a cropped head. She dropped the braids onto the floor and handed Tillijen back the knife.

"There," she said. "It's done. We can go."

Warhammer came out of hyper in Entiboran nearspace, and the cockpit console lit up with lights and alarms.

"Trouble," said Jos. "Looks like a bunch of Mages got busy while we were chewing their friends into little pieces over in the Web. Errec, fire up the message loop and start broadcasting it wideband, in the clear. That should discourage them a little."

Errec shook his head. "I don't think so. . . . Jos, we've got to hurry. Something bad is about to happen."

Jos glanced over at his copilot. Errec hadn't sounded like that since the time back in the old days when they'd taken a Magebuilt cargo ship with a hold full of looted junk from some place on Ilarna—he'd sorted through the entire load, almost, without losing it, then picked up a cheap souvenir paperweight and gone so pale he looked green. He looked worse now.

"Mage stuff?" Jos asked.

Errec nodded. "You can't imagine what it looks like . . . the auras in space . . ."

"I don't think I want to imagine it," Jos said. "Get that general message going anyway. I'll start talking to the Fleet."

He keyed on the external comm link. "Any station this net, any station this net, this is Entiboran Fleet Ship *Warhammer*, over."

The audio pickup popped and crackled. "Jos, that you?"

"Who's this?"

"Tres Brehant. Glad to see you. Are the rest of the guys going to be dropping out soon?"

"That's a negat," Jos said. "I'm carrying news only. We met the Mages off Pleyver, and we won."

"If you didn't bring reinforcements, General, we're out of luck right here. The local Mage raiders just got a lot more ships—they're hitting targets all over the planet."

"What the hell have you been doing?" Jos demanded.

More crackles and pops from the audio pickup. "The best I can. Doesn't help that I've got to run an evacuation at the same time."

"Lords of Life! What for?"

"Domina's orders. 'Lift everybody you can,' she says, and we've been pulling in merches and couriers and passenger liners and running them up to the jump points for the past ten days."

Jos felt his gut clench. *"Something bad,"* Errec said. . . . "Is Perada with you, then?"

"Negative."

Errec spoke up again from the other seat. "She has to be. The auras are shifting . . . the working is almost finished. If she stays on-planet, she's dead."

Jos glanced over at Errec—the copilot looked even worse than he had before. "What do you mean, 'the working'?"

"Circle on Circle of Mages," Errec said. "A thousand, a hundred thousand . . . who knows how many they could bring together for something like this? All of them giving up their energies to show what happens to planets that resist."

No . . . "Tres, where *is* 'Rada?"

"At the Summer Palace, coordinating the evacuation on the dirtside end."

"Conditions there?"

"Bad. Major fires and energy releases."

"Get what ships you can spare and clear me a way down. I'm going to get her away."

Jos Metadi: Ferianth
(Galcenian Dating 972 a.f.; Entiboran Regnal
Year 36 Veratina)

WARHAMMER HUNG dead in space off Ferianth, a cold and barely inhabited planet at the edge of the starless gap between the civilized galaxy and the home worlds of the Magelords. A Magebuilt merchant ship lay broken under the 'Hammer's guns, a raw-edged hole torn in the vessel's side, the external plating peeled outward where atmosphere had spilled into the hungry dark. The ship's engines were gone as well, a jagged bite taken from the edge of the ship where under normal circumstances tubes would glow.

The merchant ship spun slowly around its longitudinal axis. Warhammer moved with it, keeping position relative to the gap in the merch's hull through which the boarding party had entered. To Jos Metadi, at the controls in the 'Hammer's cockpit, the Magebuilt ship seemed to hang suspended over his own smaller vessel, the hole in its side looming large in the viewscreens.

The external comm link crackled and came to life. "Stores compartment in view," Rak Barenslee said, from somewhere in the merch's cargo hold. "Setting cutting-out charges."

"Standing by," Jos replied.

Light flashed in the *'Hammer*'s viewscreens, and part of the skin of the merchant peeled away. Jos's hands played over the lateral controls, shifting *Warhammer* into a better position for shining powerful worklights into the new-made gap. The stark white glare showed a hold full of palletized cargo, griped to the merch's deck. Rak's tiny, pressure-suited figure stood next to one of the crates, where she would be fixing the explosive charges to break the cargo free and start it tumbling across the gap into *Warhammer*'s waiting hold. Like the crates themselves, she appeared to hang inverted relative to the *'Hammer*'s viewscreens.

"Here it is," she said over the speaker. "Looks like some prime stuff. I'm ready to transfer if you are."

"Rotating to position," Jos said. He touched the controls again, bringing *Warhammer* around so that the ship's lower hatch faced the opening in the merch's hull, and hit the internal comms. "Stand by in compartment one. Opening to vacuum in five, four, three, two, now."

He made the switch. A faint shudder ran through the deckplates as the outer doors slid open.

"Got you on visual, compartment one," Rak said. "Standing by to transfer cargo."

Jos spoke over both the internal and external comm circuits. "Stand by, commence transfer."

"Transfer, now," Rak said. "That's a lift."

On the external pickups Jos saw a flash in the merch's hold. A square-edged mass broke free and began moving in the *'Hammer*'s direction.

"Captain," said Errec Ransome, from the copilot's seat. "Extraneous signal. Possibly a dropout." The Ilarnan paused. "There's no ID yet, but I think it's Mages."

"How far?"

"Wait—two more drops."

"Better speed it up down there," Metadi said over the internal comms. "We may have to boost in a hurry."

A heavy thud vibrated through the strength members of

the 'Hammer's frame as the first load of booty landed in the cargo compartment. Almost at the same time, there was another flash of light from the hold of the merch.

Rak's voice came over the external comm link. "Second load away."

"Errec," Jos said. "How far off are those contacts?"

"Distance, near. We're getting sensor data now. Signature consistent with Mage warships."

Jos picked up the external link. "Boarding party, return to the ship."

"One more load, Captain," Rak said. "I think I found something good."

Load one secure, rumbled Ferrda over the link from number-one compartment. *Standing by for load two.*

"Load two's on the way over," Jos said. "Load three is the last, and the boarding party's coming along after. Let me know when they're back with us—we need to get out of here before the bad guys show up."

Three loads aye, said Ferrda, and Rak's voice chimed in from the hold of the merch, "Third load away."

Jos thought that the last word cut off abruptly. A trick of the other ship's interior structure, maybe, blocking transmissions as Rak moved about. Then the 'Hammer's external comm crackled again. This time it was Tilly.

"We've got a problem, Captain. Rak's hurt."

"Captain," Errec said from the navigator's seat. "Those warships—"

"Get Rak out of there and get back yourself," Jos said over the external comm. "Do it now."

"Mages, definite," said Errec. "I think they've located us. I'm picking up ranging beams directed at this location."

"Maybe they're looking for the merch and don't know we're here." Jos knew he was indulging in wishful thinking, but he couldn't help it. "Tilly—can you hurry it up a bit?"

The second load of cargo arrived with a thump as he spoke. *Load two aboard,* Ferrda reported. *Waiting for three.*

"There isn't going to be a third load," Jos said. "Get

ready to bring in the boarding party. Tilly, what's your status over there?"

"Not good, Captain. The damned Mages booby-trapped that last crate. Rak's trapped—she's jammed between the bulkhead and some of the cargo."

"Keep trying. Errec—"

"The Mages have got us located," said the Ilarnan. "They've switched to fire control."

Metadi hit the internal comms. "Nannla, take number-one gun. Ferrda—the engines. The boarding party will have to close up by themselves after they come over." He switched again to the external link. "Tilly, how's it coming?"

"I'm working as fast as I can," she said. "But it's like trying to untangle a whynot's nest—if I pull the wrong thing I've lost her for good."

"I'll suit up and come help you," Jos said. He was unstrapping his safety webbing as he spoke. "The two of us can handle it, no problem."

Errec spoke up again from the navigator's seat. "Jos, I don't think we have the time. The Mages are on their way—they'll be in firing range within two minutes."

The guns on the 'Hammer's dorsal turret began to fire, sending out brilliant stabs of light.

"Jos." Rak's voice, faint and crackling, came over the external comm. "Are you under attack?"

"The shields will take it. Hold on—I'm coming over."

"No. If you stay here, they'll kill all of us. You have to take the 'Hammer and pull them away. I can hang on until you make it back."

"She's right, Jos," said Errec. "We have to leave."

Jos clenched his fist and swore under his breath. As he strapped back into the webbing of the pilot's seat, he could hear Tilly and Rak arguing.

"Tilly, go across."

"I can't—"

"I'm still in charge over here. You do what I say." Rak's voice changed pitch and volume, the better to carry over the link to the ship. "Warhammer, one to transfer."

A spray of light burst around Warhammer as the Mage

ships got into range and began firing. The power-drain indicator on the shield panel flickered.

"Jos," said Errec, "I recommend that you take evasive action *now*."

The *'Hammer'*s dorsal gun was firing continuously. The internal comm link clicked on. It was Tilly, her voice sounding tight and unhappy. "I'm across."

"Seal the doors and go take your gun," Jos said. He picked up the external comm. "Rak, hang on. We'll be back."

"Don't worry about me. Worry about the Mages. Go!"

Jos put the *'Hammer'*s realspace engines hard forward and darted around to the far side of the merchant craft. The merch dwindled away astern over the *Hammer*'s aft viewscreen.

Errec was watching the readouts. "Losing pressure in upper stores, losing pressure in engineering. The warships are still on our tail."

"Good," Jos said, tight-lipped. "That's exactly where I want them."

It took two days for Jos to fight the Mages to their destruction, in the cold dark beyond Ferianth. By the time he got back to the merch it was too late for Rak Barenslee. Though she'd been right again. This was a particularly rich load.

XXV. Galcenian Dating 978 A.F. Entiboran Regnal Year 3 Perada

Perada shifted her grip on the wooden chest holding the Iron Crown, and tried to walk faster. She didn't want to slow down Tilly and the others—not even Nivome—but she couldn't run. Some time in the past day or so the baby's weight had settled lower, and her hips ached whenever she tried to lengthen her stride.

I shouldn't have let Tilly talk me into this, she thought. Her head felt light and strangely cold without the weight of the braids she'd worn ever since her hair was long enough to plait. *I should have told them to go on without me.*

But it was too late now. Her shorn braids lay on the floor of the shelter behind her, and she was stumbling down the tunnel to the emergency hangar—the last, secret way out of the Summer Palace. The Consort-architect who'd built it, long before Veratina's day, had spoken of the project as a safety measure; not until some years after the hangar's completion had Domina Ilea learned of his clandestine departures from it to visit a common shopgirl in An-Jemayne. Ilea had dispensed with her Consort shortly thereafter, but she'd kept his well-designed private bolt-hole.

". . . if the entrance isn't blocked by rubble," Nivome was saying, when another energy strike came down on the palace somewhere above their heads. The sound was muffled and distant, but the vibration made the floor quiver underneath their feet.

Perada lost her balance—with her arms full of the chest holding the Iron Crown, and her body warped out of its normal shape and weight by pregnancy, she couldn't compensate in time. She felt Tillijen's strong spacer's hands catching her before she could fall.

"It's no good," Perada said, as soon as her feet were back under her. "I can't run, and you shouldn't have to wait on me."

Tillijen ignored her. "You," she said to Nivome. "You're the strongest of us. Pick her up and carry her."

Perada opened her mouth to protest, but the Minister of Internal Security lifted her up before she could speak. Nivome had never lacked strength; in spite of her awkward contours he carried her easily, striding down the tunnel at a pace that Tillijen and Ambassador Aringher had to stretch to equal.

The emergency hangar was deserted when they got there. A portion of the stone roof overhead had collapsed, crushing most of the waiting aircars. A fire burned in one of them, filling the air with bluish-grey smoke and acrid, choking fumes.

"Over there," Nivome said. He swung Perada to the ground and pointed to an aircar with a sleek body and stubby wings. "That one looks undamaged."

The aircar was tiny—a two-seater, which meant that Tillijen and Ambassador Aringher, as the leanest members of the party, had to squeeze in by standing against the rear bulkhead. Perada struggled to pull the safety webbing into place across her abdomen. It was a tight fit—the baby kicked and squirmed in protest, and when the latches finally clicked, she could scarcely breathe.

Nivome took the pilot's seat. He glanced over the controls, and began to snap switches with an expert hand. *I was right*, Perada thought, remembering the interminable flight up from An-Jemayne, after the attack on the Palace Major. *He can do this perfectly well when he needs to.*

The turbines fired with a whine and the aircar began to vibrate. At the same time, a booming noise from outside told of another strike. The aircar began to turn, heading toward the launch tunnel. More rumbling and booming noises came from up above. The walls of the hangar quivered and blurred as a piece of the ceiling came loose and crashed down ahead of them.

Nivome kicked the car in a tight circle around the rubble and aimed for the tunnel again, gaining speed as he went. More rocks fell behind them and to either side. Perada heard Tilly swearing under her breath in a steady monotone.

"Stand by," Nivome said. He hit a control on the console, and the car seemed to leap forward. Perada felt the seat cushions giving under the acceleration, and the separate, protesting pressure of the baby's weight inside her.

They entered the tunnel. Painted guidance and timing stripes on walls flashed by, quicker and quicker, in the glare of the aircar's landing lights. A brighter, redder light appeared in front of them, filling the cockpit with its lurid, monochromatic glow.

"Fire up ahead," said Aringher quietly. "We may well be trapped."

"We're not dying down here, Ambassador," Nivome said. The light from the approaching flames gave a grim and bloody cast to his heavy features. "I have other plans for my life."

He nudged the speed upward. Perada felt the aircar quivering with its readiness to lift—all but flying through the tunnel. The guidelines flickered past in a blur.

"Four," said Nivome. "Three, two, one. . . ."

They entered the fire. The walls and ceiling vanished in a rippling curtain of red and yellow. Nivome pulled back on the controls. Perada felt a quick, stomach-churning drop as the floor of the tunnel fell away beneath them, then a sudden heavy pressure as the aircar lifted.

The sky was black with smoke ahead, the ground was red with fire. The little aircar jerked and tossed on the updrafts.

Perada choked back the bile rising in her throat—*If I'm abandoning everything,* she pleaded with the universe, *please let me not embarrass myself while I'm doing it.* She heard a soft moan from Tillijen behind her and when she looked at the aft monitor she understood why: nothing now stood on the mountainside where the Summer Palace had once been except a heap of rubble filled with dancing flames.

Then a curl of smoke obscured the wreckage, and the aircar sped on above the burning landscape.

Warhammer drove inward toward the surface of Entibor. Tres Brehant and the few ships of the Fleet remaining in-system followed as closely as they dared, keeping the Mage warships at a distance until the *'Hammer* could reach atmosphere.

"We're losing aids to navigation," Errec said. "All the dirtside beacons are going down."

"Orbitals?"

"None active."

Jos looked at the sensor readouts. Errec was right—the screens were showing more garbage than sense. "Then we'll have to do this the hard way," he said. "Errec, you found Mages for me when I asked you to. Can you find Perada for me now?"

"I'll try."

"That's all I ask. Stand by for atmosphere translation."

Jos pulled back on the throttles and brought *Warhammer* skipping into the atmosphere, bleeding off speed with friction. When he'd slowed enough to go in without burning, he was over the nightside of Entibor, and the planetscape below him made his breath stop in his throat. The whole surface of the planet was marked and lined with fire—continents and mountain chains and archipelagoes picked out in crawling lines of scarlet and crimson and angry gold.

"Sweet fortune," Jos said. "What the hell is going *on* down there?"

"The working," said Errec. "The lives and minds of every Circle on Entibor, turned to this alone. They can't destroy the world in a single night—but they can set in motion such changes that soon nothing on-planet will be left alive."

"And 'Rada's down there in the middle of it? We have to find her, Errec—find her fast."

The sky was dark, full of smoke from the flames and rubble of the Mages' energy strikes, and from the vents that opened up in the earth below the speeding aircar like ragged, red-lined mouths. The glow of the burning world lit up the roiling clouds in shades of deep red and dull orange. Perada couldn't recognize any landmarks—the Palace Major was gone, and the Grand Plaza, and the business towers and the warehouses and the suburban shopping galleries that had spread out over the flat ground between the central metropolis and the spaceport complex.

Nivome piloted the aircar expertly through the clouds and the drifting smoke—sometimes it seemed to Perada as if he were keeping the tiny craft steady by the strength of his arms and shoulders alone. Finally, he brought the aircar down onto flat ground at what Perada supposed was the field at An-Jemayne. None of the buildings in the port complex remained standing, and grit and ash lay drifted on the cratered tarmac like snow.

"This is it, Your Dignity," he said. "We're here."

Perada needed Tillijen's help to get out of the safety webbing and down onto the field. Her legs had lost circulation during the long time she'd spent under the straps, and wanted to fold under her. The air was full of choking fumes—a vile, throat-clogging soup in which smoke from burning wreckage combined with gases belched up from underneath the earth. The smell made her gag and retch, leaning against Tilly's arm for support until the spasm passed.

"Wrap a bit of cloth around your nose and mouth," Aringher advised quietly. "It'll filter out some of the solids."

Perada swallowed hard. She wanted a mouthful of water, but she didn't think she wasn't going to get any—not now, maybe not ever—and her back and legs ached wretchedly. "I can spare a yard or two from the skirt of this gown," she said. "Tilly, you've got a knife."

Tillijen cut off strips of the finely woven fabric, and they bound them around their faces. Perada took shallow breaths and tried not to think any longer about the smell.

"Which way is the courier ship?" she asked.

Nobody answered. At last, Nivome said, "Your Dignity, there is no courier."

"But—" Her voice cracked; she forced control onto it with all the strength she had. "What happened?"

Nivome shrugged his heavy shoulders. "Who can tell, Your Dignity? You see what it's like. Maybe they came and couldn't find us, maybe they never made it down through atmosphere. Maybe they couldn't wait. We did the best we could."

"Yes," Perada said. "You've done well, all of you. And now it's over."

She opened the small wooden chest she'd carried from the Summer Palace and took out the Iron Crown. She settled the black tiara's heavy, rough-finished weight onto her head—it fit poorly on her new-cropped skull, without the thick, intertwined braids to anchor it in place.

"So I die on my planet after all," she said, "and wear the Crown to my public burning. May fortune be kind to my people who got away."

The 'Hammer was a superb starship—sturdy and well armed, and admirably constructed to run on a straight line to a jump point faster than almost anything else of her size in space—but her mass and her shape made her ill-suited for atmospheric work. Keeping the freighter on-course and stable in the thermal updrafts and the firestorms of Entibor's destruction took all the skill Jos possessed.

"The Summer Palace should be up ahead somewhere," Errec said.

"I don't have it on visual." Jos squinted at the mess outside the viewscreens. *Smoke and ash instead of atmosphere; nothing but garbage on the sensors . . . I'm lucky I haven't smashed into the side of a mountain.* "How about Perada? Can you tell me where she is?"

"Ahead," said Errec. "I can't tell how far. There's too much Magework."

"You mean we've still got Mages alive down here?"

"Not exactly."

"Can't we get under this smoke?" Nannla called over the internal comms from the gun bubble.

"I don't think so," Jos replied. "It looks like it goes right down to the ground. But this ought to be the Summer Palace."

"Maybe it is, boss, but you couldn't prove it by me."

A fireball rose from the ground below, flooding the cockpit with brilliant light, dwarfing the ship with its size.

"She isn't here, Jos," Errec said.

"How sure are you?"

"I'm sure."

"Right, people—everyone look sharp," Jos said over the intercom. "We have to stay down here a little longer. Errec, get me a new direction, fast."

"That way," Errec said. He pointed. "She's that way."

"Let me know when we're getting close."

"If I can."

Jos pushed main engines forward, and started in the direction Errec had indicated. A roar of dismay came over the internal comms from the engine room—young Wrann, who still wasn't accustomed to how much power the *'Hammer* had in her to give when she had to. After that, they flew on in silence, except for the roar of the *'Hammer* engines and the constant background rattling and chinking as firestorms and turbulence buffeted the ship.

Finally Errec said, "We're getting near."

Metadi looked over at the dead-reckoning indicator on the navicomp. "According to this, we should be right over the Palace Major, and I can't see a goddamn thing."

"She isn't here, Jos."

"Which way is she, then?"

Errec pointed again. "That way. The landing field."

Jos turned *Warhammer* in the direction Errec had indicated and slowed the ship as much as he dared. He couldn't afford the time he'd lose if they overshot the field and had to come back again from the other direction.

"This should be the An-Jemayne spaceport field," he said a few minutes later. "But I still can't see anything. We'll have to go down and take a look."

"Perada's here," said Errec. "Somewhere close. But be careful. The surface isn't what I'd call stable anymore."

"Then we won't set down on it. Stand by to lower ship."

Jos cut in the heavy-duty ventral nullgrav units that under normal circumstances would slow the final stages of the 'Hammer's landing and settle her down properly onto her legs. This time, though, he didn't hit the toggle that brought the heavy metal landing legs unfolding out of their niches in the freighter's belly. The engines growled in protest, and the nullgravs echoed the note, but they responded without stinting to the increased demand. Warhammer hovered obediently, no more than a tall man's height above the broken ground.

Jos unstrapped his safety webbing. "Hold her, Errec. I'm going to drop the ramp and see for myself what's out there."

He made his way to the 'Hammer's main hatch and hit the button to open the door and lower the ramp. The view he got wasn't encouraging—if he hadn't trusted Errec's word on it, he'd never have known that this broken-up expanse of rock and metal was the landing field for Entibor's largest spaceport.

It didn't look like there was anybody left alive. The fumes in the air made his eyes water and sting. Then he heard a voice calling his name.

"Jos! Over here!"

He jumped off the end of the ramp and ran as fast as he could over the uneven ground in the direction of the cry. He came to where four people stood close together in the lee of a small stubby-winged aircar that looked at first glance like part of the surrounding rubble. One was Tillijen, and one was—of all the people to meet again in this place and time—the pale, clerkish-looking man whom he'd surprised and tied up with curtain cords in the back room of the Double Moon. And one was Nivome do'Evaan of Rolny, and the last—the last was a small and extremely pregnant woman wearing the Iron Crown of Entibor.

She was the one who had called out his name.

" 'Rada," he said. He hadn't expected to get here in time, in spite of everything he'd said to Errec and everything he'd done. He'd hadn't expected it, but she was alive. "You've cut your hair."

"I had to," she said. "If I wanted to leave the planet. We were going to meet a courier ship, but it never came. . . . We were waiting for the fire, but then I saw the *'Hammer* come down through the smoke, and I knew that you'd come back."

The captain's cabin aboard *Warhammer* hadn't changed. It was still a spare, unadorned bit of cubic, scrupulously tidy, with the same faint but unmistakable shipboard smell to the recirculated air. Perada—too numb from the sudden change of fortune to raise a protest—let Gentlesir Aringher strap her into the acceleration couch while Jos and Tilly hurried to take their places for liftoff.

"There are, it seems, still a few Mage warships in the system," Aringher said as he worked on the buckles of the safety webbing. "After all the trouble these nice people have gone through to rescue us, it wouldn't do for us to get blown up on our way to hyper."

"No," Perada said. "I suppose not." For herself, she wasn't sure she cared. "What about you and Gentlesir Nivome? Has the captain given you places?"

"I daresay we'll ride out the lift-off on the couches in the common room," Aringher said. "Or perhaps crew berthing. At an impromptu party such as this, seating arrangements are of necessity made on an informal basis. In any case, Your Dignity, you needn't worry. We can take care of ourselves."

But I'm the Domina, she thought, as the door of the captain's cabin slid shut again behind the Galcenian Ambassador. *If I don't have my people to take care of, what reason do I have for still being alive?*

"All hands, stand by for liftoff. Stand by."

The announcement came over the shipboard speaker in the captain's cabin. Perada recognized Jos's voice, but she didn't feel a welling of renewed emotion at the sound. She'd rather expected that she would—when he had first appeared out of the smoke on the landing field, then her heart had clenched within her. Instead, now, there was nothing, only a numbness where feeling should have been. She wondered a bit about that.

The nose of the ship came up, and in the same moment, as part of the motion, the press of inertia shoved her down into the couch. It was a hard, fast launch, the gees more than she ever remembered experiencing, but this time there was no exhilaration to it. Instead there was only the relentless pressure, and a heaviness in her mind like a cold, numbing fog.

I have to decide, she thought, as the pressure shoved her deeper and deeper into the padded couch. The child inside her kicked and squirmed in furious protest against the constraints of the safety webbing—a reminder that someone, at least, still needed help that she could give. *When this is over, I won't be the Domina of Entibor any longer.*

I have to decide if I'm going to be anything at all.

Warhammer sped along the hyperspace arc to Galcen, safely out of reach of Mage warships and the firestorms of a dying planet. Jos Metadi set the cockpit controls on autopilot and headed for his cabin. Nannla and Tilly had already abandoned the gun bubbles and headed off together for a reunion in number-one crew berthing; Jos decided that he envied them. 'Rada had seemed glad enough to see him when they met on the landing field, but under the circumstances, she would probably have welcomed anybody who showed up with a working starship.

He started to palm the lockplate, then changed his mind and hit the buzzer first. Virtue, or at any rate courtesy, had its reward—he heard a muffled "Come in" and the door slid open. He entered, and the panel slid shut after him.

Perada was sitting up on the edge of the acceleration couch. She didn't look well—her face was too thin, and her skin was too pale under its coating of grit and wind-borne ash. She sat awkwardly, as though the bulge in her abdomen belonged to somebody else altogether.

"Are you all right?" he asked.

"Yes." She gave a weak laugh. "But please—don't *ever* let me ride through a lift-off when I'm this far along again. No matter how much I say I want to do it."

"I won't," he said. He nodded toward her swollen belly. "How long before . . ."

"Soon. But not right away, I hope."

"We'll be on Galcen in a few days."

"Good. I like Galcen." She sounded tired; her brief humor of a moment ago had faded. "I used to have friends there. Maybe I can stay with them until I can think of what I ought to do."

"What do you mean?"

She shrugged. "I trained all my life to be Domina of Entibor, and I don't really know what else I'm good for. Maybe I ought to put up a sign and offer private lessons in folksinging and galactic politics."

"You could do that," he said. He took a deep breath. "Or you could marry me and stick around *Warhammer* for a while."

"Marry you?" She stared; her blue eyes looked even bigger than usual without the braids to frame her face. "But you told me you weren't . . . that you didn't want to . . . that you weren't going to *do* that with me anymore."

"I told you a lot of things," he said. "Most of them were pretty stupid. And I don't believe in being stupid twice."

"I've never been married," she said. "I don't even know where I'd go to sign the papers. Or whatever it is people do."

"They share bread and wine in front of witnesses," he said. "On Gyffer, anyhow. The paperwork is optional."

"That sounds nice. Could we do it that way, do you think?"

"Right now, if you want. Tilly and Nannla can witness . . . what do you say?"

"Yes."

* * *

Festen Aringher considered himself, if nothing else, a philosopher. So it was with an air of philosophical detachment that he agreed to preside over the wedding of Josteddr Metadi, citizen of Gyffer, and Perada Rosselin, not currently a citizen of anywhere. He'd never performed a marriage, but he supposed that it was one of the things that an ambassador from Galcen had the power to do.

"I suppose," he remarked to no one in particular, as the crew decorated the common room of *Warhammer*, "that I could declare this to be the first act of the new Republic."

The thought struck him as amusing, and he smiled.

"How are we doing this?" called a female voice from the galley.

"Gyfferan-style, I guess," replied Tillijen the armsmaster, who was wiping down the mess table with a handkerchief she'd pulled from her sleeve. "Dominas don't marry, so there isn't any rite on Entibor."

"How do they do it on Gyffer?"

"I spent my life avoiding finding out that sort of thing. Don't ask me."

Jos Metadi came into the common room from the engineering spaces as she spoke. "How we do it on Gyffer," he said, "it's bread and wine, and we pour wine for each other, and break bread for each other, and then say that we're married. That's how it's done."

"Bread and wine?" Nannla said. "Jos, Cap'n, we don't have either, far as I know."

"Philosophically," Aringher said, "it's the symbolism, not the actual items. Unless you wouldn't *feel* married without the real things, of course."

"Wouldn't know how married feels," Metadi told him. "So I suppose that part doesn't matter."

Tilly dived back into the galley and emerged with a packet of compressed ready-to-eat meatmeal and a brick of dry biscuit. "This is what we've got. Lots of both, but not much variety."

"The biscuit," Metadi said. "It's closer."

"Wait a minute," Nannla said. She ducked out of the

room. In a moment she was back with a bottle wrapped in tissue. "I got this, last port call in Innish-Kyl," she said.

"Firewater? You expect anyone to drink that and be good for anything afterward?" Tilly asked.

"It's good enough, and we're honored," Aringher said. "I think everybody's ready. Shall we assemble everyone?"

"Let's do it."

The members of *Warhammer*'s temporary crew—the Entiboran Fleet ensign and young Wrann the Selvaur from Maraghai—joined the others in the common room. A moment or so later, the door of the captain's cabin opened and Perada came out. She was wearing a borrowed night-robe that clearly belonged to somebody much taller; belted high under her breasts, it skimmed her ankles in front and trailed on the floor behind.

She looked apologetic. "Nothing else on board fits me anymore."

"That's all right," Nannla told her. "Nobody's handing out points for style."

Aringher cleared his throat. "I think everybody's here who's going to be here—shall we begin?"

He stepped over to the mess table and set out two cups and two plates, with the opened bottle of firewater and the brick of compressed biscuit between them. Then he nodded to Perada Rosselin. "Pour the wine," he said; "and let him pour some for you."

She poured with a steady hand until the cup was full almost to the brim, then handed the bottle across to Metadi. He took it—Aringher noted, again with some private amusement, that the captain's hands were not nearly as steady as hers—and poured a shallow splash of firewater into the other cup.

The biscuit was white and hard, and breaking it presented a challenge. After a couple of tries, Metadi took the dagger Tilly offered and used it to break off a chunk, then handed the knife to Perada. She worked at it for a minute and managed to lever a bit off of one corner.

At another nod from Aringher they exchanged scraps of bread, and then tasted the firewater. Perada only sipped at hers, which Aringher privately considered wise under the circumstances, but Jos Metadi drained his to the bottom.

"Now," said Aringher, "do you two gentles have any statements or changes to declare?"

"Yes," Metadi said. "I declare in front of the Lords of Life and these my friends that Perada Rosselin is my wife from now henceforward."

"And I declare in front of the Lords of Life and these my friends that Jos Metadi is my husband from now henceforward."

Aringher felt a deep sense of satisfaction. "It pleases me," he said, still smiling, "as an ambassador plenipotentiary of the Republic and of Galcen, to know that I have seen both the beginning and the end of this affair. Be happy, children, and blessings on both of you."

The iridescent nothingness of hyperspace made its swirling patterns outside the 'Hammer's armor-glass viewscreens. Nothing on the console really needed tending while the ship was in hyper—the autopilot, though an older model, was reliable—but neither of the two men in the cockpit cared to attend the ceremony in the common room.

Errec Ransome, in the pilot's seat, glanced over at the man sitting next to him. "Gentlesir Nivome do'Evaan," he said. "I believe we need to talk."

Nivome frowned. "I don't think so."

"I do," said Errec. "You don't understand. The smell of what you intended to do is impossible to miss. I'm surprised that Mistress Vasari never caught it—I suppose you waited until she was dead?"

The other man's face darkened with anger. "You don't know what you're talking about."

"That's where you're wrong. I find Mages, and those who deal with Mages. And I can touch your mind, whether you will it or not."

"You're lying."

"So you say. You planned to kill the Domina in her underground shelter—you even brought her the Iron Crown as a pretext for the meeting—but you didn't find her alone.

And then you planned to abandon her on the landing field at An-Jemayne, but the *'Hammer* showed up before you could get away." Errec paused. "What did the Mages promise you, Nivome do'Evaan, in return for her death?"

Nivome exhaled heavily, like an animal pawing the ground and getting ready to charge. "I don't think I'm going to answer that. You have no proof."

"No," Errec admitted. "I don't."

"Then what's your point?"

"Just this," said Errec. "You'll leave the *'Hammer* as soon as we make planetfall on Galcen. You'll go back to Rolny, and take up whatever position you hold there. And you'll never again seek any role in the politics of Galcen, or of Entibor, or of the republic that's forming."

Nivome glowered at him. "You're nobody. You're from nowhere, and you're going nowhere. Why should I pay attention to anything you say?"

"Because if you don't comply willingly," Errec told him, "I can force compliance upon you. And if you resist me, Gentlesir Nivome, I can do things that will leave what's left of you fit for nothing except to sit on the sidewalk gibbering."

There was silence in the cockpit for some minutes. Errec watched Nivome's expression fade from belligerence to defiance and, finally, to resignation. Errec smiled.

"Good," he said. "I believe we understand one another now."

He gave a nod of satisfaction—Jos and Perada would never know about the wedding gift he had given them, but he felt happier for having given it—and went back to watching the mists of hyperspace.

"It was a nice wedding," said Perada sleepily. The captain's cabin of *Warhammer* was pleasantly dark and cool, and Jos was a comforting presence beside her on the bed. "I'm sorry we can't really ..."

"It's all right." He sounded embarrassed. "There'll be plenty of time later. On Galcen or wherever."

"That's good." She yawned and nestled close. They were lying front-to-back, like spoons; she'd almost forgotten how good it felt to drop off to sleep knowing that he was there. She was almost asleep when a bubble of curiosity worked its way up to the surface, rousing her. "Why are we going to Galcen, anyway? I forgot to ask."

"Politics," he said. "The Centrists on Galcen managed to grab the government when nobody was looking. They want to start holding talks about forming some kind of republic once the war is over."

"Do they?" She was awake again. "Who do they think is going to be in it?"

"Them, naturally, and—" It was his turn to yawn; she waited impatiently for him to continue talking. "—Gyffer and Maraghai, probably Khesat . . . I don't know all that much about it."

"What about the colonies?" she demanded. "Parezul and Ghan Jobai and Tanpaleyn and all the other little worlds? What do they want to do about *them*?"

He yawned again. "Let them in, I suppose."

"Galcen will eat them up alive. Or Gyffer." She paused. "Do you think the colonies would let me speak for them, now that I've cut my braids and all?"

"Braids grow back." He tightened his arm around her. "And I think that right now the colonies need to know that Entibor is more than just the home world. The galaxy's changing; something has to stay the same for a little while, at least. You can be that thing for them."

"It's good I didn't lose the Iron Crown, then." She could sense the political implications of the new republic unfolding themselves in her mind. It felt like circulation coming back to a deadened limb, painful and vital at the same time. "But I'll need to do more than wear the crown, if I'm going to reassure the colonies that their luck hasn't gone completely. A boy-child on the way is encouraging, but they'll want to see an heir to make certain—and fairly soon, too."

"That part's easy," he said. "Galcen's lousy with biolabs. Just find a good one and tell 'em what you want."

"I think I'd sooner do it the way I'm used to," she said. "If you don't mind helping."

Jos laughed quietly. She felt his breath stirring the short hair on the crown of her head.

"I thought I told you," he said. "I don't plan on being stupid anymore."